HORIZON

Barbara Angermeier Malcolm

Barbara Angermeier Malcolm

For my children David and Ann
You are the lights on my horizon.

Something beautiful is on the horizon.
Keep on going.

--FB/JOYOFMOM

This isn't the end...
There is much more beyond the horizon.

--DEEP

CONTENTS

CHAPTER 1

September

On the last day of my old life, I sat on my porch watching the sunset. It was the end of a perfect early September day. I sat there as I had so many times over the years, first with Bert as newlyweds planning our future, then with the boys as they grew, and again with Bert after the boys were grown and gone making their own lives. It had been eight years since my husband of more than twenty-five years had died suddenly one March day while getting the fields ready for planting. Sometimes it seemed like it had just happened but more often thoughts of Bert brought warm memories.

I kept my eyes focused on the horizon, watching the sun sink lower on its daily path. I had ended so many days on that farmhouse porch I realized I could predict where it would touch the railing as it set. I decided to start a sunset record, a sort of diary of my days spent there. A quick trip to the shed and I had a little can of black paint and a narrow brush to start immediately.

I painted a thin stripe on the porch railing at the exact spot the setting sun touched the wood. On the slat beneath the stripe, I painted "September 2." Next to the date in tiny letters I painted "Esther the chicken died." Not to imply that Esther's death had been from natural causes; Esther was at that moment in the pot becoming soup, but it seemed important to somehow mark the day.

Later that evening, eating a steaming bowl of Esther

soup, I thought about my life. All of the roles I'd played in my adult life were finished. No longer a wife, not swamped by the day-to-day routine of motherhood, done being Mrs. Logan-in-the-office to generations of local kids and their parents. Now what was I supposed to do?

The *Kingman Times* was delivered the next morning. I refilled my mug from the teapot before settling down to read the local weekly newspaper from cover to cover; farm reports, wedding announcements, obituaries, and everything in between.

Carrie Hetrick's cooking column was always interesting with its mix of traditional, foreign, and low-calorie recipes. I figured Carrie's recipe choice was based on how tight her jeans had been that week. The dinner menus of the whole area were touched by whether Carrie had been reading *Bon Appetit*, *Taste of Home*, or *Weight Watchers* magazines. This week's recipe was Moroccan lamb with apricots and cinnamon. *Bon Appetit* strikes again, I thought with a smile.

Abel Baker's garden column, "Dirty Hands," featured information on getting your plants ready for winter and when to harvest fall crops. Just below "Dirty Hands" was a tiny ad from the arts and crafts store in the mall in Simpson, ten miles away where State Highway 47, which ran through my small town of Kingman, met the interstate. "Get in Touch with Your Creative Side" it said. They were offering classes in beading, beginning crochet, and watercolor.

The watercolor class intrigued me. Friends often complimented me on the colors I used in the house, so I thought I might like painting on paper or canvas instead of plaster walls. Even as I thought about signing up for the class, I imagined I heard the voice of one of my old aunts who had never had a positive word to say about anything or anyone. Great-aunt Mame had always been ready with a negative opinion in life, and she had taken up residence in my head after she died. I had such a clear picture of her sitting in the corner of the parlor at Grandma's, her embroidery or crocheted lace resting on her lap. She always wore what I thought of as the old lady's uniform: a long black or dark gray skirt, a long-sleeved white blouse with a high collar, thick elastic stockings, and sensible shoes. I remember deciding when I was about seven that I would never become an old prune like her. Hers was the inner voice that always tried to talk me out of trying new things, but suddenly I was tired of living my life by what other people, even long-dead great-aunts, said. Before I lost my resolve, I called the number in the ad and signed up. The woman on the phone was friendly and helpful. She suggested I come in before the first night to pick up the supplies list and, of course, purchase them right there. Paid-up students got a ten percent materials discount, the clerk told me, so that didn't sound too expensive.

I grabbed a pencil and wrote "7 PM Watercolor" on Tuesday, September 10 on the big calendar from the feed store. For as long as I could remember there had been a Steve's Feeds Co. calendar in that spot. Only the style of tractor featured each month had changed as the years passed.

I read the rest of the paper, finished the crossword puzzle and it was still not yet ten a.m. I took a quick shower, not that I was in a hurry, but years of getting three boys off to school while getting ready for work myself had conditioned me to take "speed showers," as my family dubbed them.

I walked around the yard pruning and clipping with my favorite little shears, then strolled through the garden, ending up at the back door with the makings of a salad for lunch. In honor of signing up for painting class, I pulled out a pretty glass plate and spent some time arranging the tossed greens, sprinkling chopped fresh herbs, laying on slices of tomato and fresh mozzarella, and adding just a touch more vinaigrette. The recipe for the dressing was courtesy of Carrie's Provencal period.

After lunch, I pulled the recipe for my mom's bread-and-butter pickles out of the old wooden box. It made me smile to see Mom's handwriting so many years after her passing. I remembered her sitting at the table night after night in the months before my wedding. Mom said she wanted to "start our bride off with a good store of man-pleasing recipes." And the pickles made from that recipe had pleased Pop for years. I thought of all the hot fall days we'd spent in the kitchen canning vegetables and fruits for winter. Even as a girl, the rows of gleaming jars gave me a satisfied feeling.

The wooden recipe box brought back memories too. While Mom was writing out all the recipes, Pop was making the box. I loved how every dovetail was precisely the same size. I pictured Pop's rough farmer's hands smoothing the wood and fitting the joints. Even after all these years, I could still smell the oil he had painstakingly rubbed into the wood to give it a rich glow. Of all the things I had of Mom and Pop's, this box, this bridal gift and its treasure of recipes and memories meant the most.

Putting the stained and faded pickle card into the recipe holder that Matt had made in Cub Scouts, I reached into the pantry and pulled out the canning jars and kettles. "Just in time," I said, as the back door opened, and Clara came in. "How's 'the It girl' today?"

"Oh, you," she said, fists on her generous hips, "I wish you'd quit with that 'It girl' stuff. Nobody remembers Clara Bow anymore except old farts and they're dying off." She paused. "I guess that makes you an old fart, just don't you die on me."

We got to work and started the cauliflower pickles, letting the chopped vegetables for the pickles sit in big bowls with ice and salt, while we made three kinds of jam.

"You know, I'm glad your mom gave you a pickle recipe that has a lemonade break built in," said Clara as we sat on the porch after finishing the jam. "It's always so blamed hot this time of year when there's so much canning and freezing to be done."

"It sure is hot today. When I was a kid, I always volunteered to make the pickles because of that three-hour sitting time. Lydie helped with the jam because she loved it so much, but by the end of the day she looked like a wet rag. And I was as cool as a cucumber, or in this case, a cauliflower." We laughed. "Of course, we made cucumber ones, too. Pop had to have regular pickles on his sandwich every day, with cauliflower pickles on the side. He was a man who really loved pickles."

Clara reached to put her sweating glass on the porch rail and saw the stripe. "Oh, honey, you got black paint on here. You'd better get some thinner and see if you can't get it off."

"It's not a mistake, Clara." I took a sip of lemonade. "I was watching the sunset the other night and thought about how I'd sat here so many nights, I knew where it would touch the railing, so I made that little stripe." With an embarrassed chuckle I pointed at the slat below, "I dated it there."

"Esther the chicken died," Clara read. "I didn't know you named your chickens."

"Just Esther. She was the feisty old hen that always chased the grandkids, so I made her into soup the other day. Serves her right for scaring them."

The buzzing of the timer called us back to the hot kitchen to finish the pickles. It took us the rest of the afternoon.

I don't know why I didn't tell her that I'd signed up for the watercolor class. She'd been my best friend for over thirty years. We'd supported and consoled each other through the loss of our parents, Clara's stillborn baby, and Bert's sudden death—all the big and little tragedies of life. But I was reluctant to share this with her. I felt like I was taking the first step into a new part of my life and, since she was such a huge part of my past, I wanted to keep them separate for a while. Every time she got near the feed store calendar I'd watch to see if she noticed the note about class starting, but she was too interested in passing on all the gossip she'd heard at her Red Cross volunteer meeting the night before and didn't see it.

Friday morning, I stood in the kitchen surveying the

ranks of jam jars, shining like jewels in the morning light, and rows of pickle jars, with their greens, whites, and reds glimmering in brine. Admiring them, it made sense why so many of the Old Masters had put ordinary objects into their still life paintings. It felt good having things put up for the winter, even though there wasn't anyone else around anymore to eat them. I enjoyed their homey beauty. Putting the last big canning kettle back in the pantry, I decided to drive to the craft store after I showered and get the supplies for class before I chickened out.

An hour later I sat in the parking lot of the mall, staring at the row of bargain bins on either side of the entrance to the craft store. My heart fluttered and I could feel sweat trickling down my spine as I worked up the courage to go in. I studied the people coming and going, trying to figure out if I'd fit in. Fitting in had been my way of disappearing all my life. I knew that if you blended in with those around you, few people made the effort to single you out.

Giving myself a mental shake to shut up Great-aunt Mame and firm orders to quit stalling, I grabbed my purse and went in. I stopped at the service counter where the clerk checked my name off on the class roster, gave me a list of the required supplies, and pointed me toward the painting department. I grabbed a cart and strode down the aisle determined to get what I needed and get out, but a stack of baskets caught my eye. One that looked like a small picnic hamper with sturdy handles seemed just right for carrying my art things back and forth. I checked the price--$28.95, too expensive. As I reached to put it back the clerk working in the aisle pointed out a tiny sign that read "All Baskets in This Section 75% Off." A quick calculation convinced me that just over seven dollars was a good price for a nice basket. Into the cart it went.

The painting department was a sensuous revelation. It only took a minute to find the small set of watercolor tubes and the five brushes required. But I couldn't tear myself away from the brush rack. There were large, full ones with firm bristles and bamboo handles, small ones with what looked like no more than ten hairs and lacquered handles, fan shaped ones, and round and flat ones galore. I spent many minutes touching each one, stroking them on the back of my hand to see how they would feel and move on paper.

And the paints—there were large tubes of acrylics, tiny expensive ones of oils, and medium tubes of watercolors. I couldn't resist opening a few of the tubes and inhaling their rich aroma. The acrylics all smelled like the art room at Kingman Elementary, the watercolors didn't have much of an odor, and each oil color smelled different from the others. The colors were mind-boggling: luscious reds like passionate kisses, blues for every patch of ocean and sweep of sky, lemon yellow so tart it made my mouth pucker, greens for every leaf and blade of grass. I couldn't imagine how anyone would ever use them all. I also saw the metal trays with cakes of paint like I'd bought for the boys when they were little, and that had so frustrated me as a child when I couldn't make the paint do what I wanted it to.

Consulting the supplies list, I turned to the rack of sketchbooks and pads of watercolor paper. I was amazed that there were nearly a dozen different kinds of paper for watercolor alone. Checking again to make sure I had the right size, finish, and weight, I headed for the checkout. Paying for the class and supplies cost nearly eighty dollars even with the discount. Now I couldn't back out; I had too much invested.

CHAPTER 2

Sunset the next Tuesday found me back on the porch with a glass of wine. I'd painted another stripe on the porch railing near the first one, and "September 10, Watercolor Class" on the slat below. The wine was for courage. Tonight was the first night of class and I was nervous. That afternoon I had been going through my closet, for the third time, trying to find something to wear that I'd be comfortable in that would help let me blend in, when Clara knocked on the back door and came in.

"I'm in here," I called out.

"What are you doing, Gail?" Clara said, surveying the mess of discarded clothing on the bed.

I was quiet for a moment trying to decide if she would be hurt that I'd kept this from her, knowing that she would be, but I needed a little courage to get out the door, so I went for it. "I signed up for a watercolor class at the craft store in Simpson Mall. Tonight's the first class and I can't decide what to wear. Help me?"

"Okay." Clara started sifting through the clothes. "How come you're taking a painting class?"

"Oh, I don't know. Their ad last week in the *Times* caught my eye and I signed up before I thought about it too much. Guess I'm looking for a change from the ordinary in my life."

"Not me. I like my life ordinary, just the way it is." She held up a blouse, shook her head, and put it in the heap of rejects on the bed. "I take care of Hank, he takes care of me, the kids are grown and gone, and I can volunteer at church or help with the blood drive when I want to. I'm too old for changes and surprises."

I flipped through my closet and held up a flowered dress. "No, not that," we said in unison.

"Right now, I feel like change would be good," I said. "Retiring has left me feeling kind of useless and I guess I'm looking for something to fill my time. Plus, I've always liked painting the house and thought maybe painting on paper would be fun, too."

Clara's voice changed. It got softer, and smaller. "So how come you haven't said anything about it?"

I turned to look at her and was surprised to see tears in her eyes that made me feel guilty that I had kept the class to myself. "Oh, Clara, I was afraid I'd chicken out and then you'd be disappointed in me when I didn't do it. I wasn't trying to keep anything from you."

Her face relaxed at my words, and she turned back into the Clara I knew. "Do you have any idea what kind of people are going to be in class with you? Could be some sort of whacko hippies, you know."

I laughed so hard I had to sit on the bed. "Whacko hippies?" I wiped my eyes. "Good grief, Clara, I'm not going to New York. It's just a painting class in the next town and not a very big town at that. Besides, hippies went out of style in the '70s."

Clara sniffed, "Well, what do I know, Miss Up-to-date. I'm just a simple farm wife. I don't travel in the sophisticated circles you do. You'll probably make tons of new friends and forget about me."

I put my arm around her. "Don't be silly, Clara. We've been friends for some thirty-odd years and we're not going to stop because I'm taking a painting class at a craft store in a one-horse town by the interstate. Now, let's figure out what I should wear so I don't look too foolish tonight."

We finally decided on a pair of navy polyester slacks because they wouldn't wrinkle on the drive, and a long-sleeved floral blouse I had ordered from a catalog. Sensible oxfords rounded out my look.

Clara left to fix dinner for Hank, and I had a quick bowl of Esther soup before getting ready. I took a shower and twisted my long, fine, dark-brown hair, my natural color thank you, into a bun at the back of my neck, taming the wispy bits with some styling goo one of my sons had left behind after his last visit. I dressed and put my wedding pearls in my ears. Taking a look in the mirror on the closet door I decided I looked all right, a little prim and boring perhaps, but it had been a long time since I'd worried about how I looked. Too late to do something about it now. I grabbed a sweater, my basket of art supplies, my purse and keys, and was out the door.

Again, I sat in the car watching the people going into the store. I couldn't decide which of them might be in my class, so many carried bags or wore backpacks.

I dithered long enough that by the time I got directions and made my way to the classroom in the back corner of the vast store, class was about to begin.

I stood in the doorway hoping to see a familiar face but no luck. There was only one empty chair. I tucked my chin, made my way to it, and sat. I glanced to my left to see an ancient gnome of a man, his china blue eyes sparkling as he extended a hand and said, "Floyd Marley." I shook his hand with a murmured "Gail Logan" and turned to see who sat on my right.

All I could see was the back of a girl's head with black hair in tiny braids with beads on the end of each one and a narrow back clad in a colorful sweater. Before I looked away, she turned my way and smiled.

"Hi," she said, "I'm Samara."

Oh my, I thought, she's such a pretty girl but she's got her nose pierced and her eyebrow too, even one in the center of her cheek... Embarrassed to realize I was staring, I smiled back and said, "I'm Gail."

"So, have you been painting long?" Samara asked.

"Never. I just thought it would be fun."

"I've been painting my whole life, mostly on the walls, according to my mom. I plan to major in Art at college next year."

"That should be fun." I scanned the tables, which were arranged in a big square, to see what supplies everyone else had unpacked. Some of the students appeared to have everything in the list piled in front of them and others had nothing on the table in front of them. I had hoped to see someone I knew but they were all strangers to me. It looked to me like most of them already knew each other. I checked what Floyd and Samara had out, decided to emulate them, and pulled out a small notebook and pencil just as the teacher came into the room and shut the door.

"Hi everyone," the teacher said. "I'm the teacher, June. Welcome to the first fall session of Beginning Watercolor. Not beading, not crochet, so if you're signed up for either of those, you're in the wrong room." That made a little nervous chuckle ripple around the room. "Everybody got the supplies on the list?" She looked around at all eight heads bobbing yes. "Great. Let's get started." She reached into a box on the chair behind her, picked up a pile of brown paper grocery bags, and handed them to the woman sitting on her right with instructions for her to take one and pass them around. "Everyone put some water in your ice cream pail and get out your one-inch flat and your biggest round brush, #8, #9, or #10, whichever you decided to buy."

We spent the first half hour of the class using plain water and our brushes to paint shapes on the brown paper to learn how changing the brush position or the pressure used can change what it does on the paper. Then June asked us to cluster around her while she demonstrated how to prepare the paper, how to pick up paint on our brushes, and how to put the color on the wet paper. It was amazing and a bit scary to see how the drops of paint spread and changed and mixed together. Finally, June sent us back to our tables to trace a simple landscape onto a piece of paper and begin painting. I watched Samara and envied her freedom with everything. Her brush strokes were relaxed. She didn't agonize over color choices; she just painted. In contrast, I had cramps in my fingers from gripping my brush before class was half finished.

When we took a break Samara looked at my painting and said, "I like the way you control your paint. Mine's so messy."

"Free is more like it," I said. "I love the way your colors blend."

I spent the next week loving and hating painting. I used lots of paper practicing the techniques June had shown us. I also worked on not strangling my brush, if only to stave off arthritis.

On Friday Clara stopped by to deliver some lotion I had ordered from her Avon lady daughter-in-law. I had my practice paintings, as June called them, spread all over the bed in the back bedroom.

"Wow, you're really serious about this painting stuff," said Clara.

"Frustrated is more like it. See this? And this?" I picked up sheet after sheet. "Garbage. All garbage." I dropped the offending papers.

"Hey, you've only been at this for a few days. Even that Leonard daVinci guy must have had to start somewhere. Give yourself a chance to learn, for crying out loud."

"It's Leo-nard-oh."

"Yeah, I know. Leonardo, Leonard, whatever, I was just trying to make you laugh. You're so serious about all this."

She picked up a little painting of a bunch of colored blotches with green streaks below them covered with what might have been a lavender ribbon, or a lavender snake. It was hard to tell. "This really looks good. It's a bouquet, right? I like it; it's kind of, uh, impressionistic. The ribbon matches my bathroom. Can I have it?"

I snatched the painting out of her hands. "You don't

want that. It's no good. Give me a few weeks then I'll paint one like it for you, only better. I promise."

"If you say so, but remember I like this one if you're ever in the mood to give me a present," Clara said, tapping the painting.

I stood looking at the little painting in my hands. After a moment I glanced up and said, "Is Hank working late tonight?"

"Yep, till eight-thirty. Why?"

"Painting is making me crazy. Do you want to have a glass of wine with me and watch the sunset?"

"Don't mind if I do," said Clara, looking relieved when I put the little painting down and changed the subject.

We spent an hour on the porch admiring the sunset and talking about our kids and grandkids. But I was so frustrated by what I saw as my lack of painting success, my sunset glass of wine turned into two. And on the slat below the stripe for September 14 I lettered, "Painting sucks!" Clara got a big laugh out of that.

CHAPTER 3

By the end of the second night of class, I felt as if I was making friends, that I might fit in. A couple of the other women in the group had recognized me from my years of working at the school and I got a kick out of Floyd Marley. He had developed the habit of leaning on my left shoulder while I painted, giving me tips and lavish compliments and not just on my work. Since he complimented all the other women in class almost as often, and some of their work was truly awful, I figured he needed new glasses.

On the third night of class, one of the students suggested we all go out for coffee afterwards. At first, I told them I thought I'd just go home since I had a long drive, but Samara touched my arm and said, "Please, Gail, come along. You're the only one I really know." Surprised that the young woman I saw as fearless might feel shy in unfamiliar situations, I agreed.

We spent a hilarious hour sipping decadent decaf mocha lattés with real whipped cream and listening to stories of previous classes and teachers. At one point in the conversation the students discovered that everyone, except for Samara and me, had taken a class from a particular teacher none of them liked. "I should have known she was a fraud when she brought her dog, a Shi Tzu named Kiki, for a model on life-drawing night,"

As the reminiscences got louder and crazier, Samara turned to me. "I brought something for you. We made jewelry last week in Art, so I made these for you." She held out a tissue paper bundle. "They're not much."

"Why, thank you, how nice." I unwrapped the tissue

and lifted out an earring that looked like a tiny chandelier. Red, gold, and black beads dangled from silver wires. "They're beautiful, but I can't imagine what I'd wear with them."

"Anything. You'll look awesome in them. And, if you don't mind my saying this, you could use some different clothes. Your stuff's so... so old-lady-ish."

"I am old."

"You're not old. You're mature; that's what my granny says about herself and she's way older than you. Your head's stuck in some old-lady idea of what you should look like. But your heart's young; I can tell from your painting. You should dress with your heart. You need some jeans and funky tops."

"Jeans? I wear jeans when I work in the garden. Jeans are for kids."

"Hah. Jeans are for everybody. We should go shopping. I'll find you something."

I stared at the eager face, searching for ridicule but found none. I heard myself say, "Alright. When do you want to go?"

"Saturday afternoon. It's the best time to hit the shops I have in mind."

Before I had a chance to reconsider, we made a date for the following weekend.

The shopping trip was a revelation. I rediscovered an interest in clothes that made me feel good about myself. And Samara learned that even when you're in your fifties you worry if your butt looks big.

It turned out that despite the forty years difference in our ages, Samara and I wore the same size. That led to the odd experience of us in side-by-side changing rooms leaning out into the hallway exchanging things we thought the other one should try on.

We spent a lively few hours in and out of thrift shops and resale stores. Samara found some jeans I was comfortable with, that didn't squeeze me so much my middle oozed over the waist, and a whole armload of sweaters and tops in bright colors and geometric designs. My favorite thrift store find was a sweater with every primary color swirling on it and long, bell sleeves. Samara even coaxed me into some leather boots with not-too-high heels we found at the discount shoe store in the mall. When I dropped Samara off after our spree, she extracted a promise that I'd wear my new things to class on Tuesday.

That evening at home, I surveyed the purchases strewn across my bed—bright colors, natural fibers, and non-traditional designs. I stood there thinking, what possessed me? Now, when I'm fifty-seven years old, I give in to peer pressure? When I was seventeen, I worked hard to blend in, even when my friends tried to get me to change my clothes. So how come I'm listening to a seventeen-year-old now?

I pulled on a pair of the jeans, my favorite sweater, the boots, and hooked Samara's gift earrings in my ears. I looked in the mirror and barely recognized myself. But there was something slightly wrong with my new look. It's my hair, I thought, I have old lady hair.

That sunset, on the slat below the stripe I painted on the porch railing, I wrote, "New clothes, new image?"

CHAPTER 4

Monday morning at ten o'clock, I sat in the waiting area of a hair salon in Simpson Mall looking through a style magazine.

I'd been having Mavis trim my hair every six months for nearly thirty years. I had sat in that shop in the front room of Mavis' house in Kingman and caught up on all the local gossip, adding my own news to the stream.

This place, *Nine*, was unlike any place I had ever been in. Music pulsed at headache-making decibels and the people who worked there looked like they'd come to work on a spaceship. The styles in the magazine on my lap weren't much better. All the models looked fourteen, anorexic, and sulky. And some of the hairstyles featured asymmetrical swaths of hair shellacked into porcupine-like protrusions. Not one of them looked like anything I could imagine wearing.

I'd just about made up my mind to escape back to Mavis' when a young woman in a magenta Indian peasant blouse and spiky orange hair with what looked like purple chopsticks sticking out of it called my name.

"Gail Logan?"

Marshalling my courage, I stood up and smiled at her. "That's me."

"I'm Nora." The girl looked me over. "What can I do for you today, Gail?"

"Well, I've decided to update my look a bit and I'm thinking a new hairstyle might go a long way to help."

As I spoke, Nora touched my arm and led me over to her chair. I sat in the turquoise seat and Nora immediately covered me with a rose-colored drape, unpinned my trademark bun, and combed through my waist-length hair.

"Wow, your hair's sure long. Just looking for a trim?"

"No. I've decided that my bun makes me look too old. I want something easy and a little more modern. But not like the styles I saw in that magazine out there."

"Don't worry, Gail. Despite what you see on my head, I promise I won't make you look like any of those models. We had a workshop yesterday, and what you see is what I got. I kind of like the orange, but, frankly, all the gel and spray they put on it itches like crazy." We laughed. "So, what did you have in mind?"

I ran my hands through my hair and it fell around my shoulders like a protective cape. "I don't know exactly. I've worn it like this for the last thirty years because it was easy and I just don't have the hairdo gene; I'm at your mercy, Nora."

"Okay." While she was thinking, she brushed my hair. It was so relaxing I didn't care how long it took for Nora to figure out what to do. "Your hair's so heavy, I suggest we chop a bunch off first so we can better understand how to proceed. How short do you want to go?"

"Pretty short, I think. I need something simple."

Nora selected a pair of scissors and a few clips. She sectioned off my long locks and grabbed one. "Last chance to change your mind."

"Go for it." I squinched my eyes shut as the blades slashed through thirty years of hair. Methodically working around my head, Nora cut and cut, leaving it chin-length. She saved the long swaths of hair to donate to Locks of Love. I liked that idea.

"Okay, now we shampoo and see what we've got." Nora escorted me to a basin, the warm water and firm fingers on my scalp making me feel like I'd stumbled into a spa. When I was back in her chair, Nora combed through my hair, moving it this way and that. I kept quiet, letting her think.

"Here's what I suggest. You've got nice hair and it's

pretty healthy. Do you object to bangs?" I shook my head. "Okay, you've got a nicely shaped head and it looks like you've got a little natural wave. I think it will look good if we give you some bangs, not so much that you feel like a sheepdog, leave it a little longer on the top, and layer it on the sides and in the back." She stopped, obviously expecting a response.

I hesitated, having no idea whether I'd like that or not. "That's fine," I finally said. "You'll have to show me how to fix it by myself."

"No problem. If I'm right about your hair, it'll almost fix itself."

"Good. That's exactly what I'm looking for."

And with that, the final piece of my transformation began.

Again, Nora sectioned off the hair and large chunks began to rain down around me. When I could, I watched in the mirror, not sure whether to be happy or horrified as more and more of my hair fell to Nora's scissors. I peeked up to watch her face, trying to gauge how she felt about what was emerging, but Nora retained a professionally blank expression. Combing, cutting, using what looked to me like a straight razor, Nora worked to make her vision come to life. It was almost an hour later when she turned me to face the mirror again and said, "There. What do you think?"

Looking at the stranger in the mirror, I was speechless. There was a thin fringe of bangs skimming the tops of my eyebrows, soft wings of hair fell from the crown of my head, and, when I turned, I saw that my hair flipped up in little curls around the sides and back. My entire neck was exposed; I could feel a breeze and it gave me goosebumps. My head felt so light I thought it might just float away. "I...I think I like it." My hand crept up to touch my hair. "It feels very different, strange, but I like it. I like it a lot." I broke into a big grin and looked up to see Nora grinning back.

"That was fun," Nora said. "You look so much younger without all that hair weighing down your face. Let's rinse it out and then I'll show you how to do it yourself."

Twenty minutes later I left *Nine* after Nora patiently taught me how to style my hair and sold me a can of mousse. I thanked her over and over for my new look. Driving back to Kingman from Simpson, I decided I liked the anonymity of the bigger-city salon. I'd always felt that as soon as I walked out of Mavis' I became the topic of conversation among the remaining women. It was a relief to have made such a giant change among strangers. No explaining my motivation, no deflecting prying questions, just a relaxing hour and a half of pampering.

I stopped at Merrick's grocery in Kingman on my way home.

"Gail? Gail, is that you?" I heard a voice behind me.

"Clara! I didn't expect to see you."

"Yeah, like I'm not here nearly every day. I almost didn't recognize you. You look so different. That sweater's wild, you're wearing jeans, and boots. Wow, what a transformation."

"You remember I told you about Samara, the teenager in my painting class?" She nodded. "Anyway, she said last week that I dress too much like an old lady, and you know what? She was right. So, we went on a little shopping trip last Saturday." My hand went to my hair again, "Notice any other changes?"

"Oh my God, you cut your hair short." Clara put her hand on my shoulder and turned me back and forth. "I'm not used to seeing you in anything but that bun you've been wearing ever since we met. But it looks good. I think I like it."

I could see doubt on her face. "Hey, just because I bought a few new outfits and got a haircut doesn't mean I'm different. Inside, I mean."

"I guess. Pretty soon you'll be too cool to hang around with me." She shook her head, said good-bye, and walked away tugging the hem of the floral polyester blouse she had been happy to find on sale when the two of us were at Wal-Mart a few weeks ago.

I spent the next few minutes walking around the aisles in Merrick's alternating between feeling guilty because of the changes I had made and angry at Clara for making me feel that way. I fumed all the way home but as I drove past Clara's house and saw her old station wagon parked in the driveway looking a bit lonely my anger at her lack of enthusiasm evaporated. I had known Clara for over thirty years, and she had been my best friend through thick and thin. A hundred dollars worth of thrift store clothes and a city haircut shouldn't be enough to cause a rift.

I wondered why Clara wasn't right beside me making changes in her life. She was at a crossroads too; her youngest had moved into an apartment in Simpson after graduating from the tech school so she and Hank were alone together for the first time in nearly forty years. That had to be hard, and maybe it went some way toward explaining why she was sure the changes I had made would push our friendship to the brink.

The reaction from Samara and the rest of the students when I walked into the classroom on Tuesday was worth all the agonizing I'd done before I left home.

"Oh my God, you look so much younger," Samara said. "And you changed your hair." She jumped up and made me turn around so she could "get the full effect."

I touched my hair self-consciously. "You don't think it's too young?"

"Not at all. I like the way they feathered it in the back. It frames your face and looks terrific. Makes my earrings look pretty good, too." She made sure the rest of the students admired me and took credit for my transformation.

My hand fluttered in front of my blushing face, and I turned to sit down.

Floyd Marley bobbed up and held my chair. "You look especially lovely tonight, my dear."

I hope he doesn't think I changed my looks for him, I

thought. I smiled my thanks and then busied myself getting my painting things organized to deflect all the unfamiliar attention.

At the café after class, Floyd hovered nearby and snatched the chair beside me, glaring at the other man in class as if they'd been arm wrestling for the privilege of sitting next to me.

"You've got a boyfriend," Samara whispered, giggling. "See what a little wardrobe change can do?"

"Oh, hush," I whispered back. "He'll hear you. Besides I'm not in the market for another man to take care of and clean up after."

"Ok-a-ay, Gail."

During the conversation that night, I was surprised to find I had things to contribute. At first everyone was talking about The Alchemists, a new store in downtown Simpson that sold bath and body products and candles. Two of them were raving about the scented oils they'd bought, and how luxurious it was to soak in the tub with a glass of wine and a book.

One of the women had started working on a political campaign and decided to try to convince us all to vote for her candidate. Several of the other women began to fidget with their mug handles and Karen folded her arms and frowned. I was proud of myself for steering the conversation back to painting saying, "Sorry, Diane, I'm not in the mood for politics tonight. Is anyone thinking of going on that bus trip to the Art Institute that Vi mentioned? I'd love to go." I could tell the rest of the students were happy I'd spoken up. It made me proud of myself; I felt freer and more relaxed than ever before. I found myself humming along with the radio on the drive home. I couldn't wait to get my paints out when I got home and "make art," as June said.

I stayed up late painting and didn't awaken until nearly nine a.m.

I spent a couple of hours planting bulbs I'd picked up on sale at Wal-Mart. After lunch I walked over to Clara's to catch up on things. We sat chatting over coffee in Clara's sunny yellow kitchen.

"So, how did your new look go over at class?" Clara asked.

"Oh, I was a big hit. Samara took full credit for the change. And, you remember, I told you about that little gnome of a man, Floyd Marley, who sits next to me? Well, he got up and held my chair when I got to class, and when we went out for coffee later, he glared at poor Mr. Benning as if they'd been fighting over me. It was embarrassing. I'm sure everyone noticed."

"A pair of men fighting over you. Why, Gail, it's just like high school." We giggled like girls.

"Clara, what am I going to do if Floyd calls me? You should have seen him last night. All puffed up like a rooster and leaning over, breathing his old man breath all over me." The memory of it made me shudder. "Ugh."

Clara was nodding. "Yep, there's nothing quite as scary as an old coot in rut. Maybe you should get an unlisted number."

"What a thought! Clara, you take it back this instant."

"Oh, don't worry. If he's as old as you say he is, he probably doesn't remember what it's for." It took a few minutes for our laughter to die down so she could talk again. "So, how's the painting coming? You didn't throw my bouquet picture away, did you?"

I reached across the table and laid my hand on her hand. "No, I haven't thrown it away. Yet. I told you I'd make you a better one and I will. June said this week she thinks I have real talent. And I must admit, my work's coming along a lot faster than some of the others in class. Maybe I'll be a painter after all."

"I'm sure you will."

Her words might have sounded supportive, but her tone

of voice told me she wasn't interested in listening to me talk about my newfound talent. I wasn't in the mood to deal with her attitude right then so I asked her what her kids were up to and after hearing all those stories, and gossiping about most of the people in town, I thought we were back to normal.

CHAPTER 5

October

Early October was a busy season in my garden. Lots of things were ripening, so that week I spent hours in the kitchen canning and freezing my produce.

Spending so much time in the yard and garden, I found myself looking at them with an artist's eye. I was horrified to realize that everything was lined up in straight rows like soldiers on parade, and even my flowerbeds were regimented and stiff looking. I wonder if I've appeared as stiff and boring as my garden all these years, I thought.

Friday evening, I sat with a pad of graph paper and plotted out my plantings as they were. Next, I got a piece of my watercolor paper and drew and rearranged until I had something much more pleasing. Then I pulled out my paints and planned the colors, but not too rigidly. It was hard not to line things up, not to make sure there were corresponding plants or colors on either side. It went against my instincts not to make it symmetrical. But I liked how the paint blended on the moist paper and realized how much more soothing the look of the garden would be. I fell asleep planning to get a start on revamping my yard the very next day.

Bright and early Saturday morning, I drove to the garden center with my plan in my pocket hoping the last of the zone 4-hardy perennials weren't too picked over. I'd penciled in the names of the plants I already had in the garden while I had breakfast and made notes of what I could add that might look good using a seed catalog as a guide. It was a perfect autumn day, sunny and warm with just a hint of the approaching winter on the breeze.

I had already made a circuit of the greenhouses and the plants on the racks outside and was making more notes on my plan when I bumped into a tall, slender, muscular man with sparkling blue eyes and beautiful gray hair wearing a Garden Center shirt and a nametag that said "Abel."

"Oh, excuse me. I wasn't watching where I was going."

"No harm done," said the man. "I'm Abel Baker. Can I help you find something?"

"Mr. Baker, I'm so pleased to meet you. I'm Gail Logan. I enjoy your column in the *Kingman Times*."

He waved away my praise, "How can I help you, Mrs. Logan?"

"I'm thinking of redoing my flower beds and maybe my garden. My plantings look so controlled. I want something more relaxed and, well, relaxing."

"I can help you with that. Got a plan?"

I unfolded my now-crumpled paint sketch. Soon we were bent over a potting bench debating the merits of the plants I wanted to move and the ones I thought of adding. It took me a few minutes to realize that Mr. Baker had an objection to nearly everything on there. I tried to keep my temper when he said, "It's a wonder any of this stuff is growing at all. Didn't you think before you planted anything?

I could feel my fingers curl around the strap of my purse. He's just like Bert, I thought, always having to know better than I do and never hesitating to tell me what to do. "All of my plants are doing quite well, Mr. Baker." I heard the old lady echo of Aunt Mame in my voice and didn't like it one bit.

"How much shade do you have around here?" he asked, pointing to an area on the plan, ignoring my remark.

"That area gets direct morning sun and partial afternoon shade, so I thought I'd plant hostas and maybe some dahlias."

"Well, your hostas will do fine there, but your dahlias like full sun... although, I suppose they can stand a bit of afternoon shade. They might do better here in front of your porch. Did you mark the trees on your plan?"

"Yes, here, here, and here," I said, stabbing the paper. "I'm experienced enough to realize you can't plant flowers without knowing where your trees are, Mr. Baker."

He bristled. "You wouldn't believe some of the foolish ideas people have." He picked up the paper and started to walk away. "Let's see what's left on the racks and maybe we can get your new garden into the ground before winter."

I trailed after him, wishing I had run into anyone else in the place instead of this crotchety, bossy man.

An hour later I was on my way home with the trunk and backseat of my car full of plants. I had hardy perennials since it was so late in the year. And I had a list from Mr. Baker of the bulbs he thought I should plant before the first frost. When I thought of the high-handed way he'd put plants on a cart, telling me what I should buy instead of asking what I liked, I decided that in the future I'd avoid Mr. Abel Baker at all costs. I buried one bossy man, I told myself, and I'm not going to spend any time with another one.

My irritation with the garden center man gave me extra energy when I went out to dig up and rearrange plants. I found an old clothesline, as he'd suggested, to lay on the ground and figure out how I wanted to make the border. Clara stopped by and when she saw what I was doing, picked up a trowel and lent a hand. She dug out the plants to be moved while I continued to dig out the new border.

"Clara, have you ever seen that Abel Baker at the garden center?" I said to the top of her head as she loosened the soil around a peony plant.

"Can't say I have. Who is he?"

"He writes the "Dirty Hands" column in the paper. I bumped into him over there today and he was completely obnoxious."

"What do you mean?" She sat back on her heels and looked up at me. "Was he rude? Didn't he help you?"

"Help me? First, he acted as if he was the only one on earth who had ever gardened. And then he took over, throwing plants at me as if I were his student, and a not very bright one at that, pontificating about his gardening knowledge. He actually said, 'vast horticultural experience.' Can you believe it?"

Clara picked up the cultivator, leaned forward, and kept on working. She kept her eyes on the dirt as she spoke. "No, I can't. What else? I know there's more."

"Are you smiling?" I saw her back shaking and knew the truth. "You're laughing, aren't you?"

She sat back on her heels and her face was red from the effort to keep her laughter from bursting out. "I'm sorry, Gail." A laugh bubbled out. "I know you're mad, but I sure would have liked to be there to see him." She tipped to the side and sat on the grass with her wrists on her knees and her smiling face shining up at me.

The more I thought about it the angrier I got, the harder I dug, and my words came out in little bursts. "Clara, he was so patronizing I could barely be civil to the man. As I was loading the car, he came out with a list of bulbs he thought I should buy the next time I stopped in. You'd better believe if I do go in there again, I will avoid Mr. Abel Baker at all costs." I stabbed my shovel into the ground so hard I had to rock it to pull it out.

Clara tried to change the subject by complimenting me on my choice of plants and saying that the flowerbeds would be beautiful next spring, but I couldn't stop talking about what a creep Abel Baker had been.

The day was fading as we got the last of the new plants in the ground. "Thanks for all your help, Clara." I rubbed my gloved hand across the shovel to clean off the soil. "I'll finish up moving these other plants tomorrow."

As we stood back to admire our work, Clara said, "It was a good idea to use clothesline to mark the new edges."

"Well, that was the one good idea Mr. Baker gave me. I'll give him that," I said as I surveyed my new, curvy flowerbeds. "But I'll be damned if I'm listening to one more word that jerk has to say."

Clara just laughed as she dusted her knees, "I'd better get home and make Hank's supper. He's been really busy at the feed store, and you know if I have food ready when he gets home he's in a better mood. See you."

That evening I was tempted to write on the porch slat, "Abel Baker is an opinionated jerk," but contented myself with, "Redid the flowerbeds." It was a two-glasses-of-wine day.

CHAPTER 6

I was rinsing my breakfast dishes in the pale, early morning light when the phone rang.

"You ready?"

"Just about, Clara. I'll pick you up in five minutes. Give me a minute to fluff and flush and I'll be right over." Hanging up the phone, I grinned in anticipation. For the last fifteen years, this Saturday in October had been a standing date for us. Today was the biggest flea market of the year, held at the Veteran's Arena in Simpson. Being big bargain hunters and incorrigible antiquers, neither of us would dream of missing this day.

As we drove through the wide spot in the county highway that passed for downtown Kingman, I smiled at the statue of the founder in the little town square. I'd always thought that Edgar Kingman looked too crabby to have been the founder of a town renowned for its neighborliness. Residents had always been willing to lend a hand in times of trouble and, according to the town history published by the Kingman Historical Society, Edgar was a generous and helpful man. Since the Society consisted of three of his great-great-granddaughters, I supposed they wouldn't very well print something less than flattering, but it was a nice story to teach children and I decided it should be true anyway. This was just too nice a place to live to quibble about the man who started it.

We pulled into the parking lot giving each other a run-down of what to look for. We always split up, then met around noon to grab lunch and compare purchases before plunging back into the melee.

"I'm looking for some nice, every-day dishes for Dale and Kayla. Since they're just starting out, they need almost everything," said Clara. "With Dale still in college, they're on a tight budget. I miss the old days when families lived closer together and would just pass stuff around."

"Me, too. Phone calls and letters can't take the place of those good old-fashioned Sunday suppers. There's nothing like the family grapevine to have things just show up, without your having to ask. That's how Bert and I furnished our place when we were starting out. Mom put the word out, and in no time at all, aunts and cousins had shown up with pots and pans, dishes, kitchen gadgets, and all kinds of things that are so expensive to buy new. I'm still passing on some of that stuff after all these years."

"With seven children, all the things passed on to us like that are still making the rounds, but I'm sure one day they'll move back into the rest of the family. What are you looking for, Gail?"

"Picture frames. I need picture frames for my paintings." I looked up at her and she was shaking her head as if to say "all she talks about these days is her painting" but I kept on talking. "I can use any size from four by six inches to eighteen by twenty-four. I'm hoping for wood, but metal might work for some of them, too. They don't have to have glass or anything. I just need the frames. Got a tape measure?"

"Right here in my pocket." Clara patted her jeans. "And I made a copy of my list for you. Here." She handed me a piece of paper with things marked "Want" and "Need."

"What kind of prices are you thinking of for your "Need" category?" I asked.

"Oh, let's say nothing over ten dollars. That way you won't get stuck paying out too much. I thought we'd make notes of anything more expensive and then go back after lunch. How about the frames?"

"I'm hoping not to pay more than two or three dollars for any of them. I'm not interested in any of that overpriced and over-decorated stuff either. I'm looking for nice, simple ones that will showcase my art." As I said, 'my art,' I flung my head back with my right hand over my heart.

She drew in a breath, and I looked at her. I could see her frown, then she got control of whatever was bothering her, and smiled. "You might not think it's art right now, but one of these days I predict that people will fight over your paintings."

"Clara, I appreciate the thought, but I doubt it. Hey, they just unlocked the doors. Let's go."

We crossed the parking lot and joined the crush of people hoping to be the first to grab the best bargains. We paid our three-dollar admission, synchronized our watches, and agreed to meet in the food area at twelve-thirty. Once inside, Clara moved to the first booth while I started at the last so we could cover more booths faster. With any luck, we'd be able to find most of what we needed in the morning and spend a more relaxed afternoon browsing together.

At exactly twelve-thirty, I left the sales area and made my way to the food booths. We met, laid claim to a pair of chairs, and bought lunch. Over bowls of homemade soup and ham sandwiches we filled each other in on our finds of the morning.

Clara had been moderately successful filling her list. I had a few things from Clara's list too but hadn't found as many picture frames in my price range as I'd hoped. "I like to watch the program, but I'm sure unhappy that *Antiques Roadshow* is such a success," I told Clara. "Most of the vendors today seem to think that every piece of junk they're offering is a priceless antique."

"I think you're right," she said. "I had people arguing with me over the price of things that were so damaged I couldn't imagine someone buying them, even from the Goodwill. Were all the frames on your end as overpriced as the ones I found?"

"Terribly. A few of them looked like they'd fall into splinters if you touched them, and they were marked anywhere from twenty-five to fifty dollars. I figure it's just greed, pure and simple."

Clara nodded. "I know what you mean. Most of the people I tried to dicker with had huge chips on their shoulders. They were offended when I offered less than their inflated prices."

"Did you find any dishes?"

"I did. I had them put aside in the booth where I bought them. I'll pick them up on our way out. I think they're god-awful, but Kayla will like them. They're from the '70s and they were cheap. I figure they're too new to be antique and too ugly to be nostalgia."

I burst out laughing as I dug around in the bags at my feet. "I found some nice kitchen towels for you, and some canisters, and, oh, this is the best, I found six tumblers and six juice glasses that match the canisters. I hope they go with the dishes you found. I thought they were too much of a bargain to pass up; they were only three bucks." I held up a green glass with light blue flowers painted on it for Clara to see.

"Oh my gosh," said Clara, "the dishes I bought match them perfectly. It's a sign. We were supposed to be here today."

"A sign? What is it with you and signs? All these years you've talked about things being 'a sign' but you never explained what you meant."

Clara looked embarrassed. "I've always believed in signs. Portents, that's what Gram called them. She'd study the sky or the leaves in the wind or the way dogs howled in the fall. She counted the chirps of the crickets in the summer to see if a storm was on the way.

"I thought she was magic or, if I was mad at her, a witch. I overheard her telling Esther Knowling once when I was about eleven, that she could witch water. It scared me so that for a month afterward I only drank milk or juice. And I kept a real close eye on Gram whenever she drew a glass of water from the tap. I never saw her do anything to the water and she never seemed to chant an incantation over it, but I took no chances."

"Clara! That was almost fifty years ago. Do you really believe that?"

"Yes, I believe it. One day Lester Martin came over from his place complaining to Dad that his well had run dry. Gram offered to go over to help, and I tagged along to see what was going on. When we got there, Gram cut a pair of willow twigs and bound them together at one end with strips of bark. She held the other ends open in a 'V' and walked up and down Lester's pasture like she was mowing it. I couldn't figure out what she was doing, but Lester was watching her like he was praying for a miracle. Well, after a good, long time the point of those twigs dipped toward the ground. 'Here,' said Gram, 'you need to dig here.' Lester dug, and within a hundred feet, he had a new well with endless, fresh, sweet water. That made me a believer, I'll tell you."

I sat and looked at my best friend. "I've heard of water witches, but I never met anyone who knew one or was related to one. That seems so old-timey, but it's cool."

"Yeah, it was cool. I always thought I'd inherited a bit of Gram's gift; you know how good I am at finding lost keys and such. But now don't laugh at this, lately I think I can feel water in the ground too."

I was stunned. "What do you mean, you can feel water in the ground? What does it feel like?"

She scrubbed her face with her hand. "I wish I'd never mentioned this. You're looking at me like I've sprouted another head."

"I don't mean to, Clara, I'm really fascinated. Come on, tell me what it feels like. I can't believe I never asked you about this before."

She looked around to make sure no one was eavesdropping. "Okay. Well, when I walk over to your place across where it gets so muddy in the spring or when I'm walking past the old well down by the barn, I feel a kind of cold flowing over my skin. Sometimes, when it's near the full moon or I'm on my cycle, the feeling is so strong it makes my fingers get that prickly feeling you get after they've gone numb." She leaned her head in her hands. "I can't believe I'm saying this out loud."

"Why? I think it's the coolest thing I've heard in years. My friend, Clara, the water witch." I smiled when I said it, but I could see how embarrassed she was and decided to let the subject drop. "Are you ready to walk around some more?" I said, reaching down to gather up my bags. "I saw some pretty linens in one booth that might be good for Faith's new apartment. They're pricey so I didn't want to buy them without you seeing them." I could see how relieved she was to get back to shopping.

"Yep, I'm ready. All the linens I saw were too stained. Show me what you found."

We spent the rest of the afternoon together looking at the huge variety of things for sale, trying to get the sellers to lower their prices, and dreaming of owning the antique jewelry. Neither of us wore much jewelry, and never anything so fancy, but we both loved looking at it and trying it on.

On the drive home, we discussed our purchases and the difficulty we had finding bargains that year. We decided to start checking the paper for rummage and estate sales. Maybe there we'd have better luck finding what we wanted for better prices.

The next Friday afternoon I was in my studio and my attention was divided. I tried to focus on painting the last bronze chrysanthemums blooming in the garden. I could see them through the window, captured in a shaft of sunlight, shining like newly minted pennies. But I was also listening for the sound of an approaching vehicle and three special voices. Finally, I heard them.

"Mom? We're here."

"Grandma, where are you?"

Smiling, I rinsed my brush in clean water and wiped it carefully before leaving the studio, closing the door.

"Aaron, I'm so glad to see you." I hugged my middle son and then his wife. "Sara, you're positively glowing. Three more months, right?"

My daughter-in-law patted her bulging belly and said, "Yep, three more, just after Christmas. We should have planned better. Excuse me, I need..." Sara turned and headed toward the bathroom.

"And where's my little David?" I looked around, pretending not to see the child hopping in front of me.

"Right here, Grandma. I'm right here."

"This big boy is David? Aaron, are you sure gypsies didn't spirit away our little boy?"

David launched himself into my arms and nearly knocked me over.

"My, how you've grown." I shooed them toward the table. "Sit down, everyone. I made pies and they're just begging to be eaten." At the counter, I uncovered a cherry pie, handed it to Sara as she reentered the room, and took a chocolate pie out of the refrigerator. "Aaron, set out some plates please."

Years of habit die hard. Aaron's shoulders drooped just like they had when I'd asked him to do chores when he was a kid. He went to get plates from the cupboard and was amazed to find cups and glasses instead.

"Mom, what did you do with the plates? Isn't this where they always were?"

"Yes, they used to be there. I moved them." I opened another cupboard. "Here they are. Don't forget forks."

He reached in and pulled down four plates. "These are new. When did you get new plates? What happened to the old ones?" By the look on his face, you'd think I'd sold his favorite pet.

I hadn't bargained for resistance to the changes I was making quite so early in our visit. "Oh, for heaven's sake, Aaron, the old ones were chipped and ugly. I never liked them, so I bought these. Now, put them on the table. I'm sure the pie will taste fine, even on new plates."

I cut generous slices for my guests. "Whipped cream for David. Anyone else?" Two more hands were raised.

Everyone sat around the worn maple table, with pie and glasses of cold milk to wash it down, catching up on the news.

"Sara, do you have the nursery all ready?"

"Aaron just finished painting it a nice minty green. He wouldn't let me help." She reached to touch her husband's arm. "He spoils me. Says pregnant ladies shouldn't be around paint fumes. It was just latex, but he insisted."

"Good for you, Aaron. Don't want my possible future granddaughter hurt by paint fumes."

Sara continued, "I had to call Doctor MacMillan to convince him it wouldn't hurt the baby if I painted on the ends of the crib and the dresser drawers. I can't wait for you to see. I put little storybook scenes on them."

"I'm looking forward to seeing them. You've always been such an artist. I envy your ability to draw. How are you feeling? Are you planning to keep working until the very end?"

"I'm not sure how long I'll work. So far, I feel fine."

"That's great, honey. Aaron, how's your business?"

"A little slow now that school's started," he said, scraping up piecrust crumbs with his fork. "It always picks back up just before the holidays."

"I'm amazed that one of my sons sells computers. They confuse me. I had a devil of a time with the one at school and was happy to leave it behind when I retired. Besides I hear that we don't have reliable internet service out here in the country."

Aaron leaned toward me with a gleam in his eye, like an evangelist looking for converts, waving his fork in my face. "Mom, why don't you let me set you up with a nice, easy system? I can show you how to use it and then you can get on the Internet. The Wisconsin Broadband Office is working hard to get service to everyone. I'm sure you can get online here."

"I'm not ready for that level of technology. I still get confused with the microwave and the VCR."

He kept talking as if he hadn't heard me. "Instead of calling, or writing those long letters you're so famous for, you could email us. You could email Aunt Lydie, too. I get emails from her all the time."

My feelings were hurt. "Don't you like my letters?"

"Of course, we do, Gail," Sara said patting my hand. "Don't listen to him; Aaron's just computer crazy." She turned to him, "Put your fork down, dear; you're getting crumbs all over."

He set his fork on his empty plate and kept talking. "And you should see all the garden sites, Mom. There are supplies, like trowels and baskets and all that stuff, and tons of information on new varieties. Why, you can even order plants that they'll ship right to you. Save you trips to the garden center."

"I like going to the garden center, at least I used to, but I'll think about it." I turned to my grandson to change the subject. "So, David, how are your swimming lessons going?"

"I'm learning to swim really good."

Aaron interrupted, "You should say 'well', David. You're learning to swim really well."

"Okay, Dad," he rolled his eyes, "'well.'" He turned back to me. "And Grandma, I can go all the way down the pool and back without stopping."

"Can you? That's terrific. How's school?"

"Okay, but third grade's hard. We have to learn to write cursive and we started fractions last week." His little face was screwed up in a frown and looked so much like Aaron's at that age I almost cried.

"I know a good way to learn fractions. In fact, I taught your dad fractions this way. Remember, Aaron?" I got up and pulled a second chocolate pie out of the fridge. "Look, David, before we cut it, this pie makes one whole, right?"

David nodded.

"Okay, if I make one cut, like this, down the middle, what do we have?"

"Um...two halves?"

"Exactly. Now, what if I cut it in half again?"

"Uhhh..."

"How many pieces are there?"

"Four. Oh, it's quarters. That's easy."

"It sure is. And if I cut each quarter in half?"

He counted to himself. "Eighths!"

"Congratulations. You just learned fractions. Your prize is one-eighth of a chocolate pie." And I scooped a slice onto his empty plate.

"Gail, you'll spoil his dinner," said Sara.

"I think learning all that math made him very hungry, right, David?" He nodded, his mouth full of chocolate. "Besides, boys who are almost nine years old can always eat. He'll be hungry again by dinner time." I ruffled his already messy, dark brown hair. "I hope you don't mind; I've made up beds for the three of you upstairs. You don't think climbing the stairs will be too strenuous for you, Sara?"

"Not at all. Doctor Mac encourages his moms to exercise. I'm still doing aerobics three days a week. But what are you doing with the spare room? Did you finally turn it into a den, like you've threatened for years?"

"No. I, um, I'm taking a watercolor class and I turned it into a studio. It has lovely north light." I peeked at them through my lashes to gauge their reactions.

"That's great, Mom. Sara wondered what you were doing with all your time now that you're retired." Aaron got up, gathered everyone's plates, and put them into the dishwasher. "No more pie, especially for David. We don't want to spoil our supper." He leaned over to whisper in the little boy's ear. "I'll bet Grandma's cooking something dee-licious." Aaron's grin matched his son's. "Want to help me get the suitcases and carry them up, big guy?"

"No, I want to stay here with Grandma."

I patted my grandson's hand. "Why don't you go help your dad? He's getting old and I want to talk to your mom for a minute." I shooed them out the door. "Go on now."

"Sara, I want to show you... I'd like your opinion... Oh, just come with me. Please?" I was so nervous my hands were fluttering. I pulled Sara out of her chair and urged her toward the spare room. As I turned the knob to open the studio door, I paused and said, "Now, I want your honest opinion, Sara."

We both drew a deep breath and then I pushed the door open for Sara to enter first. I watched her walk around the room nibbling a cuticle. My stomach was in a knot. I valued Sara's opinion because sketching and painting had been Sara's hobby for years, even though she'd studied accounting in college.

"Oh, Gail, these are lovely." Sara looked at the paintings propped on every surface.

I exhaled heavily, not even realizing I'd been holding my breath.

Sara started around again, picking up one after the other. "I love the way you paint flowers. This is like a Monet," she said, holding a painting of the lilies in my garden. "And this little bouquet is so sweet. I love it." She looked around at the multitude of watercolors. "You've done all this since September? Wow, you've got a real talent."

"Do you really think so? You're not just saying it because you think you must?"

"Not at all. I've taken enough art classes over the years to see that you have a gift. Look at this one of the old canning jars and fruits, it's perfectly balanced and you've painted emotion into the arrangement and even hinted at the room. That takes a real eye. This is just fabulous." She walked over and gave me a hug. "I'm so happy for you, Gail. I was worried about you being lonely or depressed after you retired, but I can see I don't have to worry anymore. And I love your haircut. Makes you look ten years younger."

I patted my hair. "Ten years, huh? I'll have to tip my beautician more next time." We laughed. "I'm glad you like my paintings. I'm having so much fun in class. There's this high school girl in class, Samara, who decided I needed some modernizing. We spent a Saturday last month clothes shopping together and had lots of fun. And then there's this ancient man, who I'm afraid fancies himself a real Romeo."

"Gail," Sara giggled, "are you trying to tell me you've got a boyfriend? I'm shocked."

"Oh, you're as bad as Clara. No, Floyd's not a boyfriend. He's just an old fool with bad breath. But I'm afraid he might have a crush on me. He was awfully attentive when we all went for coffee after class last week. Every time the phone's rung I've been afraid it's him and I'll have to hurt his feelings if he asks me out. I'm too old to date. And I don't want another husband. Bert was a fine man, a little bossy I'll admit, but one was enough."

On Saturday morning, I showed them all the changes I'd been making in the flowerbeds. Aaron is as enthusiastic a gardener as I am and leaped at the chance to help with the transformation. We all piled into my car and drove to the garden center. David was fascinated with the garden ornaments, so he and Sara looked at them while Aaron and I pawed through the remaining perennials on closeout.

Aaron said, "Mom, there's an old guy following us around."

I didn't need to turn to see who he meant. "That's Abel Baker. He writes the gardening column in the *Kingman Times*. A couple weeks ago, I made the mistake of asking his opinion about what I should plant, and he did his darnedest to take over. He even gave me a list of bulbs. He's an opinionated jerk. Ignore him."

"Okay."

But when we went to pay for our purchases, Abel stepped behind the counter and told the cashier she could take a break. I glared at him.

"Nice to see you again, Mrs. Logan."

"Mr. Baker."

"How's that garden revamp coming?"

"Fine."

"I see you've got some help this weekend."

I didn't answer and Aaron felt compelled to fill the silence. "Hi, Mr. Baker. I'm Gail's son, Aaron. We're visiting Mom for the weekend."

"Must be nice for you when your family comes to visit, Mrs. Logan. Marcella and I never had kids. You're lucky to have such a fine son. That'll be $17.83."

I extended a twenty-dollar bill and said, "Yes, it is nice to have them stay. I'm sorry you and your wife never had children."

"That's eighteen, nineteen, and twenty," Abel Baker counted the change back to me. "Of course, Marcella's been gone quite a few years now. Kids would have been nice, but Marcella didn't want any. Now I think that having had children would give me someone to pass on my horticultural experience to, like you're doing with your son here."

I couldn't get out of there fast enough. Aaron trailed behind carrying the flat of plants. "Mom, how come you were rude to Mr. Baker? He seemed nice, and eager to help you fix up your garden."

"Aaron, I don't need some dried-up old widower sticking his nose into my garden. Anyway, I told you Mr. Abel Baker is a jerk."

Aaron helped me get the old house ready for winter the rest of the day. We took down screens and put up storm windows, the whole family raked, with David making forts in the leaves—generally making more work for the adults.

I was in the kitchen getting Aaron's favorite beef stew ready for supper when the screen door slammed. David rushed over holding out a bouquet, face flushed with excitement.

"Look what I picked for you, Grandma."

"Oh, David, they're beautiful. And you remembered to pick the stems long."

"Mama helped me this time."

"Let's find a vase for them. Bring them out here to the

potting bench. I think I have the perfect thing to put them in." We went out the back door to search through an old dresser I had turned into a place to store all my gardening tools. I pulled out a dark green pottery vase with geese painted on the side and held it out for David's approval.

"It's just right, Grandma. I saw some geese flying south when we were raking. I like the way they honk when they fly."

"Me, too. I think they sound like winter on the way." We took the flowers, trimmed the stems, and arranged them in the vase. "There, these will look just perfect on the table. Can you carry them in without spilling?"

David gave me a look. "Grandma, I'm not a baby anymore."

"Sorry." I was careful not to let him see me smile.

Sunset on Saturday found the four of us sitting on the porch with cups of hot chocolate enjoying the beautiful autumn colors.

Aaron took a sip of his drink and sighed. "I remember sitting out here when I was little. You'd wrap us in blankets and park us in these chairs with hot chocolate to watch the sunset. Of course, the trees were shorter then; we could see the church steeple a mile away with the sun glinting on the cross. And the hot chocolate you made for us then didn't have brandy in it." He took another sip. "This is great."

I laughed. "Maybe I should have put brandy in it then, too. With three active boys underfoot, those few minutes were about all the peace I got some days. Planting the three of you out here let me grab a breather before getting supper on the table."

"You know, Gail, I never thought of it before, but Aaron has always made a point of being home at least one evening a week to watch the sunset with David and me. He always pours us a drink, even if it's just juice. Huh... Did Bert watch sunsets, too?"

"It was his idea. We sat here watching sunsets when we were first married, planning our future. He always said it was the best in the fall, even though there was so much to do around here. He'd work until the last minute and then come racing in from wherever he was in the fields. I can still hear his boots clomping on the porch floor. And, even after all the years he's been gone, I sometimes find myself wondering if I should pour him a glass of beer when I'm getting ready to come out here."

We finished our hot chocolate in silence enjoying the fading light.

As we were getting up to go into the house for dinner Aaron said, "Mom, you've got some black paint on this railing and the slats." He was picking at the paint with his thumbnail. "I could chip it off or paint over it tomorrow before we go."

"No!" I was embarrassed at the strength of my response. "I mean, no thank you, Aaron. It's too dark to see now but I started marking the sunsets on the railing and putting little comments on the slats, kind of a sunset diary."

"What are you talking about, Mom?"

"Well, I got to thinking I'd spent so many evenings on this porch watching the sun set that it deserved some kind of recognition. So, I'm painting a stripe where the sun touches the railing and... oh, never mind." I flapped my hand to wave away the questions. "It's so silly. Just forget it. The stew's ready. Let's eat."

I watched them exchange glances that said, 'What's going on with Mom?' and 'Don't worry. It'll be okay.' Sara rubbed her husband's back as they walked in to supper, just like she did David's when he was worried or upset about something she couldn't fix.

We spent that evening toasting marshmallows around a bonfire in the fire-pit that Bert and the boys had built one year for a Boy Scout project. I told David stories of how mischievous Sam, Aaron, and Matt were when they were small. Everyone had a good laugh at the stories and Aaron looked ashamed at some of their foolishness. He warned David not to get any ideas.

On Sunday I was the first one up. Though I loved having my family visit, I was happy to have a few minutes to enjoy my tea in peace. Autumn is my favorite time of year. The colorful leaves, the sweet scent of apples from the orchard, and a hint of wood smoke from the old Ben Franklin stove in Hank's workshop down the lane all made me regret that summer was over. But being a farmer's wife, I appreciated winter because it was the only season I got to spend as much time as I wanted with Bert. He worked at the feed mill during the winter and had regular hours. I treasured the memories of evenings Bert spent at the kitchen table, poring over seed catalogs and bulletins from the county agricultural agent while I made supper.

I was sipping my tea and watching a pair of chickadees at the feeder when I noticed David's bouquet. He'd picked a mixture of bronze, deep red, and pale gold chrysanthemums. I was sure it had been Sara's idea to add a few branches with leaves still clinging to them and some bare ones. I thought it made a pretty picture with the birdfeeder and still-green honeysuckle behind it.

Picture! I promised Clara I'd paint her a bouquet picture for her bathroom. These colors would be perfect in there. I grabbed my sketchbook and pencil and got to work. I was scribbling away when Sara came down in her robe, rubbing the sleep from her eyes.

"What are you drawing?" Sara asked as she poured herself a cup of tea.

I waved the pencil at the flowers and said, "I just realized how pretty this looks with the feeder in the background and wanted to sketch it before I lost it. I promised Clara a picture and this might be just the thing."

"Good idea." We spent the half hour before the boys got up brainstorming how I could make the painting look the way I envisioned it and what colors to use. Sara promised to send me a few of her favorite watercolor books.

"I won't be painting for a while with a new baby in the

house so you might as well use them."

"Thanks, dear, I really appreciate that. I'll take good care of your books." I felt that I might be an artist after all.

I was sad to wave goodbye to my middle son and his family on Sunday afternoon, but glad there was still enough light to get back into the studio and work. I had every confidence that the phone lines between my sons and daughters-in-law would be burning as soon as Aaron and Sara got home. I imagined Merry, Sara, and Lisa assuring each other that their mother-in-law was "just going through a phase." And I could hear the boys grousing about how everything was going to change now that "Mom's gone nuts." Those three never did like change, I thought. I hope they didn't learn that from me. But, if they did, they're about to learn something new.

I spent a very pleasant and satisfying evening in the studio sketching my ideas onto paper and laying in the washes for Clara's bouquet painting.

CHAPTER 7

I spent the days after Aaron and Sara's visit fielding phone calls from the rest of my sons and daughters-in-law.

The first to call on the Sunday night after Aaron left, was Sam. Being the eldest son, he'd assumed responsibility for his brothers' well-being after Bert had died. Now it seemed that Sam felt my life was within his scope as well.

"Mother, Aaron called and said you've taken up painting, completely redone your garden, and changed the way you look. Are you all right?"

"Sam, for heaven's sake, I am a human being. Human beings change and evolve, even mothers. You can't expect me to be like some museum exhibit marked, 'Gail Logan, Midwestern Housewife and Mother (Nearing extinction).' What's really bothering you? What else did Aaron say?"

There was a considerable pause during which I assumed my eldest was marshalling his thoughts. Good thing Sam's a lawyer, I thought. I'm sure his clients appreciate the way he deliberates over things. I imagine it makes them feel he takes their every word to heart, but right now I could just shake him. Pride and exasperation warred in me, as it had since Sam was old enough to talk. Of all my sons, he was the one most burdened by the idea of doing and saying the right thing.

Sam cleared his throat and finally said, "He did mention that you seemed to have a couple of suitors." Suddenly the little boy in him burst out, "Mom, you aren't thinking of getting a boyfriend, are you?"

I almost giggled out loud. Despite his air of confidence, Sam was the most sensitive of my sons. "Sam, my dear son, I am not 'getting a boyfriend.' It's true that a gentleman in my painting class has taken a shine to me, and there's an old coot at the garden center trying to wrangle an invitation to help redo the flowerbeds, but I can assure you that your father was plenty husband for me. I have no intention of beginning to accept applications for a successor."

"Mom, I'm worried about you being out there in the country all alone. Maybe you shouldn't have retired. If you were still working, you'd have something normal to fill your days and people you know to talk to."

"Sam, I'm enjoying being alone. Besides, Clara and Hank are right down the lane like they've always been. If I get lonely or bored, or scared for that matter, they'd be here for me in a heartbeat."

"I know. But we don't even know any of these new people you're talking about. What kinds of people are in that painting class?"

"I do know them and they're regular kinds of people. There are eight of us; some know me from my years at the school, some I've just met. We go out for coffee after class and have a few laughs. I'm not hanging out in bars and I'm not picking up loose men. I've taken up painting as a hobby because it's interesting and it seems I'm pretty good at it. And I decided to dress less like an old lady and more like myself, that's all."

"But, Mom, ..."

"I know you're worried, and I appreciate your concern. But once you graduated from college, your dad and I stayed out of your life. Now that I'm retired, I want you to stay out of mine."

"Mom! Aaron said you've started keeping some sort of goofy sunset diary on the porch railing. What's that about?"

I could hear Sam's wife, Merry, in the background asking to speak to me. Reluctantly, Sam relinquished the phone.

"Hello, Gail? What has Perry Mason been saying to you?"

"It's alright. He's just concerned about me."

"Well, I heard the end of what he was saying, and I don't think he has any business telling you how to live your life."

"Thank you, dear. I appreciate you sticking up for me, but I think I handled him rather well. How have you been?"

"Fine. Listen, Sara told me how wonderful your paintings are and I, for one, want to get my order in early before her and Lisa. Anytime you have any spare paintings you think would go with our décor, you just send them right out. They don't even have to be framed. I can do that and save you the expense."

"That's very flattering, Merry. But I'm afraid Sara might have exaggerated a bit. Right now, my paintings are more on the 'refrigerator art' end of the scale. Perhaps in a year when I've taken a few more classes I'll have something better. Then I'd be happy to send you a painting."

I could picture Merry standing in her painfully modern house overlooking the Pacific, chewing on a perfectly manicured nail, and imagining herself saying to her friends, "Oh, yes, Samuel's mother had a gallery showing in Chicago. She saves her best canvases for us, of course." I loved Merry and knew she was a good wife to Sam, but I had a hard time identifying with Merry's drive to be a successful somebody, to make a real splash in the world. Merry was a realtor and collected as many 'names' as she did commissions.

"Sweetheart, it's getting late. Let me say goodbye to Sam and I'll talk to you next week."

"Okay, Gail. Goodbye, I love you."

"I love you too, honey. Have a good week."

A subdued Sam got back on the line. "Mom, I'm sorry if I sounded overbearing. It's just that we live so far apart; I feel like you might need me and I'm not there. Maybe we should move back."

I had a hard time answering around the lump in my throat, "It's okay, Sam. I wish you lived closer, too, but you and Merry are doing so well out there it'd be foolish to start over in the Midwest. Besides, I'm fine. I promise to call you if that changes. Now, you have a good week and I'll send you a letter on Friday. I love you."

"I love you too, Mom. Bye, talk to you next week."

I sat, misty eyed, looking at the phone for a long moment. For a second, I ached for the days when the boys were small, and I was the center of their world. But you're having so much fun right now, I thought. Don't wish it away.

I checked the time on the old mantle clock and decided I could paint for another hour and not be too tired in the morning. My steps were light as I crossed the kitchen to the studio. But I ended up spending an hour moving lamps around and changing the bulbs for higher wattage ones trying to shed some better light on my work, and not painting.

Monday evening brought the anticipated call from Matthew, my youngest.

"So, Mom, you're finally turning into a hippie, huh? I guess you missed it in the '70s."

I had to laugh. "No, I am not turning into a hippie. I bought some jeans and new sweaters, yes. And, yes, I took up watercolor painting. I'm not burning incense or smoking grass or anything else for that matter. Evidently Aaron called."

"Actually, it was Sam. Or should I say, Samuel, now that he's turned into an expensive San Francisco lawyer. Merry announced that we have to call him Samuel now, 'as befits his position' I was pointedly told. That woman is some piece of work."

"Be nice, Matty. I like Merry and she's a good wife for Sam. Growing up with a mother who was never satisfied with anything couldn't have been good for her. She's so insecure that she needs to build a wall of pretension around herself, that's all. Inside is a very sweet girl. So, what did Sam tell you?"

"Let's see, that you've changed your hair and clothes, that you're meeting all sorts of weirdoes and kooks in that painting class, and this is what upset him the most I think, you're attracting men left and right. Are you turning into a femme fatale, Mother?"

"Oh, you bet I am."

"Should I send you a big stick for Christmas so you can beat the men off?"

"I don't think so. One of my conquests is about a hundred years old with the worst breath on the planet, and the other one is in his late sixties or early seventies and fancies himself the world's best gardener. He works at the garden center and pontificates at length about his horticultural experience. Every time I see him, I want to run the other way. But that's enough about me, how are my brilliant grandsons and beautiful daughter-in-law?"

"The kids are great. They're getting excited about Halloween. All that candy's just what they need. Jim is just as serious as ever; he reminds me of Sam. Lisa and I have started calling him the president of second grade."

"But not in front of him, right? That would be cruel."

"Don't worry, Mom. We won't give any of them a complex. We believe in letting them get their own."

"Matthew Logan, you be nice. What about the other boys?"

"Mike and Luke have taken over their kindergarten class. Every week Lisa gets another note from the teacher asking us to come in so she can tell us about some mischief they've gotten into. And Noah's learned that the dog likes vegetables so there's a constant rain of them from the highchair. All in all, just about normal, I guess."

I thought Matt sounded like a proud patriarch talking about his rambunctious grandchildren, when in fact he was the twenty-eight-year-old father of four active boys. He had always been the most laid-back of my sons. Nothing ever disturbed his easygoing attitude.

"It sounds to me like you and Lisa are having about as much fun as your dad and I did when the three of you were small. How are things at work?"

"Good. We got in a new Sayon-214. It's a gigantic

bulldozer made in Japan. I'm having a blast learning how to fix them."

I had to smile listening to the man who'd spent his boyhood playing in the sandbox with every Tonka truck ever sold, glad that he'd followed his dreams and opened his own shop, specializing in servicing construction equipment, even if it was in a city two-hundred miles away. "I'm glad you're enjoying it. Is Lisa able to talk or is she busy refereeing?"

"Nope. We waited to call until the troops were down for the night. Here she is."

I could picture my tiny, blond daughter-in-law sitting slumped on the couch, brushing her hair out of her eyes.

"Hi, Gail. How are you doing?"

"I'm fine, sweetheart. You sound tired. The boys driving you crazy?"

"Not any more than normal. I called Sara this morning to find out what was going on with you that sent Sam into such a tizzy. Honestly, men can be such babies when things change."

I heard Matt's voice rumble in the background, then Lisa said, "Not you of course, darling. You're the most adaptable of men. Now leave me alone to talk to your mother. Go play with your new toy. There, he's gone. Now we can talk."

"What's his new toy?"

"He got a new computer."

"Matt has a computer?"

"Don't be so surprised that Wrench-boy likes them. He looks at it as just another tool. Aaron helped us pick one out, besides the kids need it for school. Matt and Jim sit there by the hour and look up things about animals and giant trucks. But I want to hear about you. What's going on?"

So for the third time in two days, I told all about my class, new friends, new clothes, and the changes I was making in the garden. I went on at length about Floyd and Abel. "Men are just too much trouble to look after. I'm having fun being by myself, doing what I want to do when I want to do it."

"Then that's what you should do. You just have to make

sure you don't encourage those guys if you're not interested. That would be mean. But men are good for some things, Gail. You know, like opening pickle jars and stuff like that."

After Matt's call, I sat staring at the wall. Now I'd seen or heard from all three of my sons. Only Matt sounded unfazed by the changes I'd made in my life. Aaron and Sam seemed ready to call in a deprogrammer.

I thought, maybe I'll resell my new clothes and let my hair grow again. I started to cry. No, I will not.

"It's my life," I said to the empty house. "I'm a grown woman, I can do what I want when I want. I let them go off and live their lives the way they want. What gives them the right to try to control mine? Did we raise them to be so narrow-minded that they expect me to stay frozen in one place?"

I had spent my entire life fitting someone else's vision. This was my time, and no amount of whining was going to derail my pleasure in my new interests. By the time I stopped crying it was too late to paint with the poor lighting in the studio. With winter fast approaching, I resolved to do something about it soon, maybe tomorrow. I locked up, grabbed a crossword puzzle book, and went to bed.

The next day dawned overcast and rainy. It was too messy outside to think about driving to Simpson Mall to buy some new lights for the studio. Instead, I decided to see if I couldn't finish the flower painting for Clara's bathroom today. I turned on all the lights in the studio, decided it was still too dim, and went upstairs to relocate a couple of lamps from the seldom-used bedrooms. Once I had a pair of lamps installed and turned on, it was much brighter, but the heat from them made the room uncomfortably warm for a woman at my age and stage in life, so I opened the window.

It was a perfect day to spend painting. No yard work could be done, there were no errands that couldn't wait, and no one called to interrupt.

I painted for hours and, for the first time, what I put on the paper matched the vision in my head. The jewel-tones of the chrysanthemums, the morning light slanting onto the vase and table, even the chickadees at the feeder outside in the honeysuckle seemed to leap off the page. It was early afternoon when I finally put down my brush.

"Now that's a painting I'll be proud to give Clara." Looking at the clock, I saw it was 1:30 and realized I was starving. I went to the kitchen to forage for leftovers in the fridge. I heated some stew in the microwave and sat at the table to eat it while watching the raindrops chase each other down the windowpane.

After only a few bites, I picked up the bowl and walked into the studio to look at Clara's painting, to reassure myself that it really was as good as I'd thought. When I entered the room, I nearly dropped my bowl.

The wind had shifted, and rain was blowing in on the painting. What had once been a bright, lively watercolor of a bouquet was now a muddy brown mess with paint dripping off the paper onto the floor.

"Oh, no."

I set my unfinished lunch on the table and slammed the window shut. I gently picked up the painting, spun around, walked through the kitchen and out the back door still carrying the wet paper. I stopped on the back porch to put on my raincoat then almost ran next door to Clara's. Bursting into Clara's kitchen, I waved the ruined painting and started sobbing, babbling incoherently.

"Gail, for heaven's sake, what's the matter? Is something wrong with one of the boys? Why are you waving that paper at me?"

I tried to talk through my hiccupping sobs, "I painted this…and…the rain…oh, Clara, I'm so sorry."

"Honey, just calm down. Here, let me get that raincoat off you and I'll fix us some coffee." She gently removed the dripping coat and hung it up and steered me into a chair. "Have you eaten?"

I nodded then shook my head, still crying too hard to talk.

"Okay, I didn't understand that, but I'm making you something anyway."

She poured me a mug of coffee and made me an egg salad sandwich on homemade bread. She set the plate on the table and sat down across from me.

"Now, eat," she said, as if to a stubborn child.

I dried my eyes on the back of my hand and smiled at her.

"I'm sorry I fell apart on you."

"It's okay. What are friends for if you can't cry all over them? What's so bad it made you cry like that?"

"Oh, Clara," I said around a bite of sandwich, "I painted that for you today." I swallowed and took a sip of coffee. "This is good. Thanks." I nodded at the smeared paper. "It was of the bouquet David picked for me over the weekend, and it was perfect. The best I've ever done. I was so happy that it was for you. I had just fixed myself some lunch and, after a few bites, I went back into the studio to admire it. In the three minutes I was gone, the wind had shifted and blew rain in the window and ruined it."

"No wonder you cried if you thought it was your best work so far. But that was an awful lot of tears over a painting. Anything else bothering you?"

I filled her in on Aaron's visit and the phone calls from Sam and Matt. "All that mistrust from the boys got to me, I guess." I groped in my jeans pocket, came up with a paint-smeared handkerchief, and blew my nose.

"You have to admit you're very different these days," said Clara. "Maybe you've changed too much too fast for them. You know how sensitive men can be about change. You and Bert put a lot of effort into making your sons' lives secure and surprise-free. Neither of you were ones for following fads; you had the same jobs for years. Everything around those boys stayed pretty much the same and only they changed. It was safe; they could depend on Mom and Dad. You and Bert were stable."

"You mean dull," I said, "Bert and I were dull. I was particularly dull. I looked the same, kept the same schedule; I even cooked the same meals year after year. Boring and dull."

"Some people might think that sort of routine is comforting. Some people don't like surprises." She got up and refilled our mugs.

"I'm usually not crazy about surprises either, Clara. I realized back in September that I didn't really know who I was anymore. I've never really felt that I fit in anywhere. Oh, I went along and did all the things women of our era were supposed to do; married a 'good' man, had children, and stayed home to raise them for a time. Then I got a job, in the school so I'd have the same vacations as the boys, was an officer in the PTA; all that stuff the experts tell you to do to have a happy and successful life."

"Weren't you happy? All these years you were pretending?"

"Yes, I was happy; I wasn't pretending. I don't know if I can explain it." I got up and looked out the window at my house in the distance. "All my life I've felt like there was a voice in me I couldn't quite hear. Telling me something really important, important to me, and I was never still enough to hear it. When I picked up that paintbrush, it was like the volume got turned up, and for the first time in my life I could hear that voice. Hear what I wanted to do, what I was supposed to do, to become myself." I turned back to my friend with a pleading look. "Does that make any sense at all, Clara? Is this some bizarre side effect of menopause? Am I nuts?" I sat back down, picked up my cooling coffee, and took a sip.

"No, honey, you're not nuts. Or maybe I should say, no more nuts than most women our age." She sighed. "All my life, all I ever wanted to be was a wife and mother. Marrying Hank, raising seven kids, feeding them, keeping them clean—that was all I ever wanted to do. I never understood those women during the feminist movement in the '70s, burning their bras and wanting to be men's equals. I never wanted to have a job out in the working world and be at someone's beck and call. Heck, I wanted to stay home and be the boss." She looked surprised at the vehemence of her statement. "Huh. I guess I never said all that out loud before." She reached across the table and covered my hand with hers. "But, Gail, if you need to change just about everything in your life to be happy, I'm on your side. All I ask is that you not forget about your old friend Clara. And that you keep coming over and telling me all about it."

I leaned over and gave her a big hug. "Clara, I knew I could count on you to be the voice of reason. Don't worry, I'll keep that path between our houses tramped open. And you'd better do the same."

I felt a lot better about myself, and all the changes I was making after talking to Clara. And I was more determined than ever to recreate that first feeling of accomplishment. The fact that the rain had ruined it, rather than a lack of skill, made the loss a bit more bearable. I went home and tacked the smeared mess up on my wall. It stayed there to remind me to be more careful.

I got out another piece of watercolor paper and sketched in the window, the birdfeeder outside in the honeysuckle, the table, and the bouquet. As I'd done before, I laid in the washes, hoping my hands remembered what they'd done earlier that day.

Sitting on the porch watching the sunset that evening, watching the light pry its way through the diminishing bars of rain clouds, the heat from my mug of tea felt good on my hands. I'd spent most of the day painting. It amazed me that I could paint and paint and never get tired of it. The ideas flowed down my arm and my fingers knew what to do. I put down my tea and flexed my right hand. I'd better rub some liniment on it before I go to bed. I don't want to wake up with cramps in the middle of the night. The red-golds and purples the setting sun washed over the sky made my fingers itch to return to the studio. But I knew in my heart that I'd never be able to reproduce them in paint. It would be frustrating to try.

I picked up my mug and sipped the tea, savoring the warmth as I drank. My life was filling up in a way I'd never experienced before. Painting, new friends, a new look, combined with the solid life I'd built added up to a deep satisfaction that warmed my soul, as the tea warmed my hands.

I lay in bed that night replaying my sons' reactions to the changes I'd made in my life. I alternated between anger and tears.

It hadn't surprised me that Sam was upset. I knew that my eldest was the most sensitive of the three. I had no idea how Merry had persuaded him to move to San Francisco. I suspected that uprooting Sam from his home overlooking the bay and his comfortable law practice would take something with the power of an earthquake.

Aaron might work with computers, which constantly changed, but he liked order in his life.

Even though Matt, the youngest and most flexible, had sounded encouraging, I couldn't help wondering if I hadn't heard a note of caution creep into his voice.

I decided that I wanted to prepare a speech designed to remind all three of them who was the mother. I sat up in bed, turned on the bedside light, put on my glasses, and grabbed the pad and pencil I kept there.

Do I need to remind you that I'm an adult? I wrote. I've managed to survive all by myself the eight years since your dad passed. I'm only fifty-seven years old and I'm not ready for the trash heap. All the changes I've made, and will continue to make, aren't about you. They're about me. You need to loosen up and give me a little encouragement like I've done for you all these years.

I reread what I'd written, put my things aside, turned off

the light, and fell asleep mentally repainting Clara's painting.

CHAPTER 8

Coming home after class, I turned off the State Highway onto the lane. My headlights cut a path through the darkness. The gravel surface forced me to slow down and watch where I was going. The lane had enough twists that you couldn't drive it on autopilot. I liked how the leaves swirled off the trees in the autumn breeze. They looked like Technicolor rain as they flew through the night. It had been years since I'd had a reason to be out regularly at night and I drank in the unfamiliarity of my view.

Passing Clara's house, I noticed a light still on in the living room. Clara must be up reading or working on a crossword, I thought. A mutual love of the word puzzles is what had drawn us together over thirty years ago.

I put the car in the garage and walked up the path to the backdoor, Clara's light winking at me through the leafless trees. I set my paint basket on the floor of the porch and decided to walk over to visit, even though it was nearly midnight. Halfway there, picking my way carefully in the dark, I looked up to see a familiar figure coming toward me.

"Couldn't sleep, Clara?"

"No. I got up about an hour ago so I wouldn't disturb Hank. I hate menopause. When I saw your headlights go by I decided to run over. So, how was class?"

"It was great. We learned about painting shadows. Come on, I'll make us some chamomile tea. Maybe that'll put us both to sleep."

We linked arms and took our time getting to my place. It was a fine autumn night.

"Look! A shooting star," said Clara. "Make a wish."

"I wish everyone could have a friend like you, Clara."

We leaned together and stood in silence watching the constellations in their slow waltz across the heavens. After a few minutes we made our way to my kitchen where we sipped tea and talked long into the night.

CHAPTER 9

As Samara and I left the classroom in the craft store on our way to the café the following Tuesday, I was surprised to see Mr. Baker looking at the display of frames nearby. I immediately stopped talking and started to steer Samara down the next aisle hoping to avoid him. But he must have been waiting for me because he turned with a smile.

"Boy, you all sure have fun in there. I could hear you laughing with the door closed."

"Yes, Mr. Baker, we do have a good time. Have a nice evening," I said and turned to catch up with Samara who was going out the door. He fell into step with me.

"I was wondering, Mrs. Logan, if you'd like to get a cup of coffee. We could maybe go to that new café down the road." He blushed and shoved his hands into his pockets.

I stiffened. That's where everyone in class was headed and I didn't want him insinuating himself into the group.

"I'm sorry, Mr. Baker. I couldn't possibly go with you. It's late and I have to get home. It's a long drive," I said, turning away again.

"Are you sure, Gail? It's only ten miles. I mean, I heard your grandson talking to his mom on Saturday about you taking this class, and I just thought it might be nice to meet you and go for coffee. We could talk about getting your garden put to bed for the winter or what you might plant in the spring..." He trailed off, sounding just like a fifteen-year-old asking out his first date.

I tried not to smile at the pleading note in his voice. Not so confident now, are you, Mr. Horticultural Experience?

I made sure to wipe any trace of a smile off my face before turning back to him.

"I'm sure, Mr. Baker. Thank you for the invitation." I walked out of the store, got into my car, and drove away. I could see him standing in the store watching me leave while the employees turned off the lights behind him.

Everyone from class was already seated when I got there. I started to place my order as I passed the waitress, but the waitress shook her head.

"I got it, honey. You're the decaf mocha latté, right?"

"I guess I'm too predictable."

The waitress laughed. "Honey, everybody's predictable about coffee. You go on sit down with your friends and I'll be right along with the drinks."

As I sat down, Mona, a young secretary, was telling everyone about a class at the museum she was thinking of signing up for.

"The instructor teaches at the University, and he's had a gallery showing in Chicago," Mona said.

Viola sighed, "A gallery showing in Chicago? Wow, that's so cool. Gail and Samara are the only ones at this table who even have a chance at that."

That took my breath away. "Me? Are you kidding, Vi? I agree that Samara has a chance, but not me. She's so relaxed and creative. I'm still strangling my brush."

A chorus of denials and reassurance that I was indeed good enough for a gallery showing answered my statement.

"You're the best in class," Joe Benning said.

"Why do you think June spends most of every class bending over your shoulder?" said Mona. "She's worried you're better than she is."

Vi said, "When I saw your first painting I almost gave my paints away."

"Gail," Samara put her hand on my arm, "you can't be serious. You've got real talent. I have plans for you and me conquering the art scene in New York just as soon as I get out of college. I'm thinking those four years will give both of us a chance to develop our own styles and then, look out, New York, Gail and Samara are on the way."

I looked at my young friend and at all the smiling faces around the table. "Thank you all for those kind words. Like I said, right now I'm just hoping to keep from giving myself arthritis. But you're all invited to my first gallery opening." I finished with a flourish.

I looked up to discover Mr. Baker standing at the cash register waiting to be seated. Samara saw the smile suddenly leave my face and whispered, "What's wrong? Who is that guy? Wasn't he waiting for you after class?"

I picked up a menu and tried to hide behind it. "That's Abel Baker. I told you about him, didn't I? He's the guy from the garden center who keeps trying to wrangle an invitation to help in my garden. He asked me out for coffee tonight and I told him I was going home. I'm so embarrassed."

I hid behind the menu while he was seated and was relieved that he sat with his back to me.

"I can't risk him seeing me. I have to leave. Make my excuses to the others, please, Samara." I gathered up my purse and jacket, tossed five dollars onto the table for my coffee, and left.

I wondered during the drive home if Mr. Baker had seen me and felt terrible for lying to him at the craft store. Maybe I'll take him a jar of pickles the next time I go to the garden center. "What am I thinking?" I said out loud. "He bugs the crap out of me. Why would I worry if I've hurt his feelings?"

I was glad that, for me, gardening season was finished so I didn't have to worry about running into Mr. Baker over the petunias for a while.

But the following Tuesday when the class arrived at the café, there he sat in the waiting area. He stood when we entered and said, "Hello, Mrs. Logan," in his deep warm-honey voice, which made every woman in the group sigh and turn and smile at me expectantly. I stifled a groan but pasted a smile on my face and invited him to join our group. Floyd was not pleased when Mr. Baker pulled out my chair and sat down on my right. Floyd plunked himself down on my left and glared at his perceived rival.

I felt like I was under a spotlight and was embarrassed by the knowing looks I received from the other women, especially Samara. I wished I could sink into the floor and just disappear.

I sat there, fuming, between the two men and looked around the table at my smiling, chatting classmates. We had only one more class and everyone had really bonded these past weeks. My eyes moved to my right where that jerk sat. He was leaning back in his chair with his left arm oh-so-casually draped over the back of my chair. I didn't want him touching me but couldn't figure out a way to get him to move it without causing a scene.

I tried leaning forward and to the left, but that put me nearly in Floyd's lap... and too close to his breath. I sat silently, fuming, and trying not to breathe.

Mr. Baker made up for my silence by being charming and funny. He introduced himself to the class and asked them about their work. He expressed an interest in their paintings and how they thought they'd progressed in the class. Listening with half an ear, I was surprised to discover that he knew a lot about art. When someone mentioned our plan to spend a weekend in Chicago at the Art Institute, Mr. Baker's eager answer silenced the whole group.

"Of course, you have to see the Picassos, the Monets —especially *On the Seine at Benncourt*—his light and colors remind me of this part of the country; and the Gauguins. But you shouldn't miss Kandinsky either; his use of color is brilliant. Be sure to look at Mary Cassatt because she was such a pioneer as a woman breaking into the Impressionist movement at that time. Of course, they all painted in oils. I know you're studying watercolor but I'm sure you can learn something from every artist." He looked at his silent audience and went on. "You have to see Manet's *Racetrack Near Paris* because those are the best skies, Jules Breton's *Song of the Lark* because of the somber mood his use of color evokes, and all of the Renoirs. Especially the Renoirs."

Eight pars of eyes stared at him, apparently stunned by the outpouring of knowledge from an unexpected source. The authority and depth of understanding from a man who looked more like a hick farmer than an art aficionado stilled the usual small conversations of the group.

"Why shouldn't we miss the Renoirs?" asked Samara.

"Because he's got it all—vivid color, great brushstrokes, excellent light, and a depth of feeling in his work that many so-called Masters could only dream about. Plus I love his choice of subject matter. I could live with any Renoir the rest of my life and be happy." He looked around at the rapt faces. "So, who do you like?"

I was disgusted by my classmates' eagerness. Each one vied for his attention, gushing about the artist that inspired them. Vi even reached across and laid her hand on his, looking soulfully into his eyes while she expounded on the depths of Edward Hopper's work.

Finally Mona asked the question that had been bothering me. "You say you're a gardener, Abel, so how do you come to know so much about art?"

He explained it by saying, "Anybody can line up flowers in a row. I'm thinking the talent to make a beautiful garden is very similar to the talent an artist needs to make a beautiful painting."

I suspected he knew more about art than he let on.

When the conversation turned to books, he had read many of the titles mentioned. He showed a surprising interest in the classics and confessed to an addiction to mysteries. I liked mysteries, too, but I was damned if I'd say that to him.

Driving home from the café I fumed that Mr. Baker had trumped my snub of last week and shown up tonight. He'd greeted me so innocently, blandly waiting for me to remember my manners and introduce him to my classmates. And then he had monopolized the conversation by being all charming and funny. And his remarks about art. I bet he'd spent the week studying art books so he could impress me with his knowledge, I thought. And then when Mona and Vi started talking about books, he'd just jumped in, giving opinions right and left as if he'd read every book ever written. The last straw was his comment about loving mysteries. Hah! That's a transparent attempt to impress me if I've ever heard one.

My irritation with that man so consumed my thoughts that I was home before I knew it. As I walked up the flagstone path to the back door I glanced up and saw Clara, wraith-like in the moonlight, making her way over for what had become our weekly midnight chat over a cup of tea after my class.

CHAPTER 10

November

The next Tuesday getting ready for our last class, I took extra care choosing my favorite red sweater and a new pair of gray wool slacks. I had gotten myself another pair of boots, red leather ones, with slightly higher heels; I wore them.

June turned the last session into what she called our "first gallery showing." She brought empty frames and invited us to mount the paintings we'd worked on throughout the last seven weeks. I was impressed that the eight of us had managed to produce quite a bit of art. Seen all together it was also easy to see which of us were artists and which were dabblers. Samara's were the most colorful and Mona's were the most precise. (I think she used three bottles of masking fluid during the class.) June went around the room commenting on each painting. She tried to compliment and encourage each of us, but I could tell by the tone of her voice that she hoped never to see some of us again. She served too-sweet punch and store-bought cookies while she told us how proud she was of our progress. We knew that the real finale would be our time at the café afterward, rehashing the evening and the class. Nine o'clock rolled around and everyone removed their paintings from their temporary frames and rushed to get to our usual table.

I spent an extra minute in the café parking lot reapplying my lipstick so I'd look nice. I was surprised at how eager I was to join the group and pushed away the hopeful thought that Mr. Baker might be waiting at the table. I was irritated with myself when I had a moment of disappointment at not seeing him. I was glad to find that the remaining empty chair wasn't near Floyd and that sitting in it would put my back to the door. I don't want anyone getting the idea I'm waiting for that obnoxious jerk to join the group, I thought as I walked around the table. I'm happy he's not here to ruin the evening.

Since it was our last class together, we stayed later than usual at the café. Joe Benning had us all cracking up at his impression of June. Vi and Mona kept asking me about Abel and teased me that we were secretly dating. I denied it, of course, since we weren't, but it was fun to be accused of having a secret life. It was nearly midnight by the time we said our final goodbyes and got up to leave. Floyd offered to walk me to my car.

As we left the café, a group of shaggy men who looked like hoodlums in black leather, chains jangling from their jeans pockets, and greasy hair piled out of a wreck of a van parked next to my car. I stopped abruptly nearly pulling Floyd, who was holding my arm, off his feet. He tottered a bit but regained his balance quickly.

"Something wrong, my dear?" Floyd said.

"I'm not sure I want to go to my car right now. Those men don't look too friendly."

"Not to worry." He patted my hand. "I'll protect you. I might not look it now, but in my day I was a bit of a scrapper."

I looked down at the wispy, white-haired man hanging heavily on my arm and smiled.

"I'm sure you were, Floyd." The men started to move toward the café door. "We might as well keep going."

The men nodded to us as they passed by. Floyd and I called a last goodbye to the other students when we reached my car.

Floyd kept hold of my arm and said, "I must tell you, my dear, I am very impressed with your painting talents. Perhaps we could plan to meet at my studio and spend an afternoon painting one day soon."

"That's a lovely idea, Floyd. I'll give you a call." I untangled my arm from his and unlocked my car door. I turned to tell him goodnight and found myself pinned against the door by his body pressing on mine. "Um, Floyd, you need to move back so I can get in my car."

"Oh, this suits me fine," he said, pressing into me harder and rolling his hips. His hands roamed up my arms and detoured towards my breasts.

I grabbed his hands and pushed them away. "That's not going to happen, Floyd." I looked around to see if any of my friends were nearby to help, but the van effectively blocked sight of my car from the rest of the lot. "I'm sorry if I gave you the wrong impression, but I'm just not in the market for a boyfriend."

"That's okay, sweetie. I'm not in the market for a relationship. I've already got a wife—and a girlfriend." He leered up at me and rocked his pelvis against my thighs. "How about a little tumble?"

"Not on your life." I shoved him so hard that he bounced off the van. "Floyd Marley, you are out of your mind. There is no way I'm giving you a tumble, ever. Now go get into your own car before I call for help."

The old man gave me a disgusted look and began to shuffle away. "You don't have to be so sore, Gail. I was just trying to be friendly. Women." He shook his head and kept on walking.

I got into the car and locked the door. I sat there watching until Floyd was in his own vehicle and driving away. Once my breathing had slowed, I wasn't certain whether to laugh or cry. I decided to laugh. I hope Clara's still up when I drive by, I thought. I can't wait to tell her about this, although she'll probably think I'm bragging again.

All the way home, I thought that maybe I'd given Floyd the wrong idea last week and brought his advances on myself.

I'd been so angry when Mr. Baker had been waiting for me at the café; so angry that he had insinuated himself into the group. When he had draped his arm across the back of my chair, I had childishly leaned away to put a little distance between us. That maneuver had put me almost nose-to-nose with Floyd. Then I had shamelessly flirted with the dirty old man. Of course, he got the wrong idea and pounced on me tonight. My cheeks burned. But on the rest of the drive home I replayed the scene in my mind, my reaction swinging from horror to embarrassment to amusement. Oh, Clara's going to love this.

Clara opened my backdoor when I got to the steps. "What took you so long? I nearly froze out there, so I let myself in."

"We stayed longer at the café. I was afraid you'd think I'd fallen in a hole. You weren't worried, were you?"

"A bit. I made the tea already. Grab a mug."

"I feel like I did coming home after a dance to find Mom waiting up for me," I said as I hung up my coat. "Clara, you are not going to believe what just happened."

"What? Did Abel show up and ask you out?"

I sat down across from her and poured myself some tea. "Floyd made a pass at me."

"The old guy? The gnome? He made a pass?" She chuckled. "Well, I'll be."

"It was awful. At first he said he admired my paintings and suggested we get together at his studio some afternoon. Then he ground himself into me and tried to grab my breasts. When I pushed his hands away and said I didn't want a boyfriend, he told me he had a wife and a girlfriend already."

"Why, that old goat."

"Exactly. His exact words were, 'how about a little tumble?' Can you believe it?"

"I don't know how you could resist that line." She tried to take a sip of her tea but snorted it up her nose instead. That

71

started the two of us giggling. "Do you think he's invited many women to his studio?" she managed to choke out.

It took me a minute to catch my breath. "Oh, maybe when he was younger he did but these days I imagine it's all in his mind."

Clara nodded. "So, when are you two getting together?" she said. "To paint, I mean."

I looked to see if she was serious, but her eyes sparkled with mischief. "Oh, Floyd's hard to resist, but I think I'll wait for a better offer. One from a man who is a little younger and not as likely to stroke out if he gets too excited, if you know what I mean."

The next weekend Samara and I were sitting in the kitchen after I showed her my studio. She was amazed at all my paintings. Her eyes kept darting around the kitchen walls. She pushed her chair back and stood up.

"Oh my God, it's like I'm in Monet's house. These flowers are fabulous." She walked around the room examining each painting in turn. "I feel like I can smell them. I told you that you were the best in class."

I had to admit that standing back and looking at my work as a whole gave me a more objective feeling about it. Maybe June was right, when you're painting you're too close to see the whole picture. You have to step back—squinting helps, too, especially with my Impressionist style.

I busied myself getting out glasses and a pitcher of fresh apple cider. While I was pouring, I said, "Samara, I have an idea."

"What?"

I put the glasses on the table and sat down. "There's going to be a craft fair at my church on December first. You know, Christmas gifts and things. What do you think about seeing if we can rent a booth and sell some of our paintings?"

Samara was stunned. "Oh my gosh, Gail. Are you serious?"

"Yes, I am."

"That would be so awesome. What brought this on? You're usually so shy about showing your work."

"Well, I was looking at the prints in that frame shop in Simpson and realized our stuff's at least as good, maybe better. Plus, I've got every surface and most of the walls in my studio covered and the rest of the house crammed full, too. I'm running out of places to hang paintings. Selling some at a craft fair might be just the thing to help clear it out. And if people liked my art, and bought it, I might start to believe what everyone in class has been saying. I'll bet your earrings would be a big hit."

"Let us give each other a sign of peace," the priest intoned near the end of Mass. "Peace be with you." He turned to each altar attendant and shook their hands and then stepped out from behind the altar to greet those in the front pew. The congregation stirred to life, murmuring, "Peace be with you" to everyone in their vicinity. It's still a surprise sometimes to see women servers, I thought. I miss altar boys and their high sweet voices calling the responses, but I suppose if the Church can move with the times, I can too.

It was the Sunday after Thanksgiving and I was glad to be standing in the relative silence of church. As I had every year for the last five, I had spent the day at Clara and Hank's with, as Clara said, all their "in-laws and out-laws." They were a rowdy and gregarious bunch and I know Clara liked having an extra pair of hands and the use of my oven to bake her green bean casserole and candied yams in.

I felt a tap on my shoulder as I disengaged myself from a rather suffocating hug from old Miss Simmons with her cloying violet toilet water. Where does she find the awful stuff? I wondered. I bet she distills it herself. I scolded myself, not very nice church thoughts, Gail. I turned to see who had tapped me and came face to face with Abel Baker. He had his hand extended and said, "Peace be with you, Mrs. Logan." I gave him my hand and responded in kind. "Are you staying for the fellowship after the service?" he asked. Before I thought, I answered yes. A satisfied look settled on his face as I turned back to the Mass.

I could have kicked myself for speaking before thinking. I was not in the market for another man in my life. It had taken me eight years to move from being Bert's wife to the place I was now. Changing the way I dress, cutting my hair and, most of all, taking up watercolor had finally opened my eyes to the endless possibilities of life. I was not interested in another husband or even a boyfriend, for that matter. I had a feeling if I was the least little bit nice or encouraging to Mr. Baker he'd take over my life in a heartbeat and I'd be right back where I started, living my life for everyone but myself.

I briefly considered making a quick getaway as soon as the final hymn began but had somehow gotten trapped between Miss Simmons and her niece, Ella, who took forever to get out of the pew and make their way down to the Fellowship Hall, and Ruby Tilden and her brood of six children, the youngest a babe in arms and the rest going up in one-year steps to the eldest, Jeremy. It took Ruby and her husband Jim an eternity to gather up all the baby paraphernalia, toys and snacks she brought along each week to try and keep them happy for the hour of Mass.

I was so distracted I was surprised to hear the beginning chords of the recessional hymn fill the church and the rustle of parishioners slipping into their coats and tucking the weekly bulletin into purses or pockets. It always amused me that the voices of the congregation were much stronger singing the ending hymn, as if people were excited to leave. Or maybe it was just that they were an hour more awake? Leaving church after Mass with that beautiful music in my ears never failed to uplift me and send me home feeling good for the entire day, but not today. All that was on my mind was how I could gulp a cup of Sister Terese's delicious coffee without scalding my gullet, say hello to a few friends and get out of there without encountering the looming charm of Mr. Abel Baker. Maybe I'd introduce him to Ella. She'd been a widow for years longer than me and maybe she was in the market for a bossy squire. Her late husband, Alfred, had been a pale, nervous man who jumped whenever Ella said jump. Maybe Ella was pining for a masterful man who could make her swoon.

The mere thought of Ella Marshall, a formidable woman dressed perpetually in shades of gray which made her look even more like the battleship her height and girth suggested, swooning over a man gave me the giggles. Which earned me a stern glare from Miss Simmons and a wink from Ralph Krinkle, the local butcher who imagined himself the Lothario of the county, leaving his pew across the aisle, his hand cupping the elbow of an overdressed woman I assumed to be his latest conquest. Must be from the city. No one around here would wear what looked like a dark blue satin cocktail dress and a little pillbox hat with a veil to Mass anymore. Those are uncharitable thoughts, Gail, I thought, and in church too. Aren't you trying to be less judgmental? I murmured a quick apology to the Blessed Mother and said a Hail Mary, hoping to appease God and whatever saints happened to be looking down.

As I passed the pew behind mine, frustrated at the stately progress of Ella and her aunt, a hand connected to an arm in a dove gray suit took my hand and I looked to see Mr. Baker thread my left arm through his.

"I was afraid you would try to avoid me, Mrs. Logan," he said. "I'm looking forward to sharing a cup of coffee and something sweet with you."

Unable to think of a quick response to his remark, I concentrated on trying to untangle my arm from his, but he had his hand over mine and refused to let go.

"I'm sorry, Mr. Baker," I finally squeaked out, "I seem to have developed a splitting headache during Mass. I think I'll go on home and lie down. I'm sorry."

Just then we emerged into the church vestibule, and I

slid between the people chatting in groups, opened the door, and set off across the parking lot toward my car.

"Mrs. Logan," Mr. Baker said from behind me, "allow me to walk you to your car." And this time the gray-suited arm slipped around my waist.

I couldn't see a way to escape without making a scene. I was sure to be the topic of gossip all over town all week long, judging from the number of hawk-eyed women who glared at me as I drove out of the lot and made my way home, wishing for a cup of Sister Terese's coffee and a little lemon bar. Darn that Abel Baker.

CHAPTER 11

December

I sat in the food area of my church's craft fair eating a cheeseburger and dreading the rest of the afternoon. It had seemed like such a good idea when I thought of it; Samara and I would sell our art at the fair and Clara would help. It would give me a chance to open up space on my walls which were quickly disappearing under my watercolors, provide an opportunity to see how strangers felt about my paintings, help Clara feel she was still a big part of my life, and make a little money to buy more supplies. So simple, so easy. Who knew that my old friend and new friend would take one look at each other and turn into the Hatfields and the McCoys?

The trouble had started earlier this morning when Clara and I approached our assigned booth. It looked like Samara had spread her jewelry over the whole table and had her paintings hung over the entire backdrop. I could feel Clara tense as we got closer.

"For Pete's sake, Gail," Clara hissed, "I thought you two were supposed to share that booth. Look at her, she has all her stuff so spread out there's no room for you."

"Clara, don't be silly. I'm sure Samara spread everything out to decide what to display first." To forestall any louder complaints, I nudged my old friend with my elbow, since my hands were filled with framed paintings. "Samara, honey, you sure got here early," I called. "Scootch some of your things over so Clara and I can unload."

The young woman looked up when she heard her name and grinned. "Hi, Gail, this is going to be great. Let me slide some of this over so you can put that box down." She took the paintings from me and piled them on the corner of the table she'd cleared. Then she smiled at the woman behind me. "You must be Clara." She put out a hand to shake before she realized that Clara's arms were full too. "Oops, sorry. Gail's told me a lot about your adventures together. So where's your booth? I hope they put us close together."

I heard Clara inhale, ready to stake out our territory, and hurried to forestall the blast. "We're sharing this booth, honey. You need to move some of your things so we can put mine out too."

Samara put her hands to her face. "Oh, I'm so embarrassed. I thought we'd each have our own." She hurried to move her jewelry and then stopped. "Wait a minute. You mean that fifty dollars I gave you was for half this booth? That's robbery!"

Clara's face reddened and she stepped around the table, still carrying the box of framed paintings. "Listen, missy, this is a church. They help out a bunch of people who are having a hard time making ends meet. That fifty bucks will buy a lot of groceries."

Tears sprung to the young girl's eyes. "I didn't mean..."

I was horrified. "Clara, I'm surprised at you. It was an honest mistake. I must not have been clear when I explained it to Samara. Now, let's help her decide what to leave on display and get my paintings put out." I glanced at my watch. "They're opening the doors in about half an hour."

It was difficult for me to decide on prices for my paintings. I walked around the booths just before the sale opened to see what prices the other artists were charging. It wasn't much help. I thought some were priced way too high; others were ridiculously low. I ended up putting twenty dollars on the smallest ones and went up to fifty on the two biggest ones. The first time someone bought a painting, I thought I'd faint. From shock or excitement, I don't know, but it was all I could do to keep from breaking out in a dance right in front of everyone. It was hard when someone spent time looking and then decided not to buy, too; kind of like they didn't like me. But I kept repeating to myself, maybe none matched their décor, and it made me feel a bit better.

The atmosphere in the cramped booth took on the air of an armed camp and I felt like I was the demilitarized zone. Clara on one side, Samara on the other darted poisoned looks at each other. Clara pointedly avoided helping people who expressed interest in Samara's jewelry, and she made a disgusted noise each time something of Samara's was sold.

Samara started the day apologizing over and over for her misunderstanding. By ten a.m. she'd turned sullen and by eleven, angry. When I finally persuaded Clara to take a break to walk around the fair and grab a bite of lunch, Samara turned to me with a sigh. "I know she's your oldest friend, Gail, but I have to tell you, she's a real pain. And she hates my work. I just know we'd have sold more without her frowning face driving people away."

"I don't know what's gotten into her." I shook my head. "Clara's been my biggest cheerleader for thirty years. Maybe that's it, she's afraid that you and I will become best friends and she'll be left out."

"Oh for heaven's sake, that won't happen." She touched my arm. "Not that I don't like you a lot, but I can't really see us becoming best buds. I'm in high school, for crying out loud, and you're, what, fifty-something?"

I laughed. "Yeah, I'm fifty-something, but I don't think we change all that much as we age. We still have the same fears and feelings we did in high school. I'll just have to work harder to make Clara feel special." I sighed. This changing your life was turning into more work than I'd bargained for. Why couldn't everyone just be happy for me?

When Clara came back from her lunch break, I encouraged Samara to go next. As soon as she was out of sight,

I turned to my old friend. "Clara Mae, I'm surprised at you. You're usually so nice to people. What has gotten into you to act this way with Samara?"

"I don't know, Gail. Something about her just rubs me the wrong way." She shook her head. "I'm sorry, I know you like her, but she's so 'me-me-me' all the time. It just drives me nuts. And her paintings! They're just paint splashed on canvas; not nice pictures like yours."

"You're right, Samara's paintings are more abstract than mine…"

"They're abstract, all right. Messy is what I'd call them."

I held up my hand, "Clara, there's all kinds of art, and just because you and I don't understand some of them doesn't make them bad. Samara's use of color and composition evokes emotion instead of representing something like my flowers or scenes. It's just different, not better or worse."

"If you say so." Clara folded her arms across her chest. "I still think she's pushing her stuff on people."

"And you're pushing mine." I peered at her over the tops of my glasses. "Right?"

Clara's lips held their sullen slant. "Yeah, you're right. I'll try to do better."

I finished my burger and went back into the sale area hoping something had changed. The atmosphere in the booth during the afternoon was calmer…a little. Clara and Samara were pointedly polite to each other and they took to giving each other the most ghastly grins each time something was sold. I was tempted to send them to separate corners for a time-out, but we were busy and really needed all our hands to handle sales.

Once all the customers had left at the end of the day, I was amazed and flattered that many of the other sellers came over to admire, and buy, most of my remaining paintings. They commented that they'd seen my work being carried around all day and everyone was talking about the watercolors at Booth 37. I decided 37 would be my new lucky number.

Samara sold most of the jewelry she'd brought but not many of her paintings. I told her that I thought her style was better suited to a more cosmopolitan clientele. Clara snorted when I said that, but she kept her mouth shut. Samara perked up and agreed that it took a more educated art connoisseur to appreciate her less-representational art.

Samara's mom, Ellen, and her granny, Jonny Lou, came to pick her up and I was happy to finally meet them. Clara struck up a conversation with Jonny Lou about raising kids and then they wandered off to track down the crafter who made the embroidered towels Clara had bought so Jonny Lou could buy some too.

Ellen and I had a laugh over Samara pushing me to transform the way I dressed.

"That girl's a force of nature," she said. "I've spent her whole life trying to slow her down. Most times I feel like I've got ahold of a comet's tail." But there was a sparkle in her big, dark eyes and a proud smile on her face.

CHAPTER 12

Canned carols drooled from the overhead speakers as I stood in Merricks' grocery store looking at the baking supplies, not at all motivated to buy what I needed to make my traditional gingerbread houses. It felt too early to start thinking about Christmas. We'd had a warm autumn; I hadn't pulled out my winter clothes and I was still wearing my corduroy jacket. It hadn't even snowed but *Frosty the Snowman* was playing in the aisles.

I have always liked Christmas. Every year, I spent days planning, baking, decorating, wrapping, and mailing. The holiday season passed in a blur of activities. Then New Year's Day arrived and I would feel like I had just emerged from a coma. The season had come and gone, and I had missed it. Missed it in the swirl of preparations and expectations—my family's and mine. On second thought, maybe I didn't like Christmas as much as I thought.

Standing in the baking aisle, sweating in my jacket, I thought about changing how I celebrated Christmas. Not exhaust myself baking and skip dragging all the old, bedraggled ornaments out of the attic and putting them in the same tired places. Maybe I'd find myself one of those aluminum trees and twist lights around the branches or make strings of beads to drape over it or maybe feathers. Maybe I'd buy cookies already decorated and pre-made candy and ship them off to the kids. They probably wouldn't notice. I thought about getting some cinnamon-scented potpourri and fooling people into thinking I'd been baking when I was really buying. I could check the phone book to find a swank bakery in

Simpson that sold cookies and things that tasted homemade. I contemplated sending for one of those gingerbread house kits you see on late night television, slapping it together, and passing it off as homemade. No one ever eats them anyway. Those things are a lot of bother, all for show. I could probably paint cardboard brown, use those tubes of icing from the store, and stick a few gumdrops and peppermints on it and no one would be the wiser. This was sounding better and better—less fuss and a whole lot less mess.

I was awakened from my reverie by a deep voice. "Good morning, Mrs. Logan. Planning your Christmas baking?" It was that darned Abel Baker. I was convinced that he'd been following me ever since I bumped into him at the garden center months ago.

"Good morning, Mr. Baker. Yes, I just need a few things. Have a nice day." I blindly threw some sugar and flour into my cart and left the aisle.

But when I got home, there was a letter from my grandson, David. "I can't wait to see the gingerbread house you make this year, Grandma," he wrote. "Remember you said you'd make a castle? I have a knight on a horse you can borrow." Damn. How could I disappoint that little face? I'd have to make one gingerbread house, but only one.

December had come in with a vengeance, cold and snowy and icy, looking like the picture on the Christmas cards I should have been addressing. To my relief, Clara called one evening, "Gail, it's December fifteenth. Time to visit Santa's workshop. Are you free tomorrow?"

"Sure," I said, "do you want to drive or should I?" I had to stop and think when we last went shopping together and was amazed to realize that it was in October, right after I started watercolor class. I wasn't really in the mood for Christmas shopping, but I didn't want to disappoint Clara. I could tell she was still troubled by all the changes I had made in the last three months.

"You drove last time, remember?" she said. "It's my

turn."

So she picked me up early the next morning and off we went to spend money we couldn't spare on gifts that would probably be returned before the holidays were over. I thought about suggesting we shop somewhere other than Wal-Mart, but she'd been rather touchy the last few times we'd spoken so I decided I'd go along with the old plan. As she pulled into a parking space in the vast lot she said, "Do you have your list, Gail?"

"I have a small one this year," I said. "I decided not to blow my budget just to get the family gifts they don't really need and won't use."

Clara pulled a handful of pages from her enormous purse. "I think I've got everything on here. Hank helped me go over it last night. He's such a good guy. All the boys would get socks and underwear if it weren't for Hank. He talks to our boys, the sons-in-law and the boyfriends too, to find out what they really want, like tools and sports stuff. That way we have at least a fighting chance of giving them something they'll really use. Saves all that returning, too."

"That's smart of you. Bert never got involved in the Christmas gift buying, not even for me. He'd pat my bottom one day in mid-December and remind me to 'get yourself something nice from me, honey.' I miss him less when I remember stuff like that."

"I'll bet. Hank better never pull a stunt like that."

We made our way toward the crowded store, picking a safe path through the rutted and icy snow. Just as we reached the end of the rows of cars, Clara's left foot decided to go its own way. She lurched, clutched at my sleeve, and started to fall. I grabbed her, trying to help, and my feet slipped too. We landed in a heap in the snow. I must have slowed her down because we kind of fell in slow motion.

"Clara, are you all right?" I asked since she was under me.

"I'm fine. Embarrassed, but fine. Get off me."

I tried to get my feet under me, but they kept slipping. I asked her to give me a push, but it didn't help. By the time I'd tried a few times, we were laughing so hard we had no strength to get up. We lay in the snow making a spectacle of ourselves. A couple of women offered their hands but it was so slippery where we'd fallen, they were in danger of falling themselves.

An impossibly young store manager ran out of the store shouting, "Don't move them. I've called 9-1-1."

We protested that we weren't hurt, just stuck, but the manager insisted that it was company policy to "activate EMS whenever someone falls at Wal-Mart." So there we lay, freezing our butts off on the ice, until a rescue squad screamed into the lot, sirens blaring, and people spilled out carrying medical bags.

The first person to reach us said, "Mrs. Logan? What are you doing down there?" It was Mike Harris. His mother was a teacher at the school I'd retired from last summer and he had been a student there.

"Clara and I slipped on the ice, Mike, and we can't get up. Not because we're hurt, but because it's so slick. Will you please get us vertical? My hind end is freezing." I held out a hand thinking he'd grab it and haul me to my feet.

"Sorry, Mrs. Logan, I can't. It's against the rules. We have to examine you to make sure you're not injured before we let you up."

"Oh, for the love of..." I put on my best school secretary voice. "Michael Harris, you give me your hand and help me up."

From behind my shoulder Clara said, "C'mon, Mike, I'm turning into a Popsicle under here. And I'm wearing my best jeans. I'm cold and wet. Now get her off me."

"Oh hi, Mrs. Simon. I didn't notice you there."

"Mike!" Clara and I yelled together. By that time we'd collected quite a crowd.

"Sorry, ladies, we'll get right to work." Mike motioned to another EMT and they knelt on the ice. He squeezed the top of my head and started moving his hands down my body.

"What do you think you're doing?"

"I have to check if you're injured, Mrs. Logan. Let me know if anything hurts when I touch it."

"Young man, you are not going to grope me in the Wal-Mart parking lot. I'm not hurt. Help me up."

He ignored me and kept right on feeling my bones, sliding his hands over my jacket, and moving from my hips to my feet. He sat back on his heels, looking disappointed. "Nothing hurt?"

"No, nothing is hurt," I said through gritted teeth, "nothing but my dignity. Will you please help me up now?"

Mike got to his feet, slipping a bit on the ice, and extended his hand. It took a little fancy footwork on both our parts, but I was finally upright. I turned to see Clara being helped to her feet by a tiny girl dressed in a uniform like Mike's. To our embarrassment, the crowd burst into applause. Clara and I linked arms and took a bow. We almost took another fall, but our rescuers grabbed our arms to keep us up.

Dusting off our pants as best we could, we made our way into the store escorted by the manager babbling apologies and excuses and headed right for the Ladies' room. I was happy to push the door shut in his face.

"Clara, this shopping trip has to be one for the record books," I laughed. "We've made a scene before we even got in the store. Are you really okay?"

She looked up from washing her hands, grabbed a wad of paper towels and started wiping off her jeans. "I'm fine, Gail. Just embarrassed. I think everyone in town was out there. How are we ever going to show our faces again?"

"I wouldn't worry about it. They'll talk about us for a day or two and then something else will happen and it'll be someone else's turn in the spotlight."

Clara kept scrubbing her knee, "That's fine for you." Her voice dropped to almost a whisper. "I suppose your new friends would think it was funny to fall and not be able to get up. Anyway, you're already the topic of most of the gossip in town."

I felt like she'd thrown cold water on me. "What do you mean?"

She straightened and pushed the wad of wet paper towels into the trash. "What I mean is you've been flaunting your new look and new talent all over town and everyone's getting pretty sick of it."

I felt my face flush. "Everyone, Clara? Or just you?"

"Well, now that you finally asked, I am getting sick of listening to you go on and on about how your paintings aren't as good as you think they should be." She folded her arms across her ample bosom.

"Anything else?"

"Yes, your fixation with Abel Baker is getting a little old. So he shows up where you are. So he's got a little crush on you. Big deal. You're not the only one with a life, you know."

I felt like someone had kicked me in the stomach. "I had no idea you felt that way, Clara. I'll try not to share my life with you anymore since you find it such a burden."

We stood looking at each other for a long time. I spoke first. "I don't think I feel like shopping after all. I'll just wait in the snack bar while you get what you need."

"I don't feel like shopping much myself. Why don't we just go home?"

"Fine."

"Fine."

The air in the car was very different on the way home, frosty even after the heater had kicked in. It was a long six miles from Wal-Mart to my house. Clara stared straight ahead when she stopped in my driveway. She didn't say a word when I opened the door and got out. I might have closed the car door a little harder than necessary. I heard the tires spin on the frozen gravel as she reversed and drove away.

Anger had kept my lips shut during the drive. It kept my spine stiff on the walk into the house. I thought of how long

Clara and I had been friends, all the heartbreaks and tears of childrearing we'd endured together, all the pots of coffee or tea we'd shared listening to each other's troubles over our thirty-year friendship. By the time I got into the kitchen, I was so mad my hands were shaking. I made a fresh pot of tea and sat at the table, warming my trembling fingers on the mug and thinking about how this whole emotional mess had started.

My untouched tea had cooled, and tears were flowing down my cheeks. I hated to argue, and it seemed like I'd been at odds with Clara for the last three months. I was surprised at her for being so angry, so hurt, so petty over a few pairs of jeans and a haircut. Okay, I suppose I had been waving my new life in her face. Had been doing the middle-aged version of skipping around the playground singing "I'm better than you are" when I shared my frustration with my painting and Abel Baker with her, but she was supposed to be my best friend. She was supposed to be on my side, be happy for me. Instead of sympathizing with me, instead of laughing with me, she kept bleating about how I had new friends, was bragging about my painting, and only thought Abel was pursuing me to make myself bigger and better than her. That thought dried my tears. Ooh, she made me so mad sometimes.

She was my oldest friend; I thought she knew me better. I loved her and I wanted her to love me—warts and all. I supposed I'd have to figure out a way to apologize, although I didn't feel like I had anything to apologize for. She was the one who got angry and said all those hurtful things.

I was working myself up to calling her, to figuring out what to say that would tell her, without apologizing, that I still wanted to be friends, when I heard footsteps coming up the back steps. I heard the screen door open and got up to open the back door.

"Oh, Gail, I'm so sorry." Clara's tear-streaked face was pinched white with cold and snowflakes covered her hair.

I pulled the door wide. "Get in here before you freeze."

She sat down in the nearest chair and put her hands

over her face. "I'm sorry, so sorry. I don't know what came over me today." Snow fell from her shoulders and head as she shivered, making a ring of melting white around her.

"Good grief Clara, how long were you outside?" I stood up and went to the bathroom to get a towel. "Get out of that wet coat and let me hang it up. Here's a towel to dry your hair. You're going to catch pneumonia."

"I don't know how long I stood out there. I just couldn't go inside and face Hank." She sat back down, twisting the towel into a knot. "You know he always wants to hear about my day, and I couldn't bring myself to tell him what I did."

I poured some tea into a mug and shoved it into the microwave to heat. "For heaven's sake, all you did was speak your mind. It wasn't World War III." The microwave buzzed and I handed her the mug. "Here, drink this before you shiver yourself off the chair." I reheated the untouched tea in my own mug and sat across from her. "So, what was all that about?"

She sipped her tea. "Mmm, this is good. Thanks." I could see color beginning to come back in her face, then she said, "I don't know. I guess I got to feeling that you're changing everything about yourself and I'm not changing anything. I'm the same old boring Clara I've always been—fat, plain, and dumb. You've gotten a new hobby, well I guess you'd call it a passion, and I'm the same. You've got all new clothes and a snappy haircut; I'm the same. You have all these different friends, young ones, old ones, and I don't know anybody new. You've got two men interested in you and all I've got is Hank."

I knew I had to stop her before she compared herself right into suicide. "Clara, you've got a terrible case of the winter blahs, that's all. You've always been an interesting person, you're active in the community, you love your kids and Hank, right?"

"I guess."

"No, don't say 'I guess.' I'm right." I reached to hold her hand. "You've always been the one on committees, active in sports booster clubs, doing volunteer work. I'm the one who sat around here staying the same all these years, keeping to myself, and never a part of the community. So in reality, I'm just catching up, that's all."

"Hey, now that you mention it, you're right." She put down her mug and smiled. "What took you so long?'

CHAPTER 13

Somewhere a bell rang. I felt like I was swimming up through thick black water, trying to find the sound that pulled me from sleep. My hand reluctantly poked out of the toasty depths of my bed and groped blindly for the phone. "Hello?" I said, sounding, I'm sure, like I had a mouth full of cotton.

"Mom? Mom, wake up."

I fought my way to the surface of consciousness and out of my tangle of sheets and quilts. "Aaron? What are doing calling me at... four o'clock in the morning? Is everything okay?"

"I want to introduce you to Elizabeth."

Elizabeth? I thought, battling the cobwebs in my brain. I don't know anyone by that name. "Aaron, who is Elizabeth and why couldn't she wait until daylight to meet me?"

A warm chuckle came down the wire. "She's your new granddaughter, Elizabeth Gail Logan. Say hello to your grandma, little one." I could hear the rasp of the phone on cloth and faint breathing. "Sorry, Mom, guess she's not up for phone conversations yet."

"Oh, Aaron, she's really a girl? We have a girl. I'm so happy for you and Sara. How is she?" I reached to turn on the bedside lamp and check the date on my clock. "Wait, isn't this early?"

"Yep, nearly two weeks. Ol' Elizabeth here was evidently anxious to appear before Christmas. We had an exciting ride to the hospital in the snowstorm around eleven last night and she popped out just after midnight. This is a girl in a hurry. Everything's fine. Mama's fine, Elizabeth's fine, and Daddy will eventually recover from all the excitement."

I felt warm inside imagining that little bundle of pink. I couldn't wait to get my hands on her. Pink! After three sons of my own and five grandsons I didn't have any girl baby clothes. Time to shop. And get the parish knitters and quilters working overtime. "Aaron, what did you do with David?"

"I scooped him up out of bed, blankets and all, and hauled him over to Bob and Julia's next door. He didn't even wake up when the snowflakes hit his face. I want to be home when he wakes up." I could hear a voice murmur something. "Mom, Sara wants to talk to you. Here."

"Gail? I made you a girl this time."

"You sure did, honey. How are you feeling?"

"Good. Happy. Tired."

"I'll bet. So tell me about Elizabeth Gail. I'm so thrilled you gave her my name."

"Aaron and I knew how excited you were about the possibility of a girl; we agreed her middle name should be yours." Sara grunted and I heard the bedclothes rustle. "Your granddaughter was in such a hurry to be born my bottom doesn't feel too sore. Anyway, she's six pounds fourteen ounces and twenty-two inches long--a real string bean. That helped her slide out pretty easy too."

"Sara! Don't you be calling my granddaughter a string bean. Have a little respect for the newest female in the Logan family. So, how long does the doctor expect to keep you in the hospital?"

"He told me in the delivery room I could go home later today, but I think I'm going to stay overnight until tomorrow afternoon. Just to make sure everything's okay with Elizabeth."

"That sounds like a good plan. It'll give me time to get packed and get out there. You still want me to come lend a hand for a few days, don't you?" I was embarrassed to hear the note of uncertainty in my voice.

"Gail, of course we want you to come. I'm going to need

to rest and get accustomed to the new baby; David will be a little lonely and having you here will help make him feel better about sharing Mama and Dad." I could hear a faint mewing like a hungry kitten. "Your granddaughter is requesting breakfast, Gail. Got to go. I'll see you when you get here. Here's Aaron." As she handed the phone to her husband, I heard her say, "Make sure your mom takes her time on the snowy roads."

"Mom? We want you to come but be careful driving out here."

"Don't worry, honey, I'll be careful. I'm going to wait until about ten o'clock to start out to give the plows and sanders time to clear the highways. I've got my cell phone all charged up and will be sure to call if I get delayed."

"Good, we don't want anything to happen to you."

"Don't you worry. Now kiss my daughter-in-law for me and tell her I love her. I love you too. I'll see you after lunch."

"Bye, Mom. I love you. See you later."

We hung up. I hugged the thought of my new baby granddaughter close. Too excited to go back to sleep, I slid my feet into my red fuzzy slippers, put on my old plaid wool robe and went to put on a pot of tea. While it steeped, I climbed upstairs and pulled out my mom's bridal trunk. It still had a wonderful cedar smell when I opened it. Deep inside, wrapped in tissue, was a quilt she'd made when I was first married and pregnant with Sam. Hoping for a girl, she'd embroidered lambs and butterflies on the blocks and trimmed and backed it with tiny pink gingham checks. After more than thirty years there was finally going to be a Logan baby girl sleeping under it. The quilt looked as beautiful as it had the day Mom finished it. I carried it downstairs and draped it over a kitchen chair to air out. I watched the sun rise on the first morning of Elizabeth's life. What exciting days she had before her.

By the time I'd finished my tea and gotten dressed, the town plow had been down the lane, so I fired up the snowblower to clear the driveway and the walk from the house to the garage. After a shower I called Clara to tell her of

Elizabeth's arrival. We talked for a few minutes about the joys of grandchildren, and I let her know I'd be away for a few days. She agreed to take in the mail. Packing only took a few minutes, then I toasted a bagel for breakfast, ate, rinsed my dishes, and left.

Turning out of the lane onto the highway, I was nearly blinded by the sun on the new snow. The roadway was clear and almost dry so I knew my two-hour drive to Aaron and Sara's in Steven's Point would be an easy one.

The trip went quickly. The plows were out shoving snow into ditches and spraying salt or sand on the pavement. I sang Christmas carols with the radio and wondered who Elizabeth looked like.

David burst out the door waving a photo as soon as I pulled in. "Grandma, guess what? I have a new baby sister."

"You do? What did you name her?" I got out of the car and hugged my excited grandson.

"I didn't get to name her. Mama and Dad did. They picked Elizabeth Gail; the Gail's for you, Grandma. Did you know that's your name?"

"Of course I did, you silly goose. You didn't think I'd spent my whole life with everyone calling me Grandma, did you?"

"Not really. Want to see her picture?" He waved the already creased snapshot in my face.

"I do. Why, David, she looks just like you did when you were born."

"You mean I was all scrunched up and covered with blankets too?" He took it back and stood frowning at it. "But not pink ones, right?"

I opened the back door and pulled out my suitcase and the bag with the quilt. "Yes, you were swaddled just like that the first time Grandpa and I saw you, and no, you weren't in pink. Can you carry this bag for me, please? Great-Grandma Hardy made a quilt for a boy and one for a girl when I was expecting your Uncle Sam and now after all these years we have Elizabeth to sleep under the girl's quilt."

He tucked the photo in his jeans pocket and carried the bag toward the house like it was fragile. "Grandma, were you waiting and waiting for a girl? Are you sorry that there's so many boys in our family?"

I set down my case as soon as we closed the door, crouched down to David's level, and looked him right in the eye. "Everyone's making a big fuss over that new baby girl, aren't they?"

"Uh-huh."

I could see he was feeling overwhelmed by all the excitement over his new sister. "I couldn't have been happier when your dad and uncles and all your boy cousins and you came along. I'm kind of nervous myself. I'm not sure I know how to be a grandma for a girl. But then, I'm a girl and your mom and aunts are girls. We'll figure it out."

"I guess." He turned and shouted, "Dad, Grandma's here."

My middle son, flushed and disheveled, poked his head around the door from the kitchen. "Hi, Mom, I'm glad you made it in one piece. Sara just called. They're kicking her out in about an hour so I'm getting things tidied up before I go get her and Elizabeth."

"So soon? I thought she was staying until tomorrow." I shrugged out of my coat and hung it in the closet. "What can I do to help? Do you have fresh sheets for your bed?"

For the next hour, the three of us moved through the house putting things away, cleaning the bathrooms, and making everything ready for the new mom. I told David that I thought he was a much better helper than his dad had ever been, which made David giggle and Aaron pretend to scowl. David and I hurried Aaron, showered and shaved, out of the house and finished the tidying. My grandson and I also made a ground beef and noodle casserole so that Sara wouldn't have to worry about feeding anyone but Elizabeth when she got home.

Sara and Elizabeth had barely gotten in the house and

settled in the rocker when David hauled the bag with Mom's quilt over to them. "Look, Mama, Great-grandma Hardy made this before Uncle Sam was born." He grabbed a corner and pulled it out of the bag.

Sara reached for it and said, "Oh, Gail, it's beautiful." She spread it over Elizabeth and ran her hand over the tiny stitches. "This is the perfect shade of pink for her skin. Look, she just glows."

I had tears in my eyes looking at my daughter-in-law and granddaughter. I thought they looked like a modern Madonna. Evidently Aaron thought so too; I could hear the click of a camera behind me.

I had the chance to get acquainted with my new granddaughter while Sara took a shower, saying she hadn't felt really clean after her speed shower in the hospital. I sat on the couch with David beside me. We unwrapped the blanket so we could see the whole baby.

"Wow, she's little, Grandma. And she looks like she'd break really easy," David said.

I had to laugh. "Oh, babies are pretty tough, but we have to be careful all the same. See the soft spot on top of her head? If you touch it gently, you can feel her pulse." I took his hand and we felt it together.

"Cool. Can you feel mine?" He tipped the top of his head toward me.

"Not anymore. As you grow that spot closes. Elizabeth's will soon enough." I planted a kiss on top of his head instead. "So, what do you think of your new sister?"

"She's okay, I guess. She doesn't seem to do much. I was hoping we could play, but she's too little."

"Don't you worry. Soon enough she'll be watching you like a hawk. Look at her; she's already turning her head toward you when you talk. And in a few short months she'll be following you around, messing in all your stuff, and you'll be wishing she was back to being this tiny."

Two mornings later when I went in to get David up for school, it took a lot of shaking to wake him. "Get up. It's time to get ready for school."

He groaned. "I'm so tired, Grandma. Can't I sleep a few more minutes?"

"I've already let you sleep an extra half hour. Mama said you need to leave at eight-thirty and it's nearly eight now. Up and at 'em, boy."

It was a hollow-eyed nine-year-old who shuffled to the breakfast table a few minutes later, shirt untucked and with one collar point nestled behind his ear. "Now here's a sleepyhead if I ever saw one. Did Elizabeth's crying wake you?"

He propped his head on his fist and said, "I think she cried every five minutes all night."

I poured his juice, refilled my mug of tea, and sat down across from him. "I know. I woke up every time too. I feel like I've been run over by a truck. Maybe I'll take a nap."

He gave a big sigh. "You're lucky, Grandma."

I had to keep after him to finish his breakfast, find his backpack, and get out the door on time. A group of neighbor kids rang the doorbell to walk with him, as they did every day. If it hadn't been for them, he would have been late.

When David got home from school that afternoon, I had a glass of milk and some fresh-baked chocolate chip cookies ready for him. "I talked to your mama and dad today about how Elizabeth has been keeping us up at night. I have an idea. How would you feel about coming home with me for a few days?"

"Today?" A big grin spread over his face, but as soon as it appeared, it disappeared. "But, Grandma, I have one more day of school before Christmas break. Tomorrow's the party. I don't want to miss it." He looked torn between his school party and a good night's sleep.

"Yes, I know; Mama said you were excited about it. How about we put cotton in our ears tonight so maybe we can get some sleep and then I pick you up after school tomorrow and we just take off?"

"Yeah," he said with a grin. Then his smile drooped, "But will I be home for Christmas?"

"I'll be happy to bring you back home on Christmas Eve. How's that? And maybe I'll stay a couple days and see if Santa can find me here."

He jumped up and gave me a hug, wiping his milk mustache on my cheek. "That'd be awesome, Grandma. I'll go pack." And he raced down the hall and into his room.

Sara came into the kitchen, smiling, and sat down. "I guess your plan was a hit, Gail."

"Are you sure you don't mind me taking David to Kingman for a few days?"

She reached across the table and patted my hand. "Not at all. You've got the laundry caught up, made wonderful chicken soup, and filled the freezer with casseroles. A few days without an energetic nine-year-old around will let me catch up on my sleep without feeling guilty. And I have to get ready for Santa to arrive. I still have a few things to wrap."

I got up and grabbed a handful of cookies to share with Sara. "If you point me in the right direction, I'll finish your wrapping."

"Not necessary," she mumbled around a mouthful of cookie. "And anyway, it's your present I still need to wrap."

"I could keep my eyes closed."

Sara shook her finger at me. "I know how curious you are, Gail. You're not fooling me into letting you anywhere near those gifts." A thin cry started in the other room. Sara groaned and stood up. "Coming, your majesty."

David and I bundled up against the cold and carried mugs of hot chocolate with us when we went out to watch the sunset from my porch. We were both in much better spirits, having gotten two uninterrupted nights of sleep.

"Mmm, this is great, Grandma. Can you make a mark

for Elizabeth on the railing?"

"I don't know, honey. I'm afraid the paint might freeze."

His little forehead frowned in thought. "But we need to make a mark for her. Do you think a black marker would work?"

"That's a great idea." I put my mug on the railing. "I have a brand new one in the desk. I'll grab it and we can try."

And that's what we did. David's idea worked perfectly, and I asked him to print "Welcome Elizabeth" on the slat below the sunset stripe for December 19.

The next day was Sunday and we dressed in our Christmas best for church. I had stopped going to the Fellowship Hour after Mass since Thanksgiving when Abel Baker had made such a pest of himself. But I was determined that David and I would go today and enjoy ourselves. The church looked beautiful with its Christmas decorations and the old Nativity scene in front of the side altar. All the students from the parish school sang the hymns and their voices sounded like angels. I had tears in my eyes when we all joined them to sing *Silent Night*.

It took a long time for the entire congregation to leave the sanctuary and make their way downstairs for Fellowship. Sister Terese stood behind the coffee pot, as usual, and David told her all about his new baby sister and showed her the crumpled snapshot he carried in his pocket. Sister told him Elizabeth was the prettiest baby she'd seen in a long time and David beamed. The crowd thinned fairly quickly, and we sat at a long table with Clara, Hank, Miss Simmons and Ella, and a few other parishioners in no hurry to leave. David finished his milk and cookies and made his way from table to table showing off Elizabeth's picture. At each one he'd say, "This is my new baby sister, Elizabeth. Don't you think she's pretty?" Everyone agreed that he had a very pretty sister. When he reached the table behind me, I heard him say, "Merry Christmas, Mr. Baker. See my sister Elizabeth? Isn't she pretty?"

And Abel said, "She sure is. Nearly as pretty as your grandma."

I could feel my face redden and Clara's eyebrows nearly wriggled right off her face. She leaned toward me and whispered, "I guess I owe you another apology for my remarks at Wal-Mart, Gail. Sounds like Abel has a big crush on you after all."

David came up behind me and leaned on my shoulder. "Are you ready to go, Grandma? This shirt's awful scratchy."

I put my arm around him. "Okay, I'm ready." We wished everyone at the table a Merry Christmas and turned to leave. Abel stood in my path saying, "Merry Christmas, Mrs. Logan. You too, young David. Will I see you at Midnight Mass?"

"No, Mr. Baker, I won't be here. I promised to take David back home on Christmas Eve so Santa will be able to find him. You have a happy holiday."

As David and I walked to the car he looked up at me and said, "I think Mr. Baker likes you, Grandma."

I sighed and said, "I think he does too, honey."

CHAPTER 14

January

I walked into the Museum feeling the return of a fear I thought I'd finally outgrown. I wished I were back in the craft store with my friends. My footsteps made a cold and lonely sound echoing in the entrance hall, making me regret I'd signed up for this class.

I'd never been in the Museum this late in the day. There weren't many people there, just a few stray figures in the distance silently surveying the exhibits. I looked around for a security guard or someone to ask directions from and found no one. But I heard the hum of voices off to my right and followed it, hoping it led in the right direction. The corridor seemed claustrophobic after the soaring space of the exhibit hall. Feeling like Alice in the maze of dim hallways, I finally popped through a door into a well-lit studio scattered with easels around the edges, and five people setting out their supplies at tables in the center of the room.

No one seemed to be in charge, no teacher stood near the front of the room. I drew a shaky breath and stepped into the light.

"Is this the watercolor class?" I asked the woman nearest me; a stupid question since I could see everyone removing tubes and cakes of paint and brushes from their carrying cases.

"Yes, it is," she said, looking up from a battered wooden box covered in paint smudges. "Are you Gail?"

"Yes, I am. How did you know?"

"I'm Renee," she said extending a hand. "Vi took a class from me last year. She told me you'd be here."

"Oh, man, now I'm really nervous. You're a painting teacher and you're taking this class? What am I doing here?"

"Don't be nervous," Renee said. "I try to take one class every year. Keeps me sharp and I can always steal other people's ideas for my own classes."

"Have you ever taken a class from this guy?"

"Nope, never. I hear he's a bit of a prima donna, but he's a dynamite artist and I intend to suck every piece of knowledge out of him I can. How about you?"

While Renee was talking, I'd started setting out my things at the table beside hers. As her words washed over me, my knees started to shake, and I was sure she could hear my heart pounding.

"I've only taken one class at the craft store. I'm afraid I've let my friends talk me into something I'm not ready for tonight."

"What do you mean?"

"Well, I think all of them telling me how good I was, hearing it for so many weeks, led me to believe it. And if you're an art teacher and you're nervous about this guy, I don't have any business being here."

"Don't be silly." Renee laid her hand on my shoulder. "Think of it this way, if this guy is as good as they say he is, you won't have too many bad habits to unlearn. I've been painting with watercolors for years and still don't feel like I have much control over them.

"Control, huh," I muttered as I dug out my favorite brushes, "I think I have too much control. I'm still strangling my brush and..."

At that moment a tall, thin man swept into the room from a door at the opposite end. Swept was the right word. He was wearing a floor-length black cape, an oversized purple velvet beret, and a silver lamé shirt. He wore a black pencil-thin mustache on his upper lip and flourished a long cigarette holder in a hand gaudy with rings. He pranced, there's just no other word for it, he pranced to the center of the room and struck a pose. Six indrawn breaths ended in a crescendo of silence as we beheld the vision of our new teacher.

A cold affected voice rang out: "I yam Jacques Tunees. I weel be your mhuse. Thees ees wataircolor clahs. I am praying you are not all stupeed." He spat the last word.

Stunned silence greeted his announcement. As we watched, the caped shoulders began to shake and he swept off his beret saying, "Man, I hate pretentious artists." in a normal, Midwestern voice. He peeled off his mustache, "that really itches," and swirled out of the cape to reveal paint-stained jeans, rolled up the sleeves of the lamé shirt, and rubbed his hands together

"Now that that's over, we can get down to business. Call me Jake," he said.

Relieved laughter relaxed shoulders among the students as Jake made his way around the room, introducing himself and getting to know each of us a bit. We spent that first evening going over the basics, the basics by Jake, that is. He was enough of a prima donna to want us to use his methods rather than the ones we'd learned in previous classes. His declared goal for the next twelve weeks was, "To teach you the right way, MY way, to paint." And he went on to assure us that using his techniques would teach us easier, more effective ways to put the paint on the paper and to make the paint do what we wanted it to do.

A few of the faces, Renee's included, showed relief rather than rebellion, which surprised me. During the break I asked Renee why she looked relieved.

"Well, I've been in a slump lately and have wasted so much paper and paint, anything this guy can teach me to help get beyond it, I'm all for." She grimaced and added a second packet of sugar to her vending machine coffee. "I told you being so new to painting would be good for you. You won't have to unlearn too much. The rest of us will be having a much harder time, you mark my words."

Renee's confidence that my status as a rank beginner would be an advantage made me feel a little better.

First Jake insisted that we put away all our brushes except for the three round brushes and three flat ones he had specified on the materials list. He said we could leave our "trick" brushes, as he called them with a sneer, home for the duration of the class. All six of us swept the offending brushes back into our boxes and baskets as embarrassed as if we'd been caught with pornography.

As for paints, Jake demanded we use only Cadmium Red Medium, Alizarin Crimson, Ultramarine Blue, Thalo Blue, Cadmium Yellow Lemon, Cadmium Yellow Medium, Burnt Umber, Burnt Sienna, and Raw Umber. He told us we should throw out any others we owned; real artists didn't need many colors, he said. But for tonight he insisted even those were too much. We were to choose any red, blue, and yellow and put all the rest away.

Then he had us tape a big piece of 140 lb. cold press paper to our boards and make sure we had a container for fresh water and one for dirty water. There was a flurry of activity as people searched for the right weight and finish paper and scrounged for a second water container.

"Now we will make colors," Jake announced. And he proceeded to spend the entire night showing us how to blend all sorts of colors and how to manipulate them to do what we wanted.

He spent a long time at my side, teaching me how to hold my brush, how not to be so tense, and how to trust myself that whatever I put on the paper tonight was right. I could see that Jake was going to help me move forward with my art but that it was going to be a long battle. My head hoped that Jake won the battle, but I was afraid my heart would fight him every step of the way.

A few days later, I was on my way to downtown

Kingman. I have always loved driving down country roads in the early morning in winter; the light on the snow all gold and pink, and everything looking newly made. I was headed to Kingman Hardware to talk to Charlie about spiffing up the plank floor Clara and I found when we took my living room carpet up the night before. As with most businesses in rural areas, Charlie opened up at seven o'clock to catch the farmers' trade. I was glad since that meant I might be able to finish my project in a day. I parked in one of the angled spaces in front of the store and admired the turn-of-the-century design of the building before going in.

"You're up early, Gail," Charlie boomed as I paused just inside the door, waiting for my eyes to adjust to the dim light.

"I want to get a jump on the day, Charlie, and I need some advice," I said.

"What can I get for you?" Charlie's voice echoed off the high ceilings and the walls filled with row upon row of wooden drawers filled with nails and screws.

"Clara and I ripped out the carpet in my living room yesterday and uncovered a beautiful old plank floor. I'd like to get something to clean it and protect it and I'm hoping you can help me."

"Come on over here and let's see what we can find."

I followed Charlie's shuffling steps to a counter in back covered by years of paint and varnish spills.

"Let's see... what kind of wood you got?"

"I have no idea. Probably pine, I guess, since it's a yellowish color. It's not dark enough to be oak."

"You're probably right, Gail. Most of those old houses had pine plank floors. Are they narrow? Wide?"

"They're a mix of narrow and wide. I'm sure they are original to the house, and it was built in 1827."

The bell hung on the door jangled and before Charlie could greet the new arrival a deep male voice spoke from behind me. "Then they're definitely pine. Probably white pine because of the forests around here in those days."

Charlie smiled. "Morning, Abel. You're out early, too. Looking for more tools?"

"Not today, Charlie," he said with a laugh. "You've already sold me more tools than my pegboard can hold. I'm just looking for a box of wood screws to finish fixing that table for Mabel Hastings." He turned and smiled at me. "Good morning, Mrs. Logan."

"Good morning, Mr. Baker." I didn't want to give him any encouragement. "Now, Charlie, about my floor. What do you suggest I use? I'm not crazy about using varnish since it takes so long to dry and makes the whole house smell."

"Now, when I did my floor," Abel said, "I used a Spar varnish and put on five coats. Very durable, Spar varnish is."

"That's very interesting, Mr. Baker," I said, "but I said I don't want to use varnish. I just said it. Excuse us." I didn't like to be rude, but I found him so annoying I couldn't help myself. "So, Charlie, what do you think?"

"Well, Gail, I'm thinking maybe this wax here. It's new and good for floors without a finish, which I assume yours is. And it's really easy to apply. See? You just use this sheepskin pad over a sponge mop. You got one of those?"

"Yes, I do."

After about fifteen minutes of discussion, I bought the wax and a couple of the sheepskin things that looked like fuzzy shower caps to apply it. Abel Baker stood by listening and offering random suggestions and even offered to carry my purchases to my car. I refused. Some people never take the hint.

I sat on my new couch with the portable walnut desk Bert made for me years ago on my lap. I remember the Christmas he gave it to me. He was so proud. He said he made it for me so I could write my weekly letters to my sister, Lydie, and the boys in comfort. He must have gotten tired of watching me try to balance a magazine on my lap and keep the stationery from sliding off. It has compartments for my pens and places for paper and envelopes, even a little drawer on top for stamps. Aaron kept bugging me to get a computer, but I liked the old-fashioned way of writing letters. I wished it were warmer; I would have been out on the porch writing my letters, but it was below zero and blowing like crazy. I had poked my nose out at sunset, but it was just too cold. So there I sat in my newly redecorated living room with Andrea Boccelli singing to me in Italian from the stereo, writing letters.

My sister Lydie is three years younger than me and she lives outside of Chicago in Bensenville. She loves to garden and has been divorced for over thirty years. After covering the usual family catch-up information, I jumped right into what I really wanted to talk to her about:

Dear Lydie, I can't decide what to do, I wrote. I want to change my life but face opposition at every turn. Clara looks hurt every time I talk about painting and, especially, about Samara. Can't she see I'm the same person I've always been? Inside, anyway. I can't believe I've been that good an actor my whole life. Or maybe it's true that people only see what they want to see. And my boys? Why, Lydie, you'd thing I'd been kidnapped by aliens and reprogrammed. I figure they'll get over it once they see how happy I am.

But anyway I have to tell you about my new watercolor class. It's long—twelve weeks—and I don't think Jake the teacher likes me. And he especially doesn't like the way I paint. He's constantly at my shoulder criticizing, correcting, pushing, pushing until I'm just about ready to scream or throw down my brush and quit for good. The rest of the students must feel neglected. I keep waiting for them to rise up and rebel. But they keep working. Maybe they're hunching their shoulders and concentrating so Jake doesn't pick on them next. One of these nights, I'm going to just burst out crying and then I'll be so embarrassed. He's not going to make me quit painting, if that's what he's trying to do. Nobody's going to make me quit, not Clara, not my boys, not Jake the painting Nazi, nobody. Every week after class I paint and paint (this

107

is costing me a fortune in supplies) but I'm determined to get Jake off my back. I must admit my work is getting better. Sometimes I just fling the paint on the paper, cram it on, mash it on, I'm so angry with him. He's not going to scare me away. I'll show him.

And Jake's not the only annoying man in my life. There's that darned Abel Baker. I wish I'd never bumped into him at the garden center; he's been like an annoying fly in my face ever since. He started out trying to take over redoing my flowerbeds and now he turns up everywhere I go. It seems like every time I get groceries at Merrick's, there he is. He was at the hardware store when I went in for new knobs for the kitchen cupboards last week. And Sunday there he was at fellowship after Mass. Sometimes I think he's following me, but then I remind myself how small Kingman really is.

Right after I started my new painting class, I got it in my head to redo the living room. I don't know why. Probably watching too many decorating shows. Anyway, I was sick of the safe boring colors and traditional furniture. I called the Salvation Army, and they sent over two guys with a big truck. They were really nice—one of them gave me his recipe for enchiladas. Anyway, I had them haul everything away. Don't worry, I kept Aunt Mary's Tiffany lamp and Grandma Wayne's marble topped table. Clara came over to see what I was getting rid of and she stayed to help me rip out that old gold carpet, roll it up, and haul it out. We ended up cutting it into strips and then rolling and taping it so we could carry it. (I love duct tape.) It was really heavy. I figure it was the dirt of the ages ground into it from all those years of farmers tramping over it. We tore the pad into pieces and stuffed it into garbage bags. After Clara left, I spent the evening scraping up the pad pieces that were stuck to the floor and ripping up the tack strips. Under all that was a beautiful old plank floor. I went to the hardware early the next morning and talked to Charlie about the best way to clean it and make it shine. That darned Abel was there too and had to put his two cents in. I froze him right out of the conversation.

I bought what Charlie recommended, drove right home and got to work. It took me the rest of the day and my back was killing me by the time I quit, but that floor just gleams. It's beautiful and worth every minute of hard work and pain.

The next morning I hobbled into Simpson to that new furniture outlet on the eastern edge of town and bought a chocolate brown chenille couch, a gold and red paisley side chair and ottoman, some side tables and a coffee table, and a floor lamp. It was the first time I ever bought brand new furniture, except for the mattress Bert and I bought for our twentieth anniversary. I was lucky they'd had a cancellation and could deliver it the very next day. So I stopped at Charlie's on my way home, bought paint and some new roller covers and brushes, and stayed up half the night painting the walls a rich cinnamon red. The next day I borrowed Clara's son Larry to help me drag an old oriental rug of Bert's mom's out of the attic and we got it unrolled just as the delivery truck pulled up. Larry hung around while the men carried in the furniture so he could help me shove it around and get it just right. Clara came over when we were almost done and couldn't believe how different the room looked. I was so proud. I hung a few of my favorite paintings in there and it looks great, the red of the walls and the chocolate of the sofa are repeated in the rug. But it makes the rest of my house look drab and dowdy. Guess I know where a bit more of my savings is going—after I take a few days to recover, that is. I'm getting too old and creaky to work this hard for very long.

I get such pleasure from the changes I'm making in my life, Lydie. The boys make me feel like I have to defend my decisions at nearly every turn, but I don't care, I'm having a blast. I've even changed my hairstyle and updated my wardrobe. I wish I'd done it years ago.

Love, Gail

CHAPTER 15

February

By the fifth week of the painting class, I was at the boiling point over the way Jake had focused so much of his attention on me. I kept waiting for one of the other students to complain to him, or at least make some disparaging remark to me before or after class.

That night was no different. As soon as class started, I could feel Jake circling around behind me and standing there with his arms folded and his eyes intent on my brush. My shoulders tensed, waiting for his criticism. Our lesson this session was how to put more light in our work. We were supposed to be leaving white areas to "sparkle in the sunlight" of our paintings. It was tricky; we needed to wet the paper, but not make it too wet so the paint would spread over the whole page. And not have too much paint on our brushes so we could control it.

Glancing around I was encouraged to see the other five students, Renee the painting teacher included, flinging their brushes aside in disgust, ripping the paper from their boards, and starting again. As I reached to do the same, I heard Jake's voice behind me.

"You can save it, you know."

I could feel my shoulders tighten even more. "I suppose I can," I said, not looking around, "but I'd rather get it right before I learn how to save it." My fingers were shaking as I removed the paper and taped a clean sheet in its place. As I picked up my brush, cleaned and dried it for another attempt, I heard Jake's boots scrape on the floor. Good, I thought, he's going away to bedevil someone else for a change.

But when I leaned toward my work, his hand covered mine and guided it. "This is what I mean. Use a light touch. Ease up on your brush and..." Jake moved my hand and brush in the motion he wanted, "just relax." I tried to relax, tried to feel what he wanted to me feel, but four weeks of being in the spotlight had just about worn me out. "See, Gail, how easy it is?" As soon as he released my hand and stepped back, I dropped the brush and whirled to face him.

"And just how easy do you think it is to learn new things with you constantly breathing down my neck? Isn't there someone else in class who could benefit from your attention?"

Every molecule in the room stopped in its orbit at my outburst; the rest of the class stood as if suddenly turned to statues. I kept my eyes fixed on Jake's, daring him to respond. After a minute, or an hour, he gave me a half-smile and turned to Renee beside me and complimented her on her efforts.

Breathless after my loss of self-control, I stooped to pick up my brush and saw the red paint that had spattered like blood on the floor. I left it there.

I plunged the brush into the rinse water and picked up another one, loaded it with paint and tried again. My hand must have learned something from Jake's guidance because the paint behaved; it did what I wanted it to do. Little white gaps stayed in the flood of color, small areas of negative space that would lighten and brighten my work.

No one commented on my outburst during the break. None of them looked me in the eye either. Renee patted my shoulder as we stood near the coffee machine but that was all. Jake kept his distance for the rest of the class session. By the time ten o'clock rolled around I had several sheets with masses of wash enlivened by "light."

As everyone began packing away their things and left one by one, I was moving slowly, thinking about how I'd yelled at Jake. I couldn't decide whether I was glad or embarrassed. The usual happy calls of good-bye were replaced by murmured "see ya"s and little waves. Renee leaned over my basket of painting things and gave me a hug. "I'm so proud of you, Gail," she said. "I can see how hard you're working to be the best painter you can be." She gathered up her things and left. I finished putting my own things together, picked up my jacket, and started to put it on.

Jake was leaning against a table near the front of the room and said, "Gail. Can I talk to you a minute?"

I glanced around to discover he and I were the only ones left. "Sure." I stayed where I was.

He pushed himself upright and walked toward me. "Do you know why I've been at you these last weeks? Any clue?"

"No." I looked down at my paint-stained fingers. "Well, maybe."

"Why then?" He stopped in front of me and crossed his arms over his chest.

"Maybe you think I can be a better painter?" I kept my chin down but peeked up at him through my lashes. Suddenly I felt like a fourth grader called into the principal's office.

"A better painter." He looked past me and smiled. "Gail, the night you walked in here you were already a better painter than anyone else in the room. Except me, of course."

That brought my chin up. "No, I wasn't. I'd only just started painting a few months before. How could I be better than people, like Renee, who've been painting for years? Renee even teaches other people to paint."

"I know Renee teaches other dabblers to paint." He flung his hand in a dismissive gesture. "I'm talking about being an artist. There's a difference, you know." He paused, obviously expecting a response. When I remained silent, he continued, "A painter slaps paint on walls or canvas or paper and usually makes a mess. Oh, sometimes their smudges might resemble what they intended, but usually it's just color over white."

That almost made me laugh, but I controlled myself, waiting to hear the rest.

"An artist, on the other hand, paints emotions—his or someone else's—and hangs them out for everyone to see." He leaned toward me and continued, almost whispering, "You, Gail Logan, are an artist."

I raised my eyes so fast our noses nearly touched. "An artist? Like you? Hah! I've seen your work. Your paintings are wonderful riots—color, emotions; they've got everything. Your paintings are masterpieces. I read that piece about you in *Art World* and nearly didn't sign up for your class." He leaned away from my waving hands. "I spend the days between classes in my studio painting, wasting paint and paper, trying to do what you ask, and I can't. For the last four weeks I've been certain that while you're standing there behind me, judging me, you're deciding when's the best time to tell me to pack up my things and just go home." I stopped because my throat had gotten tight, and I was embarrassed to feel tears on my cheeks. I reached a shaky hand up to dash them away before they dripped off my chin.

Jake's hands were firm as he reached toward me and held my upper arms. "Holy crap, Gail. Get a hold of yourself. I knew my standing behind you was pushing you, but I never imagined you would think I don't like your work. You, of all my students here or at the college, are an artist. I see so much in your work. I can see if you were happy or sad or angry when you painted each one." He released my arms and stood back. "Now I understand why your last few pieces have been so much better. You were mad at me. Good. You need to get over the silly idea that you aren't any good, that you're not worth my attention. Trust me, Gail; you're an artist. I wouldn't waste my time on you if you weren't."

His words made me feel warm with pleasure, but then a little cold voice in my head whispered, "what if I can't live up to Jake's expectations?"

"What if you're wrong?" I said with more bravery than I

felt.

"I'm not wrong." He struck a pose. "I'm older than the young stud I appear to be, Gail, and I've taught watercolor for more years than I care to count. I can feel talent in my blood. You've got it."

"Thanks, Jake, I'll try to remember that when you're breathing down my neck next week."

He reached out and touched my arm. "You mark my words, one of these days I'll get to brag that I was your teacher. Now get out of here and get some rest. Tomorrow take a good long look at your work with fresh eyes."

"Okay, Jake," I said, "and thanks." I gathered up my basket and left.

CHAPTER 16

March

Early in the month, I got an interesting catalog in the mail. It was from The Clearing, a folk school in a tiny town on the tip of Door County. It was addressed to me personally, not to occupant or resident. I didn't know how or why it was sent to me. But I took the time to page through it because when I looked at where it was located, I was surprised.

Door County was special to me. Once a summer Bert would hire one of Clara's boys to mind the farm for a couple of days and we would find a motel room to run away for a day or two. We'd take long walks in the state parks or stroll along the lake or bay and, of course, find a perfect spot on a rocky beach to watch the sunset. Once we took a picnic to Garrett Bay, just up the road from The Clearing, and planned to make a bonfire but the flies there were such vicious biters they drove us away. We ended up back in our room where Bert made a fire in the fireplace (we'd splurged that year on a suite), and we made love on the rug. It was one of my best memories of Bert.

We must have driven by the place numerous times, but never realized that it was there. I'd never heard of The Clearing but reading the catalog I was enthralled at the range of classes they offered; woodcarving, both prose and poetry writing, quilting, literature, building furniture, birdwatching, yoga, painting watercolors and oils, and many other arts and crafts; I was especially intrigued by the watercolor classes. The one taught by Laurel Andrews caught my eye in particular. Since I seemed to be having a lot of luck rushing headlong into things, I checked the dates of the class, the cost and the registration dates. Before I changed my mind, I cut out the registration form, filled it in, wrote out a check and put it right back in the mailbox

Sitting at my kitchen window, hands cupped around my mug of tea, I watched a blizzard turn the yard into an arctic wonderland. Howling winds sculpted the snow into tortured banks that carved their way around the black-green cedars. Winter-bare trees flung themselves in frenzy before the wind and surrendered to the force of nature, sacrificing twigs that rolled across the icy crust.

March is my least favorite month. Christmas with its parties and festive decorations is long gone; we have survived the sharp, sub-zero cold of January. By March I always feel like winter should start wrapping up. Every once in a while there's a warmth, a softness about the sun and breeze that teases me into thinking that spring's just around the next corner, coming with the next turn of the calendar's page. March is when I feel most tired of winter, longing to get my hands into the sun-warmed soil in my garden. I get to thinking about Bert and my pop, who both died in March. Seems like this month isn't the healthiest for farmers.

Sitting there bundled in an old plaid wool bathrobe I bought at an estate sale years ago, watching frost creep to cover the glass like the closing aperture of a camera, I thought about the six months since my birthday in September. I had always liked whatever age I was. Once I'd passed my teen years, I'd been happy, not wishing to be older or younger. But turning fifty-seven had left me feeling in a precarious position. All the things that had anchored me in my life were gone.

I eagerly embraced the changes I was making but sometimes the pace of my new life, added to the interesting hormonal changes inherent at my age, left me feeling like I was circling the edge and, frequently, in danger of going over it.

It didn't help that boys were thrown by the changes I'd made, but I couldn't tell if they were envious, worried, or irritated by it. That tantrum Clara threw in the Ladies' room at Wal-Mart before Christmas was just about the end of our friendship. She apologized and I forgave her, but I had to admit I hadn't felt the same about her since. I didn't share my new experiences and frustrations with her as readily as I did before, and I found myself censoring what I talked to her about. It was a real blow when she admitted that she was sick of hearing about my painting; and I thought she'd think my confusion over Abel's attentions were funny, or at least interesting. Though we'd talked it out, I couldn't forget that she thought I was bragging about how my life is so interesting and hers is not. I remembered standing in that cold bathroom with the florescent lights glaring off the white tiles thinking that, if not for our gray hair, we could be in junior high.

I realized that sitting brooding over my now-cold mug of tea was doing nothing to improve my mood. I was never a very good pity-party hostess, so I rinsed my mug and headed into the bathroom for a nice hot shower. Dressing myself in the brightest, loudest-colored sweater I owned and my softest jeans and comfortable shoes, I turned on all the lights in my studio and put a fresh piece of paper on my board, a big one.

Listening to the wind howl and the pellets of snow tap on the windows, I felt like doing something different. Digging in the back of the dresser drawer, I pulled out a little set of oil paints and a handful of brushes I bought at a rummage sale last fall for two bucks. I was perfectly happy with watercolors and seemed to have a knack for them, but the oils were so cheap and so tempting I couldn't resist. I had gotten a little bottle of odor-free turpentine and some linseed oil on my last trip to the craft store. All the Old Masters I really admired painted in oils, and I wanted to try them.

I put aside my painting board with the paper taped onto it and pulled out the easel Merry had sent me for Christmas. I dug in the back of the closet for a canvas board I'd gotten on sale at the craft store and put it on the easel. I squeezed tiny bits of paint onto a fresh palette and took the rubber band off the brushes. My heart beat faster as I dipped the brush into the red and made a slash on the canvas. I smeared it around and made a kind of flower shape. Another dip into the paint and more splashes, more flowers (tulips maybe?) appeared. It was fun. The paint had a rich, earthy smell that watercolors lacked.

Time passed quickly as I cleaned my brushes in the turpentine between each color and squeezed more and more paint out of the tubes. I finally got frustrated that I couldn't move more paint with my brush and squeezed it right onto the canvas.

While I painted I found myself talking, to myself... "I'm in charge of my own life."

... to Jake the painting Nazi... "I can paint the way I want."

... to my boys and Clara... "I don't need you to approve of me."

I ended up with a brush in each hand, panting with the excitement of going crazy with paint. I stepped back from my easel and looked at what I'd done. The canvas was a riot of color and vague forms. The paint hadn't acted like watercolors at all. Because oil paints take so much longer to dry, the colors had blended where they touched, where I'd smeared them together, and in other areas lay bright on the surface.

"Looks a bit like a Pollock," I said to the empty studio. "Now I know what color my emotions are, and I kind of like it."

I carefully cleaned the brushes and capped the tubes of paint. I took the canvas off the easel and, turning its face to the wall, set it on the floor behind the door where no one would see it. I wasn't ready to let anyone get a look at emotions that raw. But maybe, just maybe, letting off steam in oil paints every once in a while, would keep me circling the edge and not going over.

The Saturday after my experiment with oil paints I

invited Samara over for lunch. We talked on the phone about once a week but hadn't spent much time together since December, when we'd stolen an afternoon to exchange gifts at Christmas. I remembered how busy my boys were during their senior year in high school and laughed in sympathy over Samara's tales of trying to finish her projects and apply to colleges.

She sat hunched over a mug of herbal tea saying, "The people who invented financial aid forms are sadists."

"I remember. Do you still need to tell them everything except your mother's maiden name and blood type?"

"Yeah, that's about right. My poor mom's tearing her hair out trying to figure out what they want to know." She tugged at the braids in her hair and let them fall with a clatter of beads. "And Granny's no help. She keeps telling me to just rob a bank to pay for college."

I reached out and patted her hand. "Not the best plan, I think. Can't your guidance advisor help?"

"I try not to talk to him since he told me how lucky I was that my dad was dead."

"What?" I was stunned that anyone could be so insensitive.

"Didn't I tell you? Man, did Mom blow a gasket when I told her. It took a lot of talking for me to convince her and Granny that they didn't need to go to school and 'give that man a piece of my mind.'" She got up and refilled our mugs. "It seems that if one of your parents is dead, and you're a minority, too, you're eligible for a lot more grants and financial aid. But I think he could find a better way of putting it, don't you?"

"I certainly do. It amazes me that someone in a position to guide young people would be so crass," I said, looking out the window at the wind blowing the loose snow around. "I hate March."

Samara giggled. "You sound like Granny. She's been complaining about the cold bothering her 'rheumatiz.' Why do you hate March, Gail?"

I leaned my head in my hands. "Oh, for a lot of reasons. Bert died in March and so did my pop. The weather's usually crummy and winter's gone on way too long." I got up and started clearing the table and loading the dishwasher. "I thought that redecorating the living room would be enough excitement for this winter but now I look at the rest of the house and think it's too dull for words."

Samara looked around the kitchen. "Well, this room does look like old people live here. Maybe you could paint it a more cheerful color? Or change the knobs on the cabinets."

"I was thinking of that, but I've got a better idea. Want to help me spiff up my studio this afternoon?"

She jumped up so fast her chair nearly tipped over. Her quick reflexes caught it and she turned to me and said, "You bet. What do you want to do?"

I dried my hands on the tea towel. "Grab your jacket. I'll tell you on the way to the hardware store. Do you think your Mom would let you spend the night?"

I outlined my plan for redoing my studio on the drive into Kingman. Samara was intrigued by the idea I had gotten after watching one of those decorating shows on cable TV.

We had a fine time at the hardware store. Just as I'd thought, Charlie had everything we needed to put my studio ideas into effect: bright white paint, big eyebolts and turnbuckles, and stainless-steel cable. Samara got the giggles looking at the hardware in all the tiny drawers that went up to the ceiling and Charlie's old-fashioned manners had her blushing. He showed us new painters' tape and something called a painting pad that would make it much easier to keep the edges even. But when Charlie recommended we get a stud finder, I thought Samara was going to wet her pants laughing. I got the giggles myself trying to explain that it was for finding wood in the walls to put the bolts into, not the other kind of studs that her dirty little mind had imagined.

The weak afternoon sun was fading when we got back to my house. Samara called her mom and got permission to spend the night. Then we got started. It didn't take us long to empty out my studio. We put the painting table, a rocking chair, and the old dresser where I kept my paints and supplies in the living room and propped the bed on the back porch. Unless one of Clara's kids needed it, I'd call the Salvation Army to come pick it up later in the week. Samara and I rolled up our sleeves and started painting three of the walls and the ceiling bright white. The fourth wall, the one I thought of as the gallery wall, we painted pearl gray. Once the walls were dry, we took the painting pads Charlie had recommended and, while I painted a flat black edge all around the gray wall, Samara painted a gray edge around all the white walls. The little pads worked great and made a nice, neat stripe.

By the time we were finished with the stripes we were both pretty hungry, so we cleaned ourselves up and went into the kitchen for supper.

After eating we measured two-foot stripes from the ceiling to just above the floor on the gray wall. Then we used the stud finder to place the long eyebolts on either side of the wall in the black edges on each of our lines. We made sure that they were secure and then strung the cable between them, like steel clotheslines across the wall. The bolts stuck out about an inch from the wall when we were finished. I had bought a couple dozen shiny steel clips and I used them to clip my paintings to the cables.

We stood back and admired our handiwork. "Oh, Gail, this looks so cool," Samara said. "I wonder if I could do this in my dorm room."

"Probably not, I'm sorry to say." I threw my arm over her shoulder. "If I remember the rules from when we took Sam to college, you couldn't even hammer in a nail to hang a bulletin board."

I felt her arm go around my waist and squeeze. "Too bad. This is absolutely awesome, Gail. Everyone who sees it will be totally jealous."

By then it had gotten late, so we stopped admiring our

work to haul my table and the dresser back into the room. I let Samara shower first while I dug out some pajamas for her. After I showered, we fixed some microwave popcorn and flopped in front of the television to watch a DVD. Neither of us stayed awake to see the end.

CHAPTER 17

April

As winter faded and spring approached, I listened for the sunrise call of the cardinal and savored the frenetic antics of the chickadees at the feeder in the honeysuckle outside my kitchen window.

When I sat on the porch at sunset, the translucent green of the new leaves of the crocuses tucked next to the foundation assured me that spring, and warmth, were definitely on the way. I could finally go back out onto the porch without needing to wear every piece of wool clothing in my closet. Rare was the evening when snow flurries swirled as I sipped my drink and enjoyed nature awakening around me. I loved the sweet earthy smell of the breeze this time of year. All the farmers in the area were tilling their fields, getting ready to plant as soon as the sun dried the winter-soaked ground. The amorous bellow of bulls, coy flirtatious cows returning their calls; the bleating of newborn calves, raising their heads to the sunshine and looking a little drunk on their first few nibbles of the grass sprouts. Maybe there's a little tonic in those shoots that gave them spring fever too.

"Rain makes my flowers grow." I repeated it like a mantra as I looked out the window at sheets of rain lashing the glass for the third day in a row. It was too wet to sit on the porch to watch the sunset in the evenings.

Not that I could see the sun, even though it was nine a.m.

Hadn't seen it for days. And I knew I'd have to order a load of gravel delivered to fill in the holes in the lane that appeared each spring; gravel trucks and spring-cleaning would have to wait, I wanted to paint.

Thinking that every painting didn't have to be a cheerful one, I rounded up all my paint tubes and started mixing, trying to find a shade of gray that matched the day's mood. After I covered a sheet of paper with samples, I found that mixing ultramarine blue with raw sienna, burnt sienna, and burnt umber in turn gave me a range of three gloomy grays that would do just fine. I decided to paint the view from my kitchen window that had so depressed me earlier.

Lightly sketching the window frame and honeysuckle, I laid over a wash of faint blue that I hoped would hint at sunny days to come. A dark navy gray filled in the sky, and I painted the honeysuckle leaves beaten down by the heavy drops a dark, almost black, green. The movement of the storm across the sky almost defeated me until I remembered June at the craft store using a barbered fan brush to paint falling rain. To give the clouds depth, a piece of tissue wadded up and lightly dabbed over the wet paint made satisfactory looking cloud piles in the sky. I decided to inject a small note of hope into the painting by suggesting a thinning and lightening of the cloud cover in the upper right corner of the paper. How to paint the raindrops blurring the window defeated me, even after checking every watercolor book in my growing library. But before I depressed myself into a coma of self-pity with all the dark grays and black greens on my paper, I painted a small, bright bouquet of daffodils and crocuses in a vase on the table in the foreground.

I stepped back and looked at my morning's work. Not my best effort. But it had been an interesting exercise and led me to consider showing it to Jake and asking how to improve it. And that thought alone made me realize that I was indeed beginning to think of myself as a real artist.

I cleaned my brushes, tidied my studio, and decided to

make a pot of soup to lift my flagging spirits and quiet my stomach.

Scouring the refrigerator for ingredients, I piled vegetables on the counter. The riot of forms and colors; red tomatoes, orange carrots sporting ferny tops, white and green scallions, a handful of creamy yellow wax beans, and earthy brown potatoes gave me an idea. Instead of a paring knife I picked up a pencil and pad and sketched a still life. Back in the studio, I made my soup in paint. Warm walnut cupboards framed the jewel tones of the simple food. A slash of white and the hint of a silver glimmer suggested the stove at one edge, but the food was the star, ripe and lush and nearly tumbling off the paper. By the time I'd painted three rough sketches, rearranging each time to feature a different vegetable, the carrots were droopy, and my fingers were aching. I no longer cared about the dreary weather and the ruts in the lane. But my growling stomach wouldn't be denied any longer and I contented myself with a peanut butter and jelly sandwich and glass of milk. I just couldn't bring myself to make soup with my patient watercolor subjects.

Spring was fighting its way through winter very slowly this year. Here it was the end of April and there were still piles of dirty gray snow in the shadowy places and what should have been warm rain showed up as ice storms. My yard was littered with broken branches, which would be a pain to pick up, and even my daffodils on the north side of the house were barely peeking out. What we needed was one day of sunshine and everything would just pop.

I noticed in the latest *Kingman Times* that brave souls were starting to have rummage sales. I had so many unframed paintings stacked around the house I thought maybe I could find some cheap frames at them. I had learned that I was a better judge of my work when I saw each painting framed.

I called Clara to see if she'd be interested in launching a campaign to find some. "Sure, I'd love to go rummaging with you, Gail."

We met for coffee at my place early the next morning with the *Times* and a county map. Clara brought over pieces of her delicious cinnamon-brown sugar cake, and we plotted our plan of attack. There was an even dozen listed with a huge variety of wares advertised. A couple of them even listed frames. It wasn't the prettiest spring day; in fact, it was overcast, chilly and drizzly but I figured that might help me negotiate the prices a bit lower.

Off we went in Clara's ancient station wagon that had served so well ferrying seven kids to and from Scouts, basketball, choir, and a million other activities. What was even more amazing was that it had survived seven kids learning to drive. The paint had faded to a pale shadow of its original dark teal decorated with what looked like a rust lace skirt. But it still ran and there was plenty of room in back for frames of almost every size.

The first few sales we stopped at were mobbed. I guess everyone was as sick of the lingering crummy weather as we were. Each stop yielded a few frames, some with the most god-awful art in them imaginable. The worst were the pitiful daubs of Lorene Lewis' daughter Ruth who had spent the last fifteen years proving that if you don't have talent for painting, you can't learn it. But I could use the frames.

We hit the mother lode at Kendall's farm. Old man Kendall had made wooden furniture as a hobby, and he had a barn-full of the most beautiful handmade frames. His daughter-in-law, Sheila, was running the sale and let me have the lot, over 50 frames in every size, for only a hundred bucks.

Years of shopping together gave us the skills to cram them all in back, although I had to hold the big copper boiler Clara had bought as a planter in my lap. We drove off before Sheila realized how cheaply she'd sold them to me for.

"Gail, I can't believe how lucky we were to ask about frames. I could have just died when she pulled open that shed door and there stood all these frames."

"I know. It was hard to keep a straight face when I asked if she'd take a hundred dollars for the entire lot. And then not to jump around like a crazy woman when she said yes."

CHAPTER 18

May

It finally looked as if spring was on the way. Weeks of cold, then warm; freezing rain, then sun, then snow, had become a string of balmy days that promised more warmth in the future. I had spent the last few days poring over seed catalogs and making lists. I had enjoyed the long winter painting flowers, now I was ready to plant some.

I'd carefully planned my trip to the garden center like a general planning a campaign. Calling the store yesterday, I'd asked, "Will Mr. Baker be in tomorrow morning?"

"Sorry, tomorrow's the day he works late, so he won't be in until 1 p.m. Would you like to leave a message?"

"No, thank you. I just wanted to ask him a question. I'll see him when I stop in." I felt like a fool calling ahead so I could avoid him but decided that was better than creeping around plants and ducking behind racks of seed packets.

I was up and out early so I would have time to shop and leave before he came in at 1 o'clock. The garden center was just what I needed. Walking through the greenhouses, I reveled in the earthy smells, gently touching the pale green leaves of the young plants. I easily filled a wagon with bedding plants and seed packets, checked my watch, and was happy to see it wasn't even noon and I was ready to check out. A young man helped me load my car and I was ready to make my escape.

A sudden hard rain surprised me as I drove home, ending my gardening plans for the day. I pulled into the garage, unloaded my plants onto the shelves I'd had Matt build along the wall, and dashed up the path into the house. Guess Mother Nature is telling me to plant tomorrow. Oh well.

Leaving my muddy shoes on the back porch, I spent a pleasant afternoon baking banana bread to mail to my children and grandchildren. Living so far apart, I worked hard to stay close to my family by sending long letters every week, baking cookies for them, and reading bedtime stories for my grandchildren onto CDs. When my sons were small, sitting on their beds reading a story had been my favorite time of day. Those warm, clean little boy bodies crowded around me made up for all the hectic hours trying to keep them fed and from killing themselves around the farm.

By sunset, I had three boxes filled, taped, and addressed ready for the mailman to pick up the next day. I poured myself a glass of wine, put on a jacket to ward off the evening chill, and went out to enjoy my favorite time of day. Out came the little can of black paint, a stripe was laid on the railing, and "Banana bread on the way!" graced the slat below. Six months of stripes, the railing was about half black, and I was beginning to run out of slats. Maybe I should transfer all this to a journal and repaint over everything. Nah, it's too much fun this way.

As I sipped my tea the following morning, I was happy to see the sun drying the previous day's rain and looked forward to getting started on the flowerbeds. I dressed in my favorite gardening clothes, threw on one of Bert's old barn jackets, and went out to get to work. I loaded up the boys' old Flexible Flyer wagon and hauled my plants and tools to the north side of the house. I'd been working for about an hour when I heard a voice from behind.

"Need a hand?"

"Oh my gosh, you startled me. I didn't hear anyone pull in." I turned to face the man standing there. "Mr. Baker, what are you doing here?"

"I saw you driving out of the garden center yesterday

with your car loaded and thought I'd stop over today and see if I could help. And please call me Abel."

"That's very nice, Abel, but..."

"Come on, Gail, give me a chance. You wouldn't pass up free labor, would you? I'm a pretty good hand in the garden and I promise to put things anywhere you say. Please?"

He looked so much like the boys when they were trying to convince me they'd take good care of my car if only I'd let them use it Friday night, I couldn't resist. "Okay." I dug a folded and dirty piece of paper from my jacket pocket. "Here's the plan for this bed. The plants are in the wagon, and I marked Xs where I want them. You start at the other end, and we'll meet in the middle."

"Okay." Abel took off his jacket and draped it over the branch of a young tree, then picked up a shovel and got to work.

I was amazed, as we moved closer together as the morning progressed, that Abel managed to keep his mouth shut and not give advice about what should go where. We got to the center of the bed where I had some doubts about my plan, and I sat back on my heels.

"Abel, what do you think we should do here? I've got the Coral Bells spilling over the edge, but I don't think the Baby's Breath should be next to it after all. Both are such small flowers there might not be enough contrast."

Abel stood up and I could hear his joints crackle. "Why don't we grab a drink and stand back and look at what we've done and what's left to plant?"

"Good idea." I pushed myself up with my knuckles and my knees popped. "Guess we're too old for all this kneeling. Ooh, my back's sore." I dug my fists into my lower back and stretched. "That's better. Come on into the kitchen. I made some lemonade."

Abel stepped back to allow me to precede him. We brushed the earth from our pants legs before we climbed the steps to the back porch, took off our dirty shoes and jackets and left them there, and went into my cozy kitchen. While I got out glasses and the pitcher of lemonade, Abel looked at the framed watercolors on the walls.

"Who painted these? They're really good."

"Thanks. I painted them. I'm just learning but I'm having a good time with it."

"This one of the mums in the autumn sun is especially good. Did you frame it yourself?"

"Yes, I've been buying frames at junk shops and flea markets all winter. I can't always find exactly what I'm looking for but they're not bad—and they're cheap. Here." I handed him a glass of lemonade. "Have a seat and I'll slice up some banana bread. Would you like butter for your bread?"

He took a sip. "This is good lemonade, not too sweet. No thanks on the butter. I like to taste good banana bread without frills, and I'll bet yours is terrific."

I set a plate covered with slices of the fresh bread on the table and sat down. "Have a taste and tell me what you think." I was surprised that it mattered to me that he like my banana bread.

"It's terrific. Different from any I've ever had. What's that I taste?"

"Nutmeg. I put nutmeg in and the sugar's half white and half brown. Aaron and Sara went to Jamaica on their honeymoon and raved about it so much the chef at the resort shared his recipe. I love how fragrant it is when it's baking."

Sitting there watching him eat and drink, I found myself fascinated by Abel's hands. They were fine hands with long fingers; work-hardened but handsome. Abel gestured a lot when he talked. I could see that his nails were well cared for, and the cuticles were trimmed. I wondered how his hands would feel if they touched me. I knew he'd been a gardener all his life, so they had to be calloused. The thought of his rough hands gliding over my skin made me shiver. I took a gulp of lemonade to try and cool my heated thoughts.

"I'm sorry, Abel. What did you say?" I had been so

caught up in my fantasies that I'd missed his question.

"I asked if you might be interested in having me make some frames for your paintings. Woodworking is a little hobby of mine. That way you'd have exactly the frame you imagine."

"I don't know. Wouldn't that be a lot of work for you, take up a lot of your time?"

"Gail, I'm a widower, I work part-time at the garden center, that's it. I've got nothing but time. And I'd enjoy it."

I thought about the idea. It was becoming harder to find the perfect frames for my paintings. More and more, by the time I was finished painting one, I had a very definite idea of how the frame should look. "I don't know if I can afford custom frames."

"I wouldn't charge you. You could have them. Don't be silly."

"I'm not being silly. I can't expect you to spend your time, and the money for the wood, and just make me a gift of them. What a thought. I'd expect to pay you."

Abel ran a hand over his face and said, "You are one frustrating woman. I want to do this for you."

"Well, I won't let you, so just forget it." I stood up, put the lemonade and bread away, and put our glasses in the sink. "Thanks for your help today. I'll see you to your truck and then finish planting." I walked to the back door and put my hand on the knob.

Abel sat gaping at me. "You are the most frustrating... I mean, we haven't even talked about where to put the Coral Bells and Baby's Breath. At least let me help finish what I started. I'm not ready to leave yet."

I stood at the door thinking that Abel was even bossier than Bert had ever been, but the little things I'd learned about him made me want to know more. I was horrified, too, at myself for thinking about how his hands would feel on me. I'm probably blushing. Maybe he'll think I'm having a hot flash. "All right, we might as well go out there and finish the job."

Standing beside Abel looking at the planting plan, I was

aware of our shoulders touching and I could feel his breath on my cheek when he leaned over to point at something on the paper. My rampaging thoughts were not on his words. I tried but couldn't control myself. Just as I thought about raising my hand to touch his cheek, he moved to rearrange the plants to try a different idea.

Oh, I have got to get him out of here. I don't know what's come over me. We'd better get these plants in the ground before I embarrass myself. "That looks good just like that, Abel. Let's get them in and watered." I picked up my trowel, knelt down, and began digging holes and plopping plants into them.

"Hey, take it easy. You'll break them if you're so rough with them, and you've planted them too deep." He took the trowel from me, dug up what I'd just planted, put some soil into the hole, a sprinkle of fertilizer, and gently placed the plant in the hole, pressing firmly to fill it in. "Why don't you get the hose and I'll put in these last few."

I was glad to walk away. My cheeks felt flushed, and my hands were shaking. I took my time dragging the hose to the side of the house, stopping to unkink it, and by the time I got there Abel had finished and was putting the empty flats into the wagon. We rinsed our tools and watered in the new plants.

"Thanks again for helping, Abel. You'll have to stop by in a few weeks and see how they look once they've filled in."

"I'd like that." He took his jacket off the tree and started walking toward his truck. I walked beside him. "And I'll be happy to help if you want to work on other beds around the yard," he said. "I saw some new vines, Scarlet Cardinal Vine it's called, in a catalog that would look really nice around your mailbox."

As we neared the backdoor I touched Abel's arm, "Would you wait here a minute? I want to give you something." Not waiting for an answer, I ran up the steps and into the house. I came back carrying the painting of autumn mums he'd admired. "I want you to have this, Abel, to thank you for all your hard work today." I held it out.

"Gail. I can't take this." He reached for the painting even as he tried to refuse. "I mean, I love it, but are you sure you want to give it to me?"

"I'm sure. You like it and I can't think of a better way to thank you for today. Please, I want you to have it." I could feel myself blushing.

Abel leaned toward me and brushed a kiss on my cheek. "Thanks." He turned and walked to his truck.

I stood frozen in place, my hand stealing up to touch the cheek he'd kissed. I barely managed to wave as he drove away.

Once I got all my flowerbeds redone, I took a break and drove to visit Matt, Lisa and their boys in Pleasant Prairie for a week. It was a busy time of the year for Matt; he opened early and stayed late, trying to keep up with the work. According to Lisa, every construction company in the region had "broken their toys and dumped them on my husband."

I had great fun going along to the boys' spring events. Jim's Cub Scout troop held their Pinewood Derby while I was there, and we cheered his blocky British Racing Green car all the way to the championship. He and Matt couldn't stop trading high-fives until I pointed out that they weren't being very good sports. They stopped but then started up at home until Lisa insisted it was time for all the boys to go to bed.

The twins went on a field trip with their Tiger Cub group to a farm and came home totally bedraggled. "Luke fell in the creek," Mike yelled as they tumbled out of their leader Fred's minivan. It was bad. Not only had the poor man driven twenty miles in the enclosed vehicle with six rowdy boys but the smell coming from Luke was unbelievable. Lisa and I cracked up when we saw that Fred had wrapped Luke in a garbage bag, like a last-minute Halloween costume, to preserve his wife's upholstery and contain the stench. For myself, I was glad we were in Lisa's pickup truck and could plant our stinky boy in the back for the short drive home. It took two showers and a bath to get the smell of horse and swamp out of his hair. Lisa wadded his clothes into the garbage bag and threw them away.

I didn't have a minute of peace to paint the whole week I was there. By the time Lisa and I had gotten the boys bathed and into bed each night, Matt was just getting home. We'd open a bottle of wine and keep him company while he ate. We managed to go out to dinner, just the adults, the night before I left. I insisted on paying for dinner, and for the babysitter, despite Matt's protests that he could support his family just fine.

"I know you can; I raised you, remember? But I don't visit often, and I want to do this."

The waiter's head bobbed like he was watching a tennis match as we argued over who paid the bill. I won, of course. I was glad to visit them--and glad to go home.

I walked down to get my mail. It was a perfect sunny, spring afternoon. I admired the way the new plantings around the mailbox were filling in. The Scarlet Cardinal Vine Abel had planted there was growing fast. I loved the lacy look of its leaves and couldn't wait for the red trumpet-shaped flowers to appear. Looking through the handful of mostly junk mail I'd pulled out of the box, I glanced into the woods. I was thrilled to see that it was carpeted with trillium. The forest floor dappled with sunshine and the white trillium glowing like pearls gave me an idea.

I hurried into the house, grabbed my board to clip paper to and my paints, zipped into the basement to unearth a campstool and a TV tray, and headed right back out. I hauled my things down into the woods and found a fairly flat spot to set up my tray and stool. Made a trip back to the house because I'd forgotten water, but finally had everything arranged.

It was cool with a light breeze, perfect for sitting in the woods and painting. My hands were clumsy with excitement as I clamped a piece of paper onto the board and dug a pencil out of my basket. I took a couple deep breaths to slow myself down a bit and try to achieve the calm center that Jake said is the best place to paint from. I had to laugh at myself a bit thinking about how I had resisted Jake's teaching at first. Now it was sort of funny to remember how angry and hurt I'd been during those first few classes when he'd pushed and criticized and forced me to paint better. I didn't regret having blown up at him, because in just a few weeks after our talk, my painting had improved tremendously. Now I was grateful for the way he had pushed me.

I was about to paint outdoors for the first time. I sat quietly on my stool for a few minutes, drinking in the serenity of the woods and letting my eyes roam over the landscape. My eyes kept stopping on an area where a fallen tree had made a bigger opening, letting in a large shaft of sunlight. The trilliums in the light were incandescent in their whiteness and the trees looked almost black. Once I had my subject in view and in my mind, I carefully roughed it in with my pencil. Then I took another breath and really looked at what I planned to paint. How many colors were there? How many greens? What was the color of the shadow under the blooms? What color would I use for the background? I made notes on the small spiral pad Jake had recommended we keep with our painting supplies, dug out the tubes, and squeezed a few blobs of paint on my palette.

I had been painting for an hour, trying to capture the exact feeling I had in that place, a cross between nature appreciation and the reverence I feel at times in church, and I just wasn't getting it. I had decided to start again, for the third time, when I heard a car approaching.

That's one good thing about living on a gravel lane; you can hear your company coming before you see them. I hoped it wasn't some Jehovah's Witnesses looking to save me. Spring brought them out in droves, and I hated being abrupt with them. Their earnest pleading eyes reminded me of stray dogs that show up on your back steps hoping for a handout. But I was determined to spend this glorious afternoon painting, not listening to someone spout Bible verses at me in an attempt to save my soul.

I couldn't decide whether to be relieved or frustrated when the approaching vehicle came into sight. It was Abel's faded red pickup truck. What more does the man want? I thought. I let him help me put in the flowers and plant that area around the mailbox. I'd thanked him for the Cardinal Vines. Now what?

He must not have seen me sitting in the woods behind the mailbox because he drove past, parked next to the walk, got out and knocked on the porch door. When no one appeared, I could see him crane his neck trying to see if I was inside. Then he walked to the garden and came around the front of the house to stand by the porch. I could see he was talking to himself and had to suppress a giggle. He hitched up his khaki work pants and frowned at the sight of my car in the garage. Then he caught sight of me. I was trying not to look as if I were watching him, but I don't think I succeeded. He raised his hand in a small wave and made his way over to me.

"Gail, what're you doing hiding in the woods? Are you avoiding me?" he said when he got closer.

"Of course, I'm not avoiding you, Abel. I noticed how beautiful the trilliums look in this glade and decided to try painting outside for the first time."

"So, how're you doing?"

"Not very well. I can't seem to capture the feeling I'm looking for. Here. See what you think." I held out my first two attempts. "Be careful. They're probably still damp." Why did I hand him those? It's not like he's an art expert.

"Well, I'm no expert, but it seems to me as if you've used too dark a green for the trees and not enough gold in the flowers. Plus some of the flowers, the ones getting old, are a pale purple. But I really like your style, Gail. I hung that painting you gave me right in my kitchen where I can see it when I eat. Get lots of compliments on it too." He handed back the watercolors and peered at the blank paper on my easel.

"Going to give it another try?"

I looked at my two failed attempts and thought about Abel's comments; and I wondered who exactly had been in his kitchen to compliment him on my painting. Some woman? "I might. But the light's changed and my behind's tired of sitting on this old campstool. I know my back could use a rest." I started to clean my brushes and replace things in my basket.

"Now, don't stop on my account. I just dropped by to see how your garden's doing. I'll run along and not disturb your painting."

I put my hand out and touched his arm. "That's okay, Abel. You're not really disturbing me. I was getting too frustrated to continue. Would you give me a hand hauling this stuff back to the house? I think I could find a bottle of wine we could share if you're interested."

"That'd be just fine."

Together we gathered up my painting supplies and walked up to the house.

While I carried my painting things into the studio, I asked Abel to open one of the bottles of wine in the fridge. "I hope you don't mind white wine," I said as I gave my brushes another swish in clean water before standing them in an empty jar to dry.

"No, white's fine with me."

I could hear him grunt as he pulled on the cork and the little pop as it came out. "The wine glasses are in the cupboard above your head. I'll be right out." I ducked into the bathroom to run a quick brush through my hair and wash any paint off my hands.

He was reading the bottle as I returned. "This looks like good wine. Where'd you get it?"

"A friend had one of those wine parties a few years ago, kind of an upscale Tupperware party, I guess, and I liked this German Spatlese, so I bought a case. I know red wine's supposed to be better for your heart and all, but it's just too dry for me." I put some crackers on a plate and got a bowl of olive and nut spread out of the fridge that I smeared on them. "Let's go out to the porch."

Abel picked up the wine and the glasses and followed me through the living room and out the front door. "Maybe you and I should host one of those wine parties."

"Maybe we should," I was surprised to hear myself say, "It might be fun."

We sat on the porch and watched the sunset and talked long into the evening about gardens, and art, and local gossip, and books we'd read. I was surprised how easy Abel was to talk to once I got over thinking that he was an obnoxious jerk.

CHAPTER 19

June

I got an invitation to Lydie's son Jack's wedding, his second wedding. Or was it his third? Jack had been a charming boy, but a little wild. It always amazed me that he and Sam were such good friends. Sam was such a serious boy, thoughtful and cautious, and had become a serious man. Jack was another story. As a kid, he could be counted on to swing from a frayed rope looped over the barn rafters, fall, and break his arm. Or try to catch fish when the creek was in spring flood, fall in, scramble out on the banks nearly a half a mile downstream and try to convince Sam, who had run along the creek side screaming in fear, to "go again" with him.

The adult Jack, and I use the term "adult" lightly, had been invited to leave several colleges before he managed to graduate. And his job history covered the gamut from car sales to fast food manager and almost everything in between. Lydie said he was working as a salesman for a paper company, liked his job, and his boss, and was doing very well.

So, this expensive-looking, creamy envelope was a sign of Jack "going again," taking another turn on the marriage-go-round. I checked the date of the wedding, June 29, and the location, Madison. That gave me three weeks to find a suitable dress and wedding gift. What's appropriate for a third marriage? Luggage for yet-another divorce? Paper plates and plastic silverware so they don't have to argue over who gets what? It was a good thing Lydie couldn't hear me. She had a real blind spot where Jack was concerned. She was always convinced that this job was the perfect one, this girl was the one he'd been waiting his whole life for. If what I'd overheard my boys saying years ago was true, there were many, many Miss Rights in Jack's past. But I hoped for both Jack, and Lydie, that this was the real Miss Right, the final, permanent one who could help him live up to his mother's dreams. It would be an interesting weekend.

Sliding the invitation back into the envelope, I caught sight of a glint of gold on my left hand. My wedding ring. Eight years since Bert died and I still wore it. Wearing that ring seemed like the most natural thing in the world. But I wasn't married anymore; I was a widow.

Last week it had slipped off my finger into the dishwater. I felt panicky while groping in the water to find it. And my hands fumbled a bit when I put it back on. Then I felt a spurt of anger course through me. I knew if I took it off someone would notice and feel entitled to express an opinion.

Why shouldn't I take it off? What if I wanted to go on a date? Whose business was it but mine? It was just a plain gold band, nothing special, but taking it off and putting it away felt like I'd be denying the life and love we'd built. Maybe I'd take it off when I gardened. Just as an experiment. Then if anyone noticed, I could say I had forgotten to put it on afterwards. Maybe. Or I could quit worrying about what everyone else would say and get used to the fact that I'm a widow and getting on with my life.

Before I knew it, I'd gotten a letter from Laurel saying how happy she was that I'd be in her class and giving me a list of the things I needed to bring. I had most of the stuff and went into Simpson to the craft store to pick up the rest.

Not wanting to stick out like a sore thumb, I called the office up at The Clearing to find out what kind of clothes to pack. Kathy told me that it's usually cooler up there on the bluff and that most people wore jeans or other comfortable clothes. Good, that meant I didn't have to buy a whole new wardrobe to go to camp.

I showed the catalog to Clara when she came over for coffee a few days later and we pored over the pictures and the sample schedule. It looked like heaven—wooded grounds with old stone and log buildings, and best of all, they did all the cooking and cleaning up. There were a few pictures of painting classes, and I hauled out a magnifying glass to try to see if they were better painters than me. Clara thought it was funny, but I realized that in my first two classes I'd gotten used to being one of the better painters and wanted to be prepared if I was going to be one of the worst.

Sunday, June 15 dawned bright and beautiful. I'd laid all my clothes out on the bed the night before and figured I'd probably packed too much but wanted to be ready for anything. Check-in started at one p.m. so I left nice and early so I could spend every last minute of time up there. It was only a two-hour drive, but Door County's a big tourist destination and I hoped to avoid the worst of the traffic. I figured I could take a walk around the grounds if I got there way too early. Traffic wasn't bad, most of it was going south, so I could relax and enjoy the scenery—miles and miles of cherry and apple orchards, picturesque herds of black and white cows, small wineries and roadside stands selling fruits, jams, cherry pies, and art. Maybe I'd stop of the way home and find some special wine for Jack's wedding gift.

I turned off the highway onto Garrett Bay Road and nearly missed the driveway of The Clearing. As soon as I turned in, the blinding sunlight bouncing off the asphalt was replaced by dappled sunshine through tall old trees. The curving gravel drive wound through the woods and meadows leading me further away from my regular hectic life. A small sign directed me to the student's parking lot where I parked and sat for a moment drinking in the silence.

I saw another small sign with an arrow pointing to the Lodge for check-in. There I met a smiling woman named

Kathy who turned out to be the woman I'd spoken to when I called the office. She gave me a nametag on a string with instructions to wear it at all times, a map of the campus, and directions to my room. I couldn't afford to have a single room, so I'd have one roommate, a writer named Connie from suburban Chicago. I asked Kathy for my key and was amazed to discover that there weren't any. She said they'd never had problems with people losing things and were very aware of strangers on the grounds, but she'd get me a key if I felt I needed one. I said I guessed not if no one else felt the need and went back to my car to haul in my things. Kathy told me I was welcome to take my painting supplies down to the big room of the Schoolhouse that afternoon so I'd be ready to start early tomorrow and that I could drive down if I had a lot to carry. While I'd thought ahead and brought a dolly to haul my things, it turned out I didn't need it. The Clearing provided wheeled carts. I grabbed one and took it back to my car.

I was pleased to discover my room, number six, was right near the parking lot overlooking the propane tank. Not the most inspiring view but I didn't figure I'd be in my room much. I intended to make the most of my week in the woods.

I was pleased at how pretty the room was—a pair of twin beds with lovely handmade quilts, a desk and chair beside each bed, two built-in armoires with plenty of space for clothes, and a roomy bathroom with a shower. There was a set of towels and soap on each bed.

Leaving my painting things in the cart, I put my suitcase on the bed nearest the window since I like to have a window open when I sleep. Then I walked my art supplies in the cart down a sawdust path through the woods to the Schoolhouse. There was a couple from Illinois, Don and Jane, there who had been in Laurel's class before and helped me pick out a spot to set up my stuff. They were friendly and funny and made me feel welcome. I was glad to have met someone right away to help me settle in.

When I got back to the room Connie had arrived. She

was a short intense woman about my age who gave off an aura of suppressed energy. She was dressed in what I immediately recognized as "city" clothes, a trim black vest over tailored black and white plaid slacks topping the most amazing black and white Doc Marten wingtip shoes. I knew about Doc's from my shopping trip with Samara. I coveted them.

Connie was taking the writing class. We got acquainted while we unpacked. It didn't take me long, but I swear Connie had brought an outfit for every eventuality. I wouldn't have been surprised to see a ball gown come out of one of her suitcases. She had all these dressier casual clothes and the only thing she wore all week were jeans, t-shirts, flannel shirts and sweatshirts just like the rest of us. But she was ready, just in case.

By the time I hauled my empty suitcase back to the car to store it for the week, the campus was buzzing with students moving in, greeting old friends, and making new ones.

According to the schedule we'd gotten when we checked in, supper was at six so I had an hour to take a walk and see more of the place. I found a winding path and followed it to the edge of the bluff overlooking the bay. The sound of the waves lapping on the rock far below was a pleasant change from the noise of tractors, and the sighing of the wind in trees made my muscles relax after the long drive. Every few steps I took on the path along the bluff brought another vista worthy of painting. I couldn't imagine having enough time in a week to paint all I was inspired to paint. Good thing I'd brought a camera.

Along the path at intervals were rings of stacked limestone, some with fire pits in the center. They looked like ancient council rings. Connie was sitting in one of the rings sketching in her journal. We visited for a few minutes, and I walked on.

By the middle of the week at The Clearing I realized that I wasn't the same person with these strangers as I was at home. No one here knew me or had any expectations of my behavior so there was no reason to be anyone other than myself. I discovered that I had a lot to say and didn't hesitate to give my opinion. I stopped examining what I was going to say before I said it like I tended to do with my sons and Clara. No one at The Clearing had ever met me before so they had no preconceived ideas. They never knew me with long hair in a bun, dressed in old lady clothes, more worried about what other people think than what I think. So, I didn't have to be anyone but me, didn't have to worry about who heard me, who I sat next to at meals, or what any of them thought of me or my paintings. Didn't worry that they'd think I was weird or had changed too fast or gone too far. It was relaxing to just be Gail, the painter from Kingman who'd picked up a brush less than a year ago. I was determined to keep that feeling alive when I went home.

I was ready to be the worst in class and spent a lot of time before the drive agonizing over how I'd fit into the scheme of things. But once class got started, I found out that skill-wise I was somewhere in the middle and didn't have to worry. Merely being in class and loving to paint was enough to fit in.

Most of the students had been painting for years and many of them had followed Laurel from Rockford to take her class. For all she looked like the prototypical grandmother with her fluffy white curls, round cheeks, and ready smile, Laurel was a tough teacher demanding the best from her students and herself. As the days passed, I could see my paintings take on a life they hadn't had before.

Early in the week Connie had read me a poem she'd written called "Wise Woman" about loss. It was full of images I itched to paint. It was the first time words, instead of things I could see, made me want to pick up my brushes.

Wise woman
She stood on the shore of Lake Michigan,
feet firmly planted in the sand.
Cloak tightly wrapped to ward off the January chill.
January/Janus.

A time of looking forward – and back.
A time of reflection and change.

No matter how tightly she held the cloak,
the coldness within would not subside.
She did not expect nor seek a warming yet,
just a calming of the restlessness that roamed her soul.
Roamed through all those empty places.
Places where memories pulled her back.
Places that could swallow the joy from life
if she let them. But the woman was a wise teacher.
Healer. Truth seeker.
And knew it was time to turn inward, focusing her gifts
to heal herself.

Numbness preserves. New growth brings discomfort.
And she was greatly discomforted.
She welcomed the pain as a sign of healing.
She braced herself against the winds of change,
contemplating the paths before her.
At a time when others were storing up for the winter
of their years, she wanted to see more.
Know more. Feel more.
To fill the empty places
with new thoughts.
New teachings. New people.

A new tribe. Her old tribe had disbanded.
Her first born now dead through an act of violence.
Her daughter soon to be married, forming an alliance of
her own.
It was nearly a decade from the death of her child
to the rebirth of her spirit.
And she had survived
would continue to survive and seek the way.
For she was a woman with gifts,

a strong woman.
A wise woman.

--Connie Anderson

She gave me a copy of it and in the evenings when most of the painters went back to the Schoolhouse to work, Laurel helped me paint my impression of the woman in the poem. On Thursday afternoon I went into town and found a relatively inexpensive (it was a tourist area, after all) frame so I could give it to Connie on our last night to thank her for being a great roommate.

Mealtimes at The Clearing were fun. Not only was there fabulous food and fresh-baked bread, but it's also a rule that you sit in a different place with different people at every meal. So instead of cliques forming of painters or writers, everyone sat with everyone else, asked about how classes were going, sharing their own triumphs and tribulations both in class and in life. I'd never realized that there were so many interesting people in the world.

By the end of the week Connie and I were getting to be friends; she'd read me her writing and I'd show her my paintings. Connie had taken a watercolor class at home so she understood my frustrations and I'd been a secretary so long I could help her a bit with her grammar and punctuation.

She was touched when I gave her the watercolor I'd painted from her poem. She gave me a blank journal because she said she thought from our conversations I should be a writer too. It turned out to be a wonderful pairing. We exchanged addresses and pledged to keep in touch. On the drive home, I resolved to call Aaron and ask for his help getting a computer.

Laurel praised my work and complimented me on my skills. I had to give Jake his due; I wrote him a little thank-you note while I was still there.

A couple of the other students in class had heard of Jacques Tunis or read about him in an art magazine and

147

were very impressed that I'd actually taken a class from him. One night we sat around sharing a bottle of wine and I regaled them with stories of my adventures in Jake's class, I even told them about yelling at him and throwing my first artistic temper tantrum all over him. They thought that was hilarious. I must admit I embellished a bit, made Jake more looming and myself more courageous, but essentially, they were true stories. And no one thought I was bragging about how terrific I was. I don't know if they were thinking it, but no one said it aloud.

One of the women looked at Laurel and said, "No one could get that mad at our nice teacher." And Laurel came right back with, "Oh, don't be too sure about that. Ralph can tell you stories of students I pissed off that would curl your hair."

We all laughed but I looked at the small grandmotherly woman with her fluffy white hair and, without thinking, said, "I'll bet you can be a real witch if you think it'll pull something out of your students."

Everybody laughed. Laurel laughed loudest and said, "You got that right!"

I came back from The Clearing a changed woman. A week up there away from everyone who knew me gave me the courage to try and worry less about how others think of me and not feel like I'm living under a microscope all the time. It was a real revelation to realize that those people accepted me for who I was—and they liked me. No preconceived notions of how I was supposed to act, just Gail the painter from Kingman who had gotten to be pretty good in a really short time.

CHAPTER 20

July

It was hot and steamy already at 8:30 a.m., and I stood in the shade checking what was doing well, and what wasn't, in my gardens. In the west-facing bed across the front of the porch, I had planted bright marigolds. The reds, yellows, and oranges of the petals looked like flames against the lush foliage and the old bricks of the foundation.

Not all the flowers and shrubs I had planted with such high hopes in April and May had thrived. A bunch of them, more than I thought the law of averages should allow for, hadn't. I supposed it was naïve of me to imagine that, just because I'd planned so carefully, everything would work out the way I wanted it to.

I pulled my crumpled, soil-stained plans out of the top drawer of my planting dresser on the back porch and marked the failures with little black crosses. They looked like little graves. I used a red pencil to circle those not doing as well as I expected, kind of drawing an emergency-room circle around my horticultural patients. The number of little black crosses and red circles foretold a trip to the garden center. And right away.

Sweaty and dirt-stained from uprooting the failures, I took a shower, making sure my legs were reasonably stubble-free, and found some fresh shorts and a nice, button-down shirt to wear.

Drawing a comb through my wet hair made me glad I'd

decided to cut it short. That mare's tail dripping down my back, and the hours and aching arms it took to dry it were a thing of the past. Now I could just towel it dry and comb it into shape. Every day I thanked the instinct that led me from Mavis' "house of styles from the '80s" to Simpson for a revolutionary haircut from Nora at *Nine*. A little blush and a lick of lipstick and I was ready to go.

Pulling into the parking lot of the garden center I caught myself looking to see if Abel's red pickup was there. I was surprised to be disappointed when it wasn't. Get a grip on yourself, Gail. Must be menopause—or sunstroke.

Resolved to be more careful choosing replacement plants for my failures, I lingered at each display reading the tags detailing sun and moisture preferences. Somewhere along the line it occurred to me to invest in more perennials for my garden. They were quite a bit more expensive than annuals and wouldn't offer the instant gratification of having a drift of flowers this year, but they'd save me lots of planting time in the years to come and cut down on future backaches.

Now that I had made some decisions, I needed a cart to start hauling plants. As I looked around hoping to find one tucked in a convenient corner, I saw Abel coming toward me, smiling, and pushing a flatbed.

"Gail! It's good to see you. What can I help you with?"

Surprised at how happy I was to see him, I tried to keep from grinning, and I could feel a blush flooding my cheeks. "Abel, I didn't see your truck." Wow, Gail, way to play it cool. "I mean, I didn't think you were working today." That's a bit better.

He chuckled, "Well, it was time for old Bessie to have her check-up, so I hitched a ride to work with Norman."

"You call your truck Bessie?"

"Yep. She's old and ornery and always reminds me of one of my favorite aunts. Aunt Bessie kept everybody in line, her eighteen kids, Uncle Jack, the neighbors, the dogs.

"Is orneriness a family trait?" I asked him with a smile.

"I'll take the Fifth, Gail. So, what are you doing here this hot summer day?"

I pulled out my garden plans. "I'm sorry to say that a lot of the plants I put in last spring didn't do very well. A bunch of them have died; they're the ones marked in black. And a few are on the critical list; those are in the red circles. I'm afraid I might not have paid enough attention to what I put where as I should have."

Abel took the paper and scratched his head. "What about the ones I helped you plant?"

"Oh," I said, with a rueful laugh, "those are doing just fine. I guess I should have taken you up on your offer to help sooner than I did."

"I'll say you should have." He looked at my plans. "You probably planted them too deep. What a waste of time and money. Well, a gentleman never says 'I told you so' but…"

I felt like I'd stepped under a cold shower. "But you'll make an exception in my case?" I reached to snatch my garden plan back. "That's nice." I turned and walked away. As I strode down the rows of picked-over plants, tears blurred my vision. There I was, all ready to flirt, and thinking I might be ready to accept his next invitation and Mr. Horticultural Experience Obnoxious Jerk comes galloping out of his mouth.

"Aw, come on, Gail." He was following me down the rows of plants. I could see the heads of the other customers turn to see what was going on. "Can't you take a little joke?" He caught up to me and put his hand on my arm. "Here, let me help you pick out some more plants."

I whirled around, intending to blast him with my anger, but found I couldn't spit out the words with all those eyes looking at us. "You hurt me." I turned and kept walking toward the car.

"I didn't mean to. It's just… I was so glad to see you today. You look so pretty. Dammit, can't you give a guy a break?"

I stopped walking. What did he say? He thinks I look

pretty? The plaintive note in his voice extinguished the last of my anger. "I'm sorry, Abel. I feel so foolish to have gotten so angry. Of course, you can help me." I turned to face him and realized he had tears in his eyes. "Abel. What is it?"

He wiped his cheek and said, "Gail, I've been trying every way I can think of to get you to like me and no matter what I do or where I show up, I always seem to make you mad. What do I have to do to get you to like me? To talk to me for more than a minute before you steam off?"

I felt like I was seeing the real Abel Baker for the first time. "Well, for starters you can help me pick out some perennials that will survive in these spots, along with a few annuals to brighten it up this year. Then you can come over on your next day off and help me plant them. I'd be a fool to refuse free labor from a professional." I smiled up into the most amazing pair of ice-blue eyes I'd ever seen. Before I could stop myself, I blurted, "Have your eyes always been that color?"

He threw back his head and laughed. "Yes, my eyes have always been blue. Let's go find you something to plant."

We spent the next hour roaming all over the garden center, debating the merits of sun vs. shade, foliage shapes and shades of green. By the time the flatbed was full I knew I'd never think of Mr. Abel Baker as an opinionated jerk again.

I didn't have to wait for Abel's next day off and he didn't have to ask Norman for a ride home. Abel's shift was over, so I took him home with me. After a quick lunch of cold meatloaf sandwiches, we went out into the yard and planted and planted and planted. It was nearly nine o'clock by the time we'd cleaned up, so we ordered a pizza and sat on the porch to watch the sunset, drinking wine, and eating pizza.

We talked about art and books. I told him how much our sunset ritual had meant to Bert and me. He talked about his marriage too. I thought Marcella sounded high maintenance, but I had resolved to be less judgmental so I kept my mouth shut. Abel had obviously loved her. I had forgotten how much I liked sitting on the porch with a man and just talking.

It was nearly midnight when I gave him a ride to pick up Bessie.

Clara and I were sitting over cups of coffee in her kitchen when we heard the sound of a familiar brown delivery truck pull up.

"I'll bet that's the Avon stuff Jean said she was sending," said Clara.

We heard a knock on the back door and Clara called, "We're in the kitchen, Harry. Bring it on in, will you, please?"

The screen door opened, and heavy footsteps crossed the back hall.

"Harry's off today. I'm Justin. Will I do?" said a deep voice.

We turned expecting to see our old friend and neighbor but saw instead a pair of laughing brown eyes and dark brown hair topping a gorgeous, muscular body.

"Uh, that's fine," stammered Clara, taking the small package and setting it on the table. She reached to sign the board accepting delivery without ever taking her eyes off his face.

Justin touched a finger to his forehead, said, "You ladies have a nice afternoon," and left the way he had come.

Both of us almost fell off our chairs enjoying the view of Justin walking away. We sat in silence listening to the truck drive off.

"Oh my God, Clara, that was the most beautiful man I've ever seen."

"Did you see his eyes?" Clara asked, her hand on her heart. "I bet he'd look great in one of those tiny Speedo swimsuits. I'd pay money to see that."

"Me too. Is there such a thing as a group hot flash?" I picked up my napkin and fanned my face. "Did they even make men like that when we were younger?"

"When I met Hank, he was all tanned and muscular from working on the farm but, Gail, he never had that devilish look in his eyes. Well, maybe once or twice..."

"Clara, you are so naughty! Bert worked hard all his life and had nice muscles too, but he never ever looked at me like that young man just did. Do you think he was flirting with us?"

"Oh, I doubt it. We probably looked like two pole-axed cows, and he was laughing at us. We're way too old for a hunky, young guy like that to flirt with. Now I can guarantee you that Abel is flirting with you every time you see him."

"Do you think so? I have to admit he is kind of cute. I especially like his hands." I rested my chin in my hand and thoughts of how it would feel to have Abel touch me floated through my head.

Clara cleared her throat. "Gail, if you've finished with your coffee, maybe you'd like to be alone with your thoughts?" And she smiled the annoying smile of an old friend who can see what's on your mind.

I could feel myself blushing. "Oh, for heaven's sake, Clara, I was just... You're right, I was thinking about Abel. He's persistent, I'll give him that. I should go out with him just to get him out of my way." The smile left my face, and a frown took its place. "Do you think he's a stalker?"

Now Clara really laughed. "Gail, get a grip. We live in Kingman, Wisconsin. It's so small it barely qualifies as a town. Of course, you're going to run into Abel here and there. There are only so many places to go around here. Besides, everybody knows everybody else, and knows everybody's business, too. You can bet Mr. Baker's got his spies just like we do."

"I guess you're right."

"So, do you think Justin the delivery man is new in town or just a replacement? He sure is cute. Maybe I should engineer a meeting between him and Sharon. You know, her last boyfriend turned out to be a shiftless bum."

"I don't know, Clara," I teased. "Would you ever be able to talk to him or would his gorgeous self strike you permanently dumb the way it did today?"

"Gail! Some friend you are," Clara retorted. She turned and pulled a scissors out of a drawer. "Let's see what Jean sent." We got interested in sniffing and trying on all the goodies Clara's daughter-in-law had put in the box and the memory of the hunky UPS guy faded—a bit.

CHAPTER 21

August

Abel asked me out to dinner, a formal date. And I accepted. Despite the friendship that had slowly grown over the summer and Abel's invaluable help in my garden, this was our first actual date.

So, there I stood looking into my closet trying to decide what to wear. Most of the time I felt like I had too many clothes; that night I had too few. I didn't want to wear any of the clothes from before I went shopping with Samara, they were too old lady-ish. The clothes I bought with Samara's help, my jeans and sweaters, I loved them, but they were too casual, and too heavy for August.

Gail, get your mind back on your clothes. You'll have plenty of time later to moon over Abel. I wish I'd asked him where he's planning to take me. That would make this decision a whole lot easier. A dress is probably a good choice, but which one? So many of my dresses, okay all of them, are leftovers from working at the school--good, serviceable fabrics that don't wrinkle and don't show dirt. I have to have something pretty in my closet that I can wear.

Then I remembered the floral dress I wore to my nephew Jack's wedding. I loved the beautiful soft chiffon in a muted tropical print, but not the white eyelet shawl collar that just screamed middle-aged-aunt-of-the-groom. I pulled it out and took a look at how the collar was attached. Happily, it seemed to be barely basted on so I ripped it off and tried the dress on.

Not bad. The v-neck was a lot lower than I was used to but it wasn't too low. Maybe I could find a necklace to fill in what looked to me like an acre of bare skin.

Let's see, what time is it? Damn, nearly six forty-five and he said he'd be here at seven.

Dear Lord, please let me have one pair of panty hose without a run. Yes, here's a pair, because my only other option is a garter belt and old-fashioned hose Bert bought me from a catalog once when he was feeling sexy. I didn't think my budding relationship with Abel was ready for something that racy, at least not on the first date; the second maybe if things went well. What am I thinking? Gail, get a grip.

I checked the dress one more time for stains, tears, and loose threads. By then it was nearly seven and I was sure Abel would be right on time, even early if his persistence in getting me to agree to a date was any indicator. I got dressed, searched through my jewelry box for something the right length to fill in my neckline, and thanked God that Mom's Aunt Eunice had spent her money on jewelry. I found the perfect thing, a heavy gold chain with a free-form shape set in a few places with mother of pearl and coral beads hanging from it. It looked just right with my dress. Gold earrings, not too big, and I was ready.

As I stood in front of my dresser's mirror checking to make sure that my hair was right and I wasn't going to embarrass myself, I heard a truck pull into the drive. Abel, right on time.

I started to walk to the kitchen door to greet him because that's where everyone came in but then I heard him climb the front porch steps and ring the bell. I walked into the living room and I could see him through the window, dressed in a suit and tie, silhouetted in the sunset light. My breath caught and I thought about Bert because we'd spent so many sunsets together. For just a moment, I felt like I was cheating on my husband but pushed the thought away and opened the door.

Abel's face lit up as he saw me and he said, "Gail, you look beautiful. Here, I brought you this." He extended his hand and gave me a small white box, a florist's box.

"Oh, Abel, how nice. You shouldn't have. Would you like to come in?" I stepped back and closed the door behind him. "What is this?"

"You'll have to open it." He smiled like he had the best secret.

I carefully opened the lid of the box and there nestled in tissue paper was one perfect white rose made into a corsage with baby's breath and a little piece of fern.

"I didn't know what you were planning to wear so I thought a white rose would go with everything."

"Oh, Abel, it's beautiful," I said. "I never expected a corsage."

"Well," he said, "it's not a very big corsage and I wanted to bring you flowers but knew you wouldn't like a bouquet."

I had to laugh because he was right. I wouldn't have been happy if he'd shown up with an armload of flowers, but this was just right. "Will you pin in it on me, please?"

Abel stepped close and plucked the little flower from the box in my hand. My hands dropped to my sides and I stood very still while he pinned the rose to my dress just below my left shoulder. His spicy cologne smelled great and my breath got shallow. That made me a little lightheaded and I swayed toward him. He grabbed my shoulders, held me still and said, "There, that's got it. You smell good, Gail."

"So do you," I said with a little laugh. We stood there for a moment, eyes locked, and I figured we were each thinking the same thing, I wonder what would happen if I just leaned forward and we kissed?

Evidently neither of us was willing to risk a rebuff because after a minute his hands dropped to his sides and his eyes dropped too. He cleared his throat and said, "Guess we'd better get a move on. Our reservation is for seven forty-five."

"Oh," I said, "then we'd better go."

He still hadn't told me where we were going and I didn't

trust my voice right then. I picked up my purse, checked to make sure I had my house key, and we left.

He held the truck door for me and handed me in like a gentleman. I could see that he'd had it washed and the inside smelled like a bag of lemons had been squashed in it.

I was surprised when he turned onto the highway into Simpson and got on the bridge to cross the river. Then he took the exit as if we were going to Door County, but turned into a very nice restaurant, *Tarragon*, overlooking the bay and the sunset.

We had both been silent on the half-hour ride and as we entered the place all I could say was, "Oh."

It was beautiful--dark woods, Oriental carpets over gleaming hardwood floors, and prints of the French countryside on glowing gold walls. I stood looking around while Abel spoke to the host. I had stepped closer to the walls to check out the paintings when Abel took my elbow and we followed the host to our table. It was in the center of the wall of windows that looked west. By then it was nearly eight o'clock and I could see that the sunset would be breathtaking.

"I know how you like sunsets, Gail, so I reserved this table special for you."

"Thank you, Abel, it's perfect."

He held my chair and then seated himself next to me. Our waiter brought menus and asked what we'd like to drink. When I said I preferred wine to liquor, Abel launched into a discussion with him about the provenance of the wines and settled on one from Chile, of all places. It was an excellent wine; just the way I like it, dry and a little sweet. Does the man know about everything? After a few sips of wine, I turned back to the menu and discovered that there weren't any prices.

"Abel," I said, "does your menu have prices?"

"Yes, of course it does. I'm the host. You're the guest, so yours doesn't."

I looked at him in exasperation. "Well, then how am I supposed to know what to order?"

He laughed. "Gail, you order whatever you'd like."

"But..." I leaned toward him so no one would overhear. "But, Abel, what if what I order is too expensive?"

He reached over and covered my hand with his. "Don't you worry, I've been saving up."

"Oh, okay." I had the sneaking hunch he was laughing at me, but I found I didn't mind. It was relaxing to not have to worry about the cost of things.

We placed our orders and there were a few minutes of awkward silence, then we started talking. The food, exquisitely prepared and presented, came at a nice slow pace with plenty of time for us to enjoy it. I let Abel talk me into having a second glass of wine, but I drew the line at cognac after dinner.

"I don't have much of a head for alcohol and if I drink any more, I can't be responsible for my actions," I said.

He looked at me over his wine glass and said, "That might be interesting." The deep timbre of his voice and the smile in his blue eyes went right through me.

We were lingering over our coffee when Abel said, "Are you about ready to leave? I think they want to close."

I looked around and realized that the conversations and music that had been in the background all night had gone silent. Ours was the only table occupied.

"Oh, my heavens. What time is it?"

"Nearly eleven."

"So late? We'd better go so these nice people can close up."

I took Abel's arm as we walked out and he paused just outside the door.

"Look at the stars, Gail. Aren't they beautiful?"

I looked up at the black sky pierced by hundreds, millions of stars. "Mmm, yes, they are."

He leaned close and whispered, "But still not as beautiful as you are."

My breath stopped in my throat, and I couldn't think of a

thing to say. For once in my life, I didn't deny the compliment. "Thank you, Abel," I said. Just like a real lady.

The drive home was very different than the drive to the restaurant. We talked about art and books and gardening. I was surprised at how quickly the time had passed when we pulled into my lane. When he parked the truck and came around to open my door, my mind started racing. Should I kiss him? I wanted to. Should I invite him in? I wanted to do that too. But would he think I was being forward, inviting him in for more than coffee and conversation?

He walked me to the front door and turned me to face him. "I had a wonderful evening, Gail. I hope you did."

"Oh, I did, Abel. It was wonderful for me too."

He took both my hands in his and leaned forward to kiss my cheek. As his lips neared, I turned my head and our lips met. I could feel his hesitation but then he leaned into me, and the kiss deepened. As I reached to touch his face, he pulled back.

"Would you like to come in?" I asked.

"I, uh, I don't think I'd better. Thank you again for a lovely evening. May I have your key?"

I handed him my house key, he opened the door, handed the key back. He kissed me once again, on the cheek, and said, "Goodnight, Gail. I'll see you soon." And turned and left.

I stayed on the porch and waved as he drove away and then went indoors. As I locked the door behind me, I looked at the key in my hand and said, "Just like in the movies." It had been a night to remember.

And I couldn't wait to see him again.

I sat down Friday night as usual on the couch with my writing desk on my knees to write letters my sons and their families. Those letters were filled with the usual chat about how I was feeling, how the garden was growing, everyday stuff.

I saved the real news for my sister's letter. I couldn't

decide if I was happy about the way things had been moving on "the Abel front" or not, but I figured writing to Lydie would, if nothing else, help me gather my thoughts.

Before I took time to analyze I plunged in:

Dear Lydie, I wrote, I can't believe the way my life has changed lately. Ever since I got back from The Clearing, I've felt different. Being up there with strangers for a week, people who hadn't known me when I was a mouse, seems to have spilled over or gone on or somehow made a lasting impression on me. Those days in that utopia of painting, living in a community of artists and writers, have somehow freed me to be myself and let the rest of the world shift for itself.

Anyway, the most amazing news is that last week I finally gave in to Abel and went on a date. A date! Can you believe it, Lydie? I went on an actual date, with a "boy," and survived. I'll admit that getting ready I felt a bit like I was having an affair, cheating on Bert, but I sternly reminded myself that Bert has been dead for over eight years and wouldn't want me to cloister myself.

Abel wouldn't tell me where we were going so I just dressed up and went along for the ride. We went to that swanky restaurant, *Tarragon*, up on the bluff east of Simpson. It was gorgeous, so beautifully decorated, and the food was delicious. But the most amazing thing was how I felt with Abel. All these months I've been trying to convince myself that he was pompous and arrogant and a whole bunch of negative things, when in reality he's well-read, an art lover, and absolutely fascinating to talk to. He's got a great sense of humor and, Lydie, I have the feeling that he's not hurting in the money department, either.

But best of all, he's a really good kisser. I can't believe I just wrote that. He makes me feel like I'm in high school again, panting after some cute boy. I feel like I should pass notes in study hall and giggle at my locker with the other girls but, Lydie, when I'm with him that's just how I feel. My heart pounds, my breath gets short, and the thoughts I have ought to send me running to the confessional. Don't get me wrong, he's been a perfect gentleman and I've managed to control myself but don't know how long that will last.

The worst thing was, one of Kingman's biggest gossips, Helen Shultz (you remember her? She was a year ahead of you in school), was at *Tarragon* that same night. She didn't waste any time spreading the word that Abel and I were there, too, and holding hands. Evidently she waved at me and even called my name but I was so consumed with my own thoughts, and Abel's blue eyes, I never noticed her. Of course, she told everyone that I snubbed her and now she gives me the cold shoulder whenever she gets the chance. I am not going to revert all the way back to grade school and run up to her and fall all over myself apologizing for not seeing her. Small-minded people like Helen can just stew in their own juices as far as I'm concerned, these days.

Anyway, Abel and I have another date next week. He wants us to go to the movies. Maybe he'll put his arm around me in the dark. I can't wait. More later.

Love, Gail

Date number two was set. Abel wanted us to see a movie together and I thought I would be able sit for a couple hours in the dark next to him and not be consumed with, well, whatever it is I've been consumed with the last few times we've been together. At least I knew how to dress for the movies, a pair of nice pants, or better yet jeans, a blouse--a red one to light up my eyes, and a sweater in case it's cold in the theater.

Abel picked me up around six and I was surprised that he was in jeans too. "What movie are you taking me to?" I asked.

He laughed. "If I told you, it wouldn't be much of a surprise, now, would it?"

Not very patient, I don't like waiting for things. "Well, what kind of movie is it? Romance? Adventure? I hope it's not some violent thing with a lot of car crashes and explosions. I don't like those."

"I'm not telling. You'll have to be patient." Abel drove into Simpson but not toward the big new multiplex behind the mall. Instead, he took us to the center of the city to a neighborhood that was enjoying a renewal. Old businesses and buildings that had been vacant for years were being refurbished and reopened as boutiques, gift shops, and cafes. I'd forgotten that there was a movie theater in the district that showed art films, not mainstream movies. And that's where we stopped.

I looked at the marquee to see they were showing an Italian film. "Do you understand Italian, Abel?" I asked as he opened the truck door for me.

"Nope," he said, smiling.

"So how are we supposed to know what they're saying?"

A grin spread across his face. "Ever hear of subtitles?"

I was astounded. "You mean we'll have to read the movie? How can we concentrate on the action if we're busy reading instead of listening?"

"I think you might be surprised." And he grabbed my hand and started pulling me toward the theater door, just like a kid dragging his mom into a county fair.

We stood in line with college kids and couples in their early thirties waiting to buy tickets. The old theater had been cleaned and the beautiful original decor refurbished. It looked pretty good, better than the spaceship designs of new theaters, kind of like the movie palaces I remembered as a child. Black and white glamour shots of old movie stars graced the walls and the smell of buttered popcorn hadn't changed. I could feel Abel's warm hand on the small of my back as he guided me past the ticket-taker and into the line at the concession stand. At first all I saw were the cases filled with overpriced boxes of candy: Milk Duds, Good 'n Plentys, Mike & Ikes, red licorice whips, Dots, all the things that are so much fun to eat and are bad for you. The top shelf held beautiful pastries displayed on plates with paper doilies. And right next to that case was a bar. I'd never imagined a movie theater would sell liquor.

We moved toward the front, debating the merits of having traditional movie fare or trying something new. Abel was in favor of candy, popcorn, and soda.

"What do you think, Gail? Should we go for the upscale calories with a drink or stick with tradition and have popcorn?"

I looked at Abel and saw the twinkle in his eye. "Oh, you mean I can't have both?" I leaned more toward popcorn and a drink, a real alcoholic drink; I figured since he picked a foreign film, something I'd never experienced, I might as well go all the way over the edge.

"That's my girl. Sure, you can."

We decided on the biggest tub of popcorn they had, with extra butter of course, and a nice bottle of wine to share. Abel said it wouldn't be the movies without Milk Duds and Dots, so he bought those too.

The Velcro sound of our shoes on the theater floor as we looked for seats was the only familiar aspect of this date so far. We managed to snag one of the little bistro tables off to the side of the regular rows of seats, which I thought was a wonderful idea. It made it so much easier to pour the wine and juggle our embarrassment of snacks.

At first, I put my box of Milk Duds aside but realized that Abel was right, it wasn't a movie without candy. I found the little finger notch and opened the box. I could feel Abel watching me open it.

"What?" I said.

"Are you one of those people who carefully peels the tape off Christmas wrap too?"

"No, I rip away just like a kid. My sister Lydie is the careful unwrapper."

"So why go to the trouble to find the notch to open the box instead of just ripping off the top?"

I had to think for a minute, but then I said, "So I can fool myself into thinking I will re-close the box in case I don't eat them all in one sitting. Something I have never been able to do."

Both of us burst out laughing and were shushed by those seated around us. We looked around guiltily but, since the movie hadn't started, couldn't figure out why. Abel leaned and whispered in my ear, "Must be hall monitors all grown up," which produced a new round of smothered giggles.

After the usual ads for the concessions and innumerable previews of "coming attractions," the movie finally started. It was *Life is Beautiful* and, now that I was sitting there, I remembered the year it won Best Foreign Film at the Oscars. The director and star, Roberto Benigni, was so excited he climbed over people's heads to get to the stage. "I always wanted to see this movie," I whispered to Abel, "but that was the year Bert died and I went through life on autopilot for a while." Abel was right and after the first few minutes I didn't even realize that I was reading the subtitles while watching and listening. By the end of the film, I felt like I could sort of understand Italian.

As the credits rolled, the lights came up and I was happy to see that I wasn't the only one wiping their eyes. There was even a bit of a glimmer of tears on Abel's cheeks. He stepped back to allow me to go up the aisle first and casually put his hand on the small of my back. It was like he'd attached an electrode; the jolt weakened my knees, and I stumbled a little.

"Are you okay?" he asked.

"I'm fine. I think I hit an extra sticky spot on the floor."

"How'd you like the movie? Did the subtitles bother you?"

We had reached the lobby, so I slid my hand under his elbow as we walked side by side. "I loved the movie. And the subtitles didn't distract me at all. Thanks, Abel."

"For what?" He smiled down at me.

I snuggled a little closer. "For a new experience, for pushing me to try new things."

"Next time we're definitely going to sit in regular movie seats."

"Why? I kind of liked sitting at the table. I made it through an entire movie without dropping popcorn into my lap."

He untangled his arm from mine then I felt the weight of it settle around my waist. "Because next time we're in a darkened movie theater, I fully intend to do a little smooching."

I surprised myself by responding, "Sounds good to me."

The drive home flew by. We debated the message of the movie, marveling at the resilience of humans in a terrible situation. The moonlight made silvery patterns on the roadside as Abel steered his truck into the lane leading to my house.

Neither of us spoke when he parked under the big chestnut tree next to the driveway. The ticks and groans of the cooling engine were the only sounds except for the sigh of the wind in the tree above us. I felt Abel shift; his arm snaked around my shoulders, and he pulled me to his side. I was surprised at how right I felt nestled against his chest. I could feel him relax. I guess he expected resistance. It was nice to sit snuggled against a man's side again, hearing his heartbeat. The mixture of scents coming from him—popcorn and aftershave with an under-current of wine—was intoxicating.

He turned toward me and lifted my chin. I saw the moonlight glitter in his eyes as he leaned to kiss me. The electric charge of the contact made me catch my breath, drawing in Abel's exhalation. It was a very intimate feeling, his warm breath surging into my lungs, mixing with mine. It had been a very long time since I'd necked in a front seat but I guess it's like riding a bicycle, you don't forget. We kissed, exploring each other's face with our mouths and fingers. I turned toward him and got a surprise. "Ouch. Dammit."

"What happened?" Abel sounded confused. "Did I hurt you?"

"No, you didn't hurt me, I banged my shin on the shifter."

"Oh," I could hear the laughter bubbling in his voice, "are you okay?"

"Not funny." I rubbed the spot, hoping to keep a bruise from forming there, but I could feel my own laugh building. "Do you have insurance? I think I might be permanently disabled."

"I'd be happy to be your nurse. Do you think you need a nurse?" He wrapped his arms around me once again. "How about a therapist? We could do some physical therapy." He planted a trail of kisses from my lips, down my cheek, to my ear.

"No nibbling," I said, turning my lips to his. "I hate ear nibbling."

I could feel his lips smile against mine. "I'll try to be more careful. Is there anything else you don't like?"

It was my turn to smile. "I can't think of anything offhand. But then the last man I necked with in a truck wasn't very imaginative."

I felt him take a deep breath and his arms tightened. "I am, Gail. I'm very imaginative."

After a while, I turned to catch my breath, looked out the windshield and nearly burst out laughing.

"What?"

I leaned close and whispered, "Look at my house."

"Who is that?"

"It's Clara." I could see the indecision in her stance. "She's trying to decide whether she should walk down here or turn around and go on home."

He straightened up and I felt his arm drop from around me. "What's she doing here anyway?"

I lifted his arm and tucked myself back under it. "She always comes over when I get home from painting class and I guess she figured she'd pop over to hear how our movie date went. I'll bet she wishes she'd waited until you drove away."

Our gazes were riveted on the pale figure at the top of the walk. I was sure she was talking to herself. "Should we get out?" Abel asked.

"I can't decide which would be more embarrassing for her--for us to stay here and let her imagination run wild or get out and then she knows we've seen her." I saw Clara take a half step our way, and then she turned and started back home.

"I guess there's your answer, Gail. You'll have to wait until tomorrow for your grilling. Now, where were we?"

The next morning, I walked the path to Clara's house. I wondered what Clara would say about the night before. "Morning," I said as I opened the kitchen door.

"Oh, good morning," Clara said, turning from the mixer that was making a racket.

"What are you making?"

Clara brought over a mug of coffee and set it in front of me. "Just a cake for Kayla's birthday." She went back to the counter, turned off the mixer, and raised the beaters to let the batter drip back into the bowl. "How was the movie?" Clara's voice was higher than usual.

I sipped my coffee. "Good. I was surprised at how the subtitles didn't really interfere with the movie. In fact, by the end it was like I could understand Italian, as foolish as that sounds."

Clara kept her back turned. "It does sound kind of crazy but then I've never seen a foreign film." Silence fell. Clara used a spatula to scrape the batter into two cake pans, smoothed it out, and slid the pans into the oven. When she stood up, she said, "Oh I am so sorry that I saw you and Abel... well, in his truck. I didn't see anything, honest." She blushed to the roots of her graying brown hair.

I had all I could do not to spit out the mouthful of coffee I had just sipped. "Clara," I set down her mug and wiped my lips, "even if you'd been standing at the window all you'd have seen were two middle-aged people kissing."

Clara's shoulders sagged. "Really? Well, that's

disappointing, I spent all night imagining you two doing the deed in the front seat of Abel's truck."

I burst out laughing. "Oh Clara, if we'd done that both of us would be in traction. Have you ever done it in the front seat of a truck?" I kept giggling until I looked up at her. "Clara, you dog! Who with?"

Now it was Clara's turn to giggle. "With Hank, of course, and let me tell you it takes skill and flexibility to accomplish."

The two of us started laughing and didn't stop until the oven timer buzzed.

Clara took the cake pans out and set them to cool on the back porch. She got to work making frosting but, every once in a while, I noticed her shoulders shake with silent laughter.

CHAPTER 22

We spent an entire Saturday at the annual art fair in Simpson. I had mentioned that I wanted to go and even offered to drive, but Abel insisted that he would drive so he picked me up at nine o'clock in the morning. We drove into town and parked in a lot across the river from the fair. Abel whistled and a pedi-cab appeared. Propelled by a cheerful middle-aged woman, we were whisked across the bridge and into the hubbub of the art fair.

Irresistible smells wafted from the food area, music came from three different directions, and all around were booth after booth of all kinds of art. Paintings, watercolor and oils, glowed next to buttery soft wooden bowls and boxes, jewelry, weavings, pottery, photographs—artists of every discipline displayed their best efforts for all to see—and buy. Abel said that our first stop had to be the cotton candy booth.

"You can't be hungry," I said, "it's barely 10 o'clock."

He had the grace to blush. "I've been dreaming about this day ever since we started dating. You, me, a sunny summer day, and all this art." He handed me a cone of the shimmery pink treat with a flourish. "Sweets for the sweet."

It was my turn to blush. "You've been planning this day for months?" I said around a mouthful of the flossy sugar. "Tell me how the day's supposed to go."

"Well, so far it's going exactly according to plan." He took my elbow and steered us down the first aisle between the booths of art. "It's a beautiful sunny day, not too hot, with a nice breeze. We found a good parking place, and on the west side, so I could treat you to a pedi-cab ride. And you didn't argue too much when I bought the cotton candy."

I had to smile at the pride in his voice as if he were personally responsible for the beautiful weather and good parking place. I tilted the melting cone of cotton candy toward him. "Have some. I don't want to be the only one with sticky fingers."

He gracefully unwound a huge tuft of the candy. "Just so you know, I planned ahead. I've got a little bottle of hand cleaner in my pocket."

"You think of everything, don't you?"

The arrival of a swarm of bees, attracted by the candy I carried, forced us to find a trash bin to dispose of the tattered remains of the sticky treat.

We slowly moved up one side of the aisles and down the other admiring the art offered for sale. Couples and families walked around us and jostled us as we took our time admiring each display. I paid special attention to all the paintings, while Abel was attracted to the turned wooden bowls. At the end of each aisle, an artist in a larger booth gave a demonstration. There was a potter working his wheel, an acrylic artist painting fantastic flowers on a huge canvas, a woodcarver carving spirit faces in pieces of driftwood, a spinner making yarn from wool shorn from her own herd of alpaca, and a blacksmith hammering small hooks and decorative hangers from red-hot iron.

The blacksmith fascinated Abel. He stood staring as the artisan swung his hammer, crashing into the heated metal, causing sparks to fly in every direction. "I wonder how hot that forge has to be to make the metal soft enough to work?" he said. A young man standing at the edge of the booth stepped forward and handed Abel a printed page. "About 2200 degrees Fahrenheit," the young man said. "My dad built the forge himself." Abel finally managed to pull himself away, but not until he'd wrung every bit of info out of the men. I could see by the gleam in his eye that he was thinking of picking up a new hobby.

We got lunch from a booth called *Outback Jack's* when we were about halfway through the fair. It looked like it was built out of driftwood and stuff washed up on a beach and the food was great—two-handed wraps of grilled meat and vegetables that we washed down with huge cups of lemonade. On a stage in front of a department store a swing band played danceable music. When they launched into *String of Pearls*, Abel grabbed my hand and pulled me into the open space in front of the bandstand.

"You can't be serious," I said, trying to pull away.

"Don't you like dancing?" he said with a grin. "I love it."

Fortunately, he was a good leader because I hadn't danced in years. We must have looked like we knew what we were doing because people clapped when the song ended and I overheard a woman say to her husband as we passed, "See, Marv? They danced." Marv only grunted and shot Abel a look that said *traitor*.

As we walked away from the food area, laughing, and making sure we'd wiped all the drips from our forearms and I checked to see if I'd gotten any on my shirt, Abel bumped into a woman. She whirled around as if he'd tried to pick her pocket. She looked up and said, "You've got some nerve, Abel Baker, running into me to make certain I'd see you with your new tootsie."

It was Prudence Christian, my son Sam's mother-in-law.

Abel's jaw dropped and he said, "Prudence, what..." But that was as far as he got. She drew a breath and let him have it.

"It's bad enough I have to see the two of you make a spectacle in church on Sundays but now you follow me ten miles to the art fair to rub my nose in your sordid affair. And then you dance with her in front of God and everyone right in the middle of the place. Everyone was staring." With each word her face got redder, and she lifted her hand to shake a finger in Abel's face. Passers-by gave her a wide berth and I saw heads turn our way all up and down the aisle. "Don't think you can fool anyone with your good manners, holding the door for her, taking her out to dinner so everyone can see the two of you together. Everyone in town is talking about how you're always over there, supposedly helping her with her garden, but I know the truth and so does everyone in Kingman."

As Mrs. Christian raved, Abel's hand dropped from my waist, and he stood tall and straight. "Now you listen to me, Prudence," he said, not raising his voice when she took a breath, "you don't know what you're talking about. Gail and I are dating. What we do on our dates is no one's business but ours. Keep your nasty, unfounded accusations to yourself."

Her body was rigid with emotion, at his words her face turned from red to white. She folded her arms over her chest and looked even angrier. "I'm so glad," she hissed, "that I made you stop calling me."

His hand moved back around my waist. "Excuse us, Prudence. Come on, Gail." As we stepped past her, people turned away and the little bubble of shocked silence that had surrounded us dissolved. Abel's pace quickened, rushing us past the remaining booths in the aisle. It wasn't until we'd turned a corner and were halfway down the next block that I felt the tension leave him. "I'm so sorry, Gail. If I'd known Prudence would be here, I'd have kept an eye out for her."

I took his arm and steered him to an iron bench surrounding a tree. I sat him down in the shade and bought a cup of lemonade from a nearby vendor. "Now, drink this and then tell me what's her problem."

He took the cup from me, pulled off the top, and drank it in one gulp. "Thanks." He leaned forward, rested his forearms on his thighs, and proceeded to demolish the paper cup. "After Marcella died, I guess I went a little nuts. I was so lonely that I was chasing every single woman over 40 in the county."

I could feel a smile grow on my lips. "I think I might have heard something like that years ago."

He peeked at me. "I'm sure you did. Those cats at Mavis' are vicious."

"Not vicious, exactly, just bored, I think. Their lives are

pretty tame and repetitive. There aren't a lot of adventurous people in Kingman, especially our age, so anyone living outside the norm is bound to be the topic of gossip. And you did seem to go a little nuts. I remember."

"Yeah, well, eventually I got around to calling Prudence. We met for coffee at a place here in Simpson and within five minutes I knew I wouldn't be calling her again. That is one unhappy woman."

I reached over and took the shredded cup out of his hands and tossed it into a nearby bin. Then I lifted his chin so I could look him in the eyes. "I've known how unhappy Prudence Christian is for years. Remember, her daughter Merry is married to my Sam." I put my arms around him. "It's okay, Abel."

He hugged me back. Over his shoulder I could see Prudence Christian's lilac polyester clad form walking away from the fair toward the parking ramp. "Come on," I said, patting his back. "You promised we'd look at every booth and we're not nearly done."

He pulled away to look me in the eye. "Are you sure you want to stay?"

"I'm sure. We can't let one small-minded crazy woman ruin our day. Besides, you promised."

He got up and held out his hand to me. "Okay, let's go."

The rest of our stay was uneventful. It took a while for us to recapture the fun we'd started the day with, but by the time we'd seen every booth, bought a few small things, and sampled every kind of food and music at the fair, we had reclaimed the pleasure of the day and banished Prudence's outburst.

We decided to stay for the fireworks. We walked back across the river to stow our purchases in the truck, grab our jackets and a blanket, and found a perfect spot on the riverbank to watch the display while sipping mulled cider we bought from a stand.

It was late when we got back to my place. "Thanks for a

wonderful day, Abel. I had a great time."

"Me, too. You're not upset by Prudence's outburst?"

"Not at all." I leaned over and kissed him.

He kissed me back. "Need some help carrying your things?"

I got out of the truck. "No, thanks, I can get them. Thanks again for a fun day. Goodnight."

"Goodnight, Gail. See you in church."

I stood in the moonlight of the warm summer night watching him drive away until his taillights disappeared around a curve. I danced up the walk and into the house to the music of the cicadas.

CHAPTER 23

September

I was finally joining the computer age. Aaron promised me that the system he was bringing was simple and easy to use. To be honest, I was more excited to see David and Elizabeth. Even though they only lived a hundred miles away, they had their busy lives and I had mine; we didn't get together as often as any of us would like. I had asked Abel to help me set up the old crib in the back bedroom upstairs and I made sure to check with Sara so I had the right diapers and baby food on hand.

I loved watching David being a big brother. He vacillated between being protective of Elizabeth's crawling explorations and annoyance with how interested in his stuff she was. I remembered Aaron complaining about Matt always being in his private things, and reminded him that he'd done the same to Sam. It was comforting that some things didn't change.

By the time they arrived on Friday evening, the baby was cranky, Sara was exhausted, and David was full of energy after being cooped up in the car for a couple hours. Aaron carried in cartons marked "Handle With Care" and big arrows with "UP" printed in huge letters on all sides. He had reminded me that I'd need a phone hook-up if I wanted to get online so my original plan of hiding the computer in one of the upstairs bedrooms wouldn't work. The only other place in the house with room for a computer that already had a phone line was my bedroom. I had looked at the commercial computer desks at the Wal-Mart in Simpson but decided they were too ugly for words. I hadn't spent all those days redoing the house to put in a desk made of particleboard and wood-grained shelf paper. I found the perfect table and wooden two-drawer filing cabinet at a thrift shop and asked Clara's son Kevin, who was a carpenter, to make some shelves for the wall above the desk.

After supper, Aaron and David started setting up my system. Elizabeth crawled into the bedroom too and had a field day with the cartons as they were emptied. Big brother David was careful to keep the plastic bags and Styrofoam out of the baby's reach. I peeked in to see how things were going and was amazed at the amount of packing material heaped on the bed.

"How are things going, boys?"

Aaron waved a shooing hand and said, "It's going to be a little while, Mom. We've got most of the hardware hooked up; next we install the software and make sure it runs. You did get an internet account set up, right?"

I assured him that I had followed his instructions to the letter and that all the information was in the manila envelope on the top shelf.

Sara was eager to see my latest paintings and was satisfactorily impressed; she made all the right noises to make the artist feel flattered. She'd brought me a few more of her painting books. Her exact words were, "Gail, these are the most advanced technique books in my painting library. You're so far and away better than I ever got, maybe you'll find some little something in one of them that you can use."

I knew that by then I had borrowed most, if not all, of the books she'd collected over the years. I tried to give back some of them, but she refused saying, "Let's consider them a ninety-nine year loan. Taking care of two active kids, the house, Aaron, and my job is much more tiring than I ever imagined. With the way I feel right now, I'll just reclaim them when I retire."

To tell the truth, I was happy to have her entire library. I spent most evenings sitting in the living room with a glass of wine, poring over painting books. It made me feel virtuous when people brought up something they'd seen on TV. "I hardly ever watch anymore," I said, "I'm too busy."

By the time Sara had exclaimed over each painting, Aaron and David's patience with Elizabeth was at an end. We rescued them by dragging a few boxes into the kitchen. Within a very few minutes, Elizabeth came chugging out to find where her new toys had gone. Once she was happily chewing on a box corner, Sara quietly closed the bedroom door to give the computer guys some peace.

It was nearly 11 o'clock before Aaron came out of the bedroom declaring that my computer system was up and running. Sara and Elizabeth had gone to bed and David had fallen asleep on the floor of my room. Aaron carried him upstairs and tucked him in, then came back down to visit with me for a few minutes. We spent a half hour catching up before I saw his eyelids drooping and he couldn't stop yawning. I shooed him to bed just like I had when he was a kid.

I dreaded turning on the light in my bedroom, anticipating that Aaron would have left everything scattered all over. He'd been the messiest of the boys and I had heard Sara complain enough times about him leaving things all over the house. But evidently my yelling all those years and Sara's complaining had sunk in. All the cartons were either broken down or nested, and the packing was all in one big plastic bag ready to be thrown away in the morning.

I went over and looked at my new toy. It sat innocently on my new desk; I knew it was trying to fool me into thinking it would behave for me. After having so much trouble with the computer at the school, I wasn't fooled for a minute. I had already bought a couple of books that said they were for the complete computer neophyte, and I planned to annoy Aaron, and anyone else willing to help me, once I was brave enough to turn it on.

I was awake before everyone else the next morning.

While waiting for my tea to steep I heard Elizabeth's coos floating down the stairs. I crept up, grabbed a diaper and the baby, and brought her downstairs to have tea with grandma. Just like her Uncle Matt, Elizabeth had a sunny disposition and was happiest in the morning. After changing her, I settled her in the highchair with a handful of Cheerios. I turned the radio on low so our conversation wouldn't disturb the sleepers upstairs and we had a fine time watching the birds at the feeders. Soon enough Aaron and David came stumbling downstairs looking all rumpled and sleepy-eyed. Aaron went straight to the coffeepot and made a brew that looked like it would strip paint.

"How can you drink that stuff?" I said. "It looks like sludge."

He cocked an eyebrow at me and smiled. "Puts hair on my chest."

"Puts fuzz on your tongue's more like it. I can smell how strong it is from here."

"Want a cup?" He waved his mug in my direction.

"No thanks. I'll stick with my tea." I got up to pour David a glass of juice and find out what he wanted for breakfast.

"Just cereal for me, Grandma. Dad and I need to get your computer online."

I nearly cried at how grownup he sounded. "Are you sure, honey? I'd be happy to make you pancakes or French toast."

"Naw, that's okay. Maybe you can make French toast tomorrow before church? That'd be good. And some of those little sausages, too? They're my favorite."

"I remember," I said. "I made a special trip to Lou's Meat Market and laid in a big supply so we can all eat them till we burst." I pulled out the cereals, he kept one eye out for his Dad's reaction when he choose the Fruit Loops and poured a bowlful.

Aaron snagged the Cap'n Crunch saying, "We'd better scarf this down before Mama gets up." Father and son chuckled identical mischievous laughs.

Just then a voice came echoing down the stairs. "What are you eating I wouldn't like?"

Aaron and David traded guilty looks. "Um, nothing, dear," Aaron called, "you go back to sleep. Mom's taking good care of us."

Two spoons moved faster to scrape the bowls as a disbelieving grunt floated down followed by a dainty snore as Sara fell back asleep.

I had to laugh as they both reached to refill their bowls. "Not allowed to eat sugary cereal at home, huh?"

David looked at me with an innocent look I recognized from the days his father was his age. "Mama worries that too much sugar is bad for us, but I think a bowl or two every once in a while, won't hurt me. What do you think, Grandma?"

Feeling like an enabler, I said, "I suppose a little sugar never hurt a growing boy like you. Your secret's safe with me."

All three of us jumped when a voice came from the doorway. "Whose side are you on, Gail?" She turned to her daughter. "Good morning, sunshine." Elizabeth was so happy to see her mom, she slapped the tray of her highchair and Cheerios flew all over. "Sorry, Gail, I'll sweep those up later," Sara said, as she reached into the yellow box for another handful for the baby.

"Well, uh, Sara," I found myself stammering like I used to when my mother caught me doing something she'd forbidden, "you see, I think a little bit of something not exactly nutritious isn't always bad." Three pale guilty faces watched her cross the kitchen and take a mug from the cupboard.

"Relax, everybody." She laughed. "I'm not an ogre, you know." She grabbed a cereal bowl. "I suppose Cap'n Crunch isn't going to kill us. Hand it over." She poured her own bowl of the crisp sugary stuff, which threatened to overflow when she poured on the milk, "oops, guess I got greedy," and she dug in with enthusiasm. "Mmm, I'd forgotten how good this stuff is. I suppose it doesn't have much more sugar than the syrup we drown our waffles with."

Aaron and David looked stunned at her stuffing herself with forbidden food. They looked at each other, shrugged, and finished their own breakfasts. "Come on, assistant," Aaron said, "we'd better get dressed and finish Grandma's computer set-up."

As soon as they left the room, Sara pushed her half-finished bowl away. "Ugh, I can't eat another bite. I'd forgotten just how sweet this stuff is."

"Coffee or tea?" I asked and got up to get it for her.

"Did Aaron make the coffee?"

"Um hum."

She made a face. "Tea, please." And held out her mug. "Aaron's coffee makes great rust remover, but I won't drink it." As she sipped her tea, she asked, "Anything special on the agenda today?"

"I told Clara we'd stop over later. Kayla and Faith are home for the weekend and want to see how big the kids have gotten."

Sara smiled. "Faith's home? Oh boy, did we have fun together in college. Aaron was always a bit scandalized at our antics."

"Really? I thought he was a bit of a devil in school."

"Oh, he was. He was operating with a double standard then."

I felt a little pang of remorse. "I'm afraid that was my fault. Being such a stick-in-the-mud made him think all women were as boring as I was."

"You're not boring, Gail."

I patted her hand. "Thanks, honey. But I used to be in such a rut, I cooked the same foods on the same day every week. That's the way Bert liked it and I guess I wasn't willing to assert myself. Those days are over."

"They sure are. I liked the old Gail, but I like the new Gail a whole lot more. You're much more fun."

"Why, thanks, sweetie. I've always liked you too." I got

up, rinsed the cereal bowls, and put them in the dishwasher. "How about letting me get the baby dressed while you take a shower?"

My tired daughter-in-law gave me a grateful smile as she went upstairs for her things. "Thanks. Maybe I'll even take the time to shave. My life is so hectic that I look like a yeti half the time."

After lunch and a short visit with Clara, her daughters and the visiting grandkids, the computer boys and I left Sara and the napping baby there and walked home to have my first computer lesson. At first Aaron let David demonstrate for me but he typed too fast and left out steps, so I kept getting frustrated. Once David was sent outside to play with Faith's daughter, the lessons went more smoothly.

True to his word, Aaron had sold me a computer that seemed much better behaved than the one I'd happily left on my desk at the school when I retired. By the time Sara and Elizabeth came back to the house I had typed a letter to Lydie and printed it out. I even managed to make it print an envelope addressed to her—on the third try.

Our next adventure was getting online. After a few false starts, I was able to access the gardening website Aaron had told me about and I did a little tentative surfing. I found the website for my bank and Aaron taught me to access my account online to keep closer track of my checks and transfer money from savings to checking. Once he showed me that the bank had good security and my identity wouldn't get stolen from the site, I could see how much more convenient that would be than always having to drive into town or call someone to shift things around.

Then we set up my email account. We entered the family's email addresses and I unearthed the list of students I'd been at The Clearing with. I sent my first email to Aaron; then he went to his email box to show me that it really had worked. Drunk with my infant mastery of technology, I emailed my Clearing roommate, Connie, to tell her I'd made it into the new millennium. I also found a letter from Samara that had her email address at school on it and sent her a note.

By then everyone was starved, so we threw caution to the winds and ordered a couple of pizzas delivered. I apologized to my guests that I'd forgotten to make dinner, but they said they didn't mind. When the food came, Aaron found a bottle of red wine for the adults, poured a soda for David, and we all went into the living room to watch a DVD and stuff ourselves. Elizabeth sat on the floor with her brother and mooched crusts to gum.

Never before had I served them fast food on the living room rug while we drank cheap wine. Bert would have been scandalized. I looked at my happy family, fed and laughing all around me, and thought how glad I was that things were different.

CHAPTER 24

October

I stood in front of the rack of lingerie. All my life I had worn good, serviceable cotton bras and panties. But ever since I'd changed my wardrobe and gotten a haircut, I'd felt so much younger. I found myself lingering over the lingerie ads in women's magazines and really looking through the catalogs that I used to throw away.

So here I was in Simpson Mall, standing outside Victoria's Secret and they were having a sidewalk sale. An impossibly young clerk asked if she could help me, but I was too embarrassed to admit to a child that I'd never bought any undies except Hanes in three-packs. I flipped the racks, my fingers lingering on the cool silkiness, and I found myself making decisions about which colors might look good on my skin. And even scarier, which ones Abel might like.

We had another date last weekend and I had even more trouble controlling my rampaging imagination. I kept looking at Abel's hands and thinking about how I wanted to feel them touching my breasts. I watched his mouth and instead of focusing on what he was saying, I wondered how he would taste, how his lips would feel planting tiny kisses on the back of my neck. I don't remember ever having such thoughts about Bert. I must have been blushing because Abel asked me if I was all right. I told him I was fine, just having a hot flash. I haven't had one of those for nearly a year. Okay, maybe one or two but I seem to have them all the time when I'm with Abel.

I worked my way through every rack in the Victoria's Secret store and kept coming back to a little slip of a nightgown in alternating bands of lace and silk in a bronze color. I picked one up and asked the clerk if I could try it on.

I turned away from the mirror in the changing room to shuck my jeans and sweater and pull the gown over my head. It felt like expensive spider webs sliding over my skin; it took all my nerve to turn to look at myself. Even with the merciless lighting in the tiny cubicle I could see that it fit me perfectly, ended just below my behind, and made my skin look like cream. The only jarring note was the glare of my white cotton panties through the lace. Okay, if I'm buying this nightgown, I thought, I need to get some of those panties that look like wisps of silk to go with it.

Back into my jeans and back on the floor, I was faced with table after table of panties. I found a pair that perfectly matched the bronze silk of the gown, not a thong thank god, and since they were on sale bought five more pairs in various colors. Before I could change my mind or come to my senses I dashed to the counter and bought it all. Ninety dollars of insanity was wrapped in pink tissue and gently put in a bag that wouldn't hold four paperback novels. Resisting the urge to make the clerk take it all back, I turned to leave the store.

Walking toward the exit I passed a sale rack and couldn't resist stopping. By the time I had made my way around it, there were six hangers over my arm. Six hangers full of frothy lace, filmy chiffon, and sensual silk. Six hangers full of craziness in red, ivory, flowery prints, pale blue, and black. All in my size, all made my breath come a little faster. Before I could change my mind or come to my senses, I went back to the changing room, stripped to my undies again, and tried them on. Each one was prettier than the last; long or short, revealing or chaste, I had to have them all.

The final total was nearly two hundred and fifty dollars, and the teen-aged clerk made a sly comment about a long weekend. I was embarrassed but I smiled, winked, and got out of there. I didn't plan to show them to Clara for a while.

CHAPTER 25

November

I carried a cup of tea into the bedroom to check my email in the autumn dawn. In the two months since Aaron had set up my system, I had gotten pretty comfortable with it. Lydie and I wrote each other often. I missed getting real letters from her, but since I was busy most evenings either with painting or Abel, I had shifted to sending her my weekly letter online.

Sam and Matt were happy to get their weekly mom-report online. Aaron had told me when he installed the computer that he expected to get an email instead of a letter. I was thrilled that they responded. None of them had written me back more than a couple times when I sent paper letters. Too busy, I guess. But it seemed like we were closer, like I was more a part of their lives since I'd started using email. Even better, all of the boys had digital cameras, so I got lots more pictures online than I'd ever gotten before. Lisa even scanned in some of their kids' artwork, so my fridge had blossomed into a gallery.

Connie and I exchanged almost daily emails. She sent me the early drafts of her poems and I was, with some initial long-distance tutelage from David, able to open the attachments and read them. I'd gotten pretty good at making suggestions if I did say so myself. At least, Connie was nice enough to say I helped.

I think the most fun emails I got were from Samara. The

first one brought a real surprise.

She started with a complicated description of her arrival at the school and wickedly funny profiles of the professors she'd met. The next part sang the praises of the "incredible hottie" she'd met in her Freshman Comp. Class. I laughed picturing her lighting up the campus with her incandescent personality. When I got to the third paragraph of the email, my breath stopped.

I have a proposition for you, Samara wrote. The Art League here is having a juried show in February, and I know you've got a bunch of paintings squirreled away because you're too shy to show them to anyone. Well, Gail, if you will, I will. Enter, I mean. The deadline's December first. It doesn't cost anything to enter, and they have a thousand-dollar first prize. It's a purchase award, which means they buy your work for a thousand bucks. Wouldn't it be awesome if one of us won? I'll be home for Thanksgiving, and we can decide what to enter then. You can do it. Don't be scared.

Love, Samara.

I remembered all the positive changes I'd made since my first sweaty-palmed impulse to try watercolor painting. I thought about how my weeks in class with Jake had honed my skills and how his declaration that he thought I was a real painter boosted my confidence. How Laurel and the students at The Clearing had encouraged me. And maybe the most important of all, how that week up there among people who accepted the "new" Gail as the "real" Gail gave me the courage to stop agonizing over what Clara and my boys thought and live my life to please me.

Maybe I was brave enough to enter a contest. Maybe I was a good enough painter to have a chance. Without a fee to enter, the only thing I would risk would be my ego. I'd learned over the last year that my ego healed pretty fast and that I was stubborn enough to keep doing what made me happy.

Before I gave it too much thought and talked myself out of it, I fired an email right back to Samara. It had three words,

Okay, you're on.

True to our agreement, Samara and I spent the Friday after Thanksgiving looking at our paintings and deciding which ones to enter in the Art League's show in Madison. We stripped all my work out of the studio and used the gallery wall to line up paintings for our own juried show.

Samara went first. Seeing her work displayed all together made me appreciate her talent more and, judging by her reaction, made her much more critical of her work. "Oh my God, Gail, how can I choose?" she said. "Seeing them all together like this I can see what's wrong with every one of them. I think I hate them all."

I put my arm over her shoulders. "Don't be silly. They're not all terrible."

"Thanks a lot." She poked me with her elbow. "You're some friend."

"Hey, don't get your undies in a bunch. My turn's next." I stepped back another step. "Let's do this. First take down all the ones you really don't like. The ones that didn't turn out the way you had planned."

She moved forward, hands outstretched, saying over her shoulder, "Shouldn't I pick out the ones I like best?"

"I don't think so. We're all so eager to criticize our work, maybe taking out the ones we don't like will leave the good ones behind. Give it a shot."

"Okay." Her hands were a blur as she pulled down nearly half the canvases. She stepped back again. "Huh."

"What?" I asked. I was squinting at the remaining paintings.

"It worked. Taking those out," she motioned to the drift of canvases littered around the room, "makes what's still up there look better."

"Ha, I was right." I stuck my tongue out at her.

"Not very nice, Gail. Granny says if you stick out your tongue, a bird will come and poop on it."

"Your granny's a wise woman, but I don't think there's any danger of a bird flying in here today." I looked out the window at the dusting of snow that had arrived the day before. "Most of the smart birds have flown south."

"True, but I'm not taking any chances."

We spent the next hour debating which of Samara's paintings was art show worthy. When we'd whittled the choices down to three, we checked the rules of the contest and discovered that we could each enter two. It didn't make choosing the last one to remove any easier, but it was a heck of a lot easier than deciding on just one.

Once Samara had made her final decision, we pulled out a couple of simple black frames to see how they would look. It amazed us that the addition of those thin strips of wood made the paintings just pop off the wall. "Excellent choices."

She took them down. "You're up next," she said, a little malicious glee coloring her voice. "Don't worry, Gail, it only feels a little like standing in front of a firing squad."

"What a pal," I said, as I moved to begin hanging what I considered my best work.

When I stepped back, I understood how Samara had felt. Too many of my paintings looked amateurish, poorly executed, and, well, hideous. "Oh my." I buried my face in my hands. "These are terrible."

I heard her rich belly laugh. "What did you just tell me? Oh, yeah, 'they're not all terrible.' Uncover your face and get to work."

It was an effort to pull my hands away from my eyes and turn to face my shame. I stood there frozen with the agony of my terribleness.

A soft voice came from behind my shoulder. "Go ahead, Gail, take down the ones you really hate."

I did and, just like for Samara, the remaining paintings didn't look so bad after all. "That's better."

Another hour passed while we debated and eliminated. Finally, I was left with one of trilliums in the woods at The

Clearing that Laurel had helped me with and the other of a broken down fence section with orange daylilies nodding over it. We slipped them into frames and, just like with Samara's paintings, they came alive.

Samara turned to me. "Well, this was an exhausting afternoon, wasn't it?"

I nodded my agreement. "It sure was. Humbling, too."

"Yep. But I think we've got a chance of getting a prize."

"Do you really think so? I was just happy being brave enough to enter. Winning any sort of prize would be beyond hope for me."

Her whole little body tensed. "Oh, no you don't. You're not going to jinx our chances with any negativity. We are going to win something, even if it's just Honorable Mention."

I had to smile at my fierce young friend. "Yes, General." I snapped her a salute. "I promise to keep a positive thought. Even when my knees knock and palms sweat."

We went right into the kitchen and filled out the entry forms. We checked the rules again to make sure we had marked our work as the guidelines demanded. Then we wrapped up the four paintings, taped the entries on each, and loaded them in Samara's car so she could take them back to Madison with her.

We stood in the freezing dusk beside Samara's old car to say goodbye. "Listen," I said, "I want to pay for your gas back to school."

"Don't be silly. I have plenty of gas. Plus, Mom and Granny each slip me a twenty when they think the other one's not looking. But thanks."

"No, really, I want..."

Samara stood firm. "If you run inside to get money, I'll drive away. I will."

"Ha, fooled you." I reached into my jacket pocket and pulled out my own twenty and put it in her pocket. "I knew you'd refuse so I brought it with me. By taking my paintings back with you, you're saving me the hassle and cost of shipping them. Please take it?"

Knowing I'd won, she said, "Well, if you put it like that, I can't refuse." She hugged me. "It's been a great day. I love you, Gail."

Suddenly I had a lump in my throat. "I love you too, honey. Have a safe drive back. Tell your Mom I said hi." I waved until her taillights receded in the distance.

Then I hurried to bundle myself up in Bert's old barn coat, poured a glass of wine, and sat on the porch while I watched the sun set. I used a marker to make a stripe on the railing, on the slat below I wrote the date and "entered art contest." I felt scared and excited.

Falling asleep that night, I listened to the creaking of the old house's bones as the heat from the furnace warmed them. My last thought was that sometimes I really missed hearing the sleeping boy sounds from upstairs.

CHAPTER 26

December

It was my turn to drive Clara and I Christmas shopping. I was a little nervous about the whole day, since Clara had had her temper tantrum in the Wal-Mart Ladies' room last year. But I was hopeful that over the last few months we'd cleared the air and put all those old resentments to bed. We were still good friends, although I felt that some of the closeness had slipped away.

I was determined not to set foot in a major discount retailer this Christmas season. I had spent hours thinking about the people I bought gifts for, their tastes and hobbies, trying to choose something meaningful for them. I wanted to break the cycle of reflexively buying gifts for people I love, of being swayed by whatever's trendy or most loudly touted in the ads

I called Clara a few days before our scheduled Christmas shopping date. "Clara," I said with a bit of a knot in my stomach, "would you mind terribly if we didn't go to Wal-Mart this year?"

There was a longish pause. "Not go to Wal-Mart? But where will we shop?"

I could feel my palms begin to sweat. "I thought we might at least start out in Simpson. You know, there's been a real boom of interesting shops and boutiques opening up there this past year. I thought we could check them out and maybe surprise our families with gifts they won't see under everyone else's tree. What do you think?" I held my breath, ready for another lecture on how much I'd changed while she was the same down-to-earth person she'd always been.

"Well, that might not be such a bad idea. Hank and I were talking the other night about needing to cut the list down a bit, that I'd been getting a little out of hand. Wal-Mart always makes me feel a little drunk. Maybe shopping in places where I have to really think about what I'm buying will help."

I let out a sigh of relief. "Oh, good."

Clara laughed. "You were waiting for me to pitch a fit, weren't you?"

"A little."

"I guess watching you make such big changes in your life isn't so scary anymore. You're making me look at myself a bit and thinking I might make some changes too."

"Clara, that's great. I think we're going to have a fun day. Let's get an early start. We can have breakfast at a café in Simpson and plan."

"Okay. That sounds good. I'd better haul out my list again. Hank can help me make a few changes. Oops, gotta run, the timer's buzzing. See you Thursday."

"Bye, Clara."

Thursday promised to be one of those perfect early December days; cold and sunny with just a bit of snow to make the decorations look good. I picked Clara up early, before 8 a.m., and drove into Simpson to a little place I'd passed by a couple times. We walked into a warm steamy restaurant dotted with small tables ringed by mismatched wooden chairs, about half of them filled. The cozy room was rich with the aromas of brewing coffee and baking bread.

Clara stopped and looked around. "This looks like a nice place; kind of homey and kitchen-y."

"It smells great, too. Let's find a place to sit. I'm hungry."

We picked out a table and were waited on by a young woman in an apron with wisps of hair escaping her ponytail and a smudge of flour on her cheek. "What can I get you ladies?"

"Coffee," we said together.

"Coming right up. Regular or decaf? Flavored or plain?"

"Regular for me," said Clara, "my wimpy friend will have the decaf and we'll both have it plain, no cream or sugar."

We each grabbed a menu. It was full of the most unusual and delicious sounding things: omelets with cream cheese and chives or salsa and cheddar, scrambled eggs with sour cream and strawberry jam billed as "Jackie Kennedy's favorite breakfast," six kinds of muffins from lemon-poppy seed to pineapple kiwi, West Indian French toast with rum syrup. They also had the usual bacon, sausage, and egg offerings.

After our waitress poured our coffee, we had the devil of a time deciding what to order. It was tempting to go with the old standby of bacon and eggs but we agreed that today was the day to try new things. So Clara ordered the West Indian French toast and I had the Jackie Kennedy scrambled eggs, each of us promising to share with the other.

"That was fabulous," Clara said, as she put down her fork after the last bite. "Your Jackie special was good, but the French toast was to die for. I'd never have thought of putting vanilla and nutmeg in the egg, and that rum-flavored syrup... intoxicating. It tasted a bit like your banana bread."

I took a sip of coffee. "I liked mine too. I was a little unsure of whether I'd like sour cream and strawberry jam with eggs, but it worked."

The waitress came over to remove the soiled plates and refill our coffee as Clara pulled out her voluminous gift list and I unfolded my single sheet. "You ladies doing your Christmas shopping today?" she asked, leaning over my shoulder to pour more decaf.

"Yes, we are," I said. "We're breaking out of our Wal-Mart rut this year. Can you give us any suggestions about good, interesting places to shop?"

"Well, let me check." She turned away to a dresser near the door covered in baskets stuffed with leaflets and picked out one to bring back with her. "Here. I thought I'd seen this. It's a guide for shoppers. It just came out last week so all the newest places should be in it and there's a map, I think. Maybe you could use it to plan your day."

Clara took the pamphlet from her outstretched hand. "Thanks. I'm sure this will be a big help."

We flipped through the pages to find places we thought might have the things we were looking for, then huddled together to plan our route. The map was a big help. It was inconveniently bound into the center of the pamphlet, but we ripped it right out.

The first place we stopped was a boutique filled with imported stuff, picture frames made from exotic woods, brass urns and trays, carved stone figures, and a few clothes. It was the clothes that attracted me, and not for gifts. I wanted it all for myself.

"Gail, get a grip," Clara said, as I stepped out of the changing room in a swirly skirt and spangled peasant blouse.

"Why?" I looked up at her smiling face.

"Aren't we supposed to be buying Christmas gifts?"

I looked at my reflection. "I guess it's a bit much, too young for me, but I bet Samara would love it." I turned back to change. "See? I'm really shopping for others, I just needed to see it off the hanger."

I could hear Clara's chuckled "okay, Gail" as the curtain closed behind me and she walked away to keep looking.

That first store was a good choice. We each filled more than half our lists. I got a beautiful carved totem that I knew would be just right in Sam and Merry's modern house overlooking San Francisco bay, a brass vase that the boys couldn't break for Lisa, and that outfit for Samara. For Clara I found a beautiful fruitwood jewelry box that just glowed, and I knew she'd love seeing it on her dresser. I got a smaller one for myself, my Christmas gift from me to me, as well as an emerald and teal tunic top with ivory embroidery and little mirrors I couldn't resist. It took Clara and a clerk two trips to get her purchases to the car. As we sat there buckling our seatbelts, ready to drive off, she turned to me and said, "This was a great idea, Gail. I can't wait to see their faces on Christmas." She picked up the map. "Okay, our next stop is The Schoolhouse. It says they have a lot of educational toys. Let's go."

That store was a hit too. We were like kids racing around the aisles finding all sorts of wonderful things for our grandkids. And, best of all, we weren't spending much more than we would at that giant discount store, but the toys were much higher quality.

The sun was setting as I turned the car onto the highway toward home. Clara sat slumped in her seat, her head resting back with eyes closed. "So, Clara, what do you think of my idea now?"

My oldest friend turned toward me and opened one eye. "You've worn me out, Gail." She laid her hand on my arm. "But I don't know when I've had so much fun Christmas shopping. Thanks for jerking me out of my rut."

I could feel the I-told-you-so smile curving my lips as I drove but, in the interests of peace, kept it to myself.

CHAPTER 27

January

I looked out my kitchen window at the swirling white. For days it had been below zero and sunny. I loved sunny days in winter when the light gleamed on the snow--rainbows and stars fallen to earth.

Last night's sunset had been glorious, the soft pinks and oranges quickly fading to purple, charcoal, and then black. There would be no sunset watching tonight. I noticed it had started to snow when I locked up before bed last night. And this morning I could barely see beyond the honeysuckle hedge right outside the kitchen window. The ringing of the phone startled me.

"Hello? Oh, hi, Clara."

"Can you believe this blizzard?" Clara said. "I was supposed to work at the blood drive this morning, but I heard on the radio it's cancelled."

"I'm not surprised. They'd use up more than they'd collect if folks were out driving around in this."

"What are your plans for the day?" Clara asked.

"I don't know really. I guess I'll paint. Merry keeps pestering me for a painting. I think she sees me as a Grandma Moses locked in my studio cranking out masterpieces for her to display. I try to tell her my work is barely out of the refrigerator art stage."

"Gail, the things you say. I think your work's way beyond 'fridge art. I love the painting you did for me.

Everyone who sees it raves about it."

"Thanks."

I heard Hank's voice in the background. "How're you fixed for milk and bread and such? If the storm looks like it's going on too long, Hank says he'll get out the snowmobile and make a mercy run."

"I'm okay for now. Tell Hank I said thanks. I promise I'll call you if I need anything."

After Clara and I hung up, I went into the studio and put a fresh piece of paper on my board. What to paint? Looking out the window was no help. If I painted what I saw today, I'd be done before I started. They say that snow has many colors, but you need sunlight to make those colors in the prisms of the flakes and I defy anyone to find sunlight in a blizzard. So, I decided to paint the opposite of what I saw.

I washed the paper with a soft turquoise, deepening it at the bottom. In the left foreground I planted a couple palm trees in a crescent of beach, then I let my imagination run wild.

The hard yellow sun beat on the hibiscus and washed out the colors of the leaves and the flowers drooped under the weight of the light. Tentative clouds lurked on the horizon, dissipating before they dared to cross the sky. Out on the invisible water, a lone fisherman in a faded skiff twisted his body as he cast his net. On the beach curving up the right side of the painting a single set of footprints led to a woman asleep on a colorful beach chair in the dappled shade of a Bougainvillea. A straw hat shaded her face and a paperback with a lurid cover lay on her chest, her left hand trailing in the sand with a tiny green lizard perched on her wrist like a bracelet.

It was late afternoon when I stepped back to look at what I'd done, I heard the whine of a snowmobile engine getting louder. Who would be out in this? All of Hank and Clara's boys were grown and none of them lived at home. It couldn't be some lunatic out for a joyride. It was just too dangerous.

I went to the window in the living room to see if I could see anyone, but the snow was still falling and the wind was still whipping it into a frenzy. The engine noise got louder and louder and I followed the sound around to the kitchen. It stopped right outside my back door.

I grabbed a coat and stepped out onto the back porch. Little drifts of snow had blown under the storm windows and decorated the corners. The roar of the wind filled the small space so that I felt like I was in a tunnel.

Thinking that whoever was out there might need help, I reached to unlock the outer door just as heavy footsteps mounted the stairs. I paused a moment with my hand on the doorknob, thinking that only those up to no good would be out in weather like this, but then I chastised myself for watching too much late-night television. It was probably Hank come to check on me.

I opened the door and saw a figure emerge from the storm, covered head to boots in snow, too tall to be Hank. His eyes were the only hint that there was an actual human inside all that winter.

"Gail, are you okay? I tried to call. No one answered and I got worried."

I stepped back from the figure as he shook off the snow, still not sure who it was. He reached up and pulled off his mask, shook his head. I was shocked when I saw who was under all that white.

"Abel, what are you doing out in this? Did you ride all the way from your place just because my phone's out? Are you nuts?"

Abel started to laugh. Big clumps of snow fell from his snowmobile suit as he threw back his head. "You're really something, Gail. Here I am, riding over here feeling like a knight off to save a fair maid, thinking you were going to be in the dark, cut off from civilization, all scared and worried. And here you are just fine, giving me grief for being out in the storm. I love you."

The silence that fell over us at those words pulled the breath right out of my lungs. I don't think Abel had planned to say that. We looked at each other in shock. I moved first.

"Well, since you're already here you might as well come in and warm up. I'll put on some coffee while you get out of those wet clothes."

I turned and fled into the kitchen trying to process those three words.

I love you.

Did he mean to say that? It sounded so natural the way he said it. Bert had hardly ever said those words to me, or to anyone else for that matter, not that I ever heard anyway. Was Abel one of those people for whom those words came easy? Did he tell all sorts of people he loved them?

I love you. The words echoed in my head as I made coffee. Good thing I'd been making it for so many years because I paid no attention to what I was doing. I could have been scooping sand for all I noticed.

I love you. Not words to be taken lightly. Was I supposed to say them back? Any minute he'd be walking into the kitchen, and I felt like I was still pale with the shock of hearing "I love you" so casually. I needed to stop being so silly and just go with the flow, as the kids used to say.

I could hear him knocking the snow off his boots and shaking out his snowmobile suit as I got out mugs and pulled some vegetable beef soup out of the fridge, poured it into a pot, and put it on to heat. He came into the kitchen on a rush of cold air, rubbing his hands together.

"Brr. I was colder than I thought, and I think some snow went down my neck." He peered over my shoulder as I stirred the soup. "Oh boy, that smells good. What kind is it?"

"Vegetable beef barley. I made it yesterday. I always like to have a pot on hand in the winter. There's nothing like soup to warm you up." I looked at his feet. "Oh good, you found some shoes out there. I never could bring myself to get rid of Bert's old scuffs. They're so handy when I come in from yard work."

Abel chuckled. "These might look like Bert's scuffs but they're mine. I stuffed them in my pockets before I left home. It's my Boy Scout training. You know, be prepared?"

"Oh, I know all about being prepared. All three of my boys are Eagle Scouts and Bert was a leader for a while. Grab a couple spoons from that drawer under the dish drainer, will you please? I think everything's ready." I had poured two mugs of coffee and was ladling out the soup when, with a little pop, all the lights went out. "Oh dear, the lines must have gone down. I hope they come back on soon. It'll be awful cold without the furnace running."

Abel jumped up. "If you tell me where your firewood is, I'll get the fireplace lit."

"Sit, Abel, sit. The house won't cool off that fast. Eat your soup while it's hot. I've got a fire all laid and as soon as we're done eating, we can get it burning."

One good thing about snow is that it gathers and reflects whatever light is around. It's never really dark, even in the middle of the night, so I could see Abel in the soft glow from the window. "Wonderful soup, Gail. I can feel its warmth all the way down to my toes."

As we ate, the wind seemed to pick up and rattled the windows. "Sounds like you made it here just in time, Abel."

"Glad I'm here, huh?" And he grinned at me like a schoolboy.

"Yes, I'm glad you're here instead of out in that storm." I ate a few more bites. "But I still think you're nuts."

Once the soup was finished, we went into the living room and Abel knelt in front of the fireplace. I could see he was planning to be the big, strong man and re-lay the fire after the little woman tried her best. But years of listening to Bert instruct the boys in fire building had made me into a pretty good fire maker myself. Seeing nothing to fix, Abel took a match from the box on the mantle, dragged it on the sandpaper on the side, and touched the flame to the crumpled newspaper. Once the kindling and smaller branches had caught, he stood up, dusting off his hands as though he'd done more than just strike a match.

"You lay a nice fire, Gail."

"Thanks, Abel, I've had a lot of practice over the years. One of these days the county will finally bury the power lines and then we won't have this problem anymore."

Abel picked up the poker and started stirring the fire and put on another log.

"While you're playing with the fire," I said, "why don't I put the rest of the coffee in the thermal pot and see if I can't find some cookies for dessert?"

"Sounds great," Abel said over his shoulder.

When I got back with the tray of coffee and cookies, he had finished poking the fire and sat in one of the chairs by the hearth. He jumped up as soon as he saw me and pulled over a side table for the tray. The fire was blazing and throwing a lot of heat. "You're a good fire tender, Abel."

"Thanks. Your fireplace has a great draft. Did Bert build it?"

"No, he didn't." I sat down in the chair on the other side of the hearth. "This old house has been here way longer than any of us have been alive and I figure whoever built the fireplace needed it for warmth rather than looks and made it right."

I poured the coffee and nudged the plate of cookies toward him, a little embarrassed that there was nothing better than sugar cookies and pink spritz left.

"Mmm, I love spritz cookies," he said, taking a couple. "The red sprinkles are a bonus."

"That's polite of you to say, Abel, but these are just the Christmas leftovers. I made nut balls, molasses cookies, English toffee, and my cutouts were works of art this year. But I sent most of them to the kids and ate too many myself. You're stuck with what's left."

"Doesn't matter to me," he said around a mouthful of

cookie. "Marcella always made such a production out of Christmas, deciding on a theme, planning the tree decorations on graph paper first, and devoting an entire weekend to baking the most elaborate cookies she could find. She disdained, that's the only word for it, disdained the old traditional cookies I've always liked best. These are terrific."

My mind was boggled by the thought of having the time to make such a production of Christmas. "At least they're not stale, right?" At that moment the lights came back on with a snap.

"Well, shit!" I said, it slipped out before I could catch it. "Oh, excuse my language."

After a moment's pause Abel laughed and said, "So, Gail, did you say shit because the lights came on and I can leave or because they didn't stay off, so I'd have an excuse to stay?"

"I, uh..." I could feel a blush rising in my cheeks. "I guess a little of both. I, um, enjoy your company, Abel. But I'm not sure I want us to get too close too fast, if you know what I mean." By the time I'd stumbled through that prissy little speech, I could feel that even my ears were red. I was glad I hadn't turned on any lights in the living room. Why couldn't I spend more than ten minutes in this man's company without putting my foot in my mouth?

Before Abel could speak, the lights went out again. This time accompanied by a shower of sparks from the transformer on the pole just past the turn in the road.

"I think that's it for your electricity until the county boys can get out here tomorrow and restring the lines," he said. "And don't worry, Gail, I don't have designs on you. Well actually, I do, but I'm willing to be patient." He paused as if he expected me to say something, but I was stunned into silence. "And since it looks like someone will need to keep the fire going all night, so you don't freeze, I volunteer. And I'll sleep on the couch."

"Thank you, Abel." My voice came out in a croak, forced through my paralyzed vocal cords by sheer guts. "I'll get you some blankets and a pillow." I started to get up, but he waved me back into my chair.

"Don't be in such a rush. It's not even seven o'clock. We've got the whole evening ahead of us."

Once I was able to relax again, we spent the next few hours having the best conversation I'd had in a long time. We talked about books we'd read, Abel trying to convince me that Tom Clancy's books weren't as complicated as I knew they were and me telling him that there wasn't any such thing as "chick" lit, just stories men were too insensitive to appreciate. We were each surprised that the other loved Kurt Vonnegut, although I insisted that his short stories were better than the novels, but Abel disagreed with me. We did agree that John Steinbeck was one of the greatest authors America had ever produced. I was surprised that Abel was a big poetry fan. He recited a few poems from memory and promised to bring over his favorite poems by Billy Collins and read some to me. I'd never heard of him and was amazed to learn that he had been America's Poet Laureate a few years ago and was a contemporary poet who Abel said wrote about ordinary things with extraordinary beauty.

We'd been sitting talking when I realized by the chiming of the antique clock on the mantle that it was ten o'clock and the house was really cooling off.

I suggested to Abel that I see if I couldn't find something for him to sleep in and make up a bed for him on the couch so it would be ready when he was. He agreed so I took the flashlight and dug in the back of my dresser where I'd shoved a pair of flannel pajamas I'd bought for Bert's birthday gift his last year and never got the chance to give him. My favorite wool bathrobe was a man's style anyway, so Abel could wear it without embarrassment. While I was in my bedroom, I changed into my own flannel PJs and dug out a chenille robe Sam had given me for Christmas a few years ago. Chenille bathrobes always reminded me of the old-fashioned bedspreads that were all the rage in the 1950s, but I could either look like I was wearing a bedspread or put on an ancient quilted pink one I had with both elbows worn through and years of breakfast stains down the front.

I took some sheets and a blanket out of the linen closet and carried the whole pile into the living room. I gave Abel the pajamas and robe and he went to change in the bathroom while I made him a bed on the couch. While I was working, I thought I heard voices outside. I walked into the kitchen just as Abel came out. I whispered to him that I thought someone was outside and he came with me.

We'd only gone a few steps into the room when the back porch door burst open, and Clara walked in with Hank on her heels. "Gail," Clara was saying, "Hank and I snow-shoed over to make sure you had enough firewood." Her voice stopped abruptly when she saw Abel and I standing there in our nightclothes. "But I can see you're doing just fine." She turned around and started shooing her startled husband back out into the storm. "Come on, Hank, let's get home."

"Clara," I said.

"It's okay, Gail," she said, not turning around. "Hank and I will just be moving along."

"Clara, stop." I walked across the room and grabbed her arm. "At least stay for a cup of hot chocolate. You'll turn to icicles if you go right back out in that storm."

My old friend turned around and peeked at Abel over my shoulder. "Are you sure?" she whispered. "We don't want to interrupt anything."

"You're not interrupting, Clara. Abel, tell them to say."

He stepped forward and said, "Please, Clara, stay and have some hot chocolate with us. Hank, why don't you help me stoke up the fire?" And the two men were out of the room in a split second.

Clara grabbed my arm and pulled me toward the back door. "Holy crumps, Gail, you could have knocked me over with a feather when I opened that door and saw the two of you standing there in robes. What's going on? No, forget I asked."

Even in the dim kitchen I could see Clara's blush.

"Nothing's going on. At least not tonight. Abel came over when he couldn't get through on the phone and he was here when the power went out for good. He volunteered to keep the fire going tonight and is sleeping on the couch." I could hear the men talking in the living room. "Grab the milk, will you? I'll get out a pan and make that hot chocolate I promised. Thank goodness I've got a gas stove."

Clara and I made the hot chocolate and she called for Hank to bring the tray. He came in with a very puzzled look on his face and Clara headed off any questions with a look that promised that as soon as she learned the story, she'd tell him. I could see I'd be in for an inquisition once Clara and I were alone.

A very subdued quartet sat around the fire, sipping hot chocolate, not talking much at all. And as soon as the cups were empty, Clara stood up and announced that since the wind had stopped blowing, she was in the mood for a moonlight snowshoe home. She chivvied Hank out the house in jig time and soon they were on their way.

"Well, that was interesting," Abel said. "I suppose the news that I slept over at your place will be all over town by sundown tomorrow."

"Do you really think it'll take that long?"

"Do you mind?" he asked, a look of concern on his face.

"Oh, not really. Tongues have been wagging ever since we started dating last summer. You can bet that according to rumor we're having a much racier time than we actually are."

Abel snorted.

"But, Abel, I really appreciate you giving me time to get used to having a man in my life again."

He put his hands on my shoulders and said, "Gail, you know how I feel about you. You take all the time you need." And he leaned forward and kissed me. "You get to bed. I'll rinse the cups. Goodnight."

"Goodnight, Abel. Pleasant dreams."

I lay awake a long time before falling asleep. I heard Abel a few times in the night, up keeping the fire going. It was nice to have a man in the house again.

When I awoke the next morning, I could tell before I opened my eyes that the blizzard was over and the power was back on. Bright sunlight magnified by fresh white snow edged the shades and the wind wasn't whistling around the house. I could hear the furnace churning out heat. I rolled out of bed, put on my robe, and went into the bathroom.

It wasn't until I stepped into the kitchen that I remembered I'd had an overnight guest. By then Abel had seen me and it was too late to go back and brush my teeth and my hair.

"Good morning, Gail. How'd you sleep?" he said. "I hope you don't mind; I made coffee." He held out a steaming mug.

"Thanks." I glanced up at him and decided he'd been up for hours. He looked fresh and cheerful. At that moment I hated him. I was certain my face looked like a used paper sack and my hair was a rat's nest. "Thanks for the coffee, Abel. I'll go take a shower." I turned around and made my escape before he could get too close a look.

Fifteen minutes and one cup of coffee later, I felt like I was back in control of the situation. When I got back to the kitchen, Abel was sitting in my favorite spot at the table watching the chickadees squabble at the bird feeder.

"Breakfast?" I asked.

"I'm not much of a breakfast eater," he said. "What did you have in mind?"

Mentally going over the things in my larder, I said, "Oatmeal?"

"Oatmeal would be perfect. It'll keep me warm on the ride home."

It took only a few minutes to make two bowls of oatmeal in the microwave. I set out brown sugar, cream, and spoons.

"Can I do something to help?" he asked.

"No thanks, I've got it under control. You could pour me some fresh coffee, though, if you wouldn't mind."

He poured us each more coffee as I put the steaming bowls on the table. As he stirred the sugar into his, he asked, "What're these things?"

I had to smile. He sounded just like my boys when confronted with unfamiliar food. "Dried cherries from Door County. They served oatmeal with dried fruit every morning at The Clearing and one morning they had cherries. I loved it so much, I put them in all the time now." He handed me the brown sugar. "I hope you like it."

He did.

After clearing the dishes and helping load the dishwasher, Abel decided to go home. "I hope you aren't bombarded with gossip about me staying here last night, Gail." He put his hands on my waist and drew me closer. "I wouldn't want to do anything to make you unhappy." And he kissed me. Really kissed me, like he meant it. I realized that I was kissing him back and meaning it every bit as much. My breath was short, and I could feel my heart pound. I began to slide my hands up his arms to his shoulders. We broke the kiss at the same time. "Gail?" he said in a low voice.

The phone rang. The spell of our ardent kiss evaporated, and I rushed to answer it. "Hello?" I expected it to be the first of the busybodies.

"Mrs. Logan, my name is Lawrence Kaster and I'm with Global Life & Casualty Insurance Company…"

"I am not interested in insurance. Thank you." I hung up on him and turned back to Abel, eager to resume our interrupted kiss, to see he had put on his snow pants and was tugging on his boots. "Oh, you're leaving."

"Yeah, I thought I'd better get on home before the weather turns again. Do you want me to clear your walk before I go?"

"No, thanks. It's nice of you to offer but I kind of like getting bundled up and playing in the snow. I've got a new

210

red snowblower that's real easy to use. I'll have it cleared in no time. But thanks for asking."

He stood and put on his jacket, zipped it up, and came over to where I stood. He leaned down and kissed me again. "Well... I'm glad your phone's back on; give me a call if you need anything. Watch out for the gossips."

I laughed and kissed him back. "I will. Have a safe ride home. Call when you get there so I know you made it okay."

He picked up his helmet and gloves and left. I was tempted to call him back but let him go.

Just as I'd suspected, the news that Abel had spent the night at my place had traveled all over town before the last snowplow had finished clearing the roads. When I came in from snow-blowing my walk and driveway the phone was ringing. And it kept ringing all day long and into the evening.

Clara's was the first call I caught. It was short and to the point.

"Got the pot on?" she asked.

"I can put it on," I said.

"Great," she said, "I'm strapping on my snowshoes." And she hung up.

That meant I had about ten minutes to get the coffee made and get ready for the first interrogation. I dearly loved Clara but one of her faults was the inability to keep a secret. That was why our heart to hearts had always been more of her heart and less of mine. I knew that most of what I said to her would hit the grapevine as soon as she got home, so I had to decide, as always, what I wanted to whole town to hear.

I hadn't even finished making the coffee when the phone rang again. It was Mavis, the town beautician and chief gossip. She said she was calling to see if I wanted to take advantage of her mid-winter haircut special, but I could tell by her tone of voice that she had already heard a rumor and was hoping for a scoop.

In a town the size of Kingman, gossip was coin of the realm. It was the grease that kept the wheels moving. The base of power didn't lie in the elected town officials, it was held by the woman with the sharpest ears and fastest tongue.

Mavis deserved her spot at the top of the grapevine. Her living room beauty shop had been "gossip central" for over thirty years. Mavis' strong fingers and sympathetic eyes were masters at pulling out things you weren't sure you wanted to share while she massaged your scalp, resistance was lowered by the soothing scent of the shampoo, and the whine of the hair dryers gave an air of the confessional to the room, making you feel like no one could hear you.

On the positive side, sharing news at Mavis' meant you only had to tell things once. On the negative side, Mavis and her "stringers" had big reputations to uphold. They were not above embroidering a chance remark into something more sensational.

Friendships had been made, broken, and mended under the washed-out aqua of those beautician's drapes. Every stage of life from puberty to menopause had been discussed and survived. Divorces were diverted or dissected, and many a straying spouse found his carefully constructed web of lies unable to withstand Mavis' scrutiny. Her beauty shop was the castle of power in Kingman and Mavis was the queen.

It had been nearly a year since I'd gotten a haircut there and I was sure her nose was out of joint that I had a new look and hadn't gone to her for it. I thanked her politely for her call and told her I'd pass on the offer. She didn't miss a beat. She asked if I'd been doing anything interesting lately, the word "interesting" coyly emphasized. I said not really, just painting, both watercolors and the rooms of the house. That launched a series of questions about my redecorating; she'd obviously heard I'd given away all my living room furniture and bought new. And I wouldn't be surprised if her spies hadn't learned that I had new dishes too. It took some time, and the promise of a visit, but I finally managed to get off the phone.

By that time, I could hear Clara coming up the back steps, stamping the snow off her boots. The porch door opened, and she called out a greeting while hanging up her jacket.

"Perfect timing," I said, hearing the gurgling that signaled the end of the brewing. "Want some coffee cake to go with it? I could thaw some out."

She came over to the counter, nudged me with her elbow, and said, "I want the news."

We carried our coffee mugs to the table and sat down in our usual places. "What news? It's been snowing; there's nothing new."

"Don't tease me, Gail. You know I'm dying of curiosity, so tell."

"There's really nothing to tell. Abel and I went to our separate beds shortly after you and Hank left. We had breakfast together and he left. That's it."

"That's it? That can't be it. I see the way he looks at you when he thinks no one's looking. Come on, Gail, I'm your oldest friend. I deserve more than that sanitized version of what happened when you spent the night with a man who's not your husband."

I had to laugh. "Clara there really isn't much more to tell. He kissed me and I have to admit I kissed him back. Sorry to be such a disappointment."

"He kissed you? A lot? Is he a good kisser?" Clara's eyes shone and she leaned toward me, looking hard at my eyes as if she could read what had really occurred if she looked close enough.

"Yeah, he's a pretty good kisser. But a telemarketer interrupted us, and I guess the impulse passed. Then he went home." She looked unconvinced. "I swear, Clara, nothing else happened."

"Okay, if you say so." A sly look shaded her eyes. "But I heard Abel was real hot when he was going with Dottie Swanson a few years back and I don't think a goodbye kitchen kiss would be enough to earn him that reputation. Come on, Gail, give."

"Honestly, there's nothing more to tell. Abel was a perfect gentleman." I could feel my face turning red.

"Ha! You're blushing. Something else did happen. I knew it." While she was peppering me with questions, she walked over, picked up the coffee pot, and filled our mugs, even though neither of us had drunk more than half. "Did he get fresh? Sneak into your bedroom offering to warm you up? What?" She sat back down looking pleased with herself.

"Well, I have to admit it, he's a really good kisser. And until the phone rang, I might have been willing to go further than one kiss standing in the kitchen." I stopped and put my hand on her arm. "You have to promise me you'll only tell people that we kissed. Once. You can waggle your eyebrows at everyone like you know more but are sworn to secrecy. Promise?"

Her eyes got big and she stopped blinking. "I absolutely promise. Cross my heart." And she solemnly made a cross over the left side of her sweater.

I took a deep breath and continued. "Well, I woke up every time he got up to tend the fire, thinking he might be coming into the bedroom. And then I thought maybe I'd just go out there and attack him on the couch. But I chickened out." Both of us sighed at my lost opportunity. "Then when I got up this morning, I forgot he was here and went into the kitchen looking like the wrath of God."

Clara moaned right along with me at the thought of a new man seeing us first thing in the morning. "What did he do?"

"Well, he looked all bright and cheerful, like he'd been up for hours and had taken a shower. I have to admit I wasn't prepared for him to look so good. Anyway, he gave me a cup of coffee, and I turned right around and hid in the bathroom to take a shower and try to erase that picture from his mind. I even thought about putting on make-up but decided it would be too obvious and forward." My throat was getting dry from all the talking so I took a sip of my nearly cold coffee.

"Go on, go on."

"When I came out looking more presentable, he seemed more interested in watching the chickadees at the feeder, so I made us some oatmeal for breakfast." Just then, the phone rang.

"I'll bet it's one of Mavis' spies," Clara said.

I picked it up. "Hello? Oh, hi, Abel." I heard a sound behind me and turned to see Clara wiping up the coffee she'd spit out. "How was your ride home?"

"It was fine. The roads are mostly cleared," he said.

"Good."

"What are you doing right now?"

"Oh, Clara's over and we're having coffee."

Abel's warm chuckle came down the wire. "I suppose this is just the beginning of the All-Kingman inquisition?"

"Yes, it is." I was trying to keep a straight face but didn't think I was doing a very good job, so I turned my back to Clara.

"I'll let you go then. Let me know if the cats become unbearable and I'll knock a few heads together."

Now I did laugh. "Okay, good."

"Are we still on for the weekend?"

A warm thrill crept up my spine at the idea of seeing him again so soon. "Yep, I'll see you Saturday."

"Unless we get an even bigger storm, I guess. Of course, I'd be more than willing to come over and keep your fire lit."

"Oh really? Well, we'll see about that. I'll see you Saturday."

"Bye, Gail. Stay warm."

"You too, Abel. Bye."

When I got back to the table, Clara looked even more avid than she had before, if that's possible. "Well? What did he say?"

"He just said he got home okay. I'd asked him to call me. And made sure we still have a date for Saturday." For the first time since Abel and I had started going out, that word hit me. "Oh my God, Clara, I'm dating."

"I know, Gail." She sat back with a smug smile on her face. "You and Romeo are the talk of town."

That was not a happy thought. I'd known that tongues were wagging when I took up painting, changed my clothes and hair, but remembering the catty remarks that had flown around when other widows had started rebuilding their lives, made me wish I lived somewhere else. Somewhere, instead of this small, rural town where nothing exciting happened, so people talked about other people's lives like they were soap operas. I had always liked the warmth and neighborliness of living in Kingman, but now I wanted to be anonymous.

CHAPTER 28

The Saturday after the blizzard promised to be a perfect winter day. Sunshine sparkled on the fresh snow making the fir trees look an even darker green. The wind was minding its manners too, sending playful gusts to swirl the powder but not blowing strong enough to chill to the bone.

Abel had called on Friday night to say he'd pick me up at ten and that I should dress for a day outdoors. He wouldn't tell me what he'd planned but I'd gotten over being surprised by his date activity choices. I pulled out my polypropylene long johns, a silk turtleneck, and some space-age-fiber socks Sam had given me for Christmas. I had the boots I wore when Clara and I went snowshoeing and I supposed they'd do fine for whatever it was Abel had up his sleeve.

Precisely at 10 a.m. he pulled into my drive. Lord, that man was prompt. He got out of his old red pickup, pulled a duffel bag out after him, and came up the walk. I opened the door and invited him in. His face was lit with the smile I'd come to recognize as his adventurer's grin, the one that gave me a little knot in my stomach. Not because he scared me, exactly, but because I knew he was going to invite me to push the limits of my comfort zone.

"Now what are you planning?" I said. "You've got that Cheshire cat look about you."

He laughed. "Nothing too scary or out on a limb. We're going skiing."

Visions of hurtling down a mountain, arms waving, coming to an abrupt stop with a face full of tree flew through my brain. "Not scary? Abel, have you gone nuts? I'm 57 years old and that's too old to start sliding down mountains on barrel staves." I crossed my arms over my chest. "No thanks."

"Relax, Gail, we're not going anywhere near a mountain. Even I'm not crazy enough to take you downhill skiing. We're going cross-country skiing. It's easy. You'll see."

The first thing that popped into my head was to ask him exactly which country he was planning to cross, but bad jokes weren't the answer. There had to be another way out of this. I sidled up to him and ran my hand across his shoulders. "Are you sure you want to spend the day like that?" I purred.

His arm circled my waist, and he pulled me to him. "I'd love to spend the day the way you're implying but I don't think we're ready for that activity yet. I know you're nervous about skiing and are just trying to distract me. Won't work, Gail, not on this guy." He kissed my cheek and pushed me away. "Now, show me your outdoor things."

I shrugged and laughed; secretly glad he hadn't taken me up on my invitation. He approved my polypro long johns and my silk turtleneck. He was impressed with my super socks and said he thought my boots would do for today since they were so well broken in. But he nixed my jeans and wool sweater. "Jeans are cotton. They'll get wet and you'll get cold. Here," he pulled something out of his duffel, "I got you some ski pants." He held out a pair of navy knit pants that looked like they'd fit.

Deciding it was too much trouble to go into my bedroom to change into the ski pants, and figuring my long underwear would preserve my modesty, I slid off my jeans right there in the kitchen. "How'd you know what size to buy?" I asked as I sat down to pull them on.

There was that smug smile again. "Asked Clara, of course."

"You called Clara?" I was floored. "You told her what you were planning?"

"Yes, I did."

I had to laugh. "That little fink. She never said a word. Just wait until I talk to her again."

"Oh now, Gail, don't get on her case. I asked her to keep the secret and she did. That's a real friend."

"I'm not mad. It's just that Clara's been telling me all along that you had a hot reputation and I needed to watch my step around you and now she's helping you surprise me. Quite a turnaround."

"Clara thinks I'm hot, huh?" He stood a little straighter and preened a bit. "I hope Hank doesn't find out."

"No, Clara doesn't think you're hot. She thinks you've got a hot reputation from the rumors that have flown around town since you started chasing widows after Marcella died, that's all."

His smug look died.

"So what else have you got in that bag? I'm getting sweaty."

Abel pulled out a red, yellow, and navy jacket he said was wind-proof and matching mitts. The piece de resistance was the hat. It was unlike any hat I'd ever seen. The body of it was navy fleece but that's where the traditional look of it ended. There were stuffed multi-colored cones of fleece sticking up in a row from the middle of the front right to the back, ending in a tail, a red tail. He held it up like it was a prize he was proud of winning.

"What is it?" I said.

"It's a hat. See? This is the front."

"You expect me to wear that." I could feel my muscles tightening.

"You don't like it," he said as his smile faded, but then he brightened. "Wait till you see mine, it's even crazier." And he dipped back into the duffel bag and pulled out a purple fleece hat covered in a riot of corkscrews in day-glow colors "The guy at the sports store said they're all the rage." His hands dropped to his sides. "You really don't like them?"

"We're going to look like a couple of lunatics out there."

"Yeah, but we'll be the coolest lunatics. Come on, be a sport. Who's going to see us?" His adventurer's smile was back at full wattage.

"Everyone's going to see us. And those who don't see us will hear about it." I started to giggle and picked up my hat. I walked to the mirror hanging in the hall and tried it on. "I look silly."

He came up behind me wearing his crazy hat and put his hands on my shoulders.

"I think you're beautiful. But you're right, we look silly."

"I kind of like it. Thanks, Abel." I turned and gave him a little kiss. "If we stay here admiring ourselves, we'll never get to wherever it is we're going."

When I asked if I needed to bring anything else, Abel said he'd brought everything we would need. I put on my boots, and we left.

Not familiar with a place to go cross-country skiing in the area, I was surprised when we went west on the highway I took to get to Aaron and Sara's and turned in at the county golf course. "Why are we here?"

Abel grinned at me as he parked, "Believe it or not, golf courses are some of the best places to cross-country ski. They're well maintained, not too many hills and trees, and it makes the owners, or in this case the county, a little revenue in winter." He tapped a sticker on his windshield. "I bought a season ski pass. Another great thing is they keep the snowmobiles out so the fairways don't get torn up, so it's quiet and good for every skill level."

We got out of the truck and Abel got our skis out of the back. He had me step into the bindings and checked that they worked with my boots. They didn't. Oddly enough, I was disappointed. "Guess we can't go after all"

But he didn't seem fazed. "Not to worry. When I asked Clara your sizes, I also asked your shoe size. I never really thought your boots would work but I couldn't figure out a way to tell you to get dressed for being outdoors and not need boots." He fished a pair of boots out of that evidently bottomless duffel.

As I sat on the running board to put them on I asked, "These boots aren't new, are they? I'd hate to have my feet hurting in addition to all the bruises I fully expect to acquire learning how to work those skis."

"No, I rented the boots with your skis and poles. I don't think you have to worry too much about bruises and sore muscles either." He knelt at my feet to adjust the bindings. "You're in good shape from all the walking and snow shoveling and snowshoeing you do. I bet you'll love skiing before we're through today."

I stepped out of the bindings and stood up. "Well, let's get started. I'm ready to make a fool of myself." I pulled on my new jacket and put on that crazy hat.

Abel handed me what looked like a narrow backpack. He explained that it was a camelback, a new style of canteen with a bladder in a pack and a tube that drapes over your shoulder to drink from. He put one on too and put a normal looking backpack over it.

"What's in the pack?"

His Cheshire cat smile reappeared. "You'll see. It's a surprise." He picked up our skis and started walking toward the trailhead.

Not sure I was up for more surprises, I concentrated on not poking myself in the eye with the ski poles and followed him.

Abel was a good teacher and patient with my awkwardness. It didn't take long before I felt pretty confident. As he showed me what to do, a steady stream of couples, families and singles went by, put on their skis, and slid onto the snowy course. Everyone called a greeting and most commented on our hats. I was glad to see that many of the other skiers wore crazy hats and some had crazier clothes to go with them. Just as we were set to give it a try, he reached into a side pocket of his pack and pulled out two pairs of sunglasses. "Here." He slid a pair on me. "The sun's pretty bright today and we don't want to damage those beautiful brown eyes. Ready?"

"I'm as ready as I'll ever be."

Abel let me go first so he could keep an eye on me and pick me up when I fell. The first part of the trail was relatively flat, and I didn't have too much trouble. At intervals there were places to step off the trail to catch our breath. It was beautiful, the snow was blinding white and the course was dotted with colorful groups of skiers, like a moving Christmas tree.

I had a moment of panic when faced with the first little downhill slide, but Abel steered us off to the side and spent a few minutes teaching me to bend my knees and draw in my poles to keep my balance. We waited and watched a few people go down the hill until I felt like I might be able to ski down without falling. I made Abel go first so he could catch me before I skied off into the trees. I was glad there weren't many people behind me because I stopped at the top trying to work up the courage to plunge over the edge. Finally, I took a breath and slid my skis forward and let gravity take over. It was exhilarating. Abel had forgotten to tell me how to stop so I kept my skis in the tracks and whizzed right by him. The look on his face as I flashed by, laughing and whooping, was priceless. As I slowed, I glanced over my shoulder to see that Abel had gotten back on the trail and was following me.

The next time we stopped for a breather he spent a few minutes teaching me to snowplow, which means you turn your ski tips inward to slow your descent. When we had to go uphill, we stepped off the trail and sidestepped up so we didn't slow down the family behind us.

During one of our breaks, I asked Abel how far he'd planned us to go. He told me that just around the next bend in the trail there was a bench where he'd thought we could sit and have a little refreshment. By letting faster skiers pass us along the way, we were alone when we reached the bench, which sat in a patch of sun sheltered by a grove of pines.

I watched amazed as he pulled a bottle of wine, a pair of wineglasses, a container of sliced ham and cheese and a box of fancy crackers out of his pack. Out of his jacket pocket he pulled a very professional looking corkscrew and proceeded to open the wine and pour us each a glass. He held up his glass to me.

"Here's to the bravest woman I know."

"I don't think I'm particularly brave. Why do you say that?"

He took a sip of wine and opened the food. "I think you're brave because you're changing your life to suit yourself and no matter how unsure you are, you've been willing to try just about anything with me."

"Well, my mom always said you'd never know if you liked something unless you try, so I guess that's why I'm at least willing to try things."

"Smart woman, your mom."

We sat on the bench enjoying our wine and the snacks Abel had brought. It was like we were the audience at a play. Skiers came by in straggly lines, multicolored and cheerful. Nearly everyone commented on our feast.

By the time the last of the food was devoured and we settled back with the last of wine, the sun had dipped toward the horizon on that midwinter Saturday. I leaned back on the bench and felt Abel's arm pull me close. It was nice to be snuggled there in the crook of his arm, sheltered from the wintery wind, sipping a nice crisp wine. Eventually we finished the wine, packed up, and got back on the trail.

The trip back seemed much easier than going out. I felt like I had more control over myself. I still looked forward to the little hills to slide down, but the day was cooling fast and we kept moving to stay warm.

Skiing back to the trailhead in the rosy sunset I had the idea I had reached a crossroads. I had spent years sitting on that farmhouse porch watching the sun set and felt like this was the beginning of a new chapter in my life. Maybe today would be the first in a series of brand-new sunset adventures, active rather than passive. I helped Abel load the skis into the truck and we drove back to my place, laughing and planning more skiing.

CHAPTER 29

February

Abel and I went skiing again later that January and had planned to go more, but February blew in on the back of an arctic blast and wouldn't let go. The frost on the old house's windows spread in from the edges until the panes looked like pieces of sandblasted art glass, each etched by a different artist. The wind blew straight out of the north and wormed its way inside through every little gap in the old house; it whistled through the cracks and drummed loose shingles and shutters.

Not a flake of show fell that month because the wind blew all the clouds away. Instead the gusts picked up the January flakes and whirled them in the sun to sparkle like glitter. It frustrated me that I couldn't figure out a way to paint it.

I even called Jake for his suggestions, but he just laughed and told me to "figure it out for yourself, Gail. I gave you the tools." Humph. Even though his class had really pushed me as a painter, he still wasn't much help, still hadn't lost that bad boy personality.

So I tried and tried to paint the bright winter scenes. The pile of rejects grew around the legs of my easel and crackled underfoot as they dried.

The first Friday in February I drove to Madison for the Art League Awards Banquet. Samara and I had entered last fall with equal amounts of terror and hope, and we were about to find out what a little piece of the art establishment thought of our work. I called Samara when I got to my room, and she came right over from the university. We strolled around "the Square" and did some last-minute shopping, then headed over to the hall where all the competitors' art was hung. Walking around the exhibition of entries with Samara, I was humbled by the quality of the work on display. To my eyes my paintings looked like they'd be appropriate for a tourist area gallery and the rest of them looked like they'd be at home in a museum.

I spent the time it took to get ready for the banquet practicing my I'm-really-happy-for-the-winner smile. I didn't have to practice my smile when I looked at the dress Samara had helped me choose the day before. I had packed a navy evening suit to wear but when Samara saw it she said, "Gail, you'll look more like an executive than an artist if you wear this. We have to shop."

In a little boutique a block or two off the square we found the perfect dress, a bias-cut tank dress with an asymmetrical hem, with the greens, blues, and lavenders of the ocean swirling over it. In the same shop I bought a silver-gray shawl that glimmered like moonlight on the sea. Samara approved of the silver sandals I had brought to wear with the suit, and she gave me a pair of earrings she had made from pieces of blue and green sea glass. She even helped me with my makeup. I seldom wore any and the tiny dabs I put on were not enough according to Samara. She swept my eyelids with a green shadow that made my brown eyes look even browner; she threw away my "old lady red" lipstick and bought me a glossy dark plum that she said made my lips look luscious.

"Abel won't be able to resist kissing you when he sees this," she said, as she leaned close to apply the lip gloss.

"Give me that." I took the tube from her. "I'm not so old I can't put on my own makeup."

She giggled. "Just remember it's an evening event. Put enough on so you don't fade into the wallpaper."

We had the standard banquet dinner of watery iceberg

lettuce salad with one lonely cherry tomato, mystery meat over fake mashed potatoes, limp green beans, and orange sherbet for dessert. After dessert and too-strong coffee, a half-dozen members of the Art League got up to speak about the organization's aims, each one paraphrasing the last.

"Can't they skip all this and just get to the awards? I'm dying of suspense," Samara whispered, which earned her a glare from the pair of matrons sitting on my left.

I pulled my program out. "See?" I pointed at the list of speakers. "Only one more speech and then they announce the awards." I was nervous too. My palms began to sweat. I was glad I'd kept my napkin in my lap so I could squeeze and twist it rather than my skirt. On the off chance I'd win, I didn't want to look like a rumpled bed on stage. Then I heard my name. "Gail, you won!" Samara leaned over and gave me a hug. "Go on. Go up and get your award."

I didn't know if I could get out of my chair, let alone walk up the steps onto the stage. My ears were filled with the applause of the banquet hall full of people. As soon as I stood up the sound of the applause dimmed, the walls of the room seemed to fade into nothing, and all I could see was the spotlight on my painting on stage.

I concentrated on not stumbling over my skirt as I climbed the stairs. One of the Art League members took my arm and escorted me to center stage where the president awaited me.

"Congratulations, Gail," she said, as she hugged me and gave me an air kiss. Her embrace threw me. I'd expected a man who'd shake my hand and make some bluff remarks about art so I wasn't prepared; I was left with my arms halfway up and my lips puckered as she pulled back and turned me toward the still-applauding crowd. "Tell me, Gail, what made you enter this particular painting?"

I looked at the view of orange daylilies tumbling over a broken-down rail fence and was stuck for an answer. "I, um, I guess I disliked this one less than the rest of my paintings."

The room erupted with laughter.

Once the crowd quieted, she said, "Well, I guess that's one way to decide. Where did you find your subject?"

"On my farm in Kingman. I paint what's around me."

"How long have you been painting?"

"A couple of years, I guess."

I suppose she asked more questions; I don't remember. I know I posed for pictures with every member of the Art League Board of Directors; I have copies of the photos. I know the treasurer presented me with a check because that photo was the on the front page of the State-Journal the next morning. But I have no clear memories of the rest of the evening, I was so giddy with excitement. I do remember that Samara earned an Honorable Mention and received a check for fifty dollars. As the party started to break up, we went back to my hotel where we kicked our shoes off and lounged on the couch in my room congratulating each other and making grandiose predictions about our place in the art world. There was an empty wine bottle and two glasses on the table when I woke up the next morning. My prize, a check for a thousand dollars, was propped against the bottle.

In the morning, I called my family to tell them the news; they were all very happy for me and Merry reminded me that there were still a lot of empty walls in their house. Even Clara had to admit that winning such a prestigious prize might mean I was a real artist. Both of us laughed at that backhanded compliment, it was so classic Clara.

Samara had class that morning, so I had a light breakfast in the hotel, packed, and drove on home grinning with the joy of winning and just a tiny bit afraid of what this first success might mean.

CHAPTER 30

Abel's idea of celebrating Valentine's Day turned out to be way more than I ever expected. He invited me to dinner at his house that evening, but when I went into the kitchen Valentine's morning I found a flat basket wrapped in cellophane printed with hearts tied with a big red bow on my kitchen table. Where had it come from? I hadn't heard anybody come in during the night. My heart beat a little harder as I opened the card propped against it.

Happy Valentine's Day morning to the most beautiful woman in my world. Love, Abel, it read.

Tears sprang to my eyes and the breath caught in my throat. No one had ever done anything so romantic for me.

I set the card down, untied the bow, and unwrapped the cellophane. I couldn't believe what I saw. On a delicate white china plate, rimmed with gold scrolls and tiny red rosebuds, sat two croissants with little heart-shaped pats of butter nestled in ice chips in a matching bowl alongside. A cup and saucer in the same elegant pattern held a packet of English Breakfast Tea and another note. My fingers trembled as I opened it.

I wanted to give you roses all day. These are just the beginning. I hope you like croissants, I read in Abel's elegant script. I made the strawberry jam from my own berries. Enjoy your breakfast. I'll see you at seven o'clock tonight. My day will be empty until you arrive. Love, Abel.

I wonder how he got it in here, I thought, as I put water on to boil for tea. I'll bet Clara helped; she's the only one, besides the boys, who has a key.

I felt like a princess as I sipped my tea and ate croissants off the elegant china. The jam tasted like the berries had just been picked. As I finished the last bite, the phone rang.

"Happy Valentine's Day." Abel's deep voice sent a shiver all over me.

"The same to you," I replied, my voice shaking. My knees gave way and I plopped into the nearest chair.

"Did you enjoy your breakfast?"

"I did. It was a wonderful surprise. How did you get it in here without me hearing you?"

His throaty chuckle danced across the wires. "I'll never tell. What are you doing today?"

The night before I had made a list of things I wanted to accomplish that day, but for the life of me I couldn't remember a single one. "Paint, I guess. Or maybe clean the bathroom. I don't know. Your gift has driven everything out of my memory."

"Good. I want this to be a day to remember."

"I don't imagine I'll ever forget it. Abel, that was the most romantic gesture. It was just like in a novel. How did you do it?"

"A gentleman never reveals his sources. I'll see you this evening. I've got to get cooking. 'Bye, Gail."

"Goodbye, Abel. See you later." And we hung up. I sat there in the dim hallway wondering if these days all men treated the women they were dating like this. Bert had never been very romantic. I decided I could get used to Abel's brand of courtship very easily.

"Hey, lazy, are you still in bed?" Clara's voice from the kitchen made me jump.

"I'm right here, Clara." I got up and walked out of the

shadowy hall into the winter light of the kitchen.

"How come you were sitting here in the dark?" she said as she flipped on the overhead light. "Got any tea made?" Her voice sounded overly loud and the light seemed too bright.

"I'll make some. Turn that big light back off, please. I'll flip on the light over the stove." I refilled the kettle and put it on to heat.

She sat in the chair at the end of the table and saw the basket and the dishes. "What's this stuff? Did you make yourself a fancy breakfast?"

I pulled mugs out of the clean dishwasher and carried the steeping teapot to the table. "No, I didn't. Somehow Abel got in here last night and left it on the table for me to find this morning." I poured us each some tea and pushed the sugar bowl toward her. "Did you help him? Lend him your key?"

"Thanks. No, I didn't help him or lend him my key." She stirred two teaspoons of sugar into her tea. "Really? Abel did that. Are you sure?"

"Of course, I'm sure. He just called to see how I enjoyed my breakfast. And there was a note. Two notes, actually." I debated whether to share the contents of the notes. My instinct was not to, but I knew Clara would be hurt if I didn't. "If I let you read them," I said, holding the envelopes to my breast, "you have to promise not to tell a soul. Not any of your kids, no one in town, not even Hank."

"Wow, those must be some notes." She crossed her heart. "Okay, I promise."

I slid the two envelopes to her and watched her face as she read them.

She tucked each note carefully back into its envelope and passed them back to me. "Holy cow, Gail. Do you think he's got some sort of manual or something he got that stuff from? I'd faint dead away if Hank ever gave me something like that."

"I know. Bert would never have written anything like that either. You don't think, as our mothers used to say, Abel is out after only one thing, do you?"

Clara reddened. "Lord, Gail, I have no idea. I hardly know the man. But you'd better wear your best undies to dinner tonight, just in case. And maybe pack a toothbrush too."

I didn't tell Clara I had worn my best Victoria's Secret undies every time Abel and I went on a date. And that I'd been both relieved and disappointed that so far he hadn't gotten a look at any of it. "I'll think about it."

We jumped at a knock on the back door. "I wonder who that could be?" I asked. "Did you notice anyone drive in?" I got up to answer the knock, smoothing my hair and tugging my gaping robe shut.

"Nope." She leaned toward the window and squinted through the tiny unfrosted circle in the center of the glass. "It's a florist truck."

I opened the door to see what looked like a bouquet of red roses with legs standing on the top step. A head with a knit cap pulled down to the eyebrows and a scarf over the nose and mouth peeked at me around the flowers. "Gail Logan?" It was a young woman.

"Yes, I'm Gail Logan. Come on in before you and the flowers freeze."

The vase of roses moved closer, and I grabbed it. "Got it?" the young woman asked as she came into the warm kitchen.

"Yes, I've got it." I set the flowers on the table. "Let me give you a tip, but you're welcome to sit a minute and warm up."

Before I finished the sentence, she was pulling off her mittens. "Thanks. I'm turning into an icicle. I have got to get the heater in that van fixed." One of her small hands reached up, tugged down the scarf, and took off her hat, releasing a cascade of auburn waves. "There's no need to tip me, ma'am. The gentleman who ordered the flowers took care of that." She remained standing on the doormat.

Clara motioned to the chair nearest the door. "Sit down. Let me pour you a cup of tea." She bustled to the dishwasher for another mug. "Won't the flowers freeze if your heater's broken?"

"No, they like it cold. Besides, it's only the cab heater that's broken. The cooler for the flowers works just fine. I'm Moira Kelly, by the way. I just opened a flower shop in downtown Kingman."

Clara and I introduced ourselves, and Clara launched into a raft of questions for Moira.

"Where are you from?" asked Clara, with the look in her eyes that always made me think of those old black and white detective movies they sometimes show on the movie channel.

"I'm from Simpson."

"What made you choose a one-horse town like Kingman for your business?"

"I wanted to live in the country."

Moira weathered the barrage fairly well, answering the early questions easily, so I kept my mouth shut.

"Where are you living?"

"There's an apartment over the shop."

"When did you open?"

"I've been open two weeks."

"How old are you?"

"I'm twenty-eight."

"Are you married?"

With the last question a wary look appeared on her freckled face. "Why do you want to know if I'm married?" she asked with a little steel in her voice.

I thought it was time to interrupt. "Moira, you have to understand two things about living in Kingman. First, everyone will be talking about you before they get to know you, trying to figure out how to fit you into life out here. And second, Clara has way too many children and she's always trying to marry off the last few. I imagine she had you picked out for Dan, her youngest."

"Gail, don't be silly." Clara blushed beet red. "I was just going to suggest she take her van to Dan so he can fix the heater." She turned to Moira. "Dan's a good mechanic. Whenever anything broke around our farm when Dan was growing up, he'd be out with a wrench and fix it right up." And then she laughed. "I'm sorry, Moira. I get carried away sometimes, but I was just hoping to head off the gossips over at Mavis' beauty salon." A frown creased Clara's broad forehead as a horrible thought occurred, "You haven't been in there yet, have you?"

"No, I haven't. I've been so busy getting my shop set up the last couple of weeks, the only person I've talked to has been Charlie from the hardware store."

Clara's forehead cleared and she nodded. "Good. I'm going to get my hair done this afternoon so for once I can be the first to talk about something."

Moira looked a little scared. "Sounds like Kingman runs on gossip."

I reached over and patted her hand as it lay on the table, fingers curled under. I noticed a white line on her left-hand ring finger. "Don't you worry, honey. Gossip does make the wheels grind around here, but it's mostly well meant. It's just a faster way of getting the news than the weekly paper." I tapped her ring finger. "Just separated?"

Tears filled her jade green eyes and spilled down her cheeks.

I felt terrible. "I'm sorry. I didn't mean to make you cry." I handed her a napkin.

"It's all right." She wiped her eyes. "I've done a lot of crying over the past few months." She took a deep breath. "I might as well tell you the sad story," she smiled at Clara, "so you can spread all the juicy gossip at Mavis' this afternoon." She sipped her tea and took a deep breath. "Well, Peter and I got married right out of high school. I went to the tech school to learn landscape architecture. Peter went to State across town to study acting. He was great at it. He was in every production his whole time there and I worked for a landscaper to pay the bills. After he graduated, we moved to

New York so he could try to break into the theater. He got a few commercials and walk-ons on soap operas, things like that. I worked for a society florist and was earning a good reputation."

I refilled her tea mug.

"Thanks. Anyway, you have no idea how many people there are just like him, talented and willing to do almost anything to be successful. He got a role in a touring company last year." She stopped talking and gazed out the window. I knew she wasn't seeing the frosted pane and the snow outside. "The cast and crew of those shows get so close... You can imagine what happened."

Clara and I nodded.

"He called me from someplace in South Dakota. He and one of the actresses, the ingénue, had fallen in love. The show was going to be in Reno in six weeks, would I mind if he got a divorce there so they could get married?"

Clara couldn't control herself. "What a skunk."

She shook her head. "Not really, just an actor. It was hard for me to be sympathetic to his struggles, to be interested in the petty backbiting they all engage in. He wasn't interested in my world and seemed a little jealous that my job gave me entrée into the better parties where I met influential people from the stage and movies. He wanted me to get him into some of the parties but my boss, Luca, was totally against it once he learned that Peter was an actor. 'He will not be paying attention to the flowers. He will only think of who he can introduce himself to,' he'd say when I asked. And he was right." She sipped her cooling tea.

"I told him to get the divorce and I stayed in New York for a few months. But rent's too high and I worked so much I didn't have many friends. I was lonely and broke. So I came home, lived with my folks for a while, until I couldn't bear another chorus of 'I told you so' and moved to Kingman." She looked at her watch. "Oh gosh, I've got to go. One more delivery and then I can reopen the shop. Stop in and visit next time you're in town." She pulled her cap back on and stuffed her glorious hair under it, wrapped her scarf around her face, and left with a wave.

"She seems like a nice girl," I said as I took my first good look at the bouquet she'd delivered. "Talented, too." Baby's breath and ferns surrounded each rose; each one looked like a separate bouquet. "This is incredible."

Clara was still looking at the back door Moira had just closed. "I think I'll stop in her shop this afternoon with one of Dan's cards. She needs her heater fixed and Dan's a good listener."

"Clara, you're incorrigible. Didn't you hear a word she said? It's going to take some time for her to be ready to date again."

"Oh, I know," she said, waving away my words, "but she still needs a mechanic and I think Dan might be just what she needs. He'll introduce her to a few people, like Katie who does his books. She needs to meet young people; that's hard to do in such a small town." She glanced at the roses. "Those are nice. Got to run. I want to make Hank some lunch before I go to Mavis'."

The rush of cold that swirled around my ankles as Clara left brought me back to reality. I cleared the table and hand-washed the dishes. I didn't trust the dishwasher not to ruin them. I stood with my hands in the soapy water thinking about my crazy morning—finding a wonderful surprise from Abel for breakfast, a romantic phone call also from Abel, a visit from Clara, an absolutely gorgeous bouquet of roses from Abel delivered by an interesting newcomer to town. I felt a bit punch drunk so once the dishes were safely in the drainer I went to take a shower, hoping to clear my head.

Clean and dressed, I carried my roses into the studio and taped a small piece of paper to my board.

I washed the paper with a blue wash, dark in the upper left corner and gradually lightening to the opposite corner. To be safe I got out three more pieces of paper and repeated the process. While they dried, I pulled out every shade of red I could find. Rather than paint the entire bouquet, I decided to concentrate on one single rose.

Pulling a gooseneck lamp closer, I shined the light on the flowers and peered at them, trying to see every shade of red. One of the blooms was almost fully open and that was the one I chose to paint. I hoped a glimpse of the center of the rose would make the painting more interesting.

I got out the mask agent and dotted it all around for the baby's breath. I used a pencil to rough in the rose's shape. Then I took a few dark greens and suggested the ferns. With dark brown added to the deepest green, I put some stems under a few of the baby's breath dots.

Taking a toothpick, I masked little dots in the center of the flower so I could add yellow pollen grains to the threadlike stamens and drew little lines of masking up the inside of the petal visible above the center.

Starting with the palest, pinkest of the reds in my palette, I painted the deep center, gradually adding darker and darker reds until I finished with an almost black red. Adding even more black to the darkest red, I rolled my brush along the leading edges of the foreground petals to suggest their ragged curled edges. Since what I had produced so far resembled nothing more than a sloppy red bull's-eye, I got ready to try to turn my splotch into a realistic looking flower.

While cleaning my brushes, I peered into the bowl of the rose, learning the way Mother Nature blended her colors. Using a round brush and all the skills I had acquired over the last year I spread the rosiest reds and wine reds up the petals, letting them blend on the still wet paper so there weren't any hard edges. Once I was satisfied with the rose, I floated more of the deepest green around the foreground edges leaving jagged spaces to suggest the ferns. A few more tiny lines for the baby's breath stems and my painting was ready to dry. After cleaning my brushes, I went into the kitchen to forage for lunch.

When I opened the 'fridge I nearly fell down. There

in the center of the top shelf was another rosebud decorated china plate wrapped in plastic wrap with a note on top.

Enjoy your lunch. Love, Abel, it read, P.S. Did you notice the basket of bread on the counter?

I whirled around and, sure enough, there was a basket next to the stove. When I peeled back the linen napkin lining it, I found four tiny loaves of homemade bread—and a note.

What's bread and cheese without wine? the note said, You'll find a split of champagne and a strawberry for your flute in the crisper drawer.

I looked in the fridge and there it was. I removed the plate from the refrigerator, set it on the table, and gently peeled off the plastic wrap to discover five kinds of cheese, a small dish of olives, another of what looked like pickled vegetables, and two tiny chocolates in their paper cups. When I checked in the crisper, there was a split of champagne next to a crystal flute with a wrapped strawberry nestled inside.

"Oh my God," I said aloud. "Abel, how did you do all this without me hearing you?" I opened the bubbly, poured it over the berry, and sipped.

By the time I finished my lunch and hand-washed those dishes, I was in no shape to paint anymore. I felt as if that single glass of champagne I'd had with lunch had gone right to my head. The avalanche of Valentine's gifts made me dizzy. I decided to build a fire, sit in the living room, and read a book for the afternoon. I kind of dreaded what Abel had planned for the evening; the day had been too full of surprises.

I stayed in my chair until the light began to fade. I made myself a cup of herbal tea, pulled on a coat and hat, and went out onto the porch to watch the sunset. For the first time in over a week the clouds had flown, and the sky was tinted a beautiful rosy pink color. The spicy orange steam from the tea warmed my lips as I gazed at the horizon, thinking about how different my life had become. When I finished the last sip, the sun was sending its last rays of gold above the horizon making the sky look like a movie screen. I went inside to dress for dinner. Ignoring the feeling that I should be wearing a float-y floral dress, I pulled out a pair of beautiful charcoal wool slacks in deference to the frigid weather. I put on a thin white sweater and topped it off with a red wool blazer I hadn't been able to resist at the after-Christmas sales. Black leather boots that looked dressy but were sturdy enough for tramping through snow and ice, completed my outfit.

I checked my watch. It would take me about twenty minutes to get to Abel's, allowing plenty of time in case the roads were icy. Driving through the mid-winter dark, I could see couples leaving home, waving goodbye to children left with baby-sitters so they could enjoy dinner alone. The parking lot of Sandburg's Steaks & Beer was filled to overflowing. Every place I passed that served dinner looked jammed. It made me glad we were staying in that night. Seeing so many couples out made me think about the Valentine's Days Bert and I had celebrated. Never very romantic, Bert would usually remember to leave a card for me on the kitchen table when he left for work. A few times he'd actually bought me a gift, something practical rather than romantic. He never took me to dinner. He didn't believe in going out to dinner. He always said he worked hard to raise our food and I was a good cook. That meant he didn't want to pay someone else for a meal he could have gotten cheaper at home. A few times I had gone all out for Valentine's Day. I'd washed and ironed his mother's Irish linen tablecloth, stopped at the grocery for a bouquet of flowers, got out the silver candlesticks we'd gotten from some distant relative as a wedding gift, and made a fancy dinner. Actually, I only made a fancy dinner once. Bert had complained the entire meal that he didn't recognize anything on his plate, so the next time I made a special meal I'd made sure to prepare something just a little outside the norm. It was a disappointing way to celebrate the lovers' holiday, but I kept reminding myself that Bert's good qualities outweighed the bad. Useless nostalgic thoughts like that accompanied me all the way to Abel's.

When I'd parked and gotten out of the car, I noticed that he'd replaced the white light bulb in his porch light with a red one and had hung a heart-shaped wreath on the door. All along the walk from the street to the door were luminarias, white paper bags weighted with sand and each holding a glowing candle. He had cut out hearts on the sides of the bags so there were glowing hearts reflected on the cement. I felt like a queen on her way to her coronation. I was also worried that the wood carving I'd gotten him didn't measure up. Before I had a chance to ring the bell, the door opened and there stood my valentine, resplendent in a red v-necked sweater and a white bow tie dotted with hearts.

"Happy Valentine's Day, Gail," he said, and swept me into the house and into his arms.

"The same to you," I said nearly smothered in his embrace. When he released me and turned so he could take my coat, I said, "You're going to get a reputation with that red light over your door. Or are you thinking of running a house of ill repute as a side job?"

"What do you mean 'house of ill repute'?"

"Oh, come on, Abel," I said, laughing, "haven't you ever heard of a red light district? You know, where the ladies of the evening ply their trade."

He looked as if I'd slapped him. "I didn't mean... Of course, I've heard of them. I just thought you'd like my decorations."

"I did. I do, and this whole day has been one long romantic surprise. I'm overwhelmed. Thank you. I love your wreath, the luminarias, and even the red light bulb. It just struck me as funny." I cupped his cheek. "I didn't mean to hurt your feelings."

"That's okay." He took my elbow and escorted me into

the living room where soft music played on the stereo, a bottle of champagne sat chilling in a silver wine bucket and a tray of hors d'oeuvres rested on the coffee table. "You see, Marcella never wanted to make much of Valentine's Day. When we were first married, I brought her a bouquet of roses and took her out for a fancy dinner. She berated me for weeks for 'wasting our hard-earned money' so I never did it again." While he was talking, he popped the cork on the champagne and poured it into a pair of crystal flutes. He raised his glass to me and said, "To the woman I hope stays my Valentine forever," and took a sip.

I raised mine to him and said, "To the most surprising man I've ever had the pleasure of knowing," and sipped. I reached down beside me and handed him the red bag tied with a silver ribbon.

Spots of pink bloomed high on his cheeks as he took the package. "Gee, Gail, thanks." He sat looking at it, not even peering inside.

"Well, open it!" I said.

"Oh, okay." His long fingers were gentle as they teased apart the knot in the bow and lifted the bundle of tissue paper out of the bag, catching the card with his thumb and bringing it out too. He set the bag down on the floor and laid the gift on his lap. Carefully he opened the card, read it, smiled, and closed it. "Thanks, I feel the same way," he said, his eyes misty. He leaned toward me, and we kissed.

By that time, I was getting anxious for him to see my gift. My fingers itched to reach over and help him, but I resisted.

He unwrapped the tissue and held up the woodcarving. It was a statue of a couple dancing, but it wasn't a realistic piece, it more suggested the man and woman and their graceful movement together. "Gail," he said, "it's beautiful. Thank you." He ran his hands over the smooth wood, just as I did when I found it at the winter art fair.

"You're welcome," I said with a tight throat, "I'm glad

241

you like it. That's the way I feel when we dance."

We sat on the sofa and enjoyed the wonderful things Abel had spent the day making: stuffed mushroom caps, shrimp with a creamy dill sauce, slices of ham and cream cheese rolled around a dill pickle, and little cheese puffs.

"Everything's delicious," I said. "You must have been slaving away since dawn. You know, on my drive over here I saw a lot of couples out celebrating. It made me think of how Bert wasn't very romantic and never did much for Valentine's Day. What you said about Marcella not wanting you to spend money to celebrate it, made me think she and Bert would have gotten on just fine."

"They probably would have, but then you and I wouldn't have met." He looked into my eyes and said, "I wouldn't want to have missed meeting you for the world." He leaned toward me, put his hands on my shoulders, and pulled me to him for a long kiss. Our arms slid around each other in an embrace and we both leaned into the sofa cushions. The kiss seemed to go on forever. He nibbled his way down my jaw to my neck and his hands began to roam over my sweater.

"I hoped you'd be wearing a low-cut blouse," he murmured into my throat.

Putting a hand on either side of his face, I pulled his lips to mine and said, "It's too cold outside to expose my tender flesh."

Just as we got back to our necking, a buzzing sound erupted from the kitchen.

"Dammit," Abel said against my lips. "The potatoes are done. I've got to go finish cooking dinner." He stood up, ran a hand over his hair, and tugged his sweater down. He held out his hand to me. "Want to keep me company?"

I let him pull me to my feet and spent a moment smoothing my own hair and tugging my blazer into place. "Sure."

He refilled our glasses and carried them into the kitchen. He wouldn't let me help; he insisted I sit at the breakfast bar and watch while he cooked.

He turned off the oven so the potatoes didn't overcook. Then he melted a bit of butter in a frying pan, sautéed garlic, and slid a pair of lamb chops in. While they sizzled, he microwaved asparagus.

"Mmm, I love asparagus," I said. "Where did you find it this time of year?"

"At that new grocery in Simpson, on the east side near the greenhouse. They've got a lot of things you just can't find at Merricks'." He waggled his eyebrows at me. "Asparagus is a very erotic vegetable, don't you think?"

"I guess. I never thought of it as erotic." I sipped my champagne, wondering how the evening would end.

Abel was like a dervish, whirling from refrigerator to stove, stirring pots, turning the chops. In a very few minutes, he switched everything off, turned to me smiling, and said, "Done." He came over, picked up my wineglass, and escorted me into the dining room.

I stopped in the doorway. There were candles lit on the table and on every flat surface. The table settings gleamed in the flickering candlelight and more roses blossomed in vases around the room and in low bowls on the table. "Abel, it's beautiful."

"All for you," he said, and helped me into my chair. "I'll be right back."

I sat, snowy linen napkin in my lap, listening to him moving around in the kitchen. I heard the oven open and close, heard plates click on the countertop, and spoons scraping on cookware. In a very few minutes, he came back carrying two plates. He set mine in front of me and I just gaped at it, it was so incredible.

The lamb chops glistened on the side of the plate with a few capers sprinkled over them, the asparagus spears were bundled with a thin strip of pimento and a ribbon of hollandaise sauce lay over them, the baked potato was opened, fluffed, buttered, and there were fresh chives on top.

"Oh my God, Abel," I said, "this looks like a picture from a magazine. It seems a shame to eat it." My hands reached to pick up my fork and knife. "But I'll manage."

He picked up his own napkin, laid it across his lap, picked up his utensils, and said, "Enjoy."

Conversation while we ate was limited to a few "mmm"s and an "oh" or two. Abel's dinner was too delicious and too much of a surprise for words.

When both our plates were bare of all but a few dabs of hollandaise and a glisten of butter, he said, "I hope you saved room for dessert."

"Dessert? Oh my. I hope it's something light," I said, feeling pretty full but not wanting to miss Abel's next surprise.

"It's light, I promise," he said, getting up and removing our plates. "In fact, we have to share it. Don't go away." He disappeared into the kitchen. This time I heard the refrigerator door open and what sounded like a cardboard box lid open. He stirred another pot, and I heard the clink of spoon on plate. He hummed along with the music from the stereo as he worked. I could tell he was pleased with the success of his surprises.

I was looking at the reflection of the candle flames in the mirror over the sideboard when I heard the door open and a soft "ta da!" beside me. I looked up to see a dessert vision set down in front of me. "Oh, Abel, it's beautiful." It was a meringue bowl filled with glistening strawberries, topped with real whipped cream, all floating on a lake of hot, dark chocolate sauce.

While I stared at the amazing thing, Abel propped an envelope against my water goblet.

"What's this?"

"It's your Valentine's Day gift."

"My gift? I thought this entire day was my gift." I opened the flap and pulled out a card telling me I was getting a year's subscription to *Watercolor World*, an art magazine I'd been buying by the issue at the bookstore. "Thanks, Abel, how thoughtful; it's a wonderful gift."

"It was the only thing I could think of to give my prize-winning artist girlfriend." He leaned down and kissed me, then reached over, picked up the dessert spoon from his original seat across the table, and pulled out the chair next to mine. "I hope you don't mind that we have to share."

I shook my head, picked up my spoon, and tried to figure out where and how to get the first bite. With a twinkle in his eye, he pressed the side of the spoon's bowl onto the edge of the meringue, cracking it, sending a river of sweet red strawberry juice over the chocolate. "Ladies' first," he said with a flourish.

I dipped my spoon, managing to get a bit of each ingredient. "Oh, Abel, this is so delicious. I can't believe you made this yourself."

Managing to look humble and proud at the same time, he said, "Well, I didn't make the meringue shell; I bought it at the bakery. But I whipped the cream, hulled the berries, and made the hot fudge sauce myself. I'm glad you like it. I wanted it to be special."

I was tempted to ask more questions, keep him talking so I would get more than my share of the ambrosial treat, but he'd worked so hard to make my day special. Besides I was getting full, real full.

After we did all but lick the plate, we went into the living room for coffee in front of the fireplace. "What a lovely meal, Abel. You're quite a cook." I slid the magazines and candy dish aside so he could put down the coffee tray. "I'm glad you liked it," he said as he knelt to put another log on the fire. We sat on the couch talking late into the evening, Abel getting up periodically to poke or replenish the fire, then coming back to snuggle next to me. I remember hearing his clock strike ten o'clock but nothing after that.

The rising sun's rays shining in the front windows woke me up just after eight the next morning. We were still sitting on the couch, Abel's arm around my shoulder. His head had fallen back and each of his exhaled breaths carried a tiny snore that ruffled my hair. The fireplace was cold and the small light on the sofa table still glowed. My right arm was asleep and when I moved my head, my neck cracked. That little sound was enough to wake Abel.

"Oh, good lord, we fell asleep." He groaned. "It's been a long time since I've slept on a couch."

"Me too." I sat up and stretched, waggling my head on my neck, trying to work out the kinks. "I'll bet that's not how you imagined the evening ending."

"As a matter of fact, no it isn't. I'm sorry I fell asleep."

"Hey, don't apologize. I fell asleep too." I looked around for my purse, picked it up and got my keys out. "I hate to eat, sleep, and run, but I think I'll head on home."

Abel stood up, accompanied by a symphony of crackling joints. "Can I make you some coffee before you go?"

My negative reply was lost in a yawn that my hand wasn't big enough to cover. "I think I'd like to get out the door before all your neighbors see me and jump-start the gossip wires this early. Can you get my coat, please?"

He got my black wool coat from the hall closet and held it for me to put on. Once it was on my shoulders, he turned me to face him and began buttoning it. "Sure I can't convince you to stay?" he asked, leaning to kiss me.

I held a hand over my mouth. "No kisses, please. I have dog breath, not exactly the impression I want to leave you with. We can kiss more another time. Thanks for the lovely evening."

He walked me to the door and opened it for me. Just as quickly he shut it. "Can you wait a minute while I get out of these clothes and into a bathrobe?"

"Why?"

Pointing across the street, he said, "I just noticed Edna Watson, the gossip queen of Elm Street's light is on. If you're completely dressed and I'm in my robe, imagine the quality gossip she'll have to tell today." He laughed his slow sexy chuckle.

I grabbed his chin. "You, Mr. Baker, are incorrigible." I kissed him.

"Aha! You said you had dog breath, but I made you kiss me anyway." He reopened the door.

"Goodbye, crazy man," I said as I walked back to my car between the extinguished luminarias. "Call me later."

"Okay."

"After my shower—and nap." I unlocked my frosted car.

"Happy Valentine's Day, Gail?" he called as I got in.

I started the engine and rolled down the window. "The best, Abel, the absolute best." I drove home, smiling and humming along with the radio.

CHAPTER 31

March

March came in like a lion, as the cliché goes, but for me it was a whirlwind of art shows, painting, and dating Abel. I've always hated March; I've said that before. Bert and Pop died in March and the weather taunts you with moments of spring-like warmth and then winter races back to slap you down with icy winds and freezing rain. But this March was different.

I found myself looking forward to the days in my studio. My brushes had suddenly become obedient; what was in my head appeared on the paper. On the floor of my studio, discarded paintings that hadn't turned out the way I wanted still crackled underfoot, but there were fewer of them than ever before. Abel came over nearly every day, bringing some of the beautiful wood frames he made for my paintings. I was glad I had agreed to let him make them, certain that the reason I had sold so many pictures at the church craft fair last December was, at least partly, due to his frames.

I liked having him around too. He was so well read. He'd bring books of poetry to read in the evenings while we sat in front of the fire, or novels, classics, that we'd take turns reading aloud. It was so civilized, like a PBS mini-series.

I sometimes felt as if I were living in a novel myself; my life was so different from the life I had with Bert. Not better, because I had liked my old life pretty well, just different.

You could see the changes in my paintings too. I was much freer, much braver than I had been. Forms were softer, colors brighter or with stronger contrast, subject matter more creative.

I never imagined that you could tell the mood of the artist when he painted something but, now that my eye was trained, I couldn't believe I had missed it before. I can look at every one of my paintings and see what I was feeling when I painted it. Sometimes I felt embarrassed when I looked at a few of them. I remembered all too clearly how angry or hurt or disappointed I had been when I made the painting and was afraid that anyone looking at it would be seeing inside of me.

I spent a lot of time poring over the articles in *Watercolor World* and drooling over the beautiful expensive brushes and paints in the ads. In the back of the magazine, they listed all the art shows and exhibits in the surrounding area. Abel and I booted up his phone's GPS and plotted trips to the ones nearby. One-day trips since the weather in March in Wisconsin is so unpredictable.

I made a lot of soup and stew in March. Abel baked bread. He'd come over in the afternoons with a loaf of fresh bread under his arm and a handful of frames, arriving just as I was cleaning my brushes at the end of a long day of painting. I teased him that he must have a spy outside my window because he had uncanny timing.

"A spy?" he said. "I don't need a spy. I just keep my eye on the light and when the sun gets to a certain spot in the sky, I grab a loaf of bread, pick up some frames, and drive on over."

Art shows, art shows, art shows. Abel and I must have gone to ten of them that month. School gyms, church basements, town halls--all of them smelling of wet wool and bodies, with shuffling crowds of winter-weary people, art lovers, cabin fever sufferers, and the just plain bored looking at real art, good amateur art, and a lot of god-awful art.

By the end of our art tour that month, I thought I would scream if I saw one more crocheted dishcloth or painted wood "Welcome" plaque. At the beginning I found myself comparing my paintings, usually unfavorably, to the ones on display, but by the time the tour was winding down I had acquired a bit of objectivity and could see that my work was better than 90% of what was on offer.

"See, Gail?" Abel whispered in my ear as we passed yet another booth filled with bad watercolors. "I told you you're a real artist. Most of these people are just hobbyists or hacks."

I poked him in the ribs. "Shhh. You'll hurt their feelings," I nodded at a scowling man staring at us from the booth, "or start a fight. I think you might have insulted his wife."

He put his arm around my waist and walked a bit faster. "Not that I couldn't take him, you understand, I just don't want to make a scene."

"Of course, you don't, Tarzan," I said, laughing at my own personal macho man. Why men don't grow out of the need to flex their muscles I'll never know.

I got home from a city band concert with Abel one evening and noticed that it was chilly in the house. I tootsed up the thermostat, the furnace clicked on, but nothing happened. I had gotten a new furnace a couple years earlier and knew it didn't have a pilot light, so my only recourse was to call a repairman. Naturally, it was after-hours, so the charge was $125 just to get the guy to start his truck.

He came and, after putting little blue shoe protectors on, clomped into the basement. He called me back almost immediately and I was thrilled that he'd found the problem so quickly, but when I arrived, he launched into a ten-minute lecture on regular filter changing.

I interrupted to ask, "Is that the problem?"

"No."

"Then change the filter and keep working."

Twenty minutes later he came upstairs. "I can't find anything wrong down there; everything tests out perfect. I have to check the pipes outside."

He barely had time to get to the side of the house where

the intake and exhaust pipes poked through the wall, when he was back at the door. "Come out here, ma'am. You're never going to believe this."

I followed him around the corner and couldn't believe what he pointed at. A rhubarb leaf, a giant rhubarb leaf, had grown up and gotten sucked over the end of the pipe, blocking any air from getting in.

He graciously let me pick it myself and suggested I transplant the rhubarb to a spot where it wouldn't cause more trouble and he charged me $40 more for the service call. I stood there looking at that $165 rhubarb stalk thinking, you're going to make one expensive pie.

The next morning found me out in the yard digging up what turned out to be three rhubarb plants and moving them to a spot far away from the furnace pipes where they couldn't get into any more trouble. I made a couple of pies and froze the rest. I took one of the pies over to share with Clara and Hank; I thought Hank would split a gut laughing when I told him the story. Clara ran right outside and checked that none of her plants were in a position to suffocate their furnace. Abel thought it was pretty funny too. He threatened to write it up and post it in the garden center over the rhubarb plants as a warning to future rhubarb owners. I planted spearmint where the rhubarb had been. When Abel asked me why, I told him, "I don't want a blank spot in my garden. Spearmint leaves are too small to get sucked into the intake, and if they do get in there, maybe they'll make my house smell nice." He just shook his head.

CHAPTER 32

April

Abel escorted me into the hotel lobby, his hand on the small of my back. I stopped walking and gazed around the vast space. The wall overlooking the bay was solid glass, giving the feeling that the birches and flowers were part of the room, and enhancing the Scandinavian look of the light woods and clean-lined furnishings. The only discordant note was a lush, Persian rug woven in shades of blue, black and red. The ornate pattern and bold colors seemed too busy for the spare Northern European décor.

The pressure of Abel's hand propelled me to the desk.

"Gail? What do you say? One room or two?"

"Oh, Abel, I don't know. One, I guess. One."

I watched Abel turn to the desk clerk and arrange our room for the night.

I looked out the windows at the water, not really seeing it. My feet felt glued to the Persian rug. On the ride up I had avoided thinking about whether I would agree to spend the night together.

Last week when Abel had proposed this trip to Door County to show my paintings to his friend Gil, who owned an art gallery I hadn't considered the possibility of staying the night. It was only a two-hour drive, after all. I thought we'd leave Kingman early Saturday morning, visit the gallery, have lunch somewhere nice, and then drive home, arriving around dark. Abel's call the night before, suggesting I pack an overnight bag so we could take our time and visit more than Gil's gallery, took me by surprise. I debated with myself over whether I was ready to take that big step or not, but then realized that in wearing my "best" undies on each of our dates I had already decided. I packed my toiletries, my favorite of my unworn Victoria's Secret nighties, a robe, and fresh clothes for Sunday in a small suitcase.

The ride up the Door County peninsula was beautiful but quiet. At first Abel tried to make conversation by commenting on the daffodils, but I had trouble answering. I hoped he thought I was nervous about showing my paintings. In reality, I could feel my little overnight bag pulsing in the back seat and the thought of spending the night with a man who wasn't Bert, wasn't my husband, was making my palms sweat and my throat tighten.

What would people think? What if the girls at Mavis' found out? What if my boys found out? I had to start talking about something, anything, to keep from driving myself crazy.

"So, Abel, how did you meet Gil? It must be very interesting owning a gallery in such a popular vacation spot."

"We met about twenty-five years ago when Gil was first starting out. Marcella wanted a painting for the living room, so we went to Chicago for a weekend to walk the galleries. Gil was the manager of the first one we visited, and he was very helpful, asked all sorts of questions to help us figure out what we'd like, and walked us through the purchase. Made a nice commission, too, I'll wager. Anyway, we liked him so much and he'd been so helpful we invited him to meet us at our hotel for a drink. After that, every time we went to Chicago for a play or an exhibit, we'd call him and have dinner."

"He sounds like a very nice man."

"He is you'll like him. We even met them up in Door County for weekends a few times."

"Is he married?"

"Yes, he's married. Gil's husband is Dennis."

"Oh."

"I was a bit uncomfortable at first, but once we'd spent some time together it seemed like the most natural thing in the world. Gil and Dennis are just like every other couple. You'll like them, you'll see."

"I'm sure I will. I really appreciate you introducing us. I guess it's time I show someone other than my friends my paintings and I wouldn't have known how to find a professional or who to call. This is a real opportunity for me."

"Don't worry, Gail." He reached across and patted my hand. "I'm sure he'll like your work. It's the kind of thing that really sells in a vacation spot like this."

It wasn't a long drive to Gil's gallery in Fish Creek, a small bayside town, but it was plenty of time for the little nagging voice in my head to keep saying, you're getting in over your head, Gail.

"Gail, are you okay?" Abel's voice interrupted the defeatist chant.

"Hmm?" It took a real effort to turn to look at him, turning my eyes away from the early afternoon sun streaming in.

He took his eyes off the road for a second to cast a worried look my way. "You've been gripping the edge of the seat and staring out the window like I'm taking you to your execution. I've been talking and talking, and you haven't said a word. Are you okay?"

I looked down at my white knuckles and consciously uncurled them. "Oh, I'm okay, just nervous," I said with a little laugh. "I keep hearing this voice telling me that things are moving too fast and I'm in over my head."

"Well, do you want to go back to the motel? I can call Gil and say you don't feel well or something."

"No! I'm not letting some negative part of me scare me away." I turned to face him. "Even if Gil says my paintings aren't right for him, I won't know unless I try. Keep driving." I put my elbow on the seat back and leaned into the soft leather. "I've spent most of my life being afraid of new things, different

254

things, different people, and only this last year or so have I been brave enough to face those fears." I reached and touched his sleeve. "I really appreciate you introducing me to Gil, Abel. You're a real friend."

A little red crept up from his collar and touched his ears. "Well, thanks, Gail. I've been having a lot of fun with you, too. I know you're going to be a hit up here." He slowed, turned on his signal, turned into a gravel lot, and parked. "Here we are."

I looked out the windshield to see a converted barn and outbuildings made into six or seven little shops. The haphazard construction over what looked like a hundred years of farmers' expansion turned out to be perfect for making each little façade unique. There was a bead "shoppe," a bookstore, a gift shop, a bakery, one with garden art, an artist's studio, and Gil's gallery. Since it was early in the tourist season not all the stores were open and there were only a few vehicles in the lot. I sat staring at my potential future for a minute.

Abel slapped his hands on the steering wheel, making me jump. "Well, let's unload and go see Gil."

I laid a hand on his arm. "Wait. I think it would be better to go in and meet Gil first; once we're acquainted, we can think about showing him my paintings. In fact, let's let him ask to see them. Keep a little of the power on my side of the fence."

He turned and looked at me with amazement. "Man, for someone so nervous when we started out this afternoon, you've sure got this figured out." He opened his door, got out, and came around to open my door. He bowed low as he swung it wide, his hand extended to me. "Milady?"

I reached my hand out to his. "Thank you, kind sir." The solemnity of the gesture was broken when he tugged me into his arms for a quick hug and a kiss on the neck, which made me giggle.

"Stop that." I pushed him away and smoothed my rumpled shirt. "Gil might see and think you're bringing some tootsie to meet him instead of a serious artist."

"Hmm, I never thought of that." He adjusted his collar and brushed the front of his jacket. "Madame?" He held out his arm and I slid mine into it; his left hand covered mine and patted it. "This is going to be great."

Gil, a distinguished man with a big city air, opened the door for us. "Abel, you sly fox, how have you been?" he said, and swept Abel into a hug. Like every man on the planet, they slapped each other on the back. They stepped apart and Gil looked around at me. "You must be Gail." He shook my hand. "Abel's told me a lot about you." Then he gave me a hug too. He looked around. "But I thought he said you were bringing me some of your paintings."

I was surprised he was so eager. "I thought we might get acquainted," I said, "before I overwhelm you."

"Nonsense. I'm looking forward to it. Abel, why don't you go get Gail's paintings while she and I get to know each other a bit." He shooed Abel out the door and led me to a white sofa in front of the bay window. "Can I get you something to drink?"

"No, I'm fine, thanks." He sat beside me and asked how long I'd been painting, what I thought my style was, whose classes I'd taken. He seemed impressed that I'd studied with Jacques Tunis. I told him I called him "Jake the painting Nazi" and he laughed so hard I thought he was going to roll off the couch.

"That's the perfect name for him. He's been terrorizing students for years, but he's really got an eye. If Jake likes your work, you've got it made, at least around here."

While we talked, I kept looking at the art hung on the walls and propped everywhere in the small space. Most were pastels and oils, not too many watercolors. A few of them looked like a child had painted them; they were flat, no perspective, but I really liked their energy and bright colors. I found out later that those were Gil's own work.

By then Abel had arrived with the first box of my paintings. Gil was like a kid at Christmas, pulling them out, unwrapping them, and turning them this way and that. "These are wonderful, Gail." Abel left to get the rest. "Help me take down some of these," he flapped a hand at the wall, "and we'll hang yours so we can get a real look at them." He and I worked together making a display of my work on the largest wall. He dived right into the last box of paintings as Abel carried them in, hanging them too, arranging the dozen works in a pleasing group, and stood back. "Well, you're sure not a beginner, Gail. Are you sure you've only been painting for a year?"

Abel said, "I told you, Gil. She's got real talent."

I could feel myself blushing. "Thank you both. I'm glad you like them."

Gil turned abruptly and walked to a door in a dim corner of the room, opened it, and shouted, "Dennis, Abel's here with his friend. Come see."

A middle-aged man with soft features wearing an apron came clattering down the stairs. "Gil, one of these days you're going to make me drop something, yelling at me like that. I jumped so just now I nearly lost a whole tray of rumaki. Knock it off. Hello, Abel." He gave Abel a one-armed hug and touched his cheek to Abel's shoulder.

Abel slapped his back and said, "Dennis, I'd like you to meet my friend Gail."

"It's so nice to meet you. Abel's been raving about the new woman in his life." He wiped his hands on his apron to shake my hand. "Sorry, I've been making us some little goodies. Abel, can you help me bring things down while Gil goes gaga over Gail's paintings?"

They went up the stairs and Gil turned to me. "Don't pay any attention to Dennis. He likes to tease. I don't go gaga over everyone. Now, let's see what we have."

I sat back on the couch to give him room. I couldn't take my eyes off him as he slowly walked back and forth, rearranging a few to make a better display.

Finally, he turned and said, "These are really good. I

think the tourists will like them. Now, let's get down to business. What prices were you thinking of?"

Shocked that he expected me to set prices, I said, "I have no idea." While we waited for Abel and Dennis to bring down the food and wine, Gil led me into the world of selling art. He explained about his commission and that many artists charge for the framing and throw in the art for free. Since I got the frames from Abel for free, we went back and forth trying to set prices for the various sizes of paintings that would give me a little profit.

By the time Dennis had arranged his delicious hors d'oeuvres on the table in front of the sofa and poured us each a glass of wine, Gil was in the process of choosing which of the paintings to take. He ended up taking seven of them, various sizes and subjects. He decided that my flowers would be most popular. He also encouraged me to mat smaller paintings that he could sell in the twenty-to-forty-dollar range. He called those "bread and butter," since nearly everyone can afford them. I promised to send some as soon as I got home.

We visited for an hour or so, and I was excited that Gil kept having to get up to greet customers. I hoped to see one of my paintings sold, but no one bought anything.

Gil could see how disappointed I was and put his hand over mine. "Don't worry, Gail. It's really too early in the season for the real art buyers to be up here. The tourists up here now are more middle-class and just like to look. It'll be okay. Trust me."

"I never trust people who say, trust me," I said, "but I guess I'll have to. Promise you'll call when the first one sells?"

He promised and even crossed his heart. Abel and I said our goodbyes and left to go back to our motel, promising to call them the next time we came up to Door County.

"Happy?" Abel asked as we drove away.

"I think so. I like Gil and Dennis, and I think Gil will do his best to show my paintings in their best light. Thanks again for making this happen."

"I haven't made anything happen. I just knew someone in the art world who could give you your first opportunity. You're the artist; it's your gift that makes things happen."

The sun had nearly set by the time we got back from Gil's. I drew the drapes to let in the golden light and opened the patio doors. The music of the wind and waves rushed into the room, filling it with sound and movement. Abel opened the bottle of wine, poured two glasses, and came to sit beside me on the patio.

He raised his glass and said, "To the next successful artist in Door County."

I touched the rim of my glass to his and was surprised by the ringing it made. "This is crystal," I said.

"Yes, it is," he said, looking deep into my eyes. "I wanted our first night together to be special."

Those four little words, our first night together, threw me into a mild panic. It had been too many years since someone had seen me naked. For all my passionate thoughts of the last few months I wasn't at all sure I was ready to take my clothes off in front of a relative stranger. I turned my gaze to the setting sun and gulped my wine. Abel reached and filled my glass without a word. I kept my eyes on the horizon until all the color had faded from the sky and my second glass of wine was empty.

When the sounds of the last family on the shore had faded, his voice came out of the darkness. "Gail?" I didn't make a sound. "Gail, shall we go in?"

I drew a deep breath, nodded though I doubt he could see, and stood up on shaky legs. My knees felt like they weren't going to work and, when they did, they felt jerky and out of control, like I'd just gotten a new set.

Silently Abel followed me, closed the sliding door, and drew the drapes. I stood like a statue, my hands at my sides, in the middle of the room while he lit a rose-scented candle and turned out the entry light. He came to stand in front of me, his hands caressing my arms, and said, "We've been waiting a long time for this." And he leaned forward and kissed me very softly on the lips.

At the first touch of his lips on mine, I could feel my tight muscles relax. Abel kissed my lips again, a little nibbling kiss, and began kissing my jaw and eyes, moving to kiss my ears, sliding down my neck to my collarbone, all the time murmuring my name.

When his lips touched the hollow of my throat, a rush of heat flooded my body and unlocked the nervous tension that had frozen me. My head fell back and my hands finally came to life, gripping his arms to keep him from stopping. I pulled him closer, one hand under his chin, gently guiding his lips back to mine. We kissed, a long passionate kiss. A kiss that should have been in the movies. A kiss for the record book, if the world was smart enough to keep records of such things. A kiss I felt in every cell.

I don't know if I broke the kiss or Abel did, but soon his gentle fingers were unbuttoning my blouse and sliding it off my shoulders. I shivered, not with cold or nerves, but from the sensual feel of his hands on my skin. My fingers moved with a will of their own to find the buttons of his shirt and I concentrated on slipping the little plastic disks out of their impossibly tiny holes. Abel shrugged out of his shirt and tossed it aside.

His calloused palms raised goosebumps on my arms as they traced their way over the satin and lace of my bra. My nipples pushed at his palms, pleading to be set free. He dipped his face into the cleft between my breasts and kissed and licked the tender skin there while he reached behind me to unhook my bra. I moaned as the scrap of fabric fell away and arched my back to press my breasts to his chest. His springy gray chest hair scratched my nipples as he pulled me into his embrace. Time stood still as we reveled in the feel of our bodies entwined.

I felt Abel's hands slide down my back and slip under the

waistband of my jeans. I hadn't noticed him undoing the snap and pushing down the zipper. The warmth of his hands made me press myself to him to drink in the hint of warm cinnamon rising from our flesh. I felt for his belt, unbuckled it, and unzipped his fly. I slid my hands around his waist and felt his slacks fall away. The sound the fabric made slipping off was like a sigh or maybe he sighed, I don't know.

Abel took my hand in a courtly gesture as we stepped out of the puddles of our pants and twirled me as if we were dancing.

"Music?" he asked.

It was a struggle to form my answer. "No."

Our bodies came back together as if they were magnetized. We kissed and caressed, moving toward the king-size bed. Without breaking the kiss, Abel reached and flipped the covers back. We slid beneath the cool white sheets.

In the flickering candlelight, Abel's face loomed over me. "I love you, Gail. You're so beautiful."

"I love you too, Abel," I said, cupping his face with my hands and pulling his lips to mine.

The candle flame flickered in a pool of wax in the jar by the time we pulled the covers into some semblance of order and snuggled together to sleep.

In the morning, we walked to the Swedish pancake house a block from the motel. Sitting across from each other, surrounded by chattering families, vacationing couples, and hungry locals, I felt self-conscious as if everyone knew what we had done. But I also couldn't keep from smiling. Abel and I held hands until the waiter arrived to take our orders and pour coffee. I couldn't help but feel we were in a spotlight. People kept looking at us as if there was a flashing arrow 'ointed at us. As if they knew we were unmarried and had spent the night tangled in each other's arms.

Abel looked at me over the rim of his coffee mug. "What are you thinking? You keep blushing and then turning pale.

Are you feeling all right?"

I could feel the blush flood my cheeks again. "I'm thinking about last night," I said.

"Me too," he said with a little growl.

"As I started to say before you interrupted, I keep feeling like everyone knows and disapproves."

He set his mug down with a click. "Boy, you sure spend a lot of time thinking about what people say about what you do, don't you?"

Feeling like a reprimanded child, I shrugged and said, "I guess."

A big grin spread across his face. "Well, quit it. Nobody has the right to tell you what to do, Gail. You're a grownup, remember?"

A bit of my initial annoyance with him sparked back to life. "Yes, Abel, I do remember that I'm a grownup. This last year or so has been difficult with all my children and friends feeling like it's their duty to object to the changes I've made." I took a sip of coffee and leaned back to allow the waiter to serve my breakfast. "You have no idea how difficult it's been to dodge and deflect all the well-meaning opinions and advice." I picked up my fork and waved it under his nose. "You men have always been allowed to be yourselves. Women have had to conform to archaic roles put in place by the men who've run our society for centuries." I stabbed my fork into a sausage, nearly cracking the plate.

"Wow, Gail, that was some speech." He leaned to whisper in my ear. "I have a great idea how you can put that energy to a better use. Check-out time's not until noon." He straightened up and smiled an impish smile, waggling his eyebrows. "What do you say?"

He looked so silly sitting there leering at me, I had to laugh. "I'll consider your suggestion, sir, but I'd like to finish my breakfast first. A girl needs to keep up her strength, you know."

We finished our breakfast, walked back to the motel,

and, after arranging a late checkout at two p.m., satisfactorily dealt with those waggling eyebrows.

Abel drove more slowly on the way home. I couldn't decide if it was to prolong our time together or because he was just plain tired.

CHAPTER 33

May

I got sweaty palms every time I thought about introducing Abel to the boys. I'd been giving little hints in my weekly emails about how much time we spent together. I had told them about the trips to galleries and art shows, about meeting Gil, and having my paintings in his shop. They knew about the movies we'd seen and how Abel had completely revamped my garden, at my invitation this time.

There was no way I was going to share the more, well, intimate aspects of our relationship. I didn't expect any of them to share that part of their lives with me and I certainly wasn't ready to expose mine.

I had cleaned the house to within an inch of its life. I plumped the pillows and moved the furniture around six times. I changed the sheets on my bed twice because every time I went in the bedroom, I detected the warm cinnamon fragrance I smell when Abel and I are together. I figured that would be a dead give-away, even if Able and I managed to keep our hands off each other while they were visiting.

Only Aaron and Sara had been home since the house redecoration was complete. I couldn't imagine what Sam would say when he saw that I'd changed everything in the place. Sam had always liked things to stay the same. I had the feeling that Matt wouldn't mind or even really notice.

I had to admit I wasn't nearly as nervous about their reaction to those changes as I was terrified at the thought that one of them would figure out that Abel sometimes slept over. If I had to bet, I'd put my money on Sara and Lisa being the ones to figure it out. I had a picture of the two of them huddled in a corner swapping theories.

That reminded me of something when I was upstairs checking to make sure everything was ready for the invasion. "Abel," I called down to him from the top of the stairs, "be sure your razor and things are out of the bathroom, please. I don't want to give any of them cause for suspicion."

His sexy chuckle wafted up as he passed the foot of the stairs. I heard him mutter, "All that nervous energy wasted on grown kids. I could tell her how to use that energy."

"What was that?"

He walked back past the foot of the stairs with his aftershave and razor in his hand. "Nothing, Gail, not a thing."

I went down the stairs and slid into his arms. "Listen, I spent a good piece of the last year complaining about you to them. It's going to take them some time to get used to us dating. I just don't think it would help any if the first time they met you was also the first time they were certain we're sleeping together." We kissed.

"Sleeping together isn't the most fun part, you know," he said, sliding his hand down my back to rest it on my behind.

I pressed into him. "I know. And no butt grabbing while they're here or I'll send you home."

The pressure of his hand grew and held me closer. "What time are they supposed to arrive? It would be a whole lot easier to behave if we..." He nodded toward my bedroom, eyebrows a-waggle.

"Oh no we're not. I'm not going to get caught in the sack with you by one of my kids, not at this age." I pushed myself out of his grasp and started back upstairs. I wasn't halfway up when I heard tires on the gravel drive. "Hah! You see?" I came back downstairs and joined him in the kitchen. "You'd have had us undressed and in a compromising position when they drove up." I noticed he was still holding his shaving things.

"Hide that stuff." He put his razor and aftershave into a paper bag and shoved it into the cupboard under the stairs. I peered out the window. "That's Matt and Lisa. They were supposed to pick up Sam and Merry, but I only see children's heads."

I stopped at the mirror in the hall and made sure my hair looked okay and that I didn't have any dirt smudges on my face. I grabbed Abel's hand and pulled him outside to greet the first arrivals. "Now, behave."

"Yes, ma'am."

It tuned out that my oldest had decided he and Merry needed their own vehicle for their visit home, which turned out to be a good thing. They drove in almost before Matt had unloaded the last suitcase. By the time all three boys and their wives and kids had arrived and dinner was on the table, I was a nervous wreck. I thanked God it was May, and my grandsons, all those noisy, energetic boys, could be sent outdoors to get dirty and holler to their hearts' content once the food had disappeared. Little Elizabeth stayed inside with us.

After supper, Abel took Aaron, Matt, and all three daughters-in-law out to see the redesigned garden before it got too dark. Sam volunteered to stay inside and help me clear the table and load the dishwasher. As he carried a stack of plates to the counter he said, "Why's he here?"

Looking up from putting the silverware in the dishwasher basket, I said, "Who?"

Sam nodded in the direction of the garden. "Abel Baker, the obnoxious jerk. I thought you didn't like him."

I straightened and stood facing him, hands on hips, "Don't you read my weekly emails?"

"Yeah."

"Well, when you read them, did you get a hint that I don't think he's such an obnoxious jerk anymore?"

"I guess." He turned back to the table for more dirty dishes. "I kind of thought he was a geezer you were taking pity on and spending a little time with."

I grabbed another handful of dirty forks and spoons and

went back to work. "I did write about going cross-country skiing and hiking in Door County, right?" He nodded. "Did you think I was pushing him along in a wheelchair or something?"

"Well, no, not really."

I looked into my son's unhappy face and softened my voice. "Then, what's bothering you?"

He sat down in one of the kitchen chairs and wiped his forehead. "I don't know, Mom. It just seems like you really like this guy, and I don't know anything about him." He looked up frowning, "And what about Dad?"

I sat down next to him and put my hand on his arm. "Honey, you know I loved Dad, but he's been gone for almost ten years now. That's a long time. Abel is the first man I've met who makes me laugh, seems to like me, and doesn't want me to change into someone I'm not. I'm having a good time with Abel."

"Yeah, Mom," he said, looking at me, "what if he decides he wants to marry you or something."

I reached over and hugged him. "I appreciate your concern, but we haven't even been dating a year. Abel hasn't said a word about marriage. Don't you worry. I'll let you know before I do anything drastic." And it's too late to worry about "or something," I thought. We're already "or something"-ing like crazy.

He sat back and rubbed his eyes, just like he had when he was little. "I worry about you, Mom, living out here all alone."

"I know you do, honey, and I appreciate it. I'm fine. Clara and Hank are right next door. And I'm a big girl now, I can take care of myself."

We finished loading the dishwasher, started it, and went outside to join the rest of the family. I watched Sam stand at the edge of the group and glare at Abel. I half expected Sam to slap him across the face with a glove and call him out for a duel. It was a relief when Abel said his goodnights and drove away.

It always took Sam a while to get used to the hubbub of all those children all in one place, but it was harder on Merry. She held herself aloof for a while, even from the adults, until she felt comfortable. As the only child of an eternally dissatisfied and chronic complainer of a mother, Merry needed to take her time in our noisy family get-togethers. But soon enough she was on the floor building Legos with the littlest ones. She and Matt's eldest, Jim, got along the best. Jim was a serious boy, more interested in reading than racing around with his brothers and cousin, so he and Merry were more alike. They took walks around the place talking and talking about who knows what.

Lisa and Sara always spent the first part of any visit comparing Mom-stories. Since Merry and Sam didn't have kids, and probably wouldn't, she had nothing to contribute to those discussions.

It took a while for Merry to shed her big-city sophisticate air, too. But by bedtime of the first night she was back to the Merry we all knew. I think the other daughters-in-law were a bit intimidated by her stylish dress, her expensive haircut, and her name-dropping of places and people they'd only read about or seen in movies. But the three girls managed to find some common ground, even if it was just comparing notes about how alike, and annoying, their husbands were.

The next day Merry, Sara, Lisa and I sat on the porch watching the kids play hide-and-seek in the orchard. After a while, I went into the kitchen to put on a pot of tea. The weak afternoon sun struck rainbows from the cut glass bowl of stem-less daffodils my littlest grandsons had picked for me that morning. I opened the bag of loose tea and breathed in the scent of spices and orange peel. As the kettle on the stove started to grumble and thump, I pulled out Mom's old Brown Betty teapot and four mismatched mugs.

Sam had come in right behind me for a quick trip to the bathroom, he said. When he came out, I turned around to see all three of my sons lounging around the room. Aaron leaned on the fridge, Matt was in his childhood place at the table, and Sam stood at the sink.

"Oh, you startled me," I said. "It won't take all of you to help carry out the tea tray."

One of those looks flashed among them and I knew they hadn't just happened to all show up there accidentally. I turned to face them, hands on hips. It was the pose I had used for years to scare the truth out of them. "Okay, what's going on?"

Sam had evidently been elected speaker. He folded his arms across his chest and glared at me the way I had seen him glare at a defendant. "Mother," he said, "are you sleeping with Abel Baker? And what are his intentions?"

"Oh, for the love of God," I said, with a laugh. "Is that what brought you all in here?"

"Just answer the question."

"Don't pull that lawyer crap with me, Samuel. Remember who you're talking to."

Sam didn't change his expression or his stance. "Are you sleeping with Abel Baker?"

"What makes you ask?" I said, playing for time.

Matt pulled a paper bag off his lap and said, "Mike and Luke were looking for games; they found this in the cupboard under the stairs."

"So? What makes you think it's not left over from when Dad was alive?"

Sam leaned over, picked up the razor, and brandished it in my face. "Because it's one of those new ones with five blades. Five-bladed razors weren't invented when Dad died."

I was suddenly so angry; I couldn't see straight. "Okay, yes, it's Abel's razor and, yes, I'm sleeping with him." I turned to face my accuser. "Are you happy now, Mr. Lawyer?"

Aaron spoke for the first time. "Why didn't you tell us, Mom?"

I whirled on him. "Do any of you call me when you and your wife have sex? Did you ask my permission before you did it the first time?"

Aaron and Matt looked at their shoes and mumbled, "No." Sam remained silent.

"It's none of your business if I'm sleeping with Abel, if I'm having sex with him, or whatever I choose to do with him. Or anyone else, for that matter."

Sam finally spoke. "We want to make sure you're safe, Mom. That's all. We don't want some gigolo scamming you out of your savings or talking you into selling Dad's farm."

I rounded on him. "Have you met Abel Baker? He's a well-to-do, cultured, retired gentleman who has plenty of his own money and thinks I'm pretty terrific. I have fun spending time with him no matter what we're doing, and he usually pays, even if I try to argue him out of it." I stepped closer so we were nearly nose-to-nose. "And it's my farm. We used my dowry for the down payment when we bought the place, and my salary paid it off." I held Sam's gaze, not blinking, not looking guiltily away.

After a minute that stretched for an hour, Sam's eyes shifted, he picked up the rental car keys from the table, went outside, and drove off.

My eyes followed him. I felt sick to my stomach. I always hated arguing and I especially hated arguing with those I love.

Matt's voice came from behind me. "Good job, Mom. You won the stare-down."

I started to cry. "Oh, Matt," my knees gave way, and I sat down hard on a kitchen chair, "I didn't want you boys to find out about Abel and me this way. I wanted you all to get to know him slowly, wanted you to like Abel first, before I told you about us."

He and Aaron had the grace to look ashamed. "It wasn't our idea to confront you like that."

Aaron chimed in, "Yeah, Mom, we tried to talk Sam out of it, but he wouldn't listen."

I looked at my sons. "You let him boss you around just

like you used to do when you were kids? I thought you were all too grownup for that." I could tell by the looks on their faces that they had too. "I wondered why everyone shut up all morning when I walked into the room. This explains it; you were all discussing my sex life."

"Well, not just your sex life, Mom," Aaron said, "we were more worried about him talking you out of your money and the farm. Have you noticed that some developer has bought all the land along Westline Road? Sam heard they're going to build a raft of those mini mansions on that side of the township. There are a lot of new companies, insurance companies and such, moving to the north side of Simpson."

He turned to Matt. "Didn't you say you bid on machinery repair for one of those contractors?" Matt nodded, once, but kept his mouth shut.

Aaron continued talking, trying to work his way out of a jam with his mouth, like he had since he was a kid. "It'll be easy to sell those junior executive-type homes out this way to all the little office rats they'll be hiring; they love to pretend they're country people. How do you know Abel's not a part of that? How do you know he's not just being nice to you to get you to sell out for cheap?"

Reluctant to fall into the trap of defending an innocent man, but seeing no other way, I said, "Because Abel has been passing around petitions and trying to drum up local support to make the zoning rules so strict the developer will sell out and move on. The guy has a terrible reputation; he's the one who defaulted on that subdivision outside of Edgerton last summer. So, I know Abel's not in cahoots with the guy because he's trying to derail the project. And before you ask, I don't think Abel's a good enough actor to pretend to be against the deal when he's really for it. Every one of his emotions is plain on his face."

Aaron looked at Matt and shrugged as if to say, well, I tried, now it's your turn.

Matt straightened up and said, "Mom..."

But I had heard enough. "Don't say another word, either of you." I stood up and walked out onto the porch. "I'm going for a long walk. I need some fresh air." I put on my old barn jacket. "Don't wait supper." I left.

I walked down the driveway and turned past the mailbox to head into the woods. "Grandma, can we come?" I heard a chorus of grandsons shout at me. Then I heard their mothers call them back. I knew they had heard the argument. Good, I thought, at least they have the grace to leave me alone now, even if they aren't mature enough to keep their noses out of my business.

I took a long walk. I walked all around the edges of the farm, thinking of how sorry I was to have invited the boys home to meet Abel. Thinking, too, I should have written more about how my feelings had changed about him. Maybe they wouldn't have been as relaxed meeting him at first but knowing we were dating might have avoided the ugly words we'd just exchanged. I cried and walked, fumed and walked, until the light was fading, and I got back to the house and sat on the porch. I could hear the rest of the family in the kitchen making supper. I wasn't hungry. I sat there with my arms folded across my chest and watched as the sun set on a day I'd rather forget.

I hadn't been there long when I heard a car approaching. It was Sam. He parked the rental car in the driveway, got out, and walked directly to sit beside me on the porch. "I'm sorry, Mom," he said.

I didn't look at him. "Sorry is not enough this time, Sam."

"But…"

"No buts, Sam." I turned to look at him in the golden sunset light. "You were way out of bounds. How dare you confront me like that?"

My oldest turned his face to stare into the fading glow. "We're all worried about you. You've changed so much in the last year; we don't recognize you. Merry thought maybe you'd had a stroke, but Sara reassured her you were just finding yourself. I didn't know what that meant."

Not yet willing to be placated, I said, "I appreciate your concern, but are you so self-centered that you can't allow anyone to change? For the first time in my life, I have no one but myself to please. I spent my entire life being a dutiful daughter, an obedient wife, and a mother to three boys I'm very proud of. Or at least I was until this afternoon."

"Mom, I..."

"Let me finish. Your dad and I tried to raise you to be strong, independent men and, until today, I thought we had. That little spectacle in the kitchen leads me to believe we raised three bullies." I let the silence drag out. "It's your turn now."

Twilight had faded and the glow of the lights from the living room kept his face in shadow. "I'm sorry, Mom. I, uh, well, Merry came back from visiting her mom this morning and Prudence had told her all the gossip that's been swirling around about you. And about Abel, too. How he's had two or three girlfriends a year since his wife died. How you and he have been seen mauling each other all over town. She told Merry that Abel Baker's a money-grubbing gigolo out after only one thing."

I fell back in shock. My arms uncrossed and my hands dropped into my lap. "And you believed her?"

"Yeah, I did. I could see how much he likes you and how much you like him. I'm not used to seeing you flirt with anyone, Mom. And then when the boys found his razor hidden in the cupboard, I guess I just snapped. I feel like I've lost control."

Angry words leapt to my lips, but I tamped them down. "Prudence Christian is an unhappy woman who thinks the worst of everyone, you know that. You probably don't know she set her cap for Abel right after Marcella died and was rebuffed." I took a deep breath, my hands balled into fists in my lap. "You also know that whenever Merry visits her mother she falls right back into her nasty traps. I can't count the number of times you've complained that it takes Merry nearly a month to get back to normal after that harpy visits San Francisco. How could you just swallow her lies and half-truths so easily?"

"You're right." He shook his head. "You're right. I didn't think."

"No, you didn't." I reached out and touched his back. "And I hate to break this to you, Sam, but you're not in control of anyone's life but your own. You don't have to take your dad's place at the head of the family. I let you take over for a while right after Dad died because, frankly, I was just paralyzed by how sudden it was. When you went away to college, I thought you understood that was over. You need to take a look around." I waved toward the house where rest of the family inside gathered around the table. "All of us are adults. The three of you are married, Aaron and Matt have their own kids. I try not to interfere in your lives, it's time you let me have mine."

He sat back in his chair and took my hand. "I'm sorry, Mom. I got carried away. It's just when Merry hammers at me like that, I lose it."

"You know I love Merry. I think she's a good wife for you, but maybe you ought to think about sending her for a little counseling, maybe couples counseling. Living out in California I'm sure there's some sort of therapy on every street corner."

Sam laughed, a soft little chuckle. "Yeah, California, land of fruits and nuts. Actually, Merry's been in counseling for years, but I never thought about going too. Maybe it would help her more if we both went."

"That's a good idea. Why don't you find one of those weekend things where you're at a mountain lodge or a beach house? Get some help in a beautiful place. Getting out of your familiar rut is sometimes good medicine all on its own."

"That's why I looked for a firm out there in the first place. I thought maybe getting Merry away from here and her mom's constant barrage of complaints would be good for both of us."

"And...?"

He stood up and looked into the night, then he sat on the porch rail facing me. "It's been good. She loves her job. She's even getting better at weathering Prudence's weekly calls, but she still falls back when they're together." He pushed himself to his feet. "C'mon, Mom, something smells really great in there. We'd better grab some before the ravening hordes eat it all."

It would take a while for my hurt feelings to heal, but I was glad to start back on the road to family harmony. We'd see how things went the next day; Abel had invited us all over to his place for a picnic.

My sons and their spouses were subdued at breakfast the next morning. Sam was especially eager to help make the potato and fruit salads I planned to take to Abel's picnic. He also insisted I ride with them. "You'll be much fresher when we get there. No grandkids crawling over you in the car."

I refrained from reminding Sam that children ride in car seats these days; I was sure he'd interpret it as a dig that he and Merry hadn't produced any grandchildren. I suppose getting me to the picnic in a "fresher" state was Sam's way of apologizing for being a total bastard about my relationship with Abel the day before. I had been tempted to call Abel after everyone went to bed, but Matt and Sara decided to watch a late movie and I was tired from fighting and walking. Besides if I'd called Abel and told him about the boys' discovery and accusations, he'd have gotten angry and wouldn't be his usual hospitable self, so I was glad I hadn't called.

Merry commented on the neighborhoods and estimated property values as we drove. I could tell by her tone that Sam had told her that it was her mother's accusations that had sparked our argument the day before. She had the bright look in her eyes that told me she'd been crying, and her voice was high, bordering on squeaky, with the desire to make up. I decided to let her twist in the wind of her own words for a while. That would give both Sam and me a break.

By the time we pulled up in front of Abel's, Aaron and Matt were already there. They'd parked behind each other, gotten everyone out of the cars, and were standing in a line, their children gathered around them, all staring silently at the house.

"Oh, for heaven's sake," I said as I got out of Sam's car. "Cheer up. This picnic will only be a battlefield if you make it one."

Matt and Lisa exchanged a silent look. Matt licked his lips and said, "Are you planning to tell him...?"

I handed him the bowl of potato salad. "Not today." I looked each of my sons in the eye. "Today I'm calling a truce. No pardons yet, but you all behave here, and I'll think about it." I could see the surprised looks on the faces of my oldest grandsons. I guess they hadn't imagined that the dads who yelled at them when they misbehaved could get yelled at too. "Now, paste smiles on your faces and let's go."

I led the way up the walk. Abel had tied helium balloons on the porch posts that made Elizabeth gurgle and lean to try and grab them. I heard Merry whisper, "Looks like a kiddie party." I glared at her.

Before I could say anything, Abel opened the door. "Come in, come in." He smiled at my family as if we were just what he'd hoped to find on his porch. "Welcome, Logans."

My family filed silently into the house, standing in a cluster in the entryway. David, Jim, and the twins stood together in front of me, a grandson fence, looking like they were the ones who'd been yelled at. I leaned over them and kissed Abel's cheek. "Thanks for inviting us. What can we do to help?"

He took the bowl of fruit from my hands. "Nothing, everything's ready." He surveyed my silent family, and his smile slipped a bit. "Why don't we all go out back?" He turned to lead the way.

As we passed through the kitchen, David said, "Look, Grandma, Mr. Baker's got a painting that looks like one of yours."

"Good eye, David," Abel said, winking at me. "Your grandma painted it. I'm her biggest fan."

The backyard was beautiful. All of Abel's spring flowers were in bloom and the scent of lilacs floated on the light breeze. There were two patio tables with umbrellas set on the grass with a pile of toys between them. The boys immediately ran to sort through them. Abel put the bowl he carried on a separate table on the deck and directed Matt to put the potato salad next to it. "I'll just run inside and get the rest of the food."

Sara said, "Why don't you let us do that, Abel? Just tell us what to get." Lisa nodded her willingness to help. Merry shot Sara a glance that said she wasn't quite ready to give up her mother's opinions.

"That's very nice of you ladies; then I'll start the grill." He turned to Aaron, "Unless one of you would like to..."

Aaron looked at Sam and shrugged. "Sure thing, Mr., uh, Abel."

Abel showed him where he kept the charcoal and starter, then went to help the girls with the rest of the food. "I hope it's okay," Abel said as he followed them into the house. "I got burgers and hot dogs. Everybody likes those, right?" My daughters-in-law assured him that he'd chosen the perfect meal for a May picnic. In a few minutes the four of them were back with platters of cut-up vegetables and dip, deviled eggs, and baskets of buns that they arranged on the table holding my contributions and what looked like an entire grocery store of condiments. When I commented to Abel that I'd never seen so many kinds of mustard and pickles he shrugged and said, "I wasn't sure what everyone liked so I got it all." He slid his arm around my waist and pulled me close. "Everybody looked so solemn when you got here; anything wrong?"

I leaned on his shoulder for a minute. "Not really. Just a

little difference of opinion."

"About me?"

I looked up into his blue eyes and saw doubt reflected there, so I lied. "No. Now let's get this party going. I'm hungry."

"Whatever you say." He leaned and kissed my hair. "Your wish is my command."

As he walked away toward the grill I laughed. "Don't spoil me; you might be sorry."

"I haven't been sorry so far," he said over his shoulder

Matt had wandered toward the back corner of the yard where Abel was putting up a garden shed with an attached greenhouse. "You building this from a kit, Abel?" he asked.

Able looked up from checking the still blazing charcoal. "Yes, it's a kit but I'm adding a few improvements." He started walking toward Matt; Sam and Aaron followed him.

In no time, the grill forgotten, all four men had their sleeves rolled up and they were playing with wood, saws, and hammers.

I watched them for a while, then I spread out the coals, brushed off the grill, and got ready to put the meat on to cook.

"Isn't that just like men?" I hadn't heard Lisa approach.

"What do you mean?" I asked.

"Well," she said, "yesterday Sam had almost convinced Matt and Aaron that you were dating Satan." She gestured toward the happy, sweaty, hammering men. "Give them a way to get dirty and they're best friends."

By the time the burgers and dogs were ready to eat, all the men in my life were smiling. Sam detoured past me on his way inside to wash up. "I'm really sorry for all that stuff I said yesterday, Mom. Abel's all right. I approve."

"Well, thanks, Sam." Under my breath when he was too far away to hear me, I continued, "Not that I need your approval to live my own life, but thanks."

Just then, Jim ran up looking at me like I was nuts, and said, "Who are you talking to, Grandma?"

"Just myself. Hurry and get cleaned up, we're ready to eat." For the first time in twenty-four hours, I took a deep breath, and I could feel my muscles relax.

Abel's menu was a huge success. By the time everyone was finished eating only crumbs and smears of catsup remained, most of it decorating my grandchildren. While we women cleaned up, Abel and my sons went back to working on the shed. The grandsons had endless wars with the squirt guns they'd found at the bottom of Abel's pile of toys. Lisa confiscated all of them after receiving a blast in the face when she stepped into the line of fire while carrying an armload of dirty plates.

As the sun began to set, Abel built a bonfire in his fire pit and brought out s'mores makings. We sat on log seats toasting endless marshmallows for the boys. I gathered from the conversation among the men that they were almost done with the garden shed. I was surprised to hear Sam insist that the three of them would be happy to come back in the morning to help finish the job. I had to smile at the pleased look on Abel's face. Guess I raised them right after all.

CHAPTER 34

June

I put the phone down and sat down hard on the nearest chair. I couldn't believe what I'd just heard. It had been Gil, the Door County gallery owner, calling to tell me he'd sold the last of the seven paintings I'd left with him less than two months ago. At first when I heard his voice, I was sure he was calling to tell me he'd sold the first of my paintings. How nice, I thought, I wonder if he calls all his artists when the first of their works is sold.

Then he said, "Gail, I'm so glad I caught you at home. I need you to drive up, today if you can, and bring at least ten more paintings. I'm completely out and I can't have gaps like this for the weekend. Your work is selling like crazy. Can you come up today? Please?"

I had to ask him to repeat himself. I heard him chuckle when I said, "What? Say that again. What? You can't be serious." But he was serious. I got an immediate knot in my stomach. Fear was a familiar friend; I'd spent a lot of my life being afraid of new experiences. I'd fooled myself quite a bit this last year into thinking that I'd gotten brave, that I reveled in new challenges. And there I sat feeling sweat trace its way down my spine, feeling a cold prickling in my hands and feet.

I needed to tell somebody. I needed to find someone who could convince me that this was a good thing. I called Abel's number but got his answering machine. Then I remembered he was working. I called the Garden Center and had him paged.

"Gail, what's wrong?" he said, panting into the phone.

"Nothing's wrong, Abel, nothing at all."

"Why did you call then? It scared me half to death when Lou Ann told me you were calling."

I took a deep breath to calm my racing heart. "Gil called just now."

"What did he want? He can't want us to pick up your paintings so soon." I could hear the sound of customers and cash registers behind him.

"He wants me to drive up there today with more paintings."

"Why does he want more; didn't he say seven would be enough? Just a minute." I heard him turn away to answer a question about planting apple trees. "Okay, I'm back but you'd better make it quick. We're really swamped today."

"Okay, I'll be brief. Gil sold all of the paintings we took up there and wants more."

"Holy cow! Gail, that's wonderful. Congratulations."

I had to pull the phone away from my ear when he yelled. "Thanks. Anyway, I was hoping you could drive up with me but since you're at work and so busy, I guess you can't." I was ashamed of how whiny I sounded. I cleared my throat and tried again. "It's no big deal, Abel. I'll ask Clara to ride along. I'll call you when I get home."

"Okay, Gail, I'm sorry but I've got to run. Talk to you tonight. Love you. 'Bye."

"I love you too." But I was talking to the air.

Well, rats. Abel was my first choice to help me take a car full of paintings up to Gil. But Clara would be willing to haul paintings too, and she might get a kick out of seeing my work in a gallery. I gave her a call; she was free and more than willing to help.

It didn't take long to load the paintings in the car. Gil had asked if I had any more of the painting I'd done of my mailbox covered in flowering vines, so I packed two other ones I'd done of that part of my garden. The first ones I'd taken to Gil's were all flowers and landscapes. This time I included a couple of shore and lake views I'd done since my first trip up there with Abel. The only painting I wasn't willing to part with was the beach scene I'd painted last winter in the midst of a blizzard. After seeing it hanging in my kitchen, Abel said he'd take me to the Caribbean next winter to see things like that myself. He said we'd call it a research trip instead of a vacation. I couldn't wait.

Clara and I set off in fine good humor. Except for the backseat piled with paintings it was just like old times. We laughed and joked like we had before. I hoped this day would reassure her once again that she was still my best friend. She brought me up to date with the doings of her kids. She even reported that Dan and the new florist in town, Moira, had gone into Simpson together to see a movie the week before. She felt pretty smug that she'd scooped the gossips at Mavis' about Moira, and that her matchmaking ploy in sending the pretty young woman to Dan to have the heater in her van fixed had worked out so well.

We drove straight to Gil's gallery in Fish Creek, arriving just before noon. Gil rushed out to greet us and nearly knocked me over, he was so happy to see more paintings. It didn't take the three of us very long to unload the car. Gil spent the whole time telling me about the sale of my paintings. He was a good storyteller; he remembered every comment and compliment. It was thrilling and more than a little humbling.

Clara was quiet as we worked. I think she hadn't really believed that people would want to buy my work and I could see that listening to Gil was making her reconsider how she thought about my painting. It made me glad I'd asked her to come along.

Gil asked both of us to help hang the pictures. I loved it because he was so knowledgeable and knew just how to feature each one. He used a long pole to adjust the track lights on the ceiling to wash each painting with just the right light.

When we were ready to leave, he kissed and hugged us

both. He held my shoulders, looked me straight in the eye, and said, "I hope you're working hard, Gail. I plan to keep you busy for a long time." He reached behind him to his desk and picked up an envelope. "Here's a check for the paintings I sold. I want to take a bunch of your work along for the city gallery when we go back to Chicago in October. There are lots of people in the city who would love a little piece of Wisconsin hanging on their wall."

"Thanks, Gil," I said, "I'll keep painting."

Clara piped up, "I'll make sure she does."

I threw an arm around her shoulders. "Oh boy, I'm in trouble now. Clara can be a real task master."

Just then a car pulled up and two very well to do looking couples got out. Gil's eyes lit up. "I'd better get back to work. These are old friends and I know they're going to love your work. Thanks for racing up here today." He kissed my cheek once more and hurried over to greet them.

As Clara and I walked back to my car, we could hear one of the women say, "Gil, everyone at dinner last night was raving about a new artist you've discovered. I think her name is Gail Logan?"

Clara and I stopped walking and stared at each other, not making a sound.

"Margaret said she'd bought the last one yesterday," the woman continued. "Now that's not the truth, is it? I hope you saved one for me."

We heard Gil's smooth gallery owner voice say, "No, I didn't save you one, Emily, but Gail delivered more this morning. Why don't I show you what she brought? You just missed meeting her."

I took one look at my rumpled jeans and sweaty t-shirt, grabbed Clara's elbow, and raced us to the car. I was afraid Gil would come out and insist I go back in to meet that formidable-sounding woman and I didn't think my current attire would impress her at all.

Clara was quiet on the ride home. Even when we

stopped at *Joe's Bar* in Duval, our favorite country tavern, to eat the best burgers on the planet, she seemed distracted.

"Cat got your tongue?" I asked after we ordered.

She slowly shook her head, then said, "No, I've been thinking."

"What about?"

"Well," she showed me a little embarrassed smile, "I guess I never really believed that someone I know could be a famous painter. I mean, I like your paintings, don't get me wrong." She held up her hand to forestall any protests from me. I kept my mouth shut and let her talk.

"But the way that Gil guy was so glad to see you, and then that rich woman demanding to see your paintings... I guess I'll have to start treating you with a little more respect."

The waitress came and put our burgers and fries in front of us. I squirted catsup on the meat. I picked up my burger, careful not to let any of the fried onions slide out of the bun, and said, "You don't have to treat me with respect, Clara, but back to normal would be great."

She put the catsup bottle back in the center of the table after putting half the bottle over her fries, as usual, and picked up her burger. "Okay, it's a deal. Back to normal it is." The old Clara shone in her smile.

Neither of us said another word until our plates were empty of everything but catsup smears; food this good was meant to be gobbled.

CHAPTER 35

July

I had gotten a flier for a women's weekend of art back in May. It was kind of a kaleidoscope of things, painting, writing, pottery, papermaking, all sorts of things I'd wanted to try held at a resort in Door County. Participants stayed at the resort but went to different artist's studios for the sessions.

Clara saw the flyer on my table and looked through it. I suggested that she and I go, give her a chance to experience my new world. I had been thinking of asking Abel to come with me, even if he just stayed in the room while I did the art, the weekend was for women after all, but decided he'd be too bored and too much of a distraction. Having Clara come with me was brilliant.

We shared a room, and she was nervous that first morning as we drove to the painter's studio. I could tell because she kept saying how she'd be the worst one in class, how I'd be the best and she'd suck.

There were about half experienced painters and half beginners in the group. The artist, a vigorous man in his late seventies, gave those of us who had some experience permission to paint along or to do something different while he concentrated on the women who had never held a brush before. I decided not to paint along with the group so Clara wouldn't feel self-conscious.

The first thing he asked the beginners to do was a "glaze & silhouette" painting, a real beginner step I thought was a brilliant project to begin with.

He had a stack of templates for them to trace onto their paper and then go over with pencil. He suggested they use only indigo paint so they didn't have to deal with paints blending together, glaze the paper with a graduated wash, and then fill in the tracing with barely diluted indigo. Their choices were simple things: a tractor, an Amish buggy, a deer, two guys fishing in a boat, and an Amish guy driving a horse-drawn wagon (back view). Clara chose the last one.

When she showed it to me, I said I thought she did an okay job, although she said, "Gail, I think it looks like the horse and driver are sitting side by side, and the horse is driving." I looked at it again and I had to agree. The lack of perspective made the image flat.

The woman at the next table looked at Clara's painting when she heard us discussing it and, through a fit of giggles, said, "Honey, to me it looks like Scooby Doo driving that wagon."

We took a closer look at it and she was right. Clara had painted a watercolor of Scooby Doo on a date with an Amish guy. We laughed so hard the teacher gave us a dirty look.

Next, he asked them to try a two-color one. Clara picked the stencil of the two guys fishing since she and Hank love to fish. The teacher suggested that everyone first put a yellow glaze over the paper and then put in the sky and water with an indigo overglaze.

Clara's painting turned out pretty well, but the fishermen were turned away from each other and looked really tense. "This looks like Hank and me when nothing's biting and we've spent the morning arguing about money or one of the kids," she said, waving the paper at me. "Judging from these two failures, you don't have to worry about competition from me."

But she laughed as she said it. I agreed that perhaps painting wasn't the right hobby for her. I was relieved she wasn't angry or frustrated.

After a box lunch in the orchard near the painting studio we drove to a poet's cottage. Stepping into her space was like walking into a sorcerer's den. Sari fabric in jewel tones draped the wall of windows like a rainbow, incense and candles scented the air, and she had soft overstuffed chairs all around the room piled with pillows. She presented each of us with a beautiful, handmade book to write in and encouraged us to carefully choose a writing implement from the pots of them on the table. Clara and I each grabbed a pen from one of the pots and hurried over to claim the couch so we could compare notes on how terrible our poetry was sure to be. Elena, the poet leading the workshop, was just what I imagined a poet should be. She wore soft flowing clothes, silver bracelets that clanked when she waved her hands around, and her hair was long and curly. I whispered to Clara that I thought Elena had dramatic presence. Clara giggled and then shushed me as Elena began speaking.

Her words were not what I expected. She spoke about spilling out our lives and experiences on paper so we could enjoy them again, learn from them, and share them with others if we chose to. She read us a poem or two, free verse poems like the ones Abel likes, not the rhyming ones we'd learned in school, about summer and then asked us to write our own summer poem.

I opened the cover of my book and felt a bit intimidated by the blank page. I peeked at the other women in the circle and most of them were writing. When I looked at Clara I was amazed; in the few seconds I'd spent dithering she had nearly filled her first page. As she reached to turn the page, I heard her say, "oh" in a small voice.

Thinking I'd better get a move on if I wanted to have more than the word summer at the top of my page when Elena told us to stop, I started just making a list of the things I love about summer, the soft air, the long days, the thunderstorms. Not a real poem, I thought, but when Elena called a halt and asked people to share, most of them were like mine, a list. Not bad but then it was Clara's turn.

She started reading in a small voice but soon she got braver, and her voice got louder and a real poem came out.

Iron gray clouds pour over the horizon
filling the sky with dread.
The thunder of their approach
rolls across the day in an avalanche of sound.
Lightning forks stab the earth,
weaving the corners of the storm together.
Cold fingers of breeze snake
through the trees.

The first swollen drops explode on the ground,
laying the foundation for the coming torrent.
Hail dances on the street and pecks at the panes,
bringing a touch of ice to the sultry afternoon.
Siamese twins of thunder and lightning
boom and crack as they race by.
Sheets of rain hammer the flowers,
sluice down the gutters to foam through
parched grass.

The storm, quickly expended,
flicks diminishing drops
that sway in the shifting winds.
Blades of sunlight shred
the trailing edge of storm clouds,
summon rain ghosts
to replenish them.
The diamond sparkle of drops
on leaves makes
prisms as the sun sets.

When she finished reading no one said a thing, no one clapped, nothing. Finally, Elena said, "Well, that was impressive." You could hear everyone let out their breath in a sigh.

Instead of deflecting the compliment like she would usually do, Clara just sat looking at her notebook like she didn't recognize her own handwriting.

I leaned over to her and said, "Wow, that was great, Clara."

She looked at me with almost scared eyes and said, "I don't know where that came from."

Before we could say more, Elena was reading another poem and asking us to write again. I made another list and Clara made another terrific poem.

It was like that all afternoon; the rest of us were just pretending to make poems, Clara made them. I could see Elena's eyes shining as Clara read her words. When she thanked us for coming and said how well we'd all done, everyone in the room looked at Clara, knowing that something special had happened that day.

Clara kept staring at her hands like she didn't recognize them. She didn't complain about poetry the way she'd complained about painting that morning. She seemed almost in a trance.

As the other workshoppers got up to leave, Clara stayed put. I could see she was exhausted by what had happened; I was familiar with the feeling since that was what had happened to me when I started painting.

Elena came and sat down on the coffee table in front of us. She reached out and touched Clara's hand and said her name. Clara's head popped up like she'd had a shock and she said, "I don't know what happened to me. I'm so embarrassed."

"Embarrassed?" Elena said. "Why?"

Clara took a deep breath and said, "I came in here ready to be the worst, like I was this morning." I started to deny it, but she cut me off. "I expected to sit here beside Gail and make fun of myself and the poems everyone wrote. I expected you to be a silly caricature and for everyone to write poems like greeting cards. Instead, I made a fool of myself writing this stuff like I knew what I was doing."

"You didn't make a fool of yourself, Clara," I said.

"No, you didn't," Elena said. "You made poetry. And that's what you were supposed to do, what everyone was trying to do today. Your poems came fully grown, that's all."

I could see tears in Clara's eyes. "When we went around the circle to introduce ourselves and tell you a bit about us, nearly everyone had written poems, and a few had even been published. I made a joke that I was only here to keep Gail company and spend a weekend away from Hank doing girl things. Everyone laughed. I was happy with that. And then when you told us to write, I put the pencil on the page, and I couldn't stop."

"That's what every teacher hopes happens in her class."

Clara kept talking like she hadn't even heard Elena. "And then when I read what I'd written, it gave me goosebumps. No one spoke for a long time after I read, not even you, Elena. I thought it was because what I wrote was so terrible. And I didn't want to stop writing."

Elena leaned back and a laugh catapulted from her throat. "Terrible? Oh, my Lord, Clara, I was speechless, yes, but because what you wrote was so good, so exactly right."

Tears were streaming down Clara's face, and my face, and Elena's face. Three menopausal women, all crying over a friend's triumph. "I hope you keep writing, Clara," said Elena, as she tucked another of her handmade books into Clara's hands. "You have a lot to say that people will want to read."

Clara whispered, "I don't think I can stop."

As I drove us away from Elena's studio Clara asked if we could stop somewhere so she could buy another notebook. When I reminded her that she already had two, she said, "The way I feel right now, Gail, that won't get me to bedtime." Then she laughed, a real Clara laugh, rich and from deep inside. "Is this how you felt when you started painting?" she asked.

"Oh, it is exactly how I felt. I wasn't sure there was enough paint in the whole state for all the art I wanted to make."

I found a bookstore in one of the little towns on the peninsula where they had a whole row of journals and notebooks. Clara said she just wanted a plain old spiral notebook like the ones we sent our kids off to school with, but I insisted that, at least at first, she deserved to have the best, prettiest book we could find for her to write in. Later on, when making beautiful poetry was old hat she could scribble in the ten for a dollar ones, but for now only the best would do. We giggled over choosing the perfect one for her and then she spent an hour looking at the books of poetry on the shelf. She kept piling them in her arms until, as she said, she'd spent all her egg money for the whole year on books.

Neither of us needed the wine we had with dinner to make us drunk. We were drunk with happiness and Clara's excitement at the part of her she'd discovered that day.

Back in the room, I read for a while and finally turned out my light at midnight. I fell asleep looking at my best friend piled up in her bed with two pillows at her back and one in her lap, hunched over her second notebook, pencil flying.

CHAPTER 36

August

"Thank goodness it's cool. I'd hate to be doing this in that heat and humidity we had last week," Abel said as he carried another pair of framed watercolors to his truck.

"It's cool because the sun hasn't come up. We'll fry later, I'm afraid," I said, trailing behind him with a box of matted but unframed paintings. "Keep moving. I want to be there by six o'clock so we can get set up before the sun's too high." I set the carton on the tailgate of the truck, pushed it next to the others, and turned back to haul more things. "We should have gone up yesterday. I hate to rush."

He came out of the house with another armload of paintings and heard me. "There weren't any rooms nearby and the ones further away cost the earth, remember? It's going to be fine. We'll have plenty of time to set up and relax before the customers come." He stopped walking. "Gail, you have to stop borrowing trouble. You're going to worry yourself right into the ground." He gently laid the paintings in a big box lined with mover's blankets he'd built in the bed of his pickup to keep the framed art from getting damaged. "There. That's the last of them." He straightened up, pressed his hands into his lower back, and stretched. "Now we just need to grab the cooler and get rolling."

"You filled it with water and ice?"

"Yes, I did, Miss Worrywart. You have your easel, board, and paints?"

I went back to the truck to check. "Yep. All I need is the bag with my hat and sunscreen and I'm ready." I turned and started back to the house. "I think."

He fell into step beside me and hugged me to his side. "You'll be fine. I'll be there to fetch and carry and, besides, by noon or one o'clock at the latest, I'm sure you'll be sold out and we can come home."

"Dreamer," I said, bumping his hip with mine. "We'll probably end up hauling most of this stuff home and that'll be the end of my art career."

He held the door to the porch open for me. "Oh, right. After Gil's sold how many of your paintings in how many months?"

"He's sold about a dozen."

"That's all? In how long?"

"Three months. Okay, you're right. My paintings are doing well. I'll scale back my worrying."

He walked out of the room for one last pit stop saying, "I'll believe that when I see it."

It was nice driving up to Door County watching the sun rise. We got to the Jacksonport Town Park just after six. There were a few artists and crafters already setting up but most of the people there were huddled around an industrial sized coffeepot near the registration table. Abel parked the truck, and we walked over to check in and find out where our booth was.

The woman at the table was trying to do ten things at once, talking to volunteers, directing the placement of signs along the road, shuffling papers, and greeting artists. "Gail Logan? Hmm, let's see." I was amazed she could find anything in the mess on the table, but she dipped into the middle of a stack and came out with my entry. "Here we are. You're in Booth 37, Gail."

"Thirty-seven? That's my lucky number," I said, thinking of the craft fair I did with Samara the winter before last.

She gave me a frazzled smile and stood up to point at the rows of white tents set up all over the park. "You're right at the end of the second row. Since you've been so kind as to agree to demonstrate your art, you've got a double tent." She looked at Abel. "You can pull over by the tent to unload. Then please park your vehicle in that big field across the highway. We'd appreciate it if you'd park at the far end so the paying customers can have the nearer spots." By then, three people were standing at her elbow and there must have been a dozen artists waiting to register.

Abel drove the truck to the booth while I walked over, trying to settle my nerves with a little exercise thinking, why I ever agreed to do an art fair, much less sit in public and paint, I'll never know.

By noon, I knew why I had entered this fair. Most, if not all, of the customers shuffling past my booth had made favorable comments and many purchased something. By noon, I understood I should have brought twice the number of smaller unframed paintings. By noon, I had painted two pictures—one of Lake Michigan, which lapped at the edge of the park, the other of a patch of purple clover that was blooming merrily at the edge of the tent—and sold them, right off my easel.

"Marge! Marge! Look, I found her," a gravelly male voice called from nearby. I looked around to see what Marge was so desperately seeking. Turns out it was me.

An expensively dressed retirement age couple met and conferred before stepping into my booth. The man took an unlit cigar out from between his teeth and thrust his hand out. "Little lady, we've been looking for you all day. Haggis Chandler's my name; Marge here saw your clover painting. She wouldn't leave off pestering me until I found you."

Haggis? What kind of name is that? I guess his mother wasn't too happy when he arrived. I tried to shake his hand without touching the wet cigar. "That's very flattering, Mr. Chandler."

"Call me Hag. Everybody does." He shoved the cigar back between his teeth. "This is my wife, Marge."

"Um, Hag, Marge, nice to meet you. What can I do for you?"

He snatched the stogie out again. "Why, you can paint little Margie here one of them clover paintings. That's what you can do." Back in went the cigar.

I turned to his wife, a short dumpling of a woman with taffy colored hair. "You like clover, do you?"

She smiled at her husband and slapped him lightly on the arm. "Don't listen to him." She tucked her arm through mine and walked us over toward my easel. "We'll let the men talk. What's your husband's name, honey?"

Though my instinct was to pull my arm out and stop walking, my first morning selling art had taught me one thing —never alienate a possible customer. And a rich-looking one at that. "His name's Abel and we're not married."

Marge snorted. "Fooling around?"

It was harder to resist tugging my arm from the vise of her elbow. "Just dating." I gritted my teeth and pasted a smile on my face. "What can I paint for you, Marge?

"Bluebell." She stopped walking and looked straight at me.

"Bluebells? The flower? Are you from Texas?"

Marge giggled and slapped my arm. "No, silly, Bluebell's my cow."

I could see the commission check I had started to imagine flying away. "I've never painted a cow before. I don't know if I can. I'm not very good at drawing so I'm afraid I wouldn't do Bluebell justice."

"Oh, I wish you'd think about it. When I saw that clover you painted this morning, looking so lifelike and delicious, I just knew you were the one to paint my precious little cow."

This time I took Marge's arm and escorted her back to the front of the booth. "Why don't you leave your name and phone number with me, and I will think about whether I'm the right artist to paint Bluebell." I handed her a pen and scrap of paper, we exchanged goodbyes, and they left.

"You're never going to believe what 'little Margie' asked me to paint. Her pet cow, Bluebell. She said my clover painting looked so delicious; she knew I'm the one to immortalize Bluebell." I turned, expecting to share a laugh with Abel, but he wasn't laughing. He was staring at a piece of paper in his hand. "Abel, are you all right?" I touched his hand.

He jumped and looked at me with a dazed look in his eyes. "You know what he did?"

"You mean Hag? Isn't that a name for the books?"

"Yeah, Hag." His eyes had returned to staring at what I now saw was a check.

"What did Hag do?"

"While you and Marge were talking, he picked out eight of your paintings, all in frames, and wrote out this check for twenty-five hundred dollars. I helped load them in his car."

I looked around at the walls of the tent. They were a lot emptier than they had been a few minutes earlier. I reached over and took the check from Abel. "Twenty-five hundred dollars." I could feel my knees buckle and groped for a chair. "Eight of my paintings, even the biggest ones with the fanciest frames, don't add up to that much, do they?"

He eased into the other chair. "No, they don't. They added up to just over eighteen hundred with the tax. He said he threw the rest in to make it a round number."

Luckily, customer traffic had slowed; no one was in our booth. I guessed everyone was off finding some lunch. "What kind of car was it?"

He chuckled. "I don't think you have to worry about the check being good. It was one of those Cadillac Escalades with all the extras. Snazzy."

I folded the check in half and put it in the pocket of my shorts, buttoning it closed so I didn't lose it. "Guess I'd better learn how to paint cows."

CHAPTER 37

September

Dear Lydie,

Here I sit on the porch, just like I was when I began this adventure, but with a glass of wine. I love the play of light and color across the sky. Tonight, the sunset mirrors the autumn colors of the leaves. The sound of bells from St. Joseph's Catholic Church completes the scene.

The once-white porch railing is totally black, painted one strip at a time to mark both momentous and ordinary times. I smile to remember the first mark and its accompanying note on the slat below, "Esther the chicken died." That's a tame, almost silly note for the beginning of a life change. That was the day I read about the first watercolor class I took at the craft store in Simpson, the first time in my whole long life I did something I really wanted to do.

I had no one to blame for that. I was the one who caved in to the flood of opinion and never gave myself the space to just be me. At times I curse our Germanic ancestors with their legacy of "should's and "supposed to's" that I let shape my life for so long. And I also blame our soft French ancestors, those famous giver-uppers, for my tendency to just give in to stronger or louder voices. But now that I'm on the positive, successful end of this life change, I see that I have no one to blame for my past but me. I was the one who was too afraid to tell Bert I wanted to do something different with my life. I was the one who let what everyone else thought dictate how

I lived. I was the one who kept moving and filling up my life with so much noise, so much interference, static from being a good girl and doing what everyone said, that I just plodded along looking like everyone said I should, doing what everyone else was doing. I can't believe it's taken me so many years to be brave enough to live my life for myself.

Who knew that taking a little step, picking up a paintbrush just once, would free me in a way nothing else had done? How did I get so strong that I was able to endure Clara and my boys' being so resistant?

I have to say I think that I've been a good example for them. Sam is much less insistent that he move home to take care of me now that I'm a successful artist with paintings in galleries all over the state. Aaron and Sara have become my biggest cheerleaders, offering me a bed when I take a workshop in their area and not being too disappointed when I tell them I can only stay one night since the intensity of the class is important to preserve, so I'll be staying somewhere else. And Matt has always been the one who was on my side, joking about his hippie mother and teasing me about boyfriends. All of them are proud of me. All of them have taken something from my example and been brave enough to try something new.

Samara has been a big supporter since my very first watercolor class. She's the one who took me shopping and helped me look less like an old lady and more like myself. She's doing well in school and is coming into her own as an artist with a showing coming in Madison during the holidays.

I think Clara's changed most of all. When I first started painting, she complained that I'd find new friends and leave her in my dust, and for a while I did. We struggled, me pulling toward change and her pushing me to stay the same. We argued once, in the ladies' room at Wal-Mart of all places, and pouted and cried, but eventually our friendship stood the tests and we're the same best friends, even better, that we always were. Clara's taken up writing poetry. Can you believe it? And she's good, darned good.

And Abel. Who'd have thought that bossy man would become so important in my life? From the moment I met him I put him in a little box of my perception, and it took a lot of persistence on his part to convince me that my first impression was wrong. He has made my life much richer. He pushed me to spread my wings and is very understanding of my need for privacy. The local gossips are having a field day, wagging their tongues over the fact that Abel and I seem to have an "intimate" relationship and aren't moving in together and certainly not getting married. We've talked about it, well, he talked about it mostly, but I have managed to convince him that our dates are more fun, our sex is livelier since we don't live together, and aren't married. Abel calls us "the butterfly woman and the renaissance man" because I have made such a change, come out of my "should" cocoon, and he feels like he's grown too by being my friend. And he can dance.

I hear a car driving down the gravel lane and see headlights cutting through the night. It must be Abel. Good thing I brought out two wineglasses, just in case.

Love, Gail

THE END

ABOUT THE AUTHOR

Barbara Angermeier Malcolm

Barbara is retired from a career in retail SCUBA sales and loves to travel. She has been writing for many years for her own enjoyment. Horizon is her second published novel.

BOOKS BY THIS AUTHOR

The Seaview

Widow and scuba diver Rose Lambert uses her savings to buy a ramshackle four-room hotel on a Caribbean beach. She hires local workers, overcomes unexpected obstacles, makes friends, and works to build a new life for herself on a small island where everyone knows everyone else--and their business. She knew it would be hard work but she didn't plan on Ignatius and the way he made her feel.

ACKNOWLEDGEMENT

The poem "Wise Woman" was printed by permission of the author and writing friend, Connie Anderson. Thanks, Connie! You're a terrific roommate.

Many thanks to all the writers that listened endlessly to pieces of Horizon and gave valuable critiques. I couldn't have done it without you.

Made in the USA
Middletown, DE
18 October 2022